East End Boys
at War

East End Boys at War

David Brown

AESOP Modern Fiction
Oxford

AESOP Modern Fiction
An imprint of AESOP Publications
Martin Noble Editorial / AESOP
28 Abberbury Road, Oxford OX4 4ES, UK
www.aesopbooks.com

First edition published by AESOP Publications
Copyright (c) 2016 David Brown

A catalogue record of this book is
available from the British Library.

First edition 2016

ISBN: 978-1-910301-19-7

All through the ages we have held fast our sense of Covenant, of feeling bound to God in a special relationship that has given meaning to our existence. Because of it, and for its name's sake, we have suffered, in its name, and by its power, we have made our distinctive contribution to civilisation.

If you should seek me, you should find me, if your search for me is with all your heart.

Dedication

Many of the names in this book belong to actual people. These men and women fought against a tyrannical, sadistic regime and it is because of their staunch, never-give-in attitude that we have the freedoms we enjoy today. In this book the names of these heroic individuals live on in print.

David Brown, 2016

1

Isaac's yell of joy was whipped away by the slipstream as his flying instructor, ex World War I fighter pilot Martin Ainsworth expertly flew the bi-plane through a variety of aerobatics. They came out of an inverted roll and as they straightened out Ainsworth said down the speaking tube, 'Okay Mr Brown, the controls are yours. Do two circuits, land and take off, and concentrate this time.'

Biting his bottom lip in concentration Isaac brought the bi-plane into the wind, checked his speed – it was spot on, forty miles an hour – and pushed the stick down a fraction; the wheels touched the ground, the bi-plane leapt a couple of times like a gazelle, and then rolled smoothly along the grass. They had nearly come to a stop when Isaac pushed the throttle lever on his left forward, building up speed, pulled back on the steering column and the aircraft left the ground. Once again his landing wasn't perfect, but Ainsworth didn't say anything as they came to a stop, just undid his straps and climbed from the cockpit to stand by the fuselage level with Isaac, and leant forward, raising his voice against the sound of the idling engine. 'Mr Brown, these old bones cannot take another landing like that, and how the undercarriage had withstood it for this long beats me, so you're on your own, two circuits, land and take off.'

Isaac stared at him, his face showing disbelief, stuttering, 'But I've only—'

'Just don't break anything,' Ainsworth interrupted. 'Off you go.' Ainsworth waved a hand, turned and walked away, carrying his parachute.

Swallowing nervously Isaac pushed the throttle lever forward and the bi-plane began to move. He turned the aircraft into the wind, glanced at the speedometer, and pulled gently back on the stick.

It was by chance that Isaac had picked up a *Flight* magazine, noticing an advert: 'Learn to Fly, have a career as a pilot. Apply 60 Park Lane, London'. He did not hesitate in going there the following morning to book a lesson.

It was a clear but brisk November morning in 1938 as an apprehensive Isaac, having borrowed his father's car, drove through the gates of Heston Aerodrome, where a couple of months previously the Prime Minister Neville Chamberlain had landed after his meeting with the German Chancellor Adolph Hitler, announcing, 'I believe it is peace in our time.'

Once Isaac had checked in at reception, he was issued with a basic flying kit, overalls, a Sidcot suit (one-piece padded flying suit) helmet, goggles and a pair of gauntlets.

A man dressed in flying gear entered the room and strode over to Isaac. 'Good morning, you must be Mr Brown. I'm Mr Martin Ainsworth, your flying instructor.'

They shook hands, Isaac's eyes roaming across the weather-beaten face, the grey eyes staring steadily back as he said, 'My name's Isaac.'

Ainsworth ignored the first name by saying, 'Right Mr Brown, now you're kitted out, I'll show you around the aircraft.'

As they walked slowly around the aircraft, the instructor pointed to various parts of the bi-plane with its yellow fuselage struts and wheels. Ainsworth slid a parachute from the wing. 'Let me show you how to put this on, just in case.' Isaac wanted to ask *In case of what?* but stayed silent as Ainsworth strapped on the parachute saying, 'If you have to jump, count to three after leaving the aircraft—' he pointed to a large ring '—pull this hard. Now pop into the rear cockpit and I'll show you how to strap yourself in. Wouldn't want you falling out.'

Feeling like a trussed up chicken, Isaac sat in the cockpit listening and watching intently as Ainsworth said, 'This aircraft is a DH60 Tiger Moth. The instruments are pretty simple.'

That was seven months ago and now he was flying solo. Inhaling the clear air, a smile on his face, he moved the stick to the right to come into the wind. His eyes glanced quickly from left to right along the instrument panel: engine rev counter, air speed indictor, cross lever indicator, oil pressure gauge. His feet moved on the pedals as he straightened out, checking the speed as he came into land.

Just a slight leap and he was rolling along the grass. He revved the engine and took off again, the smile never leaving his face and letting out a whoop of triumph as he levelled out the bi-plane and looked around. A bird flew just below him in the opposite direction, the wing struts humming in tune with the engine as he looked down at the fields and houses below, knowing he could never really explain the feeling he had right now. He brought the bi-plane into the wind, licked his lips and said loudly, 'You could do it,' pulling slightly back on the stick as the wheels touched smoothly down.

He throttled back, steering the Tiger Moth to where Ainsworth was standing, and came to a stop, switched off the engine, unstrapped himself and climbed down from the aircraft, turning to see a smiling Ainsworth who grabbed his hand, 'Well done, Mr Brown, that was your best landing ever, and what a time to do it.'

Isaac's body still tingled with excitement as he drove out of the aerodrome on his way back to London. No one knew about his flying lessons. It had been hard at times keeping it a secret, especially from his wife Lily; if she only knew – he left the thought there.

It had been hard juggling flying lessons, studying for the accountancy exams and working at either the Victoria or Hanover Casino where his father was part owner. He touched his jacket pocket where nestled the letter that he had passed the accountancy exam. He opened the window, took a deep breath and yelled, letting out the pent up excitement of the day.

That evening, Wolfe, Asher, Billy and their sons leapt from their seats, the cinema erupting as Joe Louise knocked out the German Max Schmeling in four minutes and two seconds of the first round, having knocked him down three times already. The German's defeat was the icing on the cake for Isaac after a great and memorable day.

Sunday, 2 July 1939

The family's usual Sunday get-together was interrupted by a young boy asking for Sally. After speaking to the boy Sally ran back into the dining room, 'Got to go, there's been an accident at the shop.'

Sally watched Mr Bernstein the signwriter being stretchered off in an ambulance, and then turned her gaze up to the sign above her new dress shop; **SALLY B**. Mr Bernstein had fallen from his ladder before completing the **BROWN**, breaking a leg and maybe some ribs.

Her husband Phillip placed an arm around her shoulder. 'It's different.' He began to laugh. Sally pulled slightly away from him. 'What are you laughing about? It's not funny.'

'No, it's not,' but he began to laugh again. Sally hit him on the arm. He pointed to the sign. 'What if you would have used your married name, Sally H?' saying the aitch like 'ugh'.

She looked at him for a second and began to laugh, seeing the funny side of it. Just then Isaac and her father arrived to help get the shop ready for the opening the next morning.

'That's a brilliant idea.' Isaac pointed to the sign.

'Pure accident, signwriter fell off his ladder,' Phillip said.

Sally moved towards the shop entrance. 'Come on you three, there's still a lot to do.'

'Slave driver,' Phillip said, laughing as he avoided the kick.

It was just over a month ago that Sally had seen the shop in Whitechapel High Street that was for sale. She jumped off the bus at the next stop and walked back to stand in front of the double-fronted shop.

The notice said: 'Shop and Flat for Sale'. She didn't need anywhere to live, but the room, or rooms upstairs, would probably make a good workshop. She copied down the telephone number and then walked along Whitechapel High Street, looking at the shops; there wasn't a ladies dress shop, just one man's outfitters. She found a telephone box and dialled the number. As it rang, Sally knew that she was now ready to own her own dress shop. There was a click.

'Johnson and Steinbeck.' The man at the other end had a slight accent.

'Good morning,' Sally said. 'I'm interested in the property in Whitechapel High Street.'

'You want to buy, or rent?'

She hadn't thought about renting. 'How much to buy the property, Mr—'

'Steinbeck, five hundred pounds.'

'My name is Mrs Hyams; I'm interested in buying the property, I need to speak to my husband, I'll call you later.'

'Do you want me to hold the property for you?'

'Yes please.'

She hung up and called her father at the Victoria Casino. 'Papa, there is a shop for sale in Whitechapel High Street, and—'

'You want to buy it,' Wolfe interrupted.

'Yes Papa, I'm ready, I have done what you said I should do and worked for someone else, I know—'

Wolfe could hear the excitement in his daughter's voice as he interrupted again. 'How much?'

'Five hundred pounds,' she whispered, adding, 'I said I would call them back.'

'I'll meet you there, what number is it?'

She told him.

'I'll be there in twenty minutes, ask the agents to meet us there too.'

'Thank you very much, Papa.'

Wolfe parked the car outside the shop. Sally was there with a tall, thin man who held out his hand. 'I'm Mr Steinbeck.'

Wolfe took the outstretched hand. 'Wolfe Brown.'

The agent gave a well-rehearsed smile, stepping towards the shop's door. 'Would you like to look inside?'

Wolfe thought it a stupid question; of course they would, as Sally said excitedly, 'Please.'

They stepped into the shop, which was unexpectedly spacious. Wolfe stood in the middle of the room, watching his daughter wander around humming softly to herself.

'Would you like to see upstairs?' the agent asked.

'Yes please,' Sally said, a big smile on her face.

There were two rooms, plus a washroom and toilet.

Wolfe realised that it would take a lot of work for Sally to convert these rooms into a living area, but he was wrong in assuming that.

Sally stood in front of him, and whispered, 'This would make a good workshop. A couple of sewing machines to start with. What do you think, Papa?'

He was silent for a moment, trying to envisage what she would make of this place. It wasn't the first time he, Asher and Billy had lent money to someone wanting to start a business. Sally was a great dressmaker, and had drawing books filled with her designs. He would give her the money, but she would have to pay him back, otherwise this would never actually be hers.

'Yes, Sally it is a great idea, I could lend you the money, but you would have to pay me back, otherwise—'

She flung her arms around his neck. 'I promise, Papa, to—'

'Would you accept four hundred cash?' Wolfe asked the agent, interrupting Sally.

The agent stared at Wolfe, who could see him mulling it over in his mind. 'No, sorry, five hundred.'

'Come on Sally we are—'

'Four fifty,' the agent said quickly.

Wolfe smiled, holding out his hand. 'Four fifty it is.' He took out his cheque book, looking at the agent, who said, 'Make it out to Johnson and Steinbeck.' Wolfe gave the cheque to Sally. 'Meet the gentleman in the morning to obtain the documentation and keys.'

Sally flew at her father, hugging him. 'Oh thank you, Papa. I'll pay you back every penny.'

He smiled, touching her cheek. 'I know you will, but wait till the shop opens and shows some profit.'

The following day Sally took her husband Phillip with her to obtain the keys to the shop, so he could help plan the layout, knowing that his carpentry skills would be put to good use.

Now all was nearly ready. Inside the shop, her sister-in-law Lily was putting the finishing touches to a dress. Lily moved quickly across to her husband Isaac, who placed an arm around her waist and kissed her.

'Do that later,' Sally said, her face showing concern, moving away saying to know one in particular. 'It'll never be ready in time.'

At nine o'clock in the evening Sally's mother Eva arrived with sandwiches, but by that time all was ready for the opening. Dresses that Sally had designed, with the help of her friend Lily, hung on hangers.

'Come on, let's have a look from outside,' Lily said.

Hand in hand, the sisters-in-law moved outside, followed by the others, to stand a few feet away from the shop. The men stood beside their wives, arms around their waists or shoulders. All were smiling as they gazed at the shop, the lights showing off window dummies attired in their chic, individually designed dresses, with hats made by Lily.

'Oh my, doesn't it look grand,' Sally whispered.

The following day there was an excited queue outside the shop, waiting for it to open. There were gasps of surprise as Sally pulled back the shutters to reveal the four window dummies. Women surged forward as the door opened. Luckily for Sally, her sisters Freda and Lily were there to help. Gradually as morning turned to afternoon the numbers dwindled. They closed the shop at 5 pm.

'Wow that was a great first day,' Freda said, flopping onto a chair.

Sally hugged her sister and sister-in-law. 'Thank you both for today; I wouldn't have managed without you.'

Saturday, 26 August 1939

'There is definitely going to be a war,' Billy Reed said to the Brown brothers, striding step for step either side of him as they left the synagogue.

'I agree,' Wolfe, the taller of the two brothers, responded.

'The thing is—'

'We are too old to enlist,' interrupted Asher.

'You read my mind,' said Billy, adding ardently. 'We must do something in this one; we missed out on the last one.'

'That Non Aggression Pact between Germany and Russia isn't worth the paper it's printed on,' said Wolfe, adding very quickly, 'Hitler would—' he snapped his fingers '—break it just like that.'

'Poland had rushed troops to its border,' Billy said.

'No matter what Chamberlain said, I'm sure that in his heart of hearts he knew there would be a war,' Asher pointed out.

'Shelters were being handed out. By the way, have either of you received one?' Wolfe asked.

'Not yet,' Billy and Asher said in unison.

'We need to talk about what we would like to do to help the war effort when it happens,' Billy said.

Wolfe smiled. 'You're older than us; plane spotting would do you, just sit there and look at the sky, no exercise.'

Billy punched Wolfe on the arm. 'Let's go to the gym now, and I'll—'

Wolfe and Asher burst into laughter. 'It's so easy to wind you up,' Asher said.

'More important than that, they—' Billy gestured towards the women walking in front of them '—mustn't know what we decide to do until we've done it.' The other two nodded silently in agreement.

'I think it might be best if we meet at the Victoria on Monday morning and discuss it then.'

While the family had their usual Sunday get-together, the country's moveable treasures were being transferred to safety from museums, art galleries and Westminster Abbey to underground quarries in North Wales.

*

The three men met at their office in the Victoria Casino. Taking a cigarette case from his jacket pocket Billy opened it, offering it around. 'I would like to join the Fire Brigade,' he said, lighting a cigarette.

'What about the police?' Asher asked.

'Have you read the papers?' Billy reached for the *Daily Mirror*, opening the page and handing it to Asher. 'See what the bombers have done to that city? It's called *Blitzkrieg*. If we go to war, the first thing the Germans would do is bomb us. We'd be more useful as firemen.'

Wolfe blew a smoke ring across the room. 'It's a good idea, but would they accept us?'

Billy smiled. 'No problem, shall I make an appointment?'

'Yes,' the brothers said in unison.

'I've asked Frank to join us because any decision we make would concern him, as he would have to be here when the three of us are on duty.' Just then there was a knock on the door. 'Come in,' said Billy.

The door opened and Frank Mullin, who had lost a leg in the last war and had worked for the brothers for many years, even before the First World War, entered the office. 'Good morning all.'

'I'll get straight to the point,' Billy said. 'I've already spoken to Frank about managing the casino whenever we might be away.'

'Elizabeth said we could clean out the rooms upstairs to use as a flat, and we would whenever necessary move in there.'

'What about Aiden, Bridget and the stairs?' Wolfe asked, glancing at Frank's leg.

Frank smiled. 'I'm okay with the stairs. I'm expecting Aiden to be called up. He wants to join the RAF as a mechanic, and as you know Bridget's a nurse at St Bartholomew's Hospital, so us staying here when you might be on duty isn't a problem.'

'Well, that's settled then,' Billy said.

'Don't know what we would do without you,' said Wolfe.

'I second that,' said Ashley, shaking Frank's hand.

'Let's have a spot of lunch and see if the Fire Service would have us,' Wolfe said, walking towards the door, adding, 'If it takes too long, it will have to wait till Wednesday. I have a very important appointment tomorrow, and before you ask,' he shrugged his shoulders, 'I don't know anything about it, Isaac had arranged a surprise for me, I haven't the faintest idea what it might be.'

*

'Where are you taking me?' Wolfe asked his son for the umpteenth time.

Isaac, a slight smile on his face, said nothing, just looked straight ahead as they drove along the A4, and a few minute later entered Heston Aerodrome.

'What's going on?' Wolfe whispered.

'Papa, just wait a little longer, please.'

Isaac parked the car and walked into the terminal building. Wolfe followed him into the changing room as Martin Ainsworth entered. 'Good morning, Mr Brown.'

'Good morning, Mr Ainsworth, may I introduce you to my father, Mr Wolfe Brown.'

Ainsworth smiled, holding out his hand. 'It's a pleasure to meet you.' They shook hands. 'Right let's get you kitted out.'

Wolfe's face showed surprise. 'Me.'

'Papa, I know you've been wondering where I go from time to time. Well, it's here. Mr Ainsworth had been teaching me to fly an aeroplane. I knew you had always wanted to fly one too, so I've booked you a lesson.'

By the time Isaac had explained everything, Wolfe had been kitted out. 'Mr Brown, it's a nice day for flying,' said Ainsworth. 'Let me show you the aeroplane.'

Wolfe followed Ainsworth out to the DH60 Tiger Moth.

There was a big grin on Isaac's face as he watched Ainsworth put the parachute on his father, who then climbed into the rear cockpit of the aircraft; Ainsworth stood on the foothold, showing Wolfe the controls and instruments, and then climbed into the front cockpit. Within seconds they were rolling along the grass and airborne. Isaac shaded his eyes with a hand, the smile still on his face as the Tiger Moth disappeared from view.

Wolfe swallowed nervously, the aircraft rattling as they rolled along the grass, and then all was quiet apart from the engine as they left the ground. With a big smile on his face, Wolfe looked over the edge of the cockpit to see the patchwork of fields and farmhouses below and couldn't help letting out a yell of pleasure as they climbed steadily. The aircraft straightened out and Ainsworth's voice came from the speaking tube.

'Mr Brown, place your hand on the stick and your feet gently on the rudder bars.' Wolfe did as he was told, and then caught fright. 'The aeroplane is yours, Mr Brown.' They suddenly side-slipped to the right, and Ainsworth said in a calm voice, 'Gently, Mr Brown, like you were holding a woman.'

Wolfe smiled at Ainsworth's choice of words and brought the aircraft into a straight line. 'Well done, Mr Brown.'

Under the guidance of the calm voice of the instructor, Wolfe did two circuits without landing.

'OK, Mr Brown, I will take the controls.'

Wolfe felt him take the stick and reluctantly let go, taking his feet off the rudder bars, and said down the speaking tube, 'Mr Ainsworth, before we return, would you do some aerobatics?'

Without warning the aircraft suddenly pointed skyward and then dived. Wolfe let out a 'Yes, oh yes' as they went into an inverted roll and straightened out, but just for a second, as Wolfe suddenly found himself upside down. He roared with laughter yelling, 'How wonderful.'

Five minutes later they were on the ground and taxiing towards Isaac. The bi-plane came to a stop. Wolfe sat there for a second, not wanting to leave as his son moved to stand beside the Tiger Moth. He didn't need to ask. It was written all over his father's face.

Wolfe climbed down from the aircraft and hugged Isaac. 'Thank you, oh my goodness that was fantastic, thank you.' He kissed Isaac on the cheek and turned to the instructor. 'Mr Ainsworth, that was wonderful.' He grabbed the pilot by the hand, shaking it.

'My pleasure, Mr Brown. While you change I need to talk to your son.' He watched Wolfe walk away and then turned to Isaac. 'I'm very sorry Mr Brown, but I'm unable to instruct you any further.'

Isaac's face showed shock at the statement. 'What, why, is it something I have done?'

Ainsworth smiled. 'No, of course not, I have been called back into the RAF as an instructor.'

'You were about to teach me—'

'I know, but I could give you the name of a very good instructor. I'm so sorry, because I think you would be a great pilot.' He handed Isaac a card. 'This is my home address. If you ever need me for anything, and I mean anything, phone this number.' He held out his hand. 'I'm sure, Mr Brown, that we will meet again. Good luck.'

Isaac took the card. 'Thank you, Mr Ainsworth, for being so patient with me, and I hope we do meet again.'

Just as Ainsworth left, Wolfe walked in. 'Oh has he gone? I wanted to thank him.' He placed an arm around Isaac's shoulder. 'Thank you for that. I'm sure, like you, I would never be able to explain the feeling of flying. It was a dream come true.'

'It's going to happen very, very soon – war is just around the corner,' Wolfe said, slapping the newspaper he was reading with the back of his hand.

'What makes you say that?' his youngest son Saul asked.

'Hitler sent an ultimatum to the Poles, and at the same time asked the British Government to sign a peace treaty with Germany, probably having noticed that we had called up our armed forces reserves, and it was only last week that the French and British governments reaffirmed their pledged to assist Poland if they were attacked.'

'I'm going to work,' Isaac said, putting on his coat. 'If we're going to war—' placing his dark blue fedora hat on his head '—you, my young brother, would be one of the first to be called up.'

'Thanks for reminding me, but you won't be too far behind.'

'Let's keep that quiet, I don't want Lily panicking.' He touched his father's shoulder. 'I'll see you later, Papa.'

He left the house and walked towards Commercial Road. He suddenly came to a halt, a frown on his forehead. There was an eerie quietness in the air. He slowly turned a full circle, whispering, 'No children.'

The noise of children playing and shouting to each other and the yelling of mothers had disappeared. He nodded slightly: his father was right, war was imminent, the Government must know something if they were evacuating the children. He decided to walk as it was a nice day, stopping once more to watch two workmen taking down road signs. He shrugged his shoulders. Makes sense, more indication that war was around the corner. He walked on, thinking, *I wouldn't go down without a fight, but Lily, that would be different.* He lengthened his stride until reaching Gardners Corner, stopping at the crossing as four coaches full of children drove by on their way to the countryside and safety.

On entering the casino, Isaac went straight to the office. Billy was talking to a couple of croupiers.

'Sorry, I didn't know you were busy.'

'It's OK, Isaac, we had finished.' The two croupiers shook Billy's hand and left, closing the door behind them.

'They're in the army reserves and have been called up; they were worried in case we were left shorthanded, but as you know we have women croupiers who could take their place. Anyway, what can I do for you?'

'I need a gun.'

Billy, who had been leaning against the desk, stood bolt upright. 'What for, are you in trouble?'

Isaac took a step forward. 'I noticed some men taking down street signs. You know what that means: the Government must think we're going to be invaded. If that's the case, you know what the Nazis would do to Jews. I wouldn't, couldn't, let them get their hands on Lily.'

'Whoa back, you're jumping the gun, no pun intended, but nothing's happened yet, and you're panicking for no reason whatsoever.'

The worry left Isaac's face, to be replaced with a sheepish smile. 'I am, it's not like me, I'm sorry.'

'You're right, it isn't like you, but I'm pleased you came to me first. I can assure you, if they invade, I'll give you what you want.'

Isaac hesitated as though he didn't know what to say next. He pointed to the door. 'I'm going to work.'

He closed the door behind him, leaving a frown on Billy's face. Billy glanced across the room to the drinks cabinet where he kept their assortment of guns.

It had been necessary in the past to have them, and use them. His face changed to one of hatred, remembering Captain Jennings the rapist and his gang. Even after all these years it made his blood boil. He smiled, remembering his first encounter with Wolfe and Asher, who wanted to find the Irishmen who beat up their father-in-law and stole his money. He went into a boxer's stance, throwing punches. He laughed, hearing Wolfe say, *One day you and I must have a fight.*

He would never fight Wolfe; he had too much respect for him as a man and a boxer. They had won a lot of money with Wolfe's fists. He nodded as if agreeing with himself, Wolfe was a natural boxer, but with Billy's help Wolfe had been a great natural boxer. He wondered why Wolfe never took it up as a profession. He laughed, just one word: Eva. His expression changed, once again remembering the Le Feuvre twins and their younger brother. Yes, they had needed the guns then as a deterrent, but now, if there were an invasion... He lit a cigarette, he would talk to Frank, and maybe add to their arsenal.

Sunday, 3 September 1939

Everyone had arrived at Wolfe and Eva's home, and as usual the women were in the kitchen, preparing the meal and singing to a song coming from the radio, when suddenly the music came to an abrupt stop and the announcer said quietly, 'Ladies and Gentlemen, the Prime Minister, Neville Chamberlain.'

Everyone stopped what they were doing and moved into the kitchen as the Prime Minister said in a solemn voice, 'I am speaking to you from the Cabinet Room at 10 Downing Street. This morning the British Ambassador in Berlin handed the German Government a final note stating that unless we heard from them by 11 am that they were prepared at once to withdraw their troops from Poland, a state of war would exist between us. I have to tell you that no such undertaking has been received and that consequently this country is at war with Germany.'

The announcer returned, saying that the King would be broadcasting to the nation that night.

There was a profound silence in the kitchen, but there was also a silent sigh of relief that all the shinny-shenanigans with Hitler over the last few months over whether we would or we wouldn't go to war were now over.

While the family ate their meal, they discussed what they thought would happen next. 'France has also declared war on Germany,' Isaac said.

'Did you hear the newscaster?' Billy pointed his fork at no one in particular. 'An Anglo-French statement said that the two governments would avoid bombing civilians, and do not intend using poison gas or germ warfare, and have asked the German Government to say that too. That's a relief.'

'That's if the Germans agree to that,' Wolfe said.

That evening the family sat in a semi-circle around the wireless listening to the King as he said, 'We can only do the right, as we see the right and reverently commit our cause to God, may he bless us all.'

Two days later Wolfe leapt from his seat, shaking the paper in his right hand. 'Did you read this?'

'You'll have a heart attack if you carry on like that,' Eva said. 'Anyway what is it now?'

'President Roosevelt has declared that the USA will be neutral in the conflict between us and Germany.'

'So why get so excited about something you cannot control?'

He smiled. 'There are times, I hate to admit, when you're right.'

'I'm also right about the blackout curtains for the casinos. If you don't get off your backside and get to the shops they would be sold out.'

Wolfe got to his feet. 'Okay, okay, anything to stop you nagging me about it.'

'The thing is, what shall we do here? I don't fancy painting the windows black.'

'Come with me, you know—'

'I'm going to phone Sarah and Esther. If they are free we would get everything.'

He smiled. 'In that case I'm going to do the lights on the car, and get the shelter finished.'

For the next three days Eva, Sarah and Esther, with help from their daughters, made black curtains for the casinos and their respective homes.

Complaints flooded into local council and government offices from every part of London. People were spraining their ankles and knees. Without any lights at night they could not see the edge of the kerbside, or lamp posts. The Government ordered the councils to paint the bottom of lamp posts and edges of the pavement with white stripes.

Call-up began for men over twenty. The Government were adamant that there would be no exemption from call-up unless the persons were in a reserve occupation or the clergy.

'Has anyone seen Saul?' Eva asked.

'Come to mention it, I haven't seen him for over a week,' Wolfe replied.

'I'll ask Sally, she's bound to know. Those two are very close.'

2

The man uppermost in his parents' minds sat on the edge of a bed, staring at the wall through a swollen black right eye, and there were black and blue bruises on his face and body. He picked up the edge of the blanket to see that he was naked except for a pair of pyjama bottoms. Saul moaned slightly as he moved to the edge of the bed and slowly got to his feet.

For a second he felt faint, shook his head to clear his vision and then walked heavily and painfully, holding his right side, towards the window. Placing his back to the wall to hold him up, he pulled back the curtain just enough for him to peek out to see traffic moving along the street, and people passing by. He let go the curtain which dropped back into place and moved painfully back to the bed, holding onto the bedpost, lowering himself onto it, a groan of pain leaving his tight swollen lips, the face a grim mask as he propped up the pillows and settled into them, closing his eyes to recall what had happened to him.

Saul was a gambler, not big-time, but he liked to gamble. He should know better, having spent most of his teenage years in and around his father's casinos.

He had seen it a thousand times. The house always wins in the end. Even when gamblers were winning, they thought they were invincible, but the inevitable nearly always happened: their lucky streak turned against them, but instead of walking away and gambling with the casino's money another day, they would carry on, hoping upon hope that their luck would change again until they had lost their winnings and more.

Saul shook his head; it was a dead cert bet. Johnnie Gold had won ten fights, seven in knockouts; his opponent, Frank Frost, had fifteen fights and not won any of them. He owed Fred Burgess the loan shark fifty pounds. Everyone called him Bull because of his six foot four height and short neck, fifty pounds. He asked Bull for extra credit of a hundred pounds, placing the entire amount on Gold to win. He clenched his fists, the anger of being that foolish showing on his face. One lucky punch in the first round had Gold on the floor and out for the count.

Saul had tried to win the money in a card game at Bull's club, but once again he lost to the big man. That was two months ago and Burgess wanted his money, plus the interest which now amounted to about five hundred pounds, a fortune, which, with Bull's interest rates, was growing each day. Saul had won a few card games, but not the sort of winnings he needed to pay back Burgess.

It was four in the morning and he was leaving a private card party when Burgess and his two cronies caught up with him. He offered the fifty pounds he had won, but Burgess laughed, took the money and stepped back as his two henchmen attacked Saul, but they were caught unawares at his fighting skills learnt from his father, uncle and Billy Reed. It was when he had put one of the men on the floor that Bull stepped in. Although Saul got a few punches in, it wasn't enough to do any substantial damage to Bull, whose reach and hammer-like fists knocked Saul to the ground. He had the sense to roll into a ball as the beating began, especially by the two men he had blooded.

They placed him in the boot of a car and dumped him in Upper Street, Islington, close by Highbury Corner, but not before giving him another kicking.

'You have a week to find the money,' said Burgess. 'If not—' he bent, showing Saul a fist and then he was gone.

Saul heard the car drive away, and tried to get up, but it was too painful. Suddenly an arm came under his armpit.

'Let me help you.'

He peered through swollen eyes at the young woman, wondering how she would be able to help him, but she did. He staggered a few steps towards a wall and was about to fall forward when she ran in front of him placing her hands flat onto his chest. He moaned in pain.

'Turn around and take a couple of steps back to a wall, you could lean on that.'

He did as she had said, coming up against the wall and leant against it.

'I'll call an ambulance,' she said.

'No, no, please don't do that. Just call me a taxi. I'll stay at a hotel; I'll be okay in the morning.' But at that time of the morning, the streets were empty of any kind of transport.

He didn't want to go home looking the way he surmised he looked, knowing this time he had dug a hole for himself, and would probably need his father's help, which was the last thing he wanted. That was when he lost consciousness.

He looked towards the door as it opened and a pretty woman with shoulder-length chestnut hair walked into the room carrying a tray, setting it down on the dressing table.

'That's good – you're awake. I took the liberty of telephoning a number you had in your jacket pocket. It was your sister, Sally; naturally she asked where you were.' She stepped to the side of the bed. 'I'll help you sit up.' She placed an arm under his armpit. 'I hope you don't mind, but I told her.' He gave a groan of pain, but managed to sit up.

'That's okay, knowing her she'll be here in a couple of hours.' He frowned, turning to face her as she puffed up his pillows. 'How long was I unconscious?'

'Three days.'

He shook his head, watching her pour tea into a cup. 'How did you get me up the stairs?'

'Dr Franks, me and a couple of my girls, sugar?'

'Two please. Girls? You're married. What about your—'

'I'm not married,' she interrupted, smiling. 'You're in my bedroom, and this house is a brothel, my brothel to be exact.' She placed the tray across his lap.

'But you're—'

'Young,' she interrupted once again, 'and yes, it's a long story.' She turned to go.

'You don't have to go yet?' It was more a plea than a statement.

'No, not really'

I'm curious, how come you own this...' his face screwed up in pain as he swept his arm around the room '... establishment?'

'As I said, it's a long story.'

'I don't think I'd be leaving here in the immediate future.'

She smiled and sat cross-legged at the end of the bed facing him. 'Eat,' she said.

He took a bite of the cheese sandwich.

'My name is Hannah Grozenski and I was born on June 10th 1912 in Mile End Hospital. My father was killed in a tragic accident.' She held up her hand as she saw that Saul was about to ask her how. 'My mother died in that awful cold winter of 1927—'

'I remember that,' he interrupted. 'Freezing blizzards, it was below—' He saw the look on her face. 'Sorry, I won't interrupt again.'

'I was now alone. My mother had saved a little money, which she refused to use for medicine as it was to help us have a better place to live.' She looked down at her hands. 'Blout Street was a terrible place; the cobbled streets stank of urine that was thrown from flats windows, mouldy slops and dog's faeces. It was worse in the summer.

'About three weeks after my mother died I couldn't sleep so I went for a walk, which on hindsight was a pretty silly thing to do, especially as I was in unfamiliar streets. I passed heavily made-up women, who swore at me. I ended up in Chinatown, where I found people fighting for uneaten food thrown out by the restaurant. I knew where I was so I headed home.

'The very next night I awoke again in the early hours and headed for Chinatown, hoping to grab some of the unwanted food. As luck had it, I found a place, and I was the only one there. I collected chicken bones, still with pieces of chicken on them and some rice. I took my hoard of goodies home, bought some potatoes and made a soup. It was the best soup I had ever tasted.'

On seeing Saul's cup empty, she asked, 'Would you like another cup of tea?'

'No I'm fine, please continue.'

She took the tray from his lap, placing it on the dresser, and sat on the stool.

'With no food left, I decided to try my luck in Chinatown again and took a knife for protection. I turned a wrong corner and was lost once again, ending up in the street of painted women. I grasped the knife in my pocket as a woman stepped in front of me, but whichever way I turned, she blocked the way. I told her to move aside, revealing the knife. She slapped me, taking the knife from my hand and then patted my arm, telling me not to cry as slapping me was the only way to get the knife. She then said "Come with me," so I went with her. She told me her name was Ruby Newman. We stopped at a three-storey house in Ducket Street. It was strange to see this house standing alone amongst all the tenements.

'Once inside the house, Ruby took me into a kitchen that was larger than my flat, and made a cup of tea, placing some homemade biscuits in front of me.'

Hannah stopped talking for a minute a slight smile on her face. 'I could still taste them to this day. Ruby asked me about my parents. I told her I was an orphan. She asked me if I knew about the painted women and what they did. I said "Sort of."'

Hannah's face broke into a beaming smile. 'Ruby asked me to undress, bursting into hysterical laughter when I asked if she liked women. "You're a bit skinny," she commented, "but with food you would fill out." She stared at me for some minutes as I dressed and then said, "Hannah Grozenski, I would help you, not to be a prostitute on the street, but a high-class escort, I would teach you how to please a man and yourself."' A knock at the door interrupted her. She opened it stepping aside, 'Come in doctor.'

'How's the patient?'

'He woke up this morning,' Hannah said, moving to one side to allow the doctor to enter.

'That's good news,' the doctor said, entering the room, moving across to the bed and holding out his hand. 'Dr Franks.'

'Saul Brown,' he went to take the outstretched hand, but bent forward in pain.

'You might have a couple of broken ribs,' the doctor muttered, pulling back the cover, and gently placed his hands on the bruises. 'You took quiet a beating, young man.' He quickly took his hands away as Saul let out a yell. 'Sorry, I was being as gentle as I could. I think your ribs are okay, just very badly bruised, as is most of your body.'

He sat on the edge of the bed, pulling a small torch from his bag. 'Let's have a look at those eyes.'

He shone the light into the right eye, doing the same with the left, then switched off the light and patted Saul on the leg.

'You're very lucky; there's no damage to the eyes. Once the swelling goes down, everything should go back to normal.' He took a prescription book from the bag and began writing. 'I'm giving you something for the pain, and drops for the eyes.'

He went to hand it to Saul, but Hannah took it from him.

'I'll get these,' she said.

'No exertions, plenty of rest, I'll be back in a couple days to see how you're getting on.' He closed the bag, and picked it up. Hannah held door open for him and then followed the doctor out to the hallway.

'Thanks Doc, how much do I owe you?'

He smiled. 'I don't need the money, but three nights with Claire—'

She smiled. 'Why don't you ask her to marry you? It would be cheaper.'

He stepped back a pace. 'Look at me, Hannah. Who would want to marry me?'

She looked at him for a second, the slightly balding head, deep blue eyes that always seemed to be smiling, but showed care when seeing patients. She gave a slight nod. He was slim, the suit slightly too big, the trousers were baggy, and then there was the limp, a wound from the First World War. 'You're a good, caring man. If you don't ask, you don't know.'

'And what if she said no.' He shook his head. 'It's better this way.'

She shrugged her shoulders. 'Okay, Doc, Friday, Saturday and Sunday.'

There was a huge smile on his face. 'Thank you, Hannah.' He moved past her and slowly descended the stairs. Hannah moved back into the room, closing the door and said, 'I'll go to the chemist and get your medicine. Meanwhile try and sleep.'

'How could I sleep? I need to hear the rest of your story.'

She smiled. 'I'll continue it later.' She shook the prescription. 'You need these.'

An hour later Hannah entered the bedroom. Saul was asleep. She stood there for a moment, looking down at him, thinking how handsome he was. She gently touched his cheek, quickly withdrawing her hand as Saul opened his eyes. 'Sorry to wake you, but it's time for your medicine, and I've had cook make you a light meal, just eggs on toast.'

'Thanks, I'm starving.' He sat up, falling back onto the pillows, letting out a low groan of pain.

'Do things slowly,' Hannah scolded him, placing an arm under his armpit and helping him sit up, and then puffed up the pillows. Once he had settled, she placed the tray across his lap, handing him two tablets and a glass of water. 'I won't see much of you tonight,' she said, 'but I'll be close if you need me.'

He lifted the covers. 'Who undressed me? Where are my clothes?'

Hannah's face turned red. 'I did, and they're being cleaned.'

There was a mischievous grin on his face. 'Thanks, but I usual have a reason for getting naked in a woman's bedroom.' She slapped him playfully on the shoulder and he let out a yell of pain.

'Oh I'm so sorry.' There was concern in her voice and on her face.

He smiled. 'Only kidding.'

She looked at him for a second, moving slightly forward, stopping herself from kissing him and turning quickly to leave the room.

'Hey, you promised to continue the story of Hannah Grozenski.'

'Okay, but not too long – I have things to prepare.' She sat on the stool by the dresser, playing with a comb as Saul spooned a piece of toast and egg into his mouth as she went on with her story.

'Some months had gone by since moving in with Ruby when one day we were returning from an evening at the music hall and we heard screams and yelling. We both ran towards the noise to finds a man beating a young girl. We both attacked him. I jumped on his back, racking my nails across his face and Ruby kicked his legs. I jumped from his back and he ran away.

'The young girl was like many young girls coming to London from other cities that were caught up in a prostitute scam. The guy sees her on the train, chats her up, sets her up in a flat, buys her presents, until one day they are in a restaurant and a man approaches her boyfriend – well, who she thinks is her boyfriend – and threatens to kill him if he doesn't pay up. He tells her he owes a lot of money to the man, she offers to help, but how, and that's when she sleeps with the so-called enemy.'

'How do they get away with that?' Saul asked.

'The usual threats of being beaten, even killed; it's big bully tactics.' She pointed a finger at him. 'You are that girl, as you owe money, not paid within a certain time, and you're reminded that you must pay up.' Saul nodded in agreement. 'What happened to the girl?'

'Her name was Claire Wilson; I'll introduce you to her some time.'

He handed her the tray, which she placed on the dresser, and looked at his watch. 'You owe me an hour so carry on.' He settled back onto the pillows.

She smiled. 'Naturally we couldn't let Claire back into the clutches of her pimp Johnnie, so she stayed with us. Ruby had always hated pimps. A couple of days later she told me that she was going to turn the house into a brothel. That way we would get a better type of clientele and we could refuse anyone we thought undesirable.

'We then went to explore the house. Ruby had only been interested n the ground and first floors, plus installing a bath. With torch in hand, we climbed the stairs. The attic was full of old beds, chairs, trunks and other bric-a-brac. There were two rooms on the third floor. Both had beds in them, which would need replacing. Ruby was amazed at the amount of stuff there was, much of it reusable.

'Ruby, being Ruby, approached Claire about staying,' Hannah smiled, 'and Claire leapt at Ruby, nearly knocking her down. She told Claire that if Johnnie comes a calling he would regret it.

'It took us a week of planning and three months to renovate the house. There was a small desk just inside the hallway, which now had a Persian-style carpet along the middle of the tiled floor continuing up the stairs to the first and second floors. The two left-hand dining rooms had been knocked into one, with fawn velvet velour wallpaper, a mock chandelier with tables and chairs dotted around the room.' Hannah stopped for a second, a slight smile on her face, still playing with a comb.

'Hey, don't stop now.'

Hannah laughed. 'There was a drinks bar at the end of the room with French doors leading out to the small garden. On the other side of the hall the room was again papered with velvet velour but a deep red colour. In there were sofas and armchairs where the girls could relax with their clients.

'Upstairs Ruby's old bedroom had been made into two. Mine and Claire's was as before. One of the bedrooms on the third floor was Ruby's. You saw Dr Franks?'

'Yes.'

'He came in one day and befriended Claire. He's in love with her, but too scared to ask her to marry him in case she rejected him. Anyway he was our doctor, examining the women to make sure they hadn't caught anything.'

'His payment, I presume, was a night with Claire,' Saul said.

'Two nights once a month.' Just then they were interrupted by a knock at the door. Hannah opened it.

'There's a lady in the foyer, said she's the gentlemen's sister.'

'Okay, Claire, I'll come down.'

Hannah reached the bottom of the stairs and walked to the desk to greet the woman standing there. She smiled at Hannah. 'I'm Sally, Saul's sister.'

They shook hands. 'Hannah.'

'How's Saul?' Sally asked. 'Has he seen a doctor?'

Hannah smiled. 'Yes, the doctor has only just left. Would you like to see your brother?' She felt nervous in Sally's presence, which wasn't like her. 'Of course you would. Please follow me.'

'Thank you,' Sally said, following Hannah up the winding staircase, wondering what Saul was doing in a brothel. Hannah stopped at a door on the first floor, opened it and walked in, followed by Sally.

Saul was in that state of being half-awake and half-asleep when the door opened. Letting out a moan of pain as he tried to sit up, he saw Sally behind Hannah who stepped into the room. Sally's hand went to her mouth on seeing Saul's face.

'Who did that to you?' she asked in a shocked voice, but before Saul could answer she turned to Hannah. 'Thanks for looking after him, I'll get a cab and take him home with me.'

'I'm sorry, but he can't be moved at the moment – doctor's orders,' Hannah said, adding, 'It would be better if he stayed here.'

Hannah thought that Sally would object, but she didn't, saying in the scolding voice one would use to a child as she moved towards the bed, 'What have you done this time? Everyone's looking for you.'

'It was Bull Burgess.'

'What! The loan shark – I could slap you, you should know better.' She stared at him, biting her bottom lip. 'What am I going to say to Papa?'

'Don't tell him anything, please.'

'What about Burgess, how much do you owe him?'

'Probably eight hundred pounds by now,' was the quiet reply.

'I'm sorry, Saul, but I haven't got that sort of money.' She sat on the end of the bed, taking his hand. 'You must tell Papa. He will find a solution.'

Saul pointed to his face. 'If he saw that, he would be angry with me for letting it happen.'

'Was it just Bull?' Sally asked.

'There were three of them,' Hannah said. 'I saw it through my window.'

'Why didn't you call the police or ambulance?' Sally asked.

'Saul asked me not to.'

'Saul, please let me tell Mama and Papa. I'm sure Papa would understand.'

'Not about the gambling.'

'Take the chance, I guarantee he would find out somehow. You know he always does.'

'Okay, but don't tell him where I am, just that I'm being looked after and I'll be home next week when I'm feeling better.'

Sally looked at Hannah. 'Is that okay with you, Saul staying here?'

'Of course, and I agree with him.'

Sally stood. 'That's settled, and I'll tell Mama and Papa I have found you and that you will be home late next week.' She bent and kissed him on the cheek, and then turned to Hannah. 'I'll ring to see how he is getting on, if that's okay with you.'

'Of course.' Hannah moved towards the door. 'He needs to sleep.' Sally nodded in agreement and the women left the room.

At the front door they shook hands. 'Thank you for your help.'

'No problem.'

Hannah watched Sally enter the taxi, and as it drove away they waved to each other. Hannah took a couple of steps backward into the hall, closing the door and standing there for a couple of minutes, her mind on Saul. His presence there had unnerved Hannah, making her unsure of her actions in front of him, which brought back memories. She turned and walked hesitantly to the front desk, dropping onto the chair behind it. Her knee touched a whip hanging unseen from a hook. She looked around; the hall was empty of people so she took the whip from the hook, looking at the wall opposite and running her fingers along the whip, wondering when it came to that part of the story whether she should tell Saul.

That night she slept with Claire, but was up early in the morning preparing a breakfast for Saul, allowing for two cups of tea, knowing he would want to hear more about her and the brothel.

She knocked on the door and entered to see him sitting up. 'It looked like you've had a good night's sleep,' she said with a smile.

'Those tablets work wonders.'

She placed the tray onto the dresser and poured the tea. 'I've made some scrambled eggs, I didn't know what you liked for breakfast, and thought you wouldn't want anything too heavy. There's toast and jam if you want.' She took the tray over to the bed, placing it across his lap.

'For what it's worth,' Saul said, placing a piece of scrambled egg onto the end of his fork. 'Thank you, you saved my life.'

'That's too dramatic, but you're welcome.' She sat on the stool, taking a sip of tea.

'I hope you're going to continue the Hannah Grozenski story?'

'I thought you would be bored with that by now.'

'No way,' he said enthusiastically.

'Okay, but you might fall asleep. The year passed quickly as Ruby taught us the art of pleasing a man, but also pleasing ourselves. At the end of 1929 Ruby put an advert in a social paper advertising the escort agency, and placed a red light over the front door of the house. We opened for business on New Year's Eve, heralding in 1930 with a full, happy house.' Hannah stood and paced the room a couple of times, a frown creasing her forehead.

'Hannah, what's the matter?' There was concern in his face and voice.

She turned to face him. 'I'm going to tell you something that I've never told another living soul. When I've finished I would understand if you would want to go home.'

'It cannot be that terrible.'

'So, do you want me to carry on, or—'

'Come here,' he said it like an order and she moved over to the bed. He winced as he took her hands in his, saying quietly, 'I promise, no matter how bad this was, I would not condemn you.' He kissed the back of both her hands and let go, handing her the tray, settling back into the pillows.

'Twenty-first of February 1931 – that date is etched into my mind. I had an escort job at the Waldorf Hotel. I walked over to the concierge desk, smiled at him and asked if he could tell Mr Nathaniel James that Miss Green had arrived. I always used Green as a second name. Who would hire someone with the name Grozenski?'

'I would,' Saul said with a smile.

She ignored the remark and carried on. 'The concierge told Mr James that I had arrived. He covered the mouthpiece with his hand and said to me, "Mr James asked if you wouldn't mind meeting him in his suite as he was waiting for a phone call from America." I never went to a man's room I was escorting, unless there was a prior arrangement, but in this instance I told him to tell Mr James I was on my way. The concierge gave me one of those smiles, but I ignored it as he said Suite 501, and told Mr James I was on my way.

'I knocked on the door to 501, which was opened by a smiling, slightly tubby man with slicked-back brown hair with a parting to the left. His shirt collar was undone, as was the tie, and the braces of his dark brown trousers hung down his thighs. He smiled at me, showing even white teeth, "Please come in," he said. "My, you are a beauty."

'He had a southern American drawl and moved back into the room and across to a coffee table where the phone receiver lay. He said, "Honey, I'm in the middle of a call," and picked up the receiver. "My escort just arrived, Harvey, she's a beaut." I should have known then to get out of there as he said quietly, "Harvey I trust you to get it done," and then he changed, saying, "No, godammit!" yelling down the phone, at the same time pacing up and down a few steps at a time like a caged lion, shouting, "Don't fuck with me, Harvey, because when I get back, as sure as eggs are eggs, I will kill you."

'The voice said something at the other end, which seemed to calm him down. He sat on the settee, fingers stroking his brow. "I have a meeting in..." he looked at the clock on the mantelpiece "...twenty minutes." He glanced at me as Harvey said something to him. His lips twisted slightly in a smile. "I'm sure I will."

'He placed the phone on his shoulder, bringing it to his ear to stop it falling as he buttoned up his shirt and knotted the tie, saying forcefully, "They need to work an extra two hours if I'm going to pull this deal off, the boys and girls. Use the whip if you have to. I'm going now, see you at the end of the week."

'He slammed the receiver down and walked over to the mirror, at the same time picking up his jacket hanging on the back of the chair and put it on, looked in the mirror to straighten his tie, and then spread his hands and smiled saying, "Showtime." He turned to me and said, "Let's go."

'I smiled at him, asking, "Where to?" He laughed – it was one of those laughs you hoped not to hear too often, as it was loud and brash. "We're eating at the restaurant here. I don't like your weather; give me Southern sunshine any day of the week."

'In the lift he moved closer. There was a smell of pomade as he bent to kiss me, but I stopped him, saying that it was inappropriate. As luck had it, the lift stopped at another floor and two people got in. They said good evening, but he ignored then. With my arm through his, I was his escort. We entered the restaurant, stopping by the maître d's desk.

'"Good evening, sir, madam, you have a reservation?"

'"Yes, name of Mr James. Suite 501."

'The maître d' ran his gloved hand down the list, smiled and picked up some menus, saying "Follow me," and stopping at a corner table. "As you ordered, sir." He left on seeing no tip was forthcoming, returning a few seconds later with a broad-shouldered man, gesturing, "Mr James's table," and quickly turned around, returning to his station.

'James stood to greet the man, holding out his hand. "Mr Forth, I presume."

'Mr Forth smiled, taking the offered hand. "Mr James, I presume," he said in a Scottish accent and they both laughed at the simple joke. Mr James gestured to me. "Miss Green."

'Mr Forth bowed, saying, "It's a pleasure to meet you."

'He sat opposite the American as a waiter came to their table asking if we would like to order drinks. Mr James said a bottle of champagne, without asking anyone else what they might want. As he moved away, another waiter appeared to take our orders. When the champagne arrived I asked the waiter for a jug of water. James leant close to me saying he didn't ask for water. All my instincts told me to get out then, but there was this stubborn streak in me that had to face up to him.

'"Isn't the champagne good enough for you?" he asked me. I told him it was, but one glass was enough for me.

'He grabbed my arm, telling me that he was paying good money for me, and he would tell me when I'd had enough. Mr Forth could see something was happening, but stayed silent.

'As we ate they discussed business. I had finished my glass of champagne and was pouring myself a glass of water when he grabbed my hand, saying he would tell me when to drink water. I looked into his eyes.'

She shivered, wrapping her arms around herself. 'Saul, they were lifeless.'

'Why didn't you make some excuse and leave?'

'I honestly don't know. He poured me another glass of champagne, continuing with his meal and conversation as though nothing had happened. I remember the conversation as though it were yesterday. Mr Forth said he knew of no one that could deliver the amount of cotton Mr James said he could in the time stated. If he could make the delivery Mr James had a deal. The American said he would have the first shipment in three weeks.

'They spat in the palms of their hands and shook on the deal, and then that bastard Mr James wiped his hands on my dress. I took the full glass of champagne and leaned over to kiss Mr James, spilling the champagne onto his crutch. He—'

The roar of laughter from Saul stopped her for a moment, 'I'm sorry,' he said. 'Please carry on.'

'Naturally I apologised profusely. He was red in the face, telling Mr Forth he would have to cut short their meeting. "You shall have your cotton as promised." He grabbed my arm, telling me to walk in front of him. In the lift he grabbed my arm again and as the door opened on the fifth floor, he dragged me along the corridor, slamming me against the wall. He leaned his body onto mine as he opened the door to the room, pulled me into the room and began slapping me.'

'The bastard,' Saul tried to get up, but dropped back onto the bed again in pain.

'Please stay where you are,' she moved across the bedroom, handing him a tablet and glass of water. 'Painkiller.'

'Thanks, please if you are able, continue.'

'The power of the blow knocked me to the floor. He was quickly out of his trousers. I began to scream, but he stuffed his tie into my mouth, saying, "I'm going to show you what we do to whores in the South." He picked me up by my hair and threw me onto the bed, ripping my dress and panties off. I tried to resist, but he was too powerful and vicious, punching me as he … well, I passed out.

'I woke up to find the room in darkness. I tried to get up, but fell back onto the bed in pain. Taking deep breaths I managed to get to my feet, I felt sick, but stopped myself on hearing snores from the next room. I moved towards the open door. The American was in a drunken sleep. I saw his wallet on the dresser. Relieving it of the cash, I picked up my torn dress and underwear, moving as quietly as I could to the cupboard, taking a shirt and overcoat to hide my nakedness. I took his room key and a gold watch, leaving the hotel by the back entrance and took a cab home.

'It was two in the morning when I arrived home and as usual Ruby was waiting for me. Her face said it all on seeing me and she immediately ran me a hot bath, wanting to call Dr Franks as the American had damaged me. I told her later that once I had washed I was going back, and that I had the key to his room. She immediately awoke Claire.

'We entered the hotel by the rear door that I'd left slightly open, and used the back stairs to access the fifth floor, making sure we weren't seen.

'The American was still asleep when we got there. We stripped till we were naked, and then carrying a bag we brought with us, we entered Mr James's bedroom. I crawled onto the bed to lie next to him while Ruby and Claire stood either side of the bed. He stank of alcohol. I whispered one, two, three, and rammed one of his handkerchiefs into his open mouth and lay across his chest as Claire and Ruby expertly handcuffed him to the bed.

'He was so drunk that at first he didn't resist. He opened his eyes and saw me. He tried to get up, but couldn't. I jumped off the bed and helped Claire tie his left leg to the bottom of the bed, and then Ruby tied the other leg, while all the time he struggled, making noises behind the handkerchief. I placed the bag on the bed so he could see it, and withdrew a whip, half the size of the original, but just as lethal.

'I whispered in his ear, "By the time we have finished with you, you'll either be dead, or wish you were." I then lashed the whip onto his genitals. He tried to move sideways, but couldn't as the whip came down time and time again. I stopped after twenty lashes; the bed was soaked with blood and pieces of shredded skin, his face was red from trying to scream through the gag in his mouth, and he was breathing heavily through his nose.

'Ruby grabbed his face between a gloved thumb and forefinger so he could see her and said, "I wanted to cut your dick off and slam that into your mouth, but she said no."

'Without warning we untied the right handcuff from the bed and climbed over his body, dragging it across the bed and tying it down once more. This time he lay on his side, exposing his back. I said to him, "I told my two friends about you working young boys and girls to make sure your delivery was on time to Mr Forth, and we were sure the methods you used was this."

'I held the whip up so he could see it, and then stepped back and began whipping him. I stopped for Claire to take over, and then Ruby. We stopped and I looked into his eyes to see if there was any remorse, but they stared coldly back. With all the pain he was in he wanted to hurt someone, preferably me. I knew then what I had to do. I told Ruby and Claire that I had to kill him.'

Hannah stood, moving to look out of the bedroom window, and then turned to look at Saul for a minute, waiting for any comment, but he said nothing, just gestured for her to carry on.

'Ruby asked if I was sure. I told them to look into his eyes, which they did. I told them once he was better he would come looking for me.

'We cleaned up, making sure we had left nothing behind, not a fingerprint or footprints, or hair. No one must know we were there. We managed to tie him spreadeagled onto the bed taking our handcuffs. Just before we left, I slid a sharp-bladed knife across his wrists, opening the vein. He tried to get at me but his bonds held him down. I told him, "The more you struggle, the more you bleed, and as your life ebbs away, think of the amount of slaves you had whipped, and probably killed, but especially what you did to me," and then there it was, his eyes showed fear.

'I showered, washing his blood from my hands and body. We left the hotel the way we had entered, taking a taxi home.

'With Dr Franks's help, it took me six months to get over the ordeal Mr James had put me through. Luckily I was a strong person, and my revenge had been swift. There was an item in the evening papers that a Mr Nathaniel James from America had been found dead in his hotel room. No other information had been forthcoming from the newspapers then or since.'

She was silent, staring at Saul, who took a deep breath and said, 'I think you're wonderful, and brave, and your decision was the correct one. If you would have let him live, the consequences don't bear thinking about.'

There were tears in her eyes. 'Thanks, that means a lot to me.'

'Is that the end of the story?'

Hannah picked up the tray, a big smile on her face. 'Yes there's more, but you'll have to wait, I have things to do.'

'Oh come on, you cannot leave me like this.'

'Later, get some sleep.' She walked slowly down the stairs, thinking about Saul, which once again stirred up feelings she thought she would never feel again.

Gradually, over the next week, Saul became more mobile, with just a little discomfort, the painkillers that Dr Franks had given him helping ease the pain. The good doctor had visited once more, and had given him the all-clear to walk about but still be careful.

For two days after telling Saul about the American, Hannah had managed to avoid Saul, but then he cornered her in the lounge area.

'If I didn't know better I believe you were trying to avoid me.'

'I'm sorry, but I've been rather busy.'

He was moving his head, trying to make eye contact, which she was trying to avoid.

'You promised to tell me more of Hannah Grozenski's story, but...' He was silent for a minute. 'If you don't want to continue,' he said softly, 'I could leave.'

She looked up, her eyes searching his. 'Even though Dr Franks had said you could walk about, you're still in no fit state to leave.' She sighed. 'Okay I'll meet you later, and I'll bring the sandwiches, unless you fancy something else?'

He smiled. 'No that's great, your room or mine?'

She slapped him playfully on the arm. 'Mine.'

They sat at either end of the bed, a tray of food in front of them. She watched him for a moment, a slight smile on her face. He saw her looking.

'What?' he dabbed the corners of his lips.

She shook her head. 'There's nothing there.'

He looked down at the sandwich in his hand and then up at her. 'I'm sure, like in a casino, there are many funny, but serious stories in a brothel, especially where the public were concerned. There was a time when my father and his partners had to virtually fight for their own and their families' lives.'

She was about to say something, but he said, 'I'll tell you all about them one day, but only when you've finished yours.' He pointed a finger. 'Please don't leave anything out, I'm sure we could match ours with yours.'

Hannah looked at him for a moment, wiping her hands on the serviette. 'In May 1933, which I'm sure you remember, we were having a wonderful summer. I decided for no reason whatsoever to take a bus ride to Green Park. I watched the guards marching up and down outside Buckingham Palace for a while and then strolled into St James Park, which at that time of the year was in full bloom. I sat on a bench, watching some children playing tag. For no reason I turned to look at the gentleman seated at the other end looking impassively straight ahead as if seeing something that no one else could see. My view was suddenly blocked by a young man with a white-toothed smile, who said, "It's a nice day, isn't it."

'I replied politely that it was. He then sat on the bench and slid closer to me. "My name is—"

'"I don't want to know your name," I said, angry at the intrusion. But he was annoying so I told him, "Sir, would you leave me alone." He was about to say something when a voice said, "Young man, the lady isn't interested." It was the gentleman at the other end of the bench. "Be a good boy and do as she asked."

'"It's none of your business, old man, so—" the young man yelled in pain as the man's cane smacked him across his knees. I tried not to laugh as he said in that upper-class English accent. "You whippersnapper, have respect."

'The young man stood, fist clenched by his side. The elderly gentleman quickly got to his feet. Not wanting a fight I stood between them, facing the young man. He was angry at the rejection and called me a whore. He nearly fell to the ground as the old gentleman brought his cane down onto his shoulders.'

Hannah burst into laughter, 'He then said in that funny upper-class English accent. "If I had a bar of soap I'd wash your mouth out." The young man turned and ran off.

'I thanked him for being my gallant knight. He doffed his hat with a slight bow. "My name is Peter Johnson."

'I curtsied. "Hannah Green. How could I ever thank you, Mr Johnson." He smiled – he had deep green eyes that sparkled mischievously as he said, "I would like to take you to tea. I know a little place close by." I told him I would be honoured and arm in arm we left the park, ending up to my surprise at the Ritz Hotel tearoom.

'While we waited for the order to arrive he told me that he usually had tea alone and it had been a long time since he had had the company of a pretty woman. I said he was a handsome man, that any women would be happy to accompany him anywhere. He then said, "Would you accompany me anywhere?"

'I was taken aback, but there was something in his question that made me say yes. He was a widower, having lost his wife and son in a boating accident.'

She slid from the bed, taking their trays to the dresser, and turned suddenly, tears sliding down her face. In barely a whisper, she said, 'Saul, I never in my wildest dreams thought I would fall in love with him – a man old enough to be my father, but I did.'

Saul moved quickly from the bed, ignoring the pain, wrapping his arm around her, cuddling her to him as the sobs racked both their bodies. Gradually the sobbing stopped, but she didn't immediately move away, finding comfort in his arms.

'You okay now?' he asked.

She moved her head from his shoulder and nodded, wiping the tears from her face with the back of her hand. She moved from his arms onto the stool and he onto the edge of the bed.

'Peter must have been a very special person for you to have loved him like that.'

'They were wonderful days. He showed me the wonders of the ballet and opera, and he never ever talked to me like I was his daughter.'

'How did he—'

'I was going to meet him at the cinema. He was already there when I arrived. He waved when he saw me and then he suddenly collapsed. Heart attack. I never knew – he never ever told me he had a weak heart. I went to the funeral where I met his sister and brother-in-law, who knew all about me. They couldn't stop thanking me for making Peter so happy. Some weeks later I received a letter from Peter's lawyer and a cheque for ten thousand pounds that Peter had left me in his will.'

There was silence between them until Saul said, 'Come on, I'll help you carry these downstairs.'

'You will do nothing of the sort; I'll send one of the girls up for them.'

3

Poland was quickly overcome by the might of the Germans' armour and air power. Its army was in tatters. Hitler asked President Roosevelt to broker a peace deal with Britain and France, but he refused.

The German U-boats had taken no time in sinking British ships, while European countries like Yugoslavia mobilised their armed forces, but Sweden and Norway stayed neutral. Britain sent 150,000 men to France.

It was evening at Ruby's and Saul went for a walk in the garden. Hannah watched him from the lounge window. He had taken no notice of the women walking around the house, some scantily clad, and the men pairing off. She stared at him, unable to take her eyes from his face, and then that feeling, her heart racing breathing heavy, and suddenly the feeling of guilt as though she was betraying Peter.

She turned from the window, returning quickly to the desk, and sat on the stool beside it. Tears rolled slowly down her face and then she remembered Peter's sister, Claudia's words, *Put Peter somewhere in your heart and now and again let him out.* She left the desk, going into the bathroom to wash her face. As she wiped her face dry she looked steadily into the mirror.

'Do you love him?' she whispered, but she knew the answer before asking it. 'Yes,' she whispered, stepping back, knowing how crazy it was, having known him such a short time, and knew she shouldn't feel guilty about Peter – that was in the past. She made a locking motion over her heart, applied some lipstick and with a smile on her face returned to the desk just as Saul walked into the hall, stopping in front of her.

'Would it be possible for me to make a phone call?'

'Of course, there's an extension in the lounge.'

'Thanks.' He turned and walked away, Hannah's eyes following him until he disappeared into the lounge.

Twenty minutes later he appeared, heading for the desk. He stopped a few yards from her when some gentlemen arrived. He waited until they had walked past before moving to the desk. He smiled. 'You're very busy this evening, but I wondered if you would be able to continue the Hannah Grozenski story some time, perhaps...' he touched her hand resting on the desk, which sent her mind into a tizzy '... some time late tonight.'

She couldn't answer for a second, as they made eye contact, hoping he wouldn't hear the beating of her heart. 'Yes we are busy, and I might not be able to get away for some time. Surely you've have had enough of —'

'No,' he interrupted. 'Please, I'm intrigued that such a young woman like you is a madam. There must be more, and this house is nothing like the house you explained to me in East London.'

37

She held up her hands in surrender. 'Okay, I'll tell you tomorrow.'

He made a face, 'I don't think I could wait that long.'

She laughed. 'You are a glutton for punishment.'

'Being in your company is far from punishment,' he said seriously.

'Okay, but it might not be till very late, perhaps early morning.'

'Can't someone else look after the desk?' He swept an arm. 'All these women and not one of them would be able to sit there?'

'It's more than that, I have to make sure the men entering here are not drunk or on drugs, and would respect the women.'

'What about Ruby?'

The smile left her face. 'I said I would try and see you later, but I cannot say when.'

Saul quickly realised he might have overstepped the mark. He patted her hand and said timidly, 'Okay, whenever you are able, no matter what time.'

He turned away, walking towards the stairs. Her eyes followed him. Just then the bell rang.

It was three in the morning when Hannah locked the front door, switched off the red light and slowly made her way to Claire's bedroom, where she had been sleeping, to find Claire asleep. Hannah washed, undressed and took off her make-up. Tying the belt of her dressing gown, she quietly closed the door, walked along the hallway and knocked on her bedroom door.

Saul opened it, a smile on his face, and stood aside for her to enter. What he really wanted to do was take her in his arms and kiss her.

Hannah smiled back as she entered the bedroom, wishing that he would hold her and kiss her, but she sat at the end of the bed, and he on the stool by the dresser. She looked down at her hands and that sad feeling of Peter's loss engulfed her once again but disappeared as soon as she said, 'Peter's sister Claudia gave me some good advice.' She looked up at him. 'But I'll tell you about that another time.'

She stood and leaned her back against the door. 'It took me awhile before I was able to face people again, but I needed a change, a lighter mood, so I suggested that Ruby and I go to Paris, but only if Claire could look after the place for us. Claire told me not to be silly, she would look after everything and we shouldn't worry.'

Hannah smiled, brushing a strand of hair from her forehead, her mood gay as she continued. 'Ruby and I went to the Eiffel Tower, and in the evening the Moulin Rouge and... well, another time we decided to see what a top Paris brothel was like, so we bribed the concierge, explaining we were not lesbians, and went to La Belle Femme. At first we were refused entry, until we asked to speak to the madam, who luckily for us spoke English. We explained that we had a brothel in

London, and wanted to compare notes.

'The madam showed us around, opening doors to bedrooms both occupied and empty. We thanked the madam, extending an invitation to visit us in London, inwardly hoping she wouldn't. Her brothel made our house look like a hovel.'

Hannah sat back onto the bed. 'She charged her clients a lot of money, but...' Hannah had that faraway look as though she were seeing it again '... the ideas and décor of the rooms were magnificent. Ruby said our beds and furniture looked like they belonged in an old age home compared to La Belle Femme.

'We had bought so many presents and clothes for ourselves we had to buy a trunk.' Hannah laughed. 'We couldn't wait when we got home to open the trunk and hand out our presents to the girls, especially to Claire who had kept the place running smoothly.

'I couldn't get over the brothel in Paris, and a couple of weeks after our return I knocked on Ruby's bedroom door, which I had never done before. That was her private domain, but I had this idea, and I had to talk to her about it.

'She opened the door, holding a picture of a handsome man in a dress suit. "Who's that?" I asked.

'"Robert Gardner," she replied, "my one and only love."'

'That's the—'

'I'll come to that later,' Hannah interrupted him. 'I told Ruby that I couldn't get the Paris brothel out of my mind and had been comparing it with ours. She said she had too. "In that case," I said, "sell your place, and whatever you get for it, I'll match it, and while we wait for a buyer, look for a bigger better place?"

'She said it was a great idea, but a bigger, better property in that area, she didn't think so. I said, "So what? We could look somewhere else," but Ruby was unsure, saying that we had a good place there. I told her that she was putting obstacles in the way, and she knew in her heart of hearts it was the right thing for us to do, having seen Paris. She was scared in case we failed, but I pointed out that if we didn't try we would always wonder what if, and if we did fail we had tried and would have no regrets. Ruby held out her hand and said, "Okay, let's do it, partner."'

'So you bought this place,' Saul said.

Hannah's eyes shone, and there was a slight smile on her face. 'Yes we did, both agreeing that Paris was a dump compared to Compton Terrace. Ruby sold her place within a week of putting it on the market. Luckily for us the new owners didn't want to move in for a while, so it gave us time to renovate this house.'

'I must say you did a brilliant job,' he said.

'Thanks, it was a labour of love.'

'When did you open?'

'November 26th 1935. We put an article in a magazine that we knew was distributed to gentlemen's clubs. Claire worked the kitchen with a cook we had employed. We hired waitresses for the evening who wandered around with a variety of canapé's and champagne. We had a small combo playing music in the dance area. That's when I met Mr Henshaw.'

Saul leaned forward, elbows on his knees. 'Who's Mr Henshaw?'

Hannah stared at the wall behind Saul. 'Henshaw was about forty.' She made a face. 'Not handsome, but spoke well and had that sort of air that said: here I am. He asked me to dance, and I accepted. While we danced he asked if he would be able to see me if he attended the establishment, as he put it. I said he would have to wait and see. He then said, "Call me Derek." I told him we had a strict rule that we call our clients by their second name as there were gentlemen who didn't want others to know they frequented an establishment like this, and their anonymity was our main concern. He apologised.'

'Have you had any trouble from the neighbours?' Saul asked.

'There were a few moans at first, but although there were people arriving at funny hours during the day and night, it did not interfere with them. The local shops got to know us, some of them coming here, but we didn't have a name except for Number One. A year after opening we added the two portraits you see in the lounge, one of Richard Gardner and the other Peter Johnson.

'It was at this time that Ruby and I decided not to see any more clients, although I hadn't since ... you know. Ruby and I had a ritual: once a month we would go to the opera or ballet, and once a week to the Jewish Theatre in Commercial Road.'

She stood and walked over to the bed to sit next to him, but didn't look at him as she said quietly, 'It was on one of those nights in July that Derek Henshaw arrived. I hadn't seen him since the opening night. Claire in our absence was at the desk. He asked to see me. Claire explained that I wasn't there that night. He was angry, saying he didn't believe her. She asked him to keep his voice down as he was disturbing the clients. He then asked when I would be there. Claire told him the following evening. He was still angry that I wasn't there, but said that Claire should tell Ms Green that he would be back.'

'Did he return the next day?'

She ignored the question. 'I told Ruby that I had never given Henshaw any indication that I would, but when he returned I would deal with him.'

'Did he—'

Hannah held up a hand. 'Two months went by, and then one night the bell rang. We had put an intercom system in place so I picked up the phone and said politely, "Good evening, sir."

'He said, "My name is Henshaw. I was here a couple of months ago, but have been out of town. Would it be possible for me to see Ms Green?" I decided to let him in.'

'That's not a clever—'

'Please let me continue.'

He bowed, placing his finger on his lips and making a zip motion.

'"Long time no see, as they say," Henshaw said.

'"Yes, it has been some time." I said. "Where have you been?"

'"Here and there," he said.

'"You wanted to see me," I said.

'He pointed a finger upstairs. "I thought we could—"

'"I'm very sorry but I don't," I told him. "Not any more."

"Couldn't you make an exception for me?" He tried to grab me, but I avoided his hand.

'"I'm sorry," I insisted, "but no."

'He was angry, but then he said, "Okay, no is no, but is the young lady I saw last time available?"

'I told him I thought she was and he followed me to the lounge area where Claire was.

'"Claire," I said, "Mr Henshaw would like to spend time with you—"'

'Surely you aren't going to let him—' Saul interrupted.

'Saul, you have to let me carry on without—'

'Once again I'm sorry but—'

'Claire was nice to him, offering him a drink, and then they went to her room. The house at this time was nearly empty and some of the girls were dancing to a record, when suddenly a scream echoed around the house followed by others.

'I picked up my whip and ran up the stairs, hearing Claire yelling, "Please don't." I tried the door but it was locked. Ruby came along with a spare key, unlocked the door and threw it open. Shaw was naked astride Claire, punching her, yelling at her.'

Hannah got to her feet, leaning forward, using her hand like a whip. I whipped him across the back, yelling at him, "Get off!" He leapt off Claire, turning to me. He was uncontrollable yelling he was going to teach me a lesson for refusing his advances. I lashed the whip around his penis, he fell to the ground in pain and I lashed him again and again, screaming at him how dare he beat a defenceless woman, and then we heard the sound of police bells. Ruby said she had called the police, but I took no notice as I kicked and punched Henshaw. The girls pulled me off him, with Ruby asking me to stop. I told Henshaw if he ever came near one of my girls again I would kill him. Ruby whispered to me to pull myself together as the police had arrived and we went down to greet them.

'The constable said we had a call. There was someone beating a woman. "Yes, officer," Ruby said, "someone likes a certain type of, you know what, and it got a little out of hand, everything is okay now." The police left and we were immediately on the phone to Dr Franks, telling him it was Claire and an emergency. Claire's nose was broken, and there were bite marks around her nipples and bruises on her body. As he got dressed, Henshaw said he would be back. I punched him on the nose, telling him if he ever returned I would bury him in the garden. Henshaw left just as Dr Franks arrived.'

'What happened to Henshaw?' Saul asked.

'I needed information on Henshaw, so I spoke to someone who owed me a favour. Three weeks later I received a hand-delivered letter. I went immediately to Ruby's room, entering without knocking.'

Hannah knelt in front of Saul. 'Ruby was injecting something into her arm. Naturally she was angry, but I wanted to know what she was doing. She told me Dr Franks had prescribed it for her. I said, "Why has he prescribed heroin?" and then it hit me – cancer. She told me she had known for four months. She didn't want to say anything, otherwise we would fuss over her.'

Hannah smiled and got to her feet. 'She was right – we would have. She asked why the hurried entrance. I showed her the letter. Mr Henshaw was in prison for assaulting his wife and nearly killing her. As soon as he got out, he came here, and me rejecting him he took it out on Claire.

'At that moment there was a commotion downstairs, so I ran to the hallway and looked down to see Henshaw beating one of the girls. I told Ruby to call the police and ran to my room to get the whip, hiding it behind my hip as I yelled at him to stop. Henshaw began to climb the stairs as I walked down, and then he stopped a couple of stairs from me, saying he had come to teach me a lesson and pulled a pistol from his waistband.

'I goaded him: "Got an erection yet?" and wagged my little finger, saying, "Is that how big it is? Is that why you beat your wife?" I would have said anything just to get a little closer. "Did you enjoy the inmates, or did they enjoy you?" and then I was near enough and flicked the whip towards his wrist. He dropped the pistol and lunged at me.

'I stepped back and wrapped the lash around his ankle, that was luck. I pulled back on the whip, he lost his balance and tumbled head-first down the stairs just as the police entered the building to see him crashing to the floor. He was dead, broken neck. There were no charges as it was done in self-defence.'

Hannah began to cry. Saul stood and wrapped his arms around her. 'You are a very brave lady.'

'That's not why I am crying. On 2nd November 1936 Ruby passed away.'

'That's the portrait in the hall,' Saul whispered. 'She was beautiful.'

'Inside and out,' Hannah pointed out, moving reluctantly from his arms, adding, 'That's why it's called Ruby's.' She yawned, 'That's the story. Tomorrow it's your turn.' She walked to the door. 'Goodnight.'

'Thanks, Oh and where's the whip now?'

'Just hope you never see it,' she smiled closing the door behind her.

*

Since war had been declared Ruby's had been very busy, especially with young men. The house was quiet after another busy day, and Hannah decided to go for a swim in the indoor pool. After Ruby's death she had an extension built and a swimming pool installed, having seen it in a magazine. She was surprised when she got there to see Saul swimming up and down the pool. She was about to leave when he said, 'Where are you going?'

'Bed, it's been a long day.'

He pointed a finger at her. 'But you're here for a swim, why—'

'I thought no one was here.'

He laughed. 'I am, so join me.'

She smiled. Placing her towel on a chair and discarding her dressing gown, she walked to the edge of the pool and dived in, coming to the surface a couple of feet from him. 'Nice very nice.'

'Thank you, I—' It was then she noticed that he was naked.

He looked down, 'I came without any luggage. I could go if you prefer.' He began to walk to the edge of the pool.

'No, no, it's fine,' she laughed. 'It's not as if I haven't seen you naked before.'

He waded towards her. 'That's where you have the advantage on me.' He came to a halt in front of her. She looked into his brown eyes, and there it was – that feeling. He stepped closer, placing an arm around her waist and pulling her towards him. She didn't resist as his lips met hers and he began stripping the swimsuit from her. She wrapped her legs around his waist as his lips moved down to her neck and then her breasts.

'Let's finish this in my bedroom,' she whispered hoarsely.

Reluctantly they parted; she picked up her costume from the pool, draping the dressing gown around her as he pulled on his pants, and hand in hand they ran up the stairs and into the bedroom, quickly drying each other, smiling like little children. Unable to wait any longer, Hannah took his hand, pulling him towards the bed.

Hannah had a smile on her face as she lay content in Saul's arms. They had made love, showered and made love again. The light of dawn was filtering through the curtains when he said, 'I phoned my father.'

'Was he angry that you hadn't phoned earlier?'

He moved to look at her, a frown on his forehead. 'No, he didn't sound angry, just said come home when I'm ready.'

'Are you ready?'

He kissed her forehead. 'I am now, and it's silly to keep putting off the inevitable.' He moved slightly away so he could face her. 'The one thing my father does is listen. He won't jump to conclusions, he would hear what you had to say, and then see what the other person said before acting.'

'What does your father do?'

'Do you know the Victoria Casino?'

'Yes, I've been there a few times, well not for a few years, but yes I know it.'

'My father is part owner of that and the Hanover Casino in the West End.'

'And what do you do, except make an enemy of Bull Burgess? And yes I knew him. He tried to offer me protection, I did not accept.'

He stroked her left breast, kissing the nipple, 'I would have to go tomorrow, but I'll be back. For one I know I'm going to be called up pretty soon, and two, I must sort out the predicament I'm in with Bull.'

'I could give you the money,' she said earnestly, 'and then he would be off you're back.'

'Hannah, my love, it's a fantastic offer, but no thanks. This is my stupid fault, I must sort it out.' He kissed her gently on the lips; she responded, moving her hand downward until it found its objective.

On the first Wednesday of October Saul said goodbye to Hannah, having stayed an extra week and not wanting to leave. They kissed and arm in arm walked down the stairs to the front door where a taxi was waiting for him.

'I'll call you tonight,' he said, entering the cab.

Hannah watched it drive away till it had disappeared along Upper Street.

4

Saul's mother smothered him with kisses, and then smacked him on his arm. 'Why don't you call?' Her accent was more pronounced when she was angry. 'You hungry, I'll make you something to eat.'

'I'm fine Mama.' He looked at his father, the usual newspaper in his hand, surprised to see him home. 'Let's go into the dining room,' Wolfe said, folding the paper and tucking it under his arm as he rose to his feet, and walked out of the kitchen with Saul – who had been dreading this moment – in his wake.

As soon as they entered the dining room Wolfe turned to look at his son, taking his chin with his thumb and forefinger and turning his head left and right, the bruises still prominent. 'Why did you let them hit you that badly?'

'There were three of them, and they caught me by surprise.'

'I hear you owe this man a lot of money,' Wolfe said quietly, but before Saul could answer his father asked, 'Why are you gambling? Haven't you seen what it does to people?'

'Yes, Papa, you are right. I was playing cards, just small stakes, nothing big, just enjoying the game, when Fred Burgess joined in. He—'

'This the man they call Bull.'

'Yes, Papa. Well, before I knew it, we were the only two left in the game. I had a pretty good hand, three jacks and two fours.' Saul shook his head, despair in his voice. 'I was carried away by Bull upping the bet every time, until I suddenly realised what had been happening, and said "See you." He had four kings and I was into him for a fifty pounds. There was a fight that night between Johnnie Gold and Frank Frost. Frost had never won a fight, whereas Gold had won quite a few. It was a dead cert bet.'

'Nothing is a dead cert.'

'I know that now, one lucky punch and Gold was out for the count, and now I'm deeper in debt than before.'

'How much do you owe him now?'

'Burgess puts interest on interest.' Saul made a face, 'probably about a thousand pounds.' He expected his father to go mad, but Wolfe asked, 'Do you think he cheated at the card game?'

'To be truthful, Papa, I think so.'

'Okay, go clean up and change your clothes.' He held out an envelope. 'This came for you today.'

Saul took it and opened the envelope. 'I have to report for a medical next Thursday.'

Wolfe placed a hand on Saul's shoulder. 'I want you to go to the gym, every day. Next week we start training.'

Surprise showed on Saul's face. 'For what?'

'I'll let you know. Now off you go.'

As soon as Saul had gone, Wolfe picked up the telephone and dialled a number which was answered immediately. 'Frank, Wolfe here, I want you to find out all you know about a character, Fred Burgess, nicknamed Bull. Yes, as soon as possible, oh and Frank make sure he or anyone associated with him does not see you.' He listened for a moment. 'That's a better idea, thanks.' He slowly replaced the receiver, a thoughtful look on his face.

Obeying his father, Saul went to the gym, finding his cousin Abraham there. 'Where have you been? The entire East End had been looking for you.'

Saul smiled. 'That's an exaggeration even for you. How long you been here?'

'Just got here, why?'

'I'm a bit stiff and need a training partner. I haven't trained for three weeks.'

'That's not what I heard.' Abraham laughed. 'Care to tell me about it?'

'I'll see how hard you make me train.'

'By the way, have you received your medical papers?'

'Yes, for next Thursday.'

'I'm twenty-nine,' Abraham said. 'It will be ages before I get the nod. I thought of enlisting.'

Saul stopped skipping. 'Have you said anything to April?'

'Start skipping again,' Abraham ordered. 'No I haven't, and to be honest I don't know what she would say, but I feel I must go.' He dropped on all fours. 'Thirty press-ups.'

Saul dropped as his cousin counted. Two hours later, the sweat pouring from every pore, Abraham said, 'Great workout. As we shower you can tell me all about your three weeks of amour.'

It was eight o'clock the next morning when Saul returned to the gym and was surprised to see his father, Uncle Asher and Billy Reed already there and training as hard as they always did. Wolfe beckoned his son over.

'We're going to help with your training.'

'What's going on? Why this interest in my training? You have never pushed me before?'

'No, that's true, you always trained hard, but this is different. Saul, please trust me, I think you may need it.'

'Is this to do with my call-up?'

'No, but I promise you won't regret it, so this is what we're going to do.'

An hour and half later, Saul was in the boxing ring, facing Billy Reed and he hadn't landed a punch on the fifty-seven-year-old Irishman.

'You're far too slow,' said Billy. He landed two punches to Saul's helmet which shook him, but they weren't hard. Saul knew if Billy wanted to hit hard he would soon know it, but he was becoming more and more frustrated. His father had always told him if things weren't going your way, take a breather and think about it.

He moved to a corner to take stock. He had to be faster, but how? Billy Reed came at him again, landing two punches before Saul got himself out of the corner. It was then he knew he couldn't figure it out, remembering what his father had said: this was different, and Saul needed to trust him. Then that's what he would do.

Wolfe was at home when the phone rang, and picked up the receiver. 'Yes.'

'This is Frank. I have what you asked for.'

'Thanks, I'll be over in an hour.'

Wolfe walked into the Victoria Casino to be met by Frank. 'In the office,' he said.

Frank nodded and followed him. The office was empty because Asher and Billy were in the gym with Saul.

'Okay, what have you got?'

'Fred Burgess, known as Bull,' said Frank. 'Comes from Bermondsey. He was a bit of a boxer, more a bruiser, using his height and weight to overpower his lesser opponents.' Frank moved to the armchair.

'Would you like a drink?' Wolfe asked.

'It's a bit early for me, but you can—'

'Please carry on,' Wolfe interrupted.

'As I said, he fought men he knew he could beat, laying heavy bets on himself to win. He opened a card club in Jamaica Road, where he became a loan shark. Many desperate people came to him for a loan, women as well. He charged a high interest rate, doubling it if the lender missed a payment. Most of his IOUs are from people he played cards with.'

'So he's cheating?'

'Probably, but no one had proved it, and if they did know, he would soon make sure they shut up. In the past, Burgess had a run in with the police, but managed to wriggle out of it.'

'Does he still own the club, and play there?' Wolfe asked.

'Yes on both, but in the last few months he has been venturing over this side of the river.'

'Anything else I should know about him?'

'He could be dangerous, and does like beating up people.'

'Thanks, Frank, I may need you to help me bring this man down.'

'Any time, just call me,' he smiled. 'It would be nice to have a bit of excitement around here once again.'

Frank left the office and Wolfe wandered out into the casino. He stopped at one of the blackjack tables to stand beside the dealer. 'Joan, when your shifts over, could you please come to my office.'

'Thirty minutes, Mr Brown.'

He nodded and walked back to the office. Just over thirty minutes later there was a knock at the door. 'Come in,' he called out.

Joan walked in, closing the door behind her. He pointed to an armchair. 'Sit if you wish. Would you like a drink?'

Joan moved to the armchair. 'Gin and tonic please.'

He strode to the drinks bar. 'I need some help,' he said, pouring the drink, then picking up the glass and stepping towards her. 'There's a man who owns a card club in Jamaica Road, name of Burgess.'

'You mean Bull.'

'You know him?'

'Not personally, but I've heard of him.'

'He's a cheat, and not only that, the people he cheats owe him money at exorbitant interest rates, a shark.' He sat down on his high-backed leather chair behind the desk. 'Would you go to Burgess's club and find out how he cheats? I'll pay you, and give you the stake you need.'

'It could take a couple of weeks.'

'If that's what it takes, so be it.'

'Okay, I'll do it.'

Wolfe smiled, taking an envelope from his jacket pocket. 'Thanks, I appreciate that. Here's two hundred pounds. If you need more money phone me, and only me.'

*

Wolfe and Isaac stood dirt- and sweat-streaked by the back door leading to the garden. 'Eva, come here for a moment,' Wolfe called out.

Eva walked into the kitchen. 'Don't you dare come in here until you both take off those dirty clothes and the boots.'

'Eva, come into the garden. We want to show you something.'

'I'm okay.' She saw the look on her husband's face and moved forward, taking off her slippers, and put on some garden shoes. She followed Wolfe and Isaac to the rear of the garden.

'Our shelter,' Wolfe said proudly.

'Mama, you must look inside,' Isaac said, opening the door.

The two men had dug deep at an angle covering the roof with earth. Eva stepped inside. They had built a wooden floor with a bed either side of the shelter. Shelves covered the rear with a variety of tin foods and tea. 'We could make it as comfortable as we liked, and I assure you we would be safe.'

'But,' she stammered, 'nothing has happened yet. Mr Kline the butcher said this is a phoney war.' She frowned. 'What does that mean?'

'It's a pretend war,' Isaac said.

'Oh.' She turned a full circle and smiled at her husband. 'It's wonderful.' She kissed her husband and son. 'Well done.' But she wanted to scream as she walked quickly back to the kitchen, ordering over her shoulder, 'Take those muddy clothes off.'

Once the men had bathed and changed, Eva made them tea, cutting some slices of her marble cake onto a plate.

Isaac was doing the accounts. He found it easier to do them at home as it was quieter. Wolfe was reading a newspaper and Eva cooking the evening meal when Lily came into the kitchen, a big smile on her face. 'Guess what?' she looked at Isaac. 'I'm pregnant.'

'That's wonderful.' said Isaac, leaping to his feet, picking her up, turning a circle and kissing her at the same time, and then gently placing her back on her feet.

A week later Lily said to Isaac, 'My aunts are very excited about my pregnancy. Would you take me to Paris?'

Isaac looked at her in astonishment. 'Why do you want to go to Paris?'

'Well, I haven't seen my aunts since we were married, and they want to buy me clothes and things for the baby.'

'You are not going,' he said emphatically.

She leaned towards him. 'Why not?'

'Firstly we are at war; secondly Germany is now pouring troops onto its borders with France.' His voice softened. 'It's too dangerous.' He could see the spoilt Lily coming out, something he hadn't seen for a very long time. 'You could make your own maternity wear. Perhaps Sally would help you. It could be a new line. I'm sure it would sell well at the shop. You're a good knitter; you could make the babies clothes. I'm sure my mother would make something.' He knew that look as she moved to go, meaning 'one way or another I'll get my way'.

'It's not the same,' she pointed out. 'Anyway, French designs are better than here.' She turned and without another word walked out of the room.

A week went by and Isaac thought that Lily had realised he was right, and forgotten about Paris, but he should have known by now that when it comes to being spoilt by her French aunts, Paris had never left her thoughts. For two weeks Lily tried to think of a way of forcing Isaac to take her. That evening as they were getting into bed Lily said, 'Please take me to Paris.'

For a few seconds Isaac stood staring at her, and then said softly, 'Lily I love you, and you know I would do anything for you, but going to Paris now would be madness.' He walked round the bed and stood in front of her, placing his hands on her arms. 'Do you not realise that if I thought it was safe, we would be there now? It's the wrong time to go.'

She was silent as she stepped away from him and got into bed. He tried to cuddle her, but she said, 'Please take me.'

He didn't answer, knowing and hoping that she would soon accept that he was right.

*

A week had gone by, and Wolfe hadn't heard from Joan, but in the meantime he intensified Saul's training by bringing in men twice his size and weight to spar with. He took Saul for his runs and Asher pushed him with the weights, Billy Reed built up his boxing speed. Saul didn't ask any more questions, just got on with it, still with the belief that his father had a reason. Every night he spoke to Hannah on the telephone.

He reported for his call-up medical and then to the RAF recruitment. When he had finished he met Hannah and they went to the cinema. He returned home in the early hours of the morning, but was still up in time to train.

Late Sunday evening the phone rang and Wolfe answered it.

'This is Joan, Mr Brown. I have what you need.'

'Could you meet me tomorrow morning in my office?'

'Yes, Mr Brown, about ten. Is that okay with you?'

'See you at ten.'

On the dot of ten, Joan arrived. She handed Wolfe twenty pounds. 'Sorry, but that's all that's left.'

He smiled. 'No problem. What could you tell me about Mr Burgess?'

She sat down, crossing her legs. 'He's a cheat, and doesn't always use the same method.'

'Would you like a drink?'

'No thank you. As I was saying he uses a few methods. His favourite is marked cards, and he uses two ways to do so. One with the thumbnail, the other has a ring at the top of the cards marked like a clock. For example, if it's one o'clock it's the ace, two it's the king and so on. He's also had a girl serving drinks who liked to bend over to show her breasts when serving, so that the players were distracted, allowing her to see his cards.

'He only used her once, but he had two accomplices. One was a dealer, the other a watcher. A couple of occasions I saw him pick up a fresh deck, but it hadn't been sealed properly, so it meant the cards had been arranged beforehand. Your Mr Burgess is also a bully, especially if the lender hasn't made payment for a week. I saw him beat an old lady because she paid him a pound less. His two bully boys intimidate players, who in many cases play way beyond their means. This way he gets them to write an IOU. With his high interest rates they end up paying until who knows when. He keeps the IOUs in the safe in his office.'

'Thanks, Joan.' He handed her an envelope. 'For your time.'

'Can I help you in any way with whatever you have—'

'Did he notice you?'

'Sort of, he made rude remarks, but he does that to all the women.'

'I cannot put you in harm's way again,' he said quietly.

She got to her feet. 'I'll do anything to make him pay for what he does to people.' She waved the envelope, 'Thanks for this,' and left the office.

Wolfe sat at the desk, hands bridged, eyes narrowed in thought. He then picked up the phone and made some phone calls.

That same night, Wolfe, and Billy Reed entered Bull Burgess's club. Frank, with a nice-looking blonde on his arm, came a little later.

Burgess recognised Wolfe and Billy immediately, which was intended. 'Well, well, the mighty Wolfe Brown and his sidekick Billy Reed.' He looked around. 'And where's little brother?'

'He isn't here,' Wolfe replied.

Burgess bowed slightly. 'I'm honoured that you've graced my humble premises, but why?' He held up a hand. 'I know why, poor baby Saul. Has Daddy come to pay his debt?'

'As a matter of fact, no we haven't.'

'We heard about your any stakes card games, which we don't have,' said Billy.

Wolfe gave a slight smile. 'So we thought we would have a look, perhaps play a few hands.' He looked around the dimly lit room, knowing it was a cheater's paradise with the lights that low.

Burgess rubbed his hands together, 'I'm sure we could accommodate such distinguished guests. Perhaps you would like to join me?'

Billy smiled. 'Why not?'

Just then Frank moved in, saying in a broad Scottish accent, 'Can I join your game?'

Burgess smiled. 'The more the merrier.'

'Me lassie, can she play too?'

Burgess glanced at her and leered. 'Very pretty. Perhaps you would put yourself up as an IOU.'

There was a look of distain on her face as she placed a protective arm through Frank's.

'I have a separate room for honoured guests,' Burgess said, gesturing to a door. They entered a small room with a card table in the centre and six chairs. He moved past them, heading for one of the chairs, but Wolfe got there first and sat down. He looked up at Burgess, who seemed about to protest but didn't, instead taking one of the two empty chairs opposite Wolfe, who was sitting next to the young lady.

Just then another man entered the room with a box of wrapped playing cards. 'This is John, he'll be joining us.' John took the only empty seat between Wolfe and Billy.

Burgess unwrapped one of the packs and began shuffling. 'No limit draw poker.' He looked at each player as he dealt. No one objected to the play. The blonde stroked her left ear as Burgess dealt.

They had been playing for two hours; Burgess had a pile of money in front of him as did John. Wolfe was pretty low as were Billy and Frank. The blonde was nearly broke.

'I think it's about time we changed the pack, and hopefully our luck,' Billy said.

Burgess smiled. 'Certainly, you choose which one.'

Billy placed a finger on a pack.

'I think,' Wolfe said, 'that the young lady should take over the dealing.' He turned to her, looking down at the money she had left. 'I think you might want out.'

She smiled. 'You read my mind,' and turned to Burgess. 'I don't mind dealing. It would stop me being bored while I wait for Hamish.'

Burgess moved uncomfortably in his seat and was about to say something when Frank said, 'It would be fair, as this is a high stakes game, that we should all take a turns, if you object to my girlfriend dealing.'

Burgess was cornered, but he had John, 'I think—'

'It's a great idea.' Wolfe interrupted whatever Burgess was going to say.

John looked at Burgess, who handed the pack to the blonde.

Things began to move rapidly as in the next hour John lost everything, followed by Billy. The three left were about even. 'I'd like to change the pack,' Wolfe said.

Burgess looked at Wolfe, made to take a pack, but Wolfe said, 'Let the dealer choose.' Burgess removed his hand as though he had been stung, knowing he had no choice but to agree, and gave a little smile – more like a smirk – as he nodded, knowing they were all marked packs. The blonde picked up a pack and unwrapped it, throwing away the jokers, shuffled and dealt the cards.

An hour later, the only two left in the game were Wolfe and Burgess. The blonde dealt the hand, five cards to each player. Wolfe looked at his cards, 'Hundred pounds,' not looking at Burgess, who looked at his cards, running a finger across his right eyebrow, and smiled, placing a hundred pounds in the middle of the table, 'And raise you a hundred.'

Wolfe looked at his cards, taking one from his hand and laying it face down. 'One please.'

The dealer flicked him a card. He looked at his hand and closed the cards, waiting for Burgess, who discarded three cards. It was up to Wolfe to bet, 'Two hundred pounds and two more.'

Burgess looked at him and then his cards and closed them, staring at Wolfe. He pursed his lips, unfolded his cards again and picked up the money in front of him, peeling off some notes. 'Two hundred and—' he peeled of a wad of notes '—four more.'

Wolfe leaned on his right elbow, pinching his lip, staring at his opponent, placing the cards face down on the table and counting the money in front of him, saying, 'Am I right in saying this is a no limit game?' He looked up at Burgess, who licked his lips.

'Yes,' said Burgess softly.

Wolfe was still counting, placing the money in the centre of the table and taking a handful of money from his jacket pocket. 'Your four, and raise you a thousand pounds.'

There was a gasp from John and Burgess. They had never bet on anything higher than five hundred pounds, and then it would be a dead cert they would win. Burgess folded and unfolded his cards. 'I'm sorry, how rude of me, would you like something to drink?'

'No thanks.'

'I could do with—'

Wolfe smiled. 'Sorry Bull, but no one else is allowed into this room.'

'This is my club not yours, and I—'

Billy got to his feet and wandered over to the door, 'Need to stretch my legs.'

Burgess looked at his cards. 'Bet or forfeit the pot,' Wolfe ordered, adding, 'that's if you have the money?'

'I have the fucking money. You think because you have that big casino you're the only one with money.' He looked at his cards. 'I need to get some money out of my safe.'

'Hand your cards to John, so you know your cards are safe, and Shamus will go with you.'

'What – you think I'm going to cheat?'

'It has been known,' Wolfe said quietly, his eyes never leaving Burgess's.

Burgess gave the cards to John and with Frank in tow left the room, returning ten minutes later with a metal box, which he unlocked with a key attached to a chain around his neck. He gave a sneering smile. 'Now where were we?'

'The last bet, from this gentleman was a thousand pounds,' the blonde dealer said quietly.

Burgess took some money from the box tied up in one hundred pound bundles, counted out a thousand, placed his hand in the box. 'And raise you two thousand.'

Wolfe's face was impassive as he placed a hand into the inside pocket of his jacket. 'Bit of a piss-poor raise. How much you got in that box?'

'Why?'

'Humour me. How much?'

Burgess put his hand in the box and counted out the money. 'Two thousand.'

'What about the IOUs, not my sons.'

'Another five hundred,' Burgess said breathlessly.

'I raise your two thousand five hundred.' Wolfe counted out the money, placing it on the pile in the middle.

Burgess's face went white. 'That's all the money I have in the world.' He said it as a whisper, as though he didn't want anyone else to hear.

Wolfe looked around the room. 'Do you own this property?'

'Yes, why?' Burgess trembled, unable to stop answering the questions as Wolfe stared unemotionally at him.

'How much is it worth...' he circled his left hand '... rough guess?'

'Five hundred, perhaps a bit more.' Burgess was sweating.

Wolfe pointed at the pile of money and IOUs. 'Then that isn't all you have in the world.'

Burgess quickly wrote on a piece of paper, 'This is an IOU on the property.'

Wolfe placed five hundred pounds on the table. 'I'll see you.'

Burgess got to his feet, a big smile on his face, and triumph in his voice. 'Straight flush, clubs, two to the six.' He moved to swoop everything into his side of the table. Wolfe did not get to his feet as he placed his cards on the table one by one, saying, 'Nine of hearts ... ten

... jack ... queen ... king. I think I win.'

Burgess let out a yell of anguish. 'No, no.' He pointed a finger at Wolfe and then Billy Reed. 'You cheated.'

'How, they were your cards.' Burgess could not argue with that. 'Sit down,' Wolfe ordered.

Burgess stayed standing. Wolfe shrugged his shoulders, 'My son said he owes you a thousand pounds, is that right?'

Burgess nodded.

Wolfe looked the big man and said, 'I propose you fight my son in the boxing ring at York Hall on December 7th for the IOU.'

There was a big grin on Burgess's face. 'What if I win?'

'You give me the IOU and I give you two thousand pounds.'

Frank and the disguised Joan, who had discarded the wig, picked up the money and IOUs from the table as Billy Reed said, 'Don't try and claim any money from the IOUs we have.'

Burgess didn't reply.

'I'd like you to leave my premises,' Wolfe said.

Burgess stared at the blonde, pointing at her. 'I know you.' He moved towards her, but Wolfe and Billy stepped in front of him. 'I want you to stay in Bermondsey. The only time I want to see you on my side of the river would be for the fight.' He poked Burgess in the chest. 'The one thing you don't want to do is antagonise me.' He smiled. 'But you could get your own back in the ring with my son.'

'I'll see you on the 7th,' Burgess said, turned and walked out of the room.

Wolfe said to Joan. 'Could you use these premises? If so they're yours.'

'It would mean me leaving the Victoria.'

Wolfe handed her the IOU. 'We would miss you.' He smiled. 'That was flawless, I didn't see you swap over the pack. How did you do it?'

'If I tell you I would have to kill you.' They both laughed.

'Anything you need, call me, or the others.'

'I never ever thought that Bull had that much money,' Frank said to Billy as they returned the money into the casino's safe while Wolfe had gone to the gym to speak to Saul.

'Are you serious, me against that man mountain?'

Wolfe smiled. 'You would beat him easily, but you have to listen to me. From now till the seventh we – Bill, Asher and me – are going to train you even harder.'

'What about the IOU?'

'That's what you're fighting for.'

'And if I lose?'

'You won't lose.' He placed a hand on Saul's arm. 'It's not like you to be this way, and remember he had help. This time it would be just you and him.'

That evening Saul told Hannah about the fight. 'Is your Papa crazy? Have you seen what Bull had done to people?'

'Please don't worry; I have the best three people, sorry four to help me through. To tell you the truth, Hannah, I'm looking forward to having a go at him.'

'Will I see you on Saturday?'

'I'll come straight from the gym.'

'Don't tire yourself out. You'll need the energy.'

He laughed. 'Okay, see you then. Love you.'

'Love you too.'

York Hall, 7 December 1939

The atmosphere in York Hall was electric, with rival crowds from Bermondsey and East London throwing punches into the air and baying at each other across the ring where in opposite corners the two opponents waited for the announcer and referee as bets flew across the hall.

Burgess in a red dressing gown prowled his side of the ring, egging on his followers, while in the opposite corner Saul stood silent in his blue silk dressing gown as his father massaged his shoulders. Asher and Billy stood passive-faced on either side of him.

Since the fight had been announced, tickets had flown from the box office. Touts were selling them at four times the price. Everyone knew that Burgess had lost all his money as well as his club to Wolfe, except for the IOU of Saul's. Bets were still being exchanged around the hall as the announcer stepped into the centre of the ring, and suddenly there was silence.

'Ladies and gentlemen, this is the main bout of the evening. In the red corner—' he gestured towards Burgess '—the Bermondsey Bull, Fred Burgess, and in the blue corner—' he gestured again '—from East London, Saul Brown.'

The referee called the boxers into the centre of the ring. Saul did not flinch as Burgess tried to outstare him, neither hearing the referee's instructions until he said, 'Shake hands.' Burgess leaned towards Saul. 'You're going down, Jew boy.' Saul didn't say a word, just turned and walked back to his corner.

Burgess shred his dressing gown, showing why he was called Bull. Hair covered his massive muscular body; his bald head sat on broad shoulders with a small neck like a bowling ball; his legs were like tree trunks.

Wolfe helped Saul off with his dressing gown. There was a gasp from his side of the ring as they saw a six foot, broad-shouldered, confident man, muscles rippling as he moved, holding up his right arm, turning a full circle to the cheers of the East Enders.

Bull sat on the stool and on seeing there was no stool in Saul's corner stood gesturing for his to be taken away. Saul moved his head left and right, punching his fists together as the bell rang for round one.

The two fighters met in the middle of the ring. Bull threw a left, which only found air as he was hit with three quick punches to the stomach. Saul's body swayed, hands up protecting his chin, then as quick as a flash, his hands a blur, he landed two punches on Burgess's face. Burgess growled; he hadn't landed a punch, shook his head as two more punches found there mark.

Burgess moved forward, forcing Saul onto the ropes where he grabbed him on the referee's blind side, stopping Saul from moving, landing three punches to the muscular stomach. Saul leant back on the ropes, freeing his hands which landed a flurry of punches on Burgess's head as one would against a punching ball in the gym. Burgess had to let go and back-peddled away, but there was no respite as Saul followed him. The bell rang, saving him from further punishment. He flopped onto his stool, his face a red mask of hatred, staring across the ring at the standing Saul.

'He's too fast for you,' said John, his friend and second. 'You must get him in a corner; you know what to do then.'

On the other side of the ring Billy said to Saul, 'He's going to try and get you into a corner and do some dirty stuff. You know what to do.'

Saul nodded as his father placed the gum-shield in his mouth and the bell rang. Saul didn't move into the centre of the ring, but waited for Burgess to come to him and as he reached him Saul danced away, going round in a left-hand circle, forcing Burgess to turn to face him. He saw his chance and threw three quick punches to Burgess's face. As one the crowd went, 'Woo' at the quickness of the punches.

Saul continued, moving around the ring just out of the long reach of Burgess, who was getting more and more frustrated, and like a bull suddenly rushed at Saul, managing to wrap an arm around his waist, landing a hammer punch to the solar plexus. Saul tensed his stomach muscles, but even then it hurt, making him realise how powerful and dangerous Burgess was. He had to get out of the big man's clutches as he received heavy blows to the body. He tried to get away, but Burgess flung him onto the ropes and was about to land a punch to Saul's head when Saul dropped to the canvas as though he had been hit.

The referee pulled Burgess away, who was trying to punch Saul while he was on the canvas. The noise of the crowd was deafening. The referee began to count, but on four Saul got to his feet. The referee wiped his gloves, stepped back, and said, 'Box.' Just then the bell rang and the fighters returned to their corner with Burgess trying to figure a way of getting at Saul.

Billy said to Saul, 'You have to do it in this round.' He looked across the ring. 'He's trying to figure a way to get to you, and if he does, well I don't need tell you what would happen then.'

'Do you think you could do it now?' Wolfe asked.

Saul looked across to the opposite corner. Burgess was breathing heavily, and he was angry, and anger is blind. 'Yes, Papa, I could do it.'

The bell rang. Bull was hardly off his stool when Saul was in front of him, throwing punches so fast he was unable to block them. As soon as he covered his face, his body was pounded. Burgess tried to get away from his corner, but whichever way he turned he was met by a barrage of punches. Gradually he began to flounder and his head became fuzzy.

Saul could see the glassiness in Burgess's eyes as he punched his opponent as he would a punch ball in the gym. He didn't want Burgess to go down, not just yet, he hadn't hurt him enough. He threw punches at the big man's ribs, there was a yell of pain as one broke, followed by another. The crowd were silent as they witnessed a lesson in boxing. Burgess doubled over, Saul knew it was time, and with the full weight of his body threw an uppercut to the jaw. There was silence in the hall as Burgess slowly crumpled to the canvas, out for the count. The hall erupted, people stood clapping and cheering. Even Burgess's followers reluctantly applauded, many nodding their heads, having seen a fight that would be talked about in south and east London for many a year.

Saul hugged his father, Uncle Asher and Billy. 'Thank you for persevering with me.'

'You can pay for the five punching balls you broke this week, out of your winnings,' Billy said.

'How much did we make?' Wolfe asked Asher, who as always put on their bets. 'Five hundred pounds.'

'Is that all?' Billy queried.

'Each,' Asher said quietly.

'Now you're talking.' Saul held out his hand.

Asher handed him a wad of notes. 'Minus the punching balls.'

'No gambling,' Wolfe said seriously.

'No Papa, I'm going to take Hannah out for a night on the town. It may be my last chance for a long time.'

30 December 1939

'Come on, he can't wait all day to be rescued,' yelled Fire Chief McNamara as Wolfe and Billy left the extended ladder to move into the fake blazing building, while Asher and two other firemen held a hose that shot gallons of water into the building.

'You don't need water to put out the fire. McNamara's breath could do that,' Wolfe pointed out as he and Billy found the dummy. Billy bent and picked it up in a fireman's lift, carrying it to the window, where Wolfe climbed onto the ladder, taking the dummy from Billy, as the Fire Chief yelled once again, 'He'll be dead by the time you get him to the ground.' Wolfe climbed down, wanting to throw the dummy at the Chief.

Later, as they rolled up the hoses and cleaned their vehicles, McNamara came over to them. 'Well done, lads, another sixty hours under your belts.' He looked at the clipboard in his hand. 'I'll see you three on the second of January, Happy New Year to you.'

'You too, Chief,' they choroused.

Tired but happy, the three men carrying their wet uniforms headed home to clean and dry them. They had volunteered for the Auxiliary Fire Service a week after Saul's fight. Billy had pulled some strings to get them in, because of his age.

They were attached to Commercial Road Fire Station, where they had been issued with a uniform, steel helmet, rubber boots and waterproof leggings. The first few days were hard, learning to drill and obey commands. At first all three found it difficult using the Proton breathing apparatus, but gradually they had become used to wearing it. McNamara had pointed out that in a smoke-filled environment they would find it a lifesaver.

Luckily they were not scared of heights as they had to climb ladders and move into smoke-filled buildings to locate any occupants there and bring them to safety.

Entering the house after his first training session, he found Eva standing in the hallway, arms crossed, her facial expression in a 'Where have you been and what have you been doing?' look. Inside he was laughing at the sternness on her face but he didn't smile just said, 'What's the matter?'

'What's the matter? Are you *meshuggah*?[1] Do I need this *tsoris*?'[2]

He held up his hands, stopping her in midstream and smiled. 'Now you have that off your mind, what's wrong?'

She moved forward and hit him. 'What's that?' pointing at the

---

[1] mad.

[2] misery.

uniform, 'and don't give me a *gantsah megulah*.'[3]

He nodded, his mind racing to make some excuse as he hadn't told her he was joining the Fire Service. 'I was going to tell you, but what with—'

'You've been gone most days,' she interrupted, 'and here am I thinking you're at the casino and I had to find out from Esther.'

He let her yell for a while and then she began to calm down. He moved forward, dropping the wet uniform on the floor and wrapping his arms around her as she said, 'You're *schmoozing*[4] now.'

'I'm sorry; I thought if I got the training over and done with, I would tell you then.'

'I'm only angry that you didn't tell me. Promise me you won't take any chances.'

He smiled. 'Me, take chances, it's an easy job just climbing up and down ladders while they spray water into buildings.' He looked down at the uniform. 'Any chance of washing my uniform?'

'Isaac called from the Victoria. He wants to speak to you about New Year's Eve. Is Saul bringing his *kuravah*?'[5]

'Please, Eva, don't call her that. You don't know anything about her, so please, for Saul's sake, be nice.' He gave a little smile. 'Whatever Saul's girlfriend had been up to, I know you would get it out of her.' He moved away. 'I'm going to the casino. Poor girl doesn't stand a chance of hiding anything from you.' She picked up the uniform and threw it at him, but he was already closing the door.

Saul didn't know what to do or say to Hannah about New Year's Eve. He wanted to show her off to the family, but knew she liked to spend New Year's Eve with the girls. He needn't have worried as Hannah said, 'I've arranged to have a New Year's Day with the girls, and New Year's Eve with you.' His smile told her everything as she moved into his arms, but he didn't see the worried frown on her face, thinking what his family were going to say to her.

Isaac was busy getting the Victoria Casino ready for their usual New Year's Eve Party. As usual the Shafters were catering the food. There was a worried frown on his face: the champagne hadn't arrived yet. It needed to be chilled and he had made room in the cellar for it. He picked up the phone.

'Hello, this is Mr Brown once again. Could you please tell me when my champagne will be arriving.'

---

[3] tall story.

[4] buttering me up.

[5] prostitute.

The voice at the other end said something and shock showed on his face. 'Would you be able to replace it?'

He listened again. 'It must settle down and chill.' He wiped a hand across his forehead. 'All I want to know is – will I get it?' He listened again. 'Please do your best,' and broke the connection, a thoughtful look on his face. He then dialled a number, which was answered almost immediately. 'Uncle Billy, we have a problem with the champagne. The van bringing it here has had an accident and seventy per cent of the bottles were destroyed. I don't know any other supplier where we would get the amount we need at such short notice.'

'Have you called your father?'

'Yes, as far as I know he's on his way.'

'Okay, tell your father I'm coming over, and I'll phone Asher at the Hanover. He might know someone.'

No sooner had Isaac finished the call than Wolfe walked into the office. 'What's the problem?'

They received a delivery of champagne that had not broken in the crash, but by late afternoon they had still not been able to obtain the extra amount: everyone wanted champagne.

Saul paid a rare visit to the casino to make sure Isaac had put Hannah on the guest list. Seeing the worried look on his brother's face, Isaac asked him what the matter was and Saul explained, adding, 'The supplier said he would try and get us some more, but at this moment with everyone wanting champagne for New Year it's a virtually impossible task.'

Saul pursed his lips in thought and then picked up the phone, dialling Hannah's number. 'You miss me already?'

'Naturally, but there's another reason.' He explained what had happened, concluding, 'So do you know anyone that might have what we need?'

'Give me ten minutes.' Hannah closed the connection and dialled a number.

'I need some champagne for a very dear friend .... As much as you can give me .... The price is too high even for you....' She smiled. 'That's better, please send all of it, when? .... Great, see you then.' She severed the connection and dialled the number that Saul had given her. 'Hi, I've got you what you need. It's a higher price than you normally pay, but I have all the bottles you need.'

'You're a lifesaver. When can I pick it up?'

'Let's say in about an hour.'

'I get to see you twice in one day.' He blew a kiss down the phone, rang off and went looking for Isaac. He found him in the cellar. 'I've got you your champagne.'

'You're a lifesaver.'

'I'm afraid it will cost you more than you normally pay.'

'To tell you the truth Saul, at this stage of the game, I don't care.'

Isaac went with Saul to pick up the boxes of champagne with the cash Hannah had asked for. Isaac shook hands with Hannah. 'Thank you very much for your help. I'm looking forward to seeing you at the party.'

5

The New Year's Eve party at the Victorian Casino was in full swing, the war and call-up temporarily forgotten. Isaac was amused to see the family from time to time, eyeing the door, waiting for Saul to appear with his girlfriend.

Lily had asked him about her as they were getting dressed, but he said, 'Not bad.'

'That's not a description. Is she tall, thin, fat?'

He burst into laughter. 'Yes.'

She threw a shoe at him. 'You are so exasperating at times. It won't hurt you to tell me.'

'Okay, I'm going to tell you that she saved us with the champagne tonight. Otherwise we would have been in *shtoogh*.[6] She's pretty, but then some people might call her beautiful, others plain. I liked her, and you should, like everyone else in the family, make up your own mind.' He bent retrieving her shoe. 'I think this belongs to you. He gave her a peck on the cheek. 'You must practise your aim.'

For a second the room seemed to come to a standstill as Saul walked into the club with Hannah, who looked stunning in a blue halter-neck silk dress that clung to her waist, tapering down to just below the knee and then falling into folds just below the ankle. She walked confidently on Saul's arm, her other hand holding a clutch bag matching the dress. Hannah could see out of the corner of her eyes people turning to look at her as they came to stop in front of Eva and Wolfe. 'Mama, Papa, I would like to introduce you to my girlfriend, Hannah Grozenski.'

'It's very nice to meet you at last,' Eva said, shaking hands. Wolfe moved forward, giving her a peck on each cheek. 'Thank you for your help.' He swept his hand around the room. 'Without you, this would not be the party it should be.'

'No problem, I'm pleased I could help,' Hannah said, taken aback by Wolfe's friendly peck on the cheek.

'Saul, introduce Hannah to the rest of the family,' Eva said, just as a smiling Isaac appeared with Lily in tow.

'Great, you're here. Hannah this is my wife, Lily.'

They shook hands, 'That's a lovely dress,' Lily commented.

'Thank you. Your dress is stunning. Is it Coco Channel?'

'A slight copy, I'm impressed you know your dresses.' She took her

---

[6] trouble.

arm. 'The other women of the family are dying to meet you.'

Hannah looked at Saul for help. He took her hand. 'I'm coming with.'

As she was introduced to the family Hannah became more and more relaxed and was able to be herself. No one asked any awkward questions, which she knew would come one day.

As it neared midnight, waiters wandered around the casino, handing out glasses of champagne. Wolfe, Asher and Billy walked onto the stage. Wolfe looked at his watch and tapped the bandleader on the shoulder. The music stopped. Isaac moved over to a radio as Billy picked up the microphone.

'Ladies and gentlemen, as we end this year, we,' he gestured to Wolfe and Billy, 'hope the war in Europe will soon end, and that 1940 will be a year of peace.' Then he, Wolfe and Asher alternately counted down the minutes. The sound of Big Ben rang out from the radio, and in unison everyone yelled, 'Happy New Year.' The trio moved quickly off the stage to embrace their wives, the rest of the family and some of their guests.

Saul and Hannah were swamped as, one by one, people came over to kiss them and wish them a Happy New Year. The band began to play Auld Lang Syne and a circle was quickly formed. Everyone was smiling and singing at the top of their voices and the sound echoed out into the garden and Queen Victoria Street.

Saul danced cheek to cheek with Hannah.

'I like your family,' she said.

He pulled away slightly. 'I have to report for training on the eight of the month.'

She nodded and cuddled into him, holding him tight and whispering, 'Would you stay with me until then?'

'Hadn't thought otherwise,' and then he kissed her.

On the other side of the dance floor Abraham was trying to think of a way to tell April that he had enlisted, and had received orders to report to Infantry Officer Cadet Training Unit, at Mons Barracks, Aldershot the same day as Saul for four months' training. He bent to kiss her and just before their lips met, April said, 'I know.'

He took half a step back, the shock of her knowing on his face. 'I was going to tell you tomorrow, I only received the letter yesterday.'

'It came on Friday. I'm sorry, but I opened it.'

He gave a fleeting smile. 'Why didn't you say anything?'

'You didn't have to enlist yet. You're twenty-nine, they are calling up men of Saul's age and younger. I need you, they don't, at least not yet.'

'I'm sorry, but I thought they would tell me to go home and wait, but the sergeant said that I was officer material, so now you know. I'm sorry you had to find out that way.'

April stepped close to him. 'Well, sir, kiss me now and we can dance the night away.'

It was nearly two o'clock in the morning and most of the guests had left. The band was playing the last waltz.

Wolfe cut in on Saul. 'Go dance with your mother.'

Saul smiled. 'Don't step on her toes.'

'I'm happy you came,' Wolfe said, adding, 'I hope it wasn't too daunting.'

'No, everyone had been so kind, and I have made some new friends. It's been one of the best New Year's Eve's I have had for many years.'

Sunday, 7 January 1940

Eva wasn't smiling as she and the other women prepared the table. Wolfe saw how sad she was and followed her into the kitchen. 'What's the matter, something happened?' he asked quietly in Yiddish.

'Saul and Abraham are going away, and how many other mothers' sons. It feels like this could be the last time we would ever be together,' she answered in the same language.

'You must keep a brave face, and try not to think about that.'

'Look at April; she hasn't left Abraham's side, and Hannah too with Saul. I want to scream and tear the heart out of that Hitler for what he's doing to our families.'

'There are other families going through the same thing,' Wolfe uttered softly.

'I know, but it doesn't make it any easier.' Hannah couldn't stop smiling, even though Saul was going away for ... she didn't know how long. Everyone was talking. Eva and her friend Sarah in English with a slight accent, Billy Reid with his Irish brogue mixed with Yiddish and English. There were no arguments, everyone seeming to know what to do.

The dining table looked amazing with bottles of wine and different garnishes. Saul and Isaac counted the seats, knowing how many were needed. Baby Samuel lay in the crook of his father Jack's arms as his mother Sophie helped with the cooking.

Eva yelled from the kitchen, 'Everyone sit down, dinner will be served in five minutes.'

There was an orderly rush to the dining room as Eva walked from the kitchen, carrying a tureen of chicken soup with *lokshen* and *knaidlach*. A smiling Hannah followed with another tureen.

As people spoke, Hannah tried to identify their names, watching in amazement at the orderly way things were done. Everyone helped, even the men.

After the dessert was cleared away and the washing up had been done, there was a sleepy lull. No one talked about the war, just silly things that had happened to them during the week. Suddenly, as if there had been a signal, chairs were moved, the carpet rolled back, and the music began.

Slowly, one by one, family made their goodbyes to return home. Saul took Hannah's hand and then climbed the stairs to his bedroom. Abraham and April had said goodnight just after midnight as he had to catch an early train to Aldershot.

As she undressed, Hannah said, 'Your family's amazing.'

'They are, aren't they.' He stared at Hannah as she stood naked in front of him. 'You are so beautiful it takes my breath away.'

She smiled with pleasure. 'You're not too bad yourself.'

They didn't sleep, making love, whispering silly little things to each other. As dawn arrived they bathed and went downstairs, and were surprised to see that Eva was already up.

'Would you like some breakfast?'

'Tea and toast,' Saul said.

'Can I help?' Hannah asked and, not waiting for an answer, picked up the kettle, filling it and placing it on the gas ring.

They heard footsteps in the hall and Isaac walked in. 'Mama, why are you up so early?'

'Couldn't sleep thinking about ... well, just couldn't sleep.' Saul had taken the cups and saucers from the cupboard and then moved across the room to his mother, bending to wrap his arms around her. 'Please Mama, don't worry, I'm joining the RAF as a mechanic, I would not be fighting, just repairing the aircraft.'

'Are you sure?'

He smiled, kissing her on both cheeks. 'Positive.' He turned to his brother. 'Have to be somewhere?'

'No, just a light sleeper, I heard voices and, well, to tell you the truth I just wanted to wish you good luck.'

The two men hugged and Wolfe walked into the kitchen. 'What's for breakfast?'

It was time to go, Saul had persuaded Hannah not to go with him to Euston Station, but to say goodbye at the house. She had argued for a little while until he said, 'It would be too hard for me to leave you at the station, whereas if we say goodbye at my home I know someone will be with you.'

She cried bitterly as the taxi drove away. Eva was also crying. the two women comforting each other. 'He would be home before you know it,' Wolfe said quietly.

At Waterloo, April clung to Abraham. 'Please be careful, don't do anything silly.'

He smiled. 'I'm only going for training, so I can shout at men as they march.' They kissed; both reluctantly parting. He entered the carriage, closing the door and leaning out of the window. The guard blew his whistle, waved to the driver and climbed aboard as the train began to move. April waved until the train disappeared around a bend.

*

Two months had gone by since the boys had left. Both April and Hannah received letters virtually every day.

In mid-January as Britain trained its troops for war, heavy snow and freezing conditions throughout Europe brought transport to a complete halt. The Thames froze over for the first time since 1888. Many people took the chance to enjoying the freedom to skate outside the Houses of Parliament and under Westminster Bridge.

Eva was in the kitchen singing when Freda and Max entered, attired in army uniform. 'My God, you've—'

'No Mama we haven't,' Freda quickly interrupted. 'Max and I have joined ENSA. It's an organisation to entertain the troops.'

'But you will have to go where there's fighting.'

'No, it's to entertain the troops here,' Max pointed out.

Relief showed on Eva's face. 'Tea?'

Wolfe, Eva and Isaac were in the kitchen listening to the radio when William Joyce, dubbed Lord Haw-Haw by the British public because of his nasal speech, said, 'Germany calling on 1st March 1940.'

On the second Sunday of the month, the family met at Billy and Esther's house. The main topic of conversation was rationing.

'I am sure meat will be rationed soon,' Esther commented, adding, 'I'm going to have chickens in the garden, and Billy is going to plant some vegetables.'

'That's a brilliant idea,' Eva said. 'I'm going to copy that.'

'Me too,' Sarah smiled. 'I spoke to Mrs Smith in the grocery shop on Friday. She asked if I could swap my bacon and ham coupons for her sugar and butter, I said yes on the spot.'

'That's what we need, ideas to help each other,' said Eva.

'I heard you were angry with Wolfe about volunteering to be a fireman,' Esther smiled. 'I wish I had been there.'

Eva laughed. 'He looked like a little boy caught with his fingers in the biscuit jar.'

The following day, Eve, Esther and Sarah each bought six chickens and one cockerel to share between them for mating. They were to be delivered the following day. From there the three women went to the vegetable market to buy potato, carrot, pea and green seeds.

That afternoon the women arranged for their husbands to meet at Billy's home. After very little discussion or arguments from the men, who knew it would be futile to argue, it was agreed that they should help each other build a hen coop in each garden and plant the seeds.

Sunday, 31 March 1940

Lily and Isaac had just returned from Asher and Sarah's house when Lily took an envelope from her bag. 'I have two provisional tickets on the Golden Arrow to Paris on 5th April. Would you come with me?'

Isaac was angry. It showed on his face and in his voice. 'How dare you go behind my back and book those tickets. You know my thoughts about you going to Paris.' He pointed to his forehead. 'What entered your brain to even think I would change my mind?'

'I thought—'

'That's the problem,' he interrupted, 'you don't think.' He pointed at the radio. 'Every day you hear things about the war.' He picked up the newspaper, slapping it with the back of his hand in anger. 'It's there in black and white, yet you wish to ignore it, or your own safety.'

'Nothing was going to happen. The Germans, as you once said, were sabre rattling. So they attacked Poland and our army was sent to rescue them. In the meantime I'm going to Paris. Naturally I would like you to come with me, but if you don't, I shall go alone. It's up to you.'

Isaac wanted to lash out at something. He turned and walked out of the room and the house before he said or did something he would regret. After an hour of working up a sweat in the gym he entered a telephone box, taking a card from his wallet and dialled the number, which was answered after three rings.

'Hallo,' a young voice said on the other end.

'Could I speak to Mr Ainsworth please?'

'Yes, one minute, Dad, it's for you.'

A second went by and Ainsworth came on the line. 'Hello, who is this?'

'I'm sorry to bother you, Mr Ainsworth, it's Isaac Brown.'

'How are you, are you still flying?'

Isaac smiled. 'No, I haven't had a chance. You said that if I ever needed your help to call.'

'That's true, so how could I help you?'

Lily had tried at the last minute to persuade Isaac to go with her, but he had refused. He knew there was nothing he could say to stop her from going and just said, 'Have a good trip,' kissing her on the cheek.

He watched the train disappear, and then turned towards the taxi rank. Ten minutes later the taxi pulled up outside Adastral House in Kingsway. He paid off the cabbie, hesitated for a moment and then walked up the stone stairs, taking an envelope from his jacket pocket. At the desk he showed it to a commissioner with World War One Campaign medals pinned to his chest.

'Follow me, sir,' he smiled and took him to a waiting area.

'Won't be too long sir.'

Isaac took an empty seat, feeling out of place as the room was full of young boys.

Two hours later he was called into the Selection Board Room. His hands were sweating and felt sick as he entered the room. Three men sat at a table facing him. The middle of the trio with silver grey hair and a warm smile said, 'Please, Mr Brown, take a seat,' pointing to a chair in front of them.

He then asked, 'Why do you want to enlist in the RAF?'

Isaac smiled. 'That's easy, sir, I love flying.'

'You have flown before?'

'Yes, sir, I soloed at Heston last year. My tutor was a Mr Martin Ainsworth.'

The man on the right, his thin brown hair parted to the right hiding his baldness, asked, 'What about the war, you are—'

'That is why I'm enlisting to fight for my country,' Isaac interrupted, avoiding an awkward situation, and for a moment there was silence as Isaac looked from one to the other. They asked him a variety of maths questions, and then it went quiet again. Isaac waited with bated breath, feeling a little more confident, having answered everything.

The man on the left smiled, holding out a blue slip. 'Take this to the doctor, and good luck Mr Brown, and may I say you could not have had a better tutor than Mr Ainsworth. We were in the last shindig together.'

Isaac took the slip. 'Thank you.'

After a day of medicals, where they tested every part of his body, Isaac walked out of Adastral House, a big smile on his face. He knew that Lily wouldn't like it, and because of his love for her he had put this off for far too long. This was what he wanted, and had done so since the declaration of war. He found his father in the casino, watching a crowd of people around the roulette wheel. 'I've enlisted in the Royal Air Force as a trainee pilot.'

Wolfe looked at his son. 'I'm not going to say I like it, but I know that's what you have wanted for a long time, and to tell you the truth, if I were in your shoes, I would do the same.'

That night Lily telephoned. 'I've arrived safely. Everything is okay. My aunts were disappointed that you hadn't come too.'

Isaac could hear the excitement in her voice and said, 'Have a great time, give them all my love, I'll speak to you soon.' He saw no reason to tell Lily he had enlisted in the RAF.

Two weeks later he was on his way to RAF Bridgenorth, where he spent the next four weeks in what was called square bashing.

6

Abraham looked in the mirror and straightened his tie. It had been a hard, gruelling four months, both physically and mentally, but the Second Lieutenant pip on his shoulder showed it had been worth it. He turned towards the bed, picked up his cap, placing it squarely on his head, rubbed the tip of his shoes on the back of his trousers, and picked up his travel documents.

A head poked round the door. 'Transports ready,' then disappeared. In one movement Abraham shouldered his kitbag and walked out of the barracks to a lorry waiting outside, threw his kitbag into the back and followed it. He smiled at the man sitting opposite him, who smiled back, slapping him on the knee. 'We did it.' The smile left his face. 'Thanks to you, I wouldn't—'

'Yes you would have,' Abraham interrupted, 'but you did help me learn to shout louder.' They both laughed as the lorry moved off.

Abraham took a taxi from the station, eager to get home. He hadn't told April about the two week leave as he wanted to surprise her.

April didn't turn when he entered the salon as she took the rollers from a client's hair. 'Be with you in moment.'

'I can wait,' he said.

She turned with a yell, moving quickly across the salon and leaping into his arms, saying between kisses, 'Why didn't you tell me you were coming home? I look a mess.'

'You look lovely, and—'

'Excuse me,' the lady in the chair said, pointing at the rollers in her hair.

'Oh, I'm so sorry Mrs Bernstein,' April said, still holding on to Abraham. 'I'll—'

'April, just take the damn curlers out. I'll brush it out myself.'

April was quickly by the chair to take the curlers out. Mrs Bernstein pulled the cape from around her neck and got to her feet, handing it to April. 'If I had a husband as good looking as that, I'd put "Closed" on the door, and … well, I'll say no more.'

April helped Mrs Bernstein on with her coat. 'Thank you. It's a free perm next time.'

As soon as she closed the door, April turned the 'Open' sign to 'Closed' and pulled down the shutters, engulfing the shop in darkness. She moved over to Abraham, wrapping her arms around Abraham's neck. 'Now where were we?'

*

71

Saul had written to Hannah almost every day. He smiled as the train entered the station to see her waiting for him. 'I love a man in uniform, especially you.' She wrapped her arms around him, the kiss passionate and wanting.

'I have ten days, and then I have to report at— well I cannot say,' he pointed to a poster, WALLS HAVE EARS. 'Would you mind if we went to my parents first?'

She nodded. 'Okay, but then—' She left the rest to his imagination.

*

Eva looked at the family, a frown on her forehead. 'You'll have wrinkles,' Sally said.

Eva looked up, a startled look on her face. 'What?'

Sally squatted. 'Mama, what's the matter, you haven't smiled all day?'

'Look, our family isn't complete, and I wonder if it ever would be again.'

Sally placed her arms around her mother, 'Mama you mustn't think like that.'

'Saul and Abraham are in uniform, Freda is entertaining troops, Isaac is, I don't know where, wanting to be a pilot.' Eva gestured towards Phillip. 'He will be next, and then Jack, and then there's your father, uncle and Billy becoming firemen, all putting themselves in danger.'

Wolfe was suddenly by her side. 'Eva, what's the matter?'

'Matter,' she reverted to Yiddish. 'Everyone's *meshuggah*, smiling and laughing as though nothing's the matter. We are at war, look,' she pointed at Abraham and Saul. 'They are going to war, and could be killed, doesn't that worry you?'

'Of course it worries us,' Billy said in Yiddish.

'The best thing for all of us,' Wolfe joined in, 'would be to carry on as normal, well as normal as we possibly can, and to support our children who want to fight—'

'Mama,' Saul interrupted his father, and knelt beside his mother, 'we must fight Hitler and his Aryan army. All those years ago you fled to escape the pogroms. What do you think Hitler has in store for the Jews of Europe?'

She stopped crying, placed her hand on Saul's cheek and then kissed it. 'You are a clever son.' She looked around the table. 'Please forgive me for my outburst.'

One by one they went over to kiss her. Sarah sat next to her. 'I think it's about time we girls decided what we could do to help the war effort.'

Before leaving, Billy Reid took Abraham by the arm, leading him slightly away from everyone. 'I'm going to give you a bit of advice: make sure your men are fit. Fitness breeds confidence, as you well know, and don't ask them to do anything you wouldn't do yourself – that would earn you respect. And one last thing, trust your sergeants and corporals.'

'Thanks, Billy. It's good advice.'

Two weeks later Abraham reported for duty with the East Surrey Regiment at their barracks in Kingston-upon-Thames. Thirty minutes after reporting at the barracks Abraham was standing in front of a Major Smithson. He saluted, 'Second Lieutenant Brown reporting for duty, sir.'

'Stand at ease, Brown.' He glanced down at the file in front of him and tapped it with his finger. 'Very impressive report. Get squared away in the officer's quarters. The sergeant there would be able to give you a room.' He hesitated for a moment and then said, 'B Platoon needs another officer. Their CO is Lieutenant Johnson. We embark for France in two weeks. Off you go.'

Abraham saluted, turned smartly and left the office.

'I'm sorry, sir, but you'd be sharing a room with Lieutenant Johnson.' The billet sergeant said to Abraham as he helped carry his gear to the first floor. 'I've had your bed made as we were told to expect you.' He dumped the case on the floor. 'If there's anything else you need, sir, please tell me and I'll see what I can do.'

The sergeant saluted and left the room. Abraham unpacked and was about to leave when a lieutenant entered.

'I'm Mike Johnson.'

The two shook hands.

'Abraham Brown, I was just—'

'It's nearly lunchtime,' Johnson interrupted. 'I'm just going to wash and we'll go over together.'

'Thanks, that would be great.' Fifteen minutes later they walked over to the officers' mess.

The next day Johnson put Abraham in charge of red section, and for the rest of the week, he and his men settled down to army routine.

It had been a long day, and an even longer week, Abraham was asleep in an instant, but awoke on hearing Mike being sick. Abraham got out of bed and walked across to the toilet. Through the open door he saw Mike on the floor, his face as white as a sheet, holding his stomach. 'I'm going to call the doctor,' Abraham said.

Within minutes the doctor and an orderly arrived. 'We need to get him to hospital; I'm sure its appendicitis.'

Abraham went with the ambulance to the hospital, where the doctor's diagnosis was confirmed. Although it was four in the morning, Abraham contacted Major Smithson who said, 'Report to me at my office at 1000 hours.'

Before he could reply the line went dead.

After morning inspection, and exactly at ten Abraham knocked on Major Smithson's door. On hearing 'Enter,' he opened the door and walked into the office, noticing a staff sergeant to his left. Abraham stood to attention and saluted.

'Stand at ease,' the major said, picking up a pipe from his desk and began to fill it while saying, 'We have a sticky situation with Lieutenant Johnson in hospital. I don't have another senior lieutenant that could take over B platoon – well, not at such short notice as we leave for France next Thursday.' He pointed the stem of the pipe at Abraham. 'So you are going to be in charge of B platoon until one arrives.'

'But sir, I—'

'Yes I know it's not protocol and all that, and yes I have requested another lieutenant, but until then, Staff Sergeant Newark would be your second in command.'

Abraham turned to look at the staff sergeant: the tip of his boots shone like glass, the uniform pressed with the creases in the right places. He looked impassively at Abraham who could see the staff sergeant inwardly flinch at having such an inexperienced officer in charge of his troop.

The major said, 'Because of what's happened, you two should get to know each other very quickly.' He waved a hand, 'That's all, dismissed.'

The two men saluted and left the office. As they exited the building Abraham said, 'Staff Sergeant, you know this place better than me. Is there somewhere we could go and have an informal chat?'

Staff Sergeant Newark stared at Abraham for a second, and then said, 'My room would probably be the best place, and we could pretend we are inspecting the barracks again.'

'Good idea, lead the way.'

Five minutes later they were in the staff sergeant's room attached to Barrack Six. Abraham was impressed the room was an extension of Newark, its appearance immaculate.

'Have you been to war, Staff?' Abraham asked.

'No sir.'

Abraham smiled. 'Well, that's something we have in common.' He took a cigarette case from his pocket, offering it to Newark, who said 'Thanks' as he took one, lighting Abraham's before adding the match to his own.

'Look sir,' Newark leant forward, 'I've been with the troop since the beginning. The only reason I'm a staff sergeant was because I was in the Territorials.' He smiled. 'I worked for the Prudential Insurance Company. My boss, Mr Tolliday, was an officer in the last war, and had joined the Territorials, and talked me into joining, and to be honest I quiet enjoyed it.' He took a puff of his cigarette, blowing the smoke into the air. 'I know every one of the forty men under your command, and I think if you don't mind me saying, you should too.'

'I agree with you,' Billy's advice came to mind. He looked at his watch. 'I want the men on the parade ground in thirty minutes.'

'What do you have in mind?'

'I want to see how fit they really are.'

Thirty minutes later Abraham stood in front of the men and yelled, 'Parade right turn.' As one, the men turned. There was a crash of boots on the ground. Newark smiled chest out. Not a man moved.

'Staff sergeant, I want two sergeants at the rear to help stragglers, and corporals at the sides,' Abraham ordered. He then marched to the front of the men and yelled, 'Parade on the double quick march.' He set off around the parade ground and after four laps yelled, 'Parade halt.' He moved across to stand facing the middle of the column, as did Newark. 'Parade, left turn.' The sweating men did as he ordered. 'Stand at ease.' Abraham with the staff sergeant in tow moved to the first man in the front line, the sweat pouring down his face. Abraham didn't say anything as he slowly moved along the three columns and then the sergeants. 'Sergeant Booth, how many stragglers?'

'Not one, sir.'

Abraham smiled. 'Thank you, Sergeant.' He returned to the front. 'Well done, everyone, get showered and go to lunch.' He turned to Newark. 'March them up to barracks then dismiss them, Staff.'

He watched the men march away and then ran back to his billet. Showered and dressed, he walked over to the officer's mess, pleased with what he had done and seen so far.

All leave had been cancelled pending their embarkation to France, which peeved Abraham, knowing he was just a train ride away from April. He telephoned her, but couldn't tell her he was going to France.

Abraham stepped up his men's training, gradually getting to know the names to their faces, but most important of all they didn't moan. Many were happy to be doing something other than square bashing.

On Friday night he went to the small chapel where he was told the Jewish Sabbath service would be held. He was surprised to see Staff Sergeant Newark there. 'I didn't know you were Jewish.'

'Not the usual typical nose,' Newark said pointing to it.

Abraham laughed. 'I suppose not, but it's better no one knows in case we are captured.'

'Agreed,' Newark said, placing a prayer shawl around his shoulders.

Abraham, with Staff Sergeant Newark beside him, stood to one side of the gangplank as his men boarded the ship to take them across to France. Every day leading up to their departure from barracks he had worked the men hard, doing everything they did and more. After each exercise he would talk to the men, trying to get to know them. Most were single, but the section sergeants were married. One of the men – a fruiter from East London – asked Abraham, 'Got a fag, sir?'

'Scrounging again, White, and yes I have a fag thanks.'

The men burst into laughter.

*

Isaac lit a cigarette just as a voice said, '*Oui.*'

'Aunt Sarah, could I speak to Lily please?' There were muffled voices and then Lily was on the line. 'Lily, you have to come home now. The Germans are only sixty miles from Paris.'

'I have tried to get train home, but most of the trains are being used for the troops. There's a train leaving the Gare du Nord tomorrow. If I can't get on it I would accompany my aunts to Nice.'

He stared exasperated out of the booth's window. 'Do your best, love you.'

'See you in a couple of days.' The line went dead.

He dropped the cigarette onto the floor, stubbing it out with the sole of his shoe, and stepping from the booth, straightened his uniform jacket and headed for the barrack. He saw no need to tell Lily he was in the RAF.

In Paris Lily slowly replaced the receiver. She knew Isaac had been right about her going to Paris, but that stubborn streak whenever he said no had reared its ugly head, and now she was in trouble. Twice she had tried to board a train going to Calais, and twice she had failed. Tomorrow was her last chance, after that… she shuddered to think any further than getting on the train.

Lily couldn't sleep and woke up her aunts. 'I must go to the station now, and if need I would queue all night to ensure I board the train.'

Her aunts agreed with her, and thirty minutes later they were at the Gare du Nord. There were four people in front of Lily at the closed ticket office. At five in the morning the ticket office opened, by then the queue was about a mile long.

With her tickets in her handbag and a porter stowing her luggage away, Lily stood facing her aunts by the open carriage door. 'Please write and tell me you are safe and send an address so I can tell you when the baby arrives.' She kissed each aunt on either cheek; all had tears running down their faces, not knowing if they would ever meet again.

She waved until they had disappeared from view. Lily entered her carriage and stretched out on the overnight bed and was instantly asleep. The porter woke her. 'Madam, we should be arriving at Victoria in one hour.'

'Thank you,' she said, handing him a tip and closing the door to wash and change her clothes, not believing that she had slept the entire journey. She had telephoned the house as soon as she had her tickets with the time of her arrival.

The train came to a gradual stop as an anxious Lily looked out of the window, searching the faces for Isaac. She spotted Wolfe and Eva and waved. As the porter loaded her luggage onto a taxi, she asked, 'Where's Isaac?'

'He enlisted as a pilot in the RAF,' Wolfe said.

Lily nodded and hugged her parents-in-law. 'I'm happy to be home.'

*

As Abraham embarked for France, Saul was at Biggin Hill, his head inside a Spitfire's engine. He smiled, wiping his greasy hands on a rag, and replaced the cowling over the engine, making sure it was secure before stepping down from the gantry, sliding it away from the fighter. He looked up at the sergeant sitting in the cockpit and raised a thumb. There was a slight stutter – a sound like a cough – and the engine came to life. They let it run for a couple of minutes and then turned it off.

'Sounds good, Serg,' said Saul.

A flight sergeant appeared. 'Hey Brownie, I've another Spit in Hangar Two,' the pilot said. 'It's a carburettor problem. Mind you they all say that.'

Saul pointed to the fighter. 'I'll just sign this one off, and I'll go straight over there.'

7

'Take cover!' Abraham yelled as once again Stukas dived down with their distinctive banshee howl onto the retreating British troops, adding to the continuous noise of artillery fire and exploding bombs.

Abraham and his men had been in constant battle with German forces since their arrival in France. They had counter-attacked a couple of times, but as soon as they made progress they were pounded by Stukas, the Germans using them as mobile artillery.

The East Surreys had been ordered to retreat to Dunkirk, their progress hampered by abandoned handcarts, vehicles, fallen trees, dead cattle, and bodies of men, women and children that littered the roads and hedgerows. The diving Stukas did not discriminate between civilians or troops as they dropped their bombs, pulling out of their dive to strafe the column. Once they had gone, so began the cries of the wounded, and the wailing of a mother or father, holding their dead child in their arms. A young boy wandered around in a stupor, calling for his parents. A young girl pulled her mother's arm, telling her to wake up.

Abraham, with Staff Sergeant Newark, checked the men. They were carrying two of their wounded with them as Abraham heard the Germans were shooting wounded prisoners, and he was not about to leave anyone behind. Once again he checked his men and found two more wounded, one with a broken leg, and the other with a nasty bullet wound on his right side. While the medic helped the wounded, Abraham and the men quickly made two stretchers from various materials. He ordered two men to take one stretcher while he and Newark the other. They changed stretcher-bearers every fifteen minutes; this was where his men's fitness shone through.

As they trudged on, Abraham's thoughts were on April, wondering how she was, and hoping that he would soon be back in her arms. His thoughts were interrupted once again by diving Stukas.

Unbeknown at this time by Abraham and his men, Vice Admiral Ramsey had put into place Operation Dynamo, the evacuation of British troops from Dunkirk. The Germans had destroyed most of the piers and only the East Mole was usable. Ramsey had commandeered vessels with a minimum of thirty foot in length. Cabin cruisers, fishing boats and barges, all were now making their way to the French coast.

Bone-weary and hungry, having fought a rearguard action for the last four days, Abraham and his men, their uniforms dirt- and sweat-streaked, some like Abraham with superficial wounds and with very little ammunition left, walked slowly through the burning town of Dunkirk. His shoulder throbbing from the bullet that luckily went through the fleshy part of his shoulder, he led his men onto the beach to be met by a cacophony of sounds.

He stopped for a moment to survey the scene of carnage, his eyes near to tears whispering, 'If there was a hell, this was it.' The beach was littered with wrecked lorries, heavy equipment, dead animals and men. The noise deafening as shrieking Stukas wheeled around like birds in the sky looking for their prey, and then went into a screeching dive, one following the other, dropping their bombs, coming out of the dive and flying low along the beach; their guns spitting out a stream of bullets at the waiting soldiers who dived into the sea to avoid them. Exploding bombs and thunder of guns drowned the screams of wounded men and animals. Isaac stared with disbelief as, once the Stukas had gone, the soldiers formed orderly lines which snaked towards the sea, some shoulder deep in the water waiting patiently to be picked up.

Major Smithson suddenly appeared, his right arm in a sling. Abraham didn't salute. 'Brown—' he pointed '—take your men to the end of that line and join up with A platoon.' He gave a slight smile. 'See you later.'

Before Abraham could reply, he turned and strode quickly away. Staff Sergeant Newark yelled, 'Down everyone.' Abraham dived onto the sand, bumping into Newark, who grinned at him. 'Nice day for a swim, sir.'

Abraham laughed. 'You're an idiot staff.' For a second there was silence, and then came the screams for help. Abraham was instantly on his feet, moving swiftly amongst the men shouting, 'Everyone okay.' He had already lost six killed and four wounded, who he hoped were already on their way back in England, having taken them to the first-aid station. He breathed a sigh of relief as someone said in a cockney voice, 'Got a fag sir, I'm out.'

Abraham smiled; with all they had been through the last two weeks the only thing White wanted was a fag. He took the cigarette case from his pocket, opening it as he walked over to White and offering it to him. White went to take the cigarette from the case. 'That's your last one, sir.'

'That's okay, just make this one last.'

White hesitated for a second, but Abraham gestured for him to take it. 'Thank you, sir, you're a toff.'

He took the cigarette from the case placing it in his mouth. Abraham gave him a box of matches. 'I suppose you'll need these.' White took the matches just as someone yelled, 'Here they come again.'

White, the cigarette hanging from the corner of his mouth, crouched in the sand, his Bren gun pointing at a diving Stuka. Just before it dropped its bomb, White let out a stream of swear words as he fired. Abraham could see the bullets arching towards the German plane, thinking, 'Just one lucky shot.' As the bomb left the belly of the aeroplane, it flew straight into the Bren's bullets. White and Abraham let out a yell of triumph as bits flew off the wing; smoke curled behind the Stuka as it pulled out of the dive, bullets spitting from its guns in anger as it flew low across the beach; black smoke billowing out from the aircraft as it flew over the flotilla of boats picking up the soldiers. Three lorries careered down the beach, their drivers driving them into the sea to form an improvised mole.

A Messerschmitt 109 came in low, firing its cannon and machine guns, the bullets whipping up the sea, hissing as they entered the water, some finding their targets. Abraham held his breath, diving into the cold sea away from the danger. He rose quickly, wiping his eyes to look back to his men. He was quickly beside Newark who had been hit. Abraham gently lifted him to his feet, the pain showing on the staff sergeant's face.

'Where are you hit?' Abraham asked, looking for the wound.

'Right side,' Newark whispered.

Abraham saw White close by. 'White – over here, give me a hand with Staff.' He then grabbed the nearest soldier by his sleeve, pulling him towards him. 'Burke, help White.'

He left them to wade back along the line checking the men. 'Help each other,' he said as he passed counting the men.

He saw two floating face down, backward and forward with the movement of the sea. He reached one, turning him over, his face hard and angry. It was their medic. He slid the backpack from the dead medic and then turned, wading back to Newark as the line moved slowly forward. He had White and Burke hold Newark above the waves, as he pulled open his jacket, lifting the shirt.

'It's okay, Staff. I'm going to put some disinfectant powder into the wound, yell if you want.'

He wiped the wound with gauzed and poured in the powder, and then placed a large pad against the wound wrapping a bandage tight around him. He placed the shirt and tunic back in place. 'Okay Staff, try and get to your feet.' White kept hold of him as Newark got to his feet, trying not to show the pain he was in, all shivering from the icy cold sea.

Once again the Stukas came, the soft sand absorbing some of the bombs impact, but their machine guns caused havoc amongst the waiting soldiers, who without a word, once they had gone moved back into line.

Abraham waited patiently, making sure all his men boarded the boat, urging them on. 'Not long now and we'll be back home. Keep your chin up, Smith. You don't want to drink that.' Smith straightened up, a smile on his face. 'Nah sir, them up front had been pissing in it.'

There was a titter of laughter as Abraham took his position as the last man passed by. The boat pulled away and he looked back to see the devastation on the beach littered with bodies and mangled, broken, burning vehicles, tanks and guns. Black smoke from burning tyres blew across the beach, littered with vehicles of war left by a retreating army. Abraham heard that doctors and medics had drawn lots to see who stayed behind to tend the wounded. He moved slowly amongst his men, giving them words of encouragement until reaching Newark. 'How's the wound, Staff?'

Newark tried to smile. 'Hurts like fuck if you must know, sir.'

'Soon be back, and then we'll get you to hospital.'

'How many we lose?'

'Ten dead, five wounded.' He gestured towards Dunkirk. 'Had to leave three there, too badly hurt to bring them with us.'

'I'm sure the Swiss would let us know in due course if they were okay.'

'I hope so, sir, I hope so.'

Abraham was surprised at the welcome they received when the boat docked, not as a defeated army, but as victors. Ambulances lined the quay, taking the wounded to be treated. Abraham made sure that Newark was aboard an ambulance and then walked among the men, ensuring those that needed it were looked after by a medic.

'Excuse me, sir.'

'Yes, White, you okay?'

'Yes sir, just wanted to give you these.' He handed Abraham a pack of cigarettes. 'Thanks, sir.' And White turned, disappearing with the other men onto the train.

He was about to board a train when a nurse accosted him. 'Excuse me, Lieutenant, may I look at your wound?'

'I'm fine.'

'I still insist on looking at the wound. Please come with me.'

He nodded silently and went with her to a building with a red cross on its side, leading him to a cubicle.

'Strip,' she ordered.

He smiled. 'You first.'

She gave him a look that said 'do not mess with me', so he undid his webbing belt with his pistol, placing them on a table and stripped.

'Sit,' she ordered, taking a sterile pack from a tray and cleansed the wound. 'Lucky,' she whispered. 'You know this could have become gangrenous, and believe me you don't want that to happen.'

He stayed silent, knowing he was getting a very quiet telling off.

'Stay here, don't even twitch, I'll be back.'

Ten minutes later, the nurse returned with a doctor, who looked at the wound. 'Clean it thoroughly, you know what to do.' He stood in front of Abraham. 'The wound must be cleansed. The nurse will dress it and then you will be able to return to your unit. Make sure the medics there keep an eye on it.'

He touched Abraham's arm, saying, 'Well done,' and turned and walked out of the cubicle. He did not know what the 'well done' really meant: they had retreated, a beaten army, but through it all, surprisingly, he wasn't scared, he was far too busy trying to keep his men alive.

Two hours later Abraham, his arm in a sling, boarded a train for London. C platoon were on board, what was left of them. Their two officers had been killed. The sergeant was relieved to see Abraham. He was nearly in tears as he told him, 'The Germans hit us just as we were evacuating Nieuport. The Stukas caused havoc and we lost our two officers. There were just twenty of us left when we hit the beach.'

Abraham placed his good arm around the sergeant's shoulders. 'You did great; your efforts brought those men home.'

B and what was left of C platoons' walking wounded were checked over by the doctors at Axminster. The doctor looked at Abraham's wound. 'It's clean…' He hesitated for a second. 'If I let you go on leave would you make sure the wound stays clean. Don't shower for a week. I'll give you some dressings; get someone to redress it in three days, do not get it wet.'

He turned to the nurse. 'Give the Second Lieutenant dressing for a fortnight.' He signed a piece of paper. 'Take this to the orderly room; they'll give you a pass for two weeks' leave. When you return I want you straight back here, or if you think the wound becomes infected, return here immediately. Is that clear?'

'Yes sir, thank you.' He was about to salute but the doctor turned and left the cubicle. Two hours later Abraham was on the train to London, knowing he could never tell anyone about the horrors he had witnessed, and the feeling of utter despair and helplessness he felt, standing waist deep in the freezing ocean. He was thankful that he was able to hide it from his men.

Meanwhile High Command licked their wounds, knowing that an impossible feat had happened. It was a miraculous escape by the BEF, but the blunder of the Germans stopping their advance when only one day away from Dunkirk would haunt the Germans for many years.

The fact was that 338,226 men were rescued from the brink of death or capture. Now the wounded were being tended to, and rebuilding the army, ready for the coming battles against Italy and Germany had begun, plus the plans for the Allies' return to Free France and other German-occupied countries.

Monday, 27 May 1940

While Abraham stood in the frozen Channel, Isaac was boarding a train to Netheravon. Placing his case on the rack and sat down. The carriage was full of very young fresh-faced boys in RAF uniform, which made him ancient at twenty-four. Opposite him sat a red-headed, freckle-faced man with a fixed grin on his face. He leant forward and held out his hand. 'I'm Liam Robinson, my friends call me Ginger,' he said in an Irish brogue. Isaac smiled, taking the hand. 'Isaac Brown.'

'Are you going to Netheravon?'

Isaac laughed, 'I think the entire trains going there.'

Isaac opened the newspaper with the news that British forces were being pushed back to the sea. Lily had been lucky and had taken the last boat train to England. He had telephoned her that very morning. 'I won't be able to contact you for a few days, but as soon as I can I'll call. Love you.' He threw a kiss down the phone.

'I understand. I love you too,' she said, replacing the receiver.

Arriving at Netheravon, they were assigned their billets. Isaac and Ginger were in the same billet, quickly moving across the room to take the beds next to each other.

The next morning they were marched into a Nissan hut to await the arrival of the Chief Flying Instructor. Suddenly a voice yelled, 'Attention.' As one everyone stood as two men, both squadron leaders, marched into the room mounted a stage at one end of the room and for a second surveyed the men in front of them.

One of them stepped forward. 'At ease, smoke if you want.' There was the rustle of cigarette packets being opened and the flare of matches.

'I am Squadron Leader Andrew Gold, your Chief Flying Instructor.'

He took off his hat, placing it on the lectern in front of him to reveal close-cropped brown hair. Green eyes gazed at the men around the room. 'You pupil pilots would have to pass an ab initio flying course on a DH82 Tiger Moth.' He took a couple of paces to the side. 'If you are not bowler-hatted[7] by then you will advance to a much faster aeroplane. By the end of the course you will be able to do everything in the way of flying that the RAF requires of you: aerobatics, cross-country and night flying.' He turned to his companion. 'Squadron Leader Jim Roscoe is the

---

[7] dismissed.

Chief Ground Instructor.'

Roscoe was slim and tall, with a bushy moustache and thin, stern lips. He stepped forward. 'Anyone who thinks that this is an easy course better think again. Navigation and other ground work must be spot on, there would be no errors, errors cost lives, yours.'

Isaac realised that these two men had his fate in their hands, having the power to pass or fail him.

'Gentlemen, you are free for the rest of the afternoon,' Squadron Leader Gold said.

Both men walked off the stage; a corporal by the door shouted loudly, 'Attention.'

The room stood and the Squadron Leaders left.

Isaac went to leave; Ginger moved beside him. 'Where're you going?'

'See the aircraft, coming?' Ginger nodded and they left the room.

There was a smell of petrol and oil in the air as they approached the airfield. Isaac stopped for a moment on seeing the line of Tiger Moths. He had never seen so many in one place before. He walked slowly over to the nearest one, running his hands lovingly along the fuselage.

'They are—'

'Magnificent,' Isaac finished Ginger's sentence.

The following day, after being kitted out, Isaac and the other trainee pilots met their instructors.

Flight Lieutenant John Morgan, a thirty-nine-year-old Scotsman from Glasgow, was Isaac's instructor. Isaac saluted, Morgan returned the salute, his brown eyes with tiger claws at the edges stared into Isaac's as though reading his mind. 'Don't kill us,' was all he said and then turned and walked away, saying over his shoulder. 'See you in the morning, laddie.'

Dressed in flying gear and carrying his parachute, Isaac walked towards his allotted aircraft. Morgan stood beside the aircraft, arms crossed, face showing no expression, as Isaac saluted. He tried to smile but failed and said, 'Good morning, sir.'

'Good morning, Brown,' Morgan returned the salute and moved forward to help with the parachute, but Isaac was already putting it on. Morgan gave a slight smile, unseen by Isaac.

'Brown, I know you've had some flying lessons. I want you to forget most if not all that you have been taught because this is going to be a different ball game.'

*

The disastrous month of May was over and Britain now stood alone against the might of Nazi Germany. The country waited for the onslaught to come and once again the people were stirred into patriotism with another of the Prime Minister Winston Churchill's speeches to Parliament and the nation: 'We shall defend our island, whatever the cost may be. We shall fight on the beaches, we shall fight on the landing grounds, we shall fight in the fields and in the streets, we shall fight in the hills; we shall never surrender.'

There was a murmur of approval from the men of the East Surrey Regiment at their barracks at Kingston-upon-Thames, including Saul listening to the radio at RAF Biggin Hill, repairing aircraft in Hangar Two. Saul stopped for a moment looking out to the airfield wondering how Isaac was getting on.

Isaac never heard the speech: he was four thousand feet in the air. 'I'm going to show you a few tricks,' Morgan said down the voice pipe, 'that I hope will keep you out of trouble and alive.' For the next twenty minutes Morgan patiently showed Isaac various moves, making him duplicate them until he was satisfied that Isaac could do it automatically. They were approaching Netheravon when Morgan said, 'Take the controls, Mr Brown, and bring us in.'

There was a slight bump as they landed and taxied to the dispersal area. Isaac waited until Morgan had exited the plane and climbed down. 'Very good, very good, but don't get too complacent on your landing. It must become second nature so that if need be you could land blindfolded.'

Throughout the country, especially London, there was an atmosphere of expectancy. People went about their business with one eye on the sky, their ears heightened, waiting for the air-raid sirens to go off, but they stayed silent, adding to the tension. The Germans had offered the French that Paris would be a non-belligerent zone if they surrender immediately. The French accepted the offer.

Tears ran down Lily's face as she heard the newscaster reporting, in a sombre voice, 'Today, 14th June 1940, the Nazi flag flies over the Eiffel Tower and the Arc de Triomphe. Grim-faced Parisians, many crying, watched the Germans marching up the Champs Elysées for the first time since 1871. It would be for many Frenchmen a day of mourning for Paris, and France.'

Lily felt the baby kick and got slowly to her feet, letting out a gasp of pain and sat down quickly, yelling, 'Mama.'

At ten minutes past nine in the morning of 15 June 1940, Lily had a baby boy. She and Isaac had agreed that if they had a son he would be named Daniel.

Within the hour, and thirty minutes before Isaac was about to take off on his first navigational flight, he received the telegram. With a big smile on his face he showed it to Morgan. 'Congratulations, laddie, do you want to fly to East London and parachute down, or take me to, Andover, Salisbury and back here in time for lunch.'

Isaac laughed, but it was cut short by the unsmiling expression on the Scotsman's face, 'Andover, sir.'

On landing Morgan stepped down, Isaac was about to follow when Morgan said, 'Stay where you are, laddie, two circuits two landings,' he pointed a finger. 'Don't let the new bairn down.' He swung his parachute over his shoulder and walked away. Isaac gunned the engine and within seconds was airborne. His yell, 'I'm a father,' was lost in the slipstream.

Both landings were perfect. He climbed down from the Tiger Moth, flung the parachute over his shoulder, and for the first time saw a smile on Morgan's face.

He had just enough time for some lunch, a shower and then onto the classroom. He had just emerged from the shower when there was a knock at the door. Wrapping the towel around his middle he opened the door to see Morgan standing there holding out a piece of paper. 'Be back here by lights out Sunday, now get dressed and go see your family.'

'Thank you, sir.'

Morgan nodded, turned and as he walked away said, 'Well done today, laddie.'

There were tears in Isaac's eyes as he held his son, whispering, 'No matter what happens to me, I live on in you.' He knelt beside Lily, handing her the baby and from his pocket took a little Star of David with a red ribbon and pinned it on Daniel's vest, saying to his son, 'My father gave me this when I was born. I hope one day you would pass it on to your first born child.' He turned to look at his mother. 'He knows he smiled.'

'It's wind,' Eva said.

Wolfe and Eva left to make arrangements for the *Briss*.[8] Leaving Lily and Isaac alone. It was the first time they had been alone since she left for Paris.

'I'm sorry—' she began, but he placed a finger on her lips. 'It's done, and you are both safe, that's all that matters.' He kissed her passionately on the lips, and then pulled slightly away. 'I hope you understood me enlisting?'

'I do, and I promise that I would never ever do that again.'

He smiled. 'Let's not say ever.'

---

[8] circumcision.

The next day, before going to the hospital Isaac caught up with the family. He had a quiet chat with Abraham who would be returning to barracks in a few days. He couldn't stay long as he wanted to see Lily and Daniel before leaving for Netheravon.

He arrived at the airfield late that night, and before going to bed looked up the roster for the following day. He had an entire day of classes.

*

Since the evacuation of British troops from Dunkirk, the Luftwaffe had continually attacked British shipping in the Channel. Goering's plan now, having been told by his intelligence staff that RAF had only fifteen hundred fighters and were short of pilots, was to lure them into dog-fights over the Channel believing a plane lost over the sea was also a pilot lost. Hitler had told Goering that unless he destroyed the RAF the invasion of Britain could not take place. Goering promised he would wipe the RAF from the skies.

Suddenly on 18 August the Luftwaffe switched their attacks from the English Channel to British fighter bases in the south of England. The Battle of Britain had begun.

Radar which could detect aircraft seventy-five miles away was crucial to the British defences, allowing British fighters to intercept the Germans before they reached the English coast, but some did get through.

Saul placed the cowling over the engine on a Spitfire he had just finished working on when the siren blared out through the loud speakers. Pilots that had been sitting in their planes at the end of the runway tried to take off, but they were too late: Messerschmitt 109s swooped low over the field guns blazing. They hit one Spitfire just as it was leaving the ground. The pilot never stood a chance, while another's wing broke off the pilot leapt to safety, and then the bombers arrived. The entire attack lasted an hour and then they were gone.

The all-clear sounded and Saul emerged from the shelter, fists clenched, his face a mask of hatred, as he surveyed the scene of devastation, hearing the cries of the wounded above the bells of the fire engines and ambulances. Among the craters were dead and wounded pilots and anti-aircraft gunners. The administration building was on fire and precious Spitfires and Hurricanes were aflame or badly damaged. The roof on Hangar Two was on fire; airmen wheeled out aircraft in various states of repair. Saul ran over to help them.

By evening the craters had been filled in, the fires were out and Saul with other mechanics had begun repairing damaged aircraft.

8

Wolfe arrived home from another three days at the fire station to find Eva on the kitchen floor, surrounded by aluminium utensils.

'What are you doing?'

'The government needs aluminium to make fighter planes. Isaac's a fighter pilot and he needs an aeroplane to fight the Germans.'

Wolfe smiled. 'So you think those,' he pointed to the saucepans and frying pans, 'would make an aeroplane.'

She looked up at him. 'Don't be silly, but it could make a wing – well, a tail wing.'

He bent, taking her hands and gently pulled her to her feet and kissed her, saying, 'There are no children here to see us.'

Eva responded to his kiss and then pulled slightly away. 'Lily and Daniel are here.'

He burst into laughter. 'Daniel cannot walk yet, so there would be no surprise entrance.' He leant closer, but she bent her body back. 'Lily could walk in any—'

'Morning,' Lily said gaily, holding baby Daniel as she walked into the kitchen coming to an abrupt stop on seeing the floor covered in utensils. 'Mama, you spring cleaning?'

Eva looked at Wolfe and raised an eyebrow. He just laughed, planted a kiss on her lips, and then walked out of the kitchen. Eva pointed to the morning paper. 'The government said they need aluminium to build fighter planes, and that if we had any aluminium utensils could we help the war effort and hand them in.'

Lily smiled. 'Let me feed your hungry grandson and I'll help you.'

Wolfe quickly realised how clever the Government were when he met up with Asher and Billy at the Victoria Casino. 'Sarah's gone mad, piling up her aluminium pots and pans.'

'Eva too,' said Wolfe.

'Esther has emptied every cupboard in searching for them,' Billy joined in, looking at the brothers. 'Now that's the way to get housewives thinking they're helping the war effort.'

They watched as housewives pushed prams and carts loaded with aluminium utensils to pick-up points throughout London and other cities. Every housewife felt they were now helping the war effort; that it was personal, whenever they saw a Spitfire or Hurricane, they wondered with pride if it was their pots and pans that helped build it.

On 20 August, the same day, the Prime Minister made a stirring speech to the nation and Parliament. 'Let us brace ourselves to do our duty and bear ourselves that if the British Commonwealth and Empire last a thousand years men would say this was their finest hour. Never in the field of human conflict had so much been owed by so many, by so few.'

Isaac, the thin pilot officer stripe on his sleeve and pilot wing on his left breast arrived at RAF Turnhouse in Scotland some seven miles from Edinburgh. He had sadly left Ginger who had been posted to Manston.

Once he had settled into his billet, he reported to a Flying Training Officer, Flying Officer Jones, who, when he entered his office, was perusing Isaac's file. He smiled at Isaac, returning the salute. 'Stand at ease, Brown.' He took a cigarette from a packet on his desk, offering one to Isaac, who refused the offer. 'How many hours have you had on Spits?' He lit the cigarette.

'Six sir,' Isaac stuttered, knowing full well it wasn't enough.

The training officer sighed, letting out a cloud of smoke. 'What are they playing at?' He closed the file. 'Before you fly any combat missions, you'll have to do a lot more hours.' He pointed a finger at Isaac. 'Be at the stores at eight sharp in the morning.'

'Yes sir.' Isaac went to salute. 'Forget that bullshit for now, report to the Adjutant.' He held out Isaac's file. 'Give him this, and don't read it on the way.'

Isaac opened the door and left the office, arriving five minutes later in front of a door with a sign Squadron Leader Pilkington Adjutant. He knocked on the door opening it on the command of 'Enter'.

The following morning, Isaac entered the store to obtain his flying gear, helmet and goggles; fleece-lined flying jacket, gloves and boots. He had just finished when the flying training office entered. 'Great, let's get changed, grab a parachute and we'll be off.'

An hour later, Isaac stood by a Spitfire with the large letters XT, a circle looking like a target and then the letter G. A rigger helped him with his parachute straps and then jumped down. Isaac checked the oxygen through his mask and pressed the start button. There was a slight whine and the propeller began to turn slowly; he pushed the throttle slightly forward, foot on the brake pedal. There was a puff of white smoke from the exhausts. He held up a thumb to the fitter on the ground, who pulled away the chocks, hearing the flying instructor's voice in his ears. 'Blue two, take off, climb to twenty thousand feet and then level off.'

'Roger Blue Leader,' Isaac said, opening the throttle and the Spitfire gathered speed. Isaac weaved slightly to see Jones's Spitfire just in front and to his right lift off the ground. Isaac looked at the speedometer, pulled back on the stick and the aircraft left the ground, the wheels moving into their housing as he climbed steadily into the blue skies.

*

Saul took cover in the hangar as once again the German bombed Biggin Hill. A 109 flew low along the airfield strafing it, hitting parked aircraft, which burst into flames. A stationary vehicle flew into the air, crashing down on its roof. He saw one of the gun crews take hits fifty yards away. He yelled angrily at the German fighter and, without thinking, ran to the gunpit, diving for cover as the German came around for another attack. One of the soldiers moaned in pain, blood seeping down his left side.

'Can you load the gun?' Saul asked. The soldier nodded, a moan escaping his lips as he grabbed a box of ammunition and loaded the machine gun. The ME streaked low across the field. Yelling obscenities in English and Yiddish, Isaac pressed the button, the machine gun shuddering in his hands, but he missed, quickly realising he had to fire in front of the fighter.

'Can you load it again?' The soldier's white face showed the pain he was in, his lips drawn tight as he loaded, smacked Saul on the arm dropping into the bottom of the pit and passed out. Once again the enemy fighter came across the field. Saul judged his height and began firing, once again yelling obscenities at him. The 109 flew straight into the stream of bullets.

The pilot tried to gain height, flames flowing backward from the engine which stalled and the German fighter dived into the ground and exploded. For a second there was silence, which was broken by the bells of fire engines as they raced towards burning Spitfires and buildings. Ambulances and fire engines from outside the aerodrome raced in to help with the wounded, and put out the fires. Saul looked down at the soldier: he was still breathing.

He sat on the sandbags on top of the gunpit, waving his hands yelling, 'Medic! medic!'

Two medics ran over with a stretcher. One of the soldiers had died, but the other that helped Saul was still alive. Just as they moved to take him to the first-aid station, Saul said, 'Thanks.'

The soldier gave a white-faced smile and closed his eyes. A car pulled up and a squadron leader got out; blood seeped from a thigh wound as he limped over to Saul.

'What's your name airman?'

'3153807 SAC Brown, sir.' He pointed to the officer's thigh. 'Excuse me, sir, but you've been hit.'

'Just a flesh wound, I'm Squadron Leader Ambrose, report to me 1000 hours tomorrow morning.'

He didn't wait for an answer, turned and moved back to the car.

Saul looked around the airfield, smoke billowing upward from burning aircraft, including the German fighter. He looked over to his right to see a Hurricane he had just finished servicing leaning over onto its port wing. The pilot was about to take off when the sirens wailed and everyone ran for the nearest cover. The warning had come a little late, and the pilot just managed to leap into one of the gunpits. Saul walked from the gunpit. Above the crackling flames could be heard the cries of the wounded as firemen tried to put out the flames.

Saul clenched his fists. He needed to fight, repairing aircraft to fly against the Germans was all well and good, but he needed to do something other than cower in a bunker.

Saul helped repair damaged aircraft from the raid while soldiers filled in the craters.

*

On an assault course in Gosport, their wounds healed, the newly promoted Lieutenant Abraham Brown and Warrant Officer Gus Newark, carrying the same amount of equipment as their men, raced side by side towards the wall. In one leap Abraham grabbed the parapet and hauled himself to the top and sat astride it, hanging his right hand down for the shorter warrant officer to grab. In one movement Abraham grabbed the outstretched hand and hauled Newark to sit beside him, a big grin on his face.

'This is fun, you'll have to grow a couple of inches, Gus,' and then yelled, waving his arm forward. 'Come on you lazy lot.'

He leapt from the wall. 'You coming?' he said to Newark, who grinned. 'I suppose this is fun.' He leapt from the wall, following his commanding officer to the next obstacle.

In East London, Wolfe was running up a smoke-filled staircase, followed by Asher, both wearing their Proton breathing apparatus. Wolfe reached the top, moving into a smoke-filled room, heading for an open window. He came to a stop and looked down: the ladder was there. Asher walked into the room; without a word Wolfe picked him up into a fireman's lift and climbed through the window and onto the ladder, climbing slowly down. On reaching the ground he dropped Asher onto the floor.

'Take it easy – that hurt.'

Taking off his mask and goggles Wolfe gave a slight grin. 'Either beat me to the top so you could carry me, or lose weight and then I won't drop you.'

Asher turned to Billy who was working the ladder. 'You think I've put on weight?'

Billy shook his head. 'I'm not getting in the way of a brotherly argument.' He stared at Asher for a second, and then said, 'Wolfe might be—' Asher leapt at Billy, who was laughing.

Sally held baby Daniel, who smiled at his aunt. 'He's so handsome.' She looked up at her sister-in-law, who was arranging a hat she had made onto the head of a dummy in the window. 'You're getting broody.'

Sally pursed her lips. 'Mm, yes and no.' She stood and walked over to the window. 'That hat would go in a second. You should make more.'

'Haven't got the time, that little monster keeps me busy most of the day. I'm lucky to be living with your mother. She washes all his nappies and clothes.'

Sally smiled. 'Mama is like that, and her washing is always so soft. I would like a child, but I have the shop, and for the moment, I'm content to hold yours.'

A couple of miles away, April was being sick. She looked at her complexion in the mirror: she looked terrible. She must be okay for next week as Abraham was coming home for a week's leave. She cleaned her teeth, took a swig of water and walked back into the shop, a smile on her face. She would go later and see the doctor. Her sister Dora could open the shop on Sunday. Even though she had not changed her religion when marrying Abraham, she never opened on Saturdays out of respect for her parents and husband.

*

Making a sound like a machine gun Flying Officer Jones yelled, 'Blue two, you're dead.' Isaac's squadron leader was putting him through a gruelling combat flying exercise.

He was sweating, three times now Jones had caught him, it wasn't good. In combat he wouldn't last a minute.

'Okay, Blue Two, let's go home and talk about what went wrong.'

Isaac manoeuvred his Spitfire to fly in formation with Jones. Once he had landed, Isaac stood by his aircraft as Jones approached.

'Canteen,' was all he said, and led the way into the canteen. Jones poured a mug of tea from an urn in the corner, offering it to Isaac, and then poured one for himself, dropping his parachute onto the floor and sat down. Taking off his flying helmet, he ran his fingers through brown curly hair, an exasperated look on his face. Isaac dropped onto the chair opposite him.

Jones took a sip of tea and then said, 'You don't weave enough, and you fly straight for far too long. You're a sitting duck for any German fighter pilot.'

He took a sip of tea, while Isaac looked into the cup held between his hands.

'Don't kick yourself, we all start somewhere, and hope to live and learn from our mistakes. The next time you'll be better, and by the time we face the enemy, which I'm sure won't be many weeks away, it would become second nature.'

'Thanks. If the weather's okay, could we go up tomorrow?'

Jones smiled. 'Who said anything about tomorrow? Get some lunch and meet me by your Spit at 1400 hours, I've already ordered your fitters to fuel her up, we'll try something different this time.'

At 1400 hours, wondering what Jones had in store for him, Isaac found his CO waiting by his Spitfire with the other pilot from Blue Section, Pilot Officer Ron Cole. At twenty years of age he was already an experienced pilot, having fought in France with two kills to his credit. He had the blondest hair Isaac had ever seen. He smiled at Isaac. 'I want you to do exactly as I do,' he said.

In a line the three Spitfires of Blue Section took off. For the next hour, Isaac followed everything Cole did. Every time Jones attacked, Cole changed the manoeuvre, sometimes falling in behind Jones and attacking him. They landed back at Turnhouse with a smiling Isaac, who knew that today he had had a master class in flying, and knew that he would never forget the lesson Cole had taught him. He was as ready as he would ever be for combat, and hoped it would be soon.

Saul reported to Squadron Leader Ambrose as ordered. 'Stand at ease, Brown. I'm recommending you for a medal for your bravery yesterday.'

He slapped a file in front of him. 'I see here that you are requesting pilot training, why?'

Before Saul could reply, Ambrose went on, 'I'm told you are a great mechanic.' He frowned, looking up at Saul. 'It's people like you that keep the pilots in the air, and your sergeant says you seem to enjoy what you do.'

'Yes sir, I know that, but I'm fed up with the Germans attacking the field, and I'm unable to do anything about it. To be honest, sir, it's not in my nature to just take it, I have to fight back.'

'I understand what you are saying,' The Wing Commander leant forward. 'But you may not make the grade as a pilot.'

'I would like the opportunity to try, sir.'

The Wing Commander looked at Saul for a moment and then said, 'Have another medical, I'll send in a request for you to start pilot training as soon as possible.

Saul stood to attention. 'Thank you very much sir, I appreciate your help.'

'Okay Brown, dismissed.'

Throughout history unplanned accidents had changed the course of a battle or war. German pilots were forbidden to bomb London as German High Command feared retaliated air strikes against Berlin.

On the night of 27 August a flight of Heinkel 111s were to target the aircraft factories in Rochester and Kingston, and oil refineries at Thames Haven. They missed their target and by mistake bombed the City of London. The following night British bombers attacked Berlin, which was hit four more times over a ten-day period. Hitler threatened to raise British cities to the ground.

On 28 August the twelve aircraft of 603 Squadron landed at RAF Hornchurch. Isaac couldn't have been happier. It wasn't far to East London, Lily and Daniel.

9

It was almost five o'clock in the afternoon when the sirens screeched their warning throughout London. Some people carried on working, thinking that it was another false alarm, but many ran to their shelters and underground stations. Wolfe, Asher, Billy and other firemen stood outside the fire station, looking skyward as above the dying wail of sirens could be heard a low humming sound like a swarm of bees.

Shading his eyes with a hand, Wolfe could see in the distance tiers of black shapes that at first looked like migrating birds, but as they grew closer they were now noticeable as aircraft that covered miles of sky. The humming became louder and louder, the air vibrating from the thunderous sound from the engines of three hundred German bombers, with double the number of fighter escort.

Con trails criss-crossed the sky as Hurricane and Spitfire fought a running battle against Messerschmitt 110s and 109s as British fighter planes tried to get to the bombers. Now and again a speck fell from the sky, plummeting downward, black smoke trailing behind before hitting the ground and exploding, leaving behind men floating down on their parachutes.

The firebell rang as Fire Chief McNamara put down the phone. 'Come on,' Billy yelled, running towards their fire tender with Wolfe and Asher close behind and Billy saying over and over again, 'This is it, this is it.'

They sped out of the fire station with the bell ringing.

'Shut up,' Wolfe and Asher yelled together.

Wolfe looked upward to see slender Dornier and heavier Heinkel bombers darkening the sky. Suddenly shapes left the bellies of the aircraft. People who had stood curiously looking upward suddenly realised the danger and fled in panic to shelters to avoid the bombs that fell slowly at first, their speed increasing and making a whistling sound on their way downward. The ground shook as explosion followed explosion in one consecutive roar.

Gas and power stations were hit, with Surrey Docks seeming to be the primary target. Shrapnel bounced off cobbled streets. Flames rose hundreds of feet in the air, seemingly alive as embers floated lazily on the breeze to start new fires that spread from street to street.

Wolfe clung to the side of the fire engine as they sped along Commercial Road, its bell ringing shrilly as they turned into West Ferry Road and through the entrance to London Docks, coming to a screeching halt. Other fire tenders were already there, their hoses snaking along the piers. Wolfe, Asher and Billy leapt from the fire tender, ignoring the exploding bombs, and within minutes they were tackling the fires that raged on the water, and the surrounding warehouses. Chief McNamara was yelling instructions, but they had already anticipated what he was going to say.

Wolfe, Asher and Billy held the bucking hose steady as it poured gallons of water into the raging conflagration. Wolfe let out a scream, watching in horror as a building collapsed, the flames engulfing the firemen trying to put out the blaze.

A thousand gallons of water a minute poured into warehouses from the twin hoses on fire boats. The task seemed hopeless, the heat blistering paintwork forcing the boats back. Barges, wooden warehouses, even the wooden blocks on the road's surface were aflame. It seemed an impossible task for Wolfe and his fellow firefighters to put out the raging fires. One station officer sent out a message: 'Send all the bloody pumps you've got, the world's on fire.'

Surrey Dock was ablaze from end to end. Barrels of rum exploded inside burning warehouses, sending a stream of rum into the river; paint drums flared white in the heat; black, choking smoke billowed upward from melting rubber. Burning sugar united with the rum floated slowly downstream. Billy, Asher and Wolfe covered their faces as best they could against the throat-searing hot pepper floating in the air from burst sacking and barrels. Swarms of rats fled the flames that threatened to engulf them, some running in panic into the flaming River Thames.

The bells of fire engines and ambulances added to the roar of the flames as firemen tried to stem the wall of fire. Wolfe's eyes roamed the area around them. The bombers had gone, and they seemed to be winning, but then another wave of bombers guided by the still raging fires arrived. Wolfe swore at them in English and Yiddish, punching his fists skyward as wave after wave of bombers unloaded their lethal cargoes and then flew along the River Thames, turning back towards Calais, leaving destruction and mayhem in their wake.

The brothers and Billy were, like the others, dirt streaked from the smoke, soaking wet and tired. McNamara walked quickly over to them with three firemen in tow. 'I want you three to rest. I have a replacement crew to take your place.'

'Thanks, Chief,' Asher said through dry lips.

'There's a mobile canteen around the corner. Get some tea and sandwiches.'

Gradually as dawn broke, the firefighters had most of the fires under control. The streets were crisscrossed with hoses snaking down towards the river as many water mains had been destroyed by the bombs. Salvage workers worked their way through the wreckage looking for survivors. Bomb dispersal units were called to various sites where a bomb had not exploded.

Back at the station Wolfe and the others cleaned their fire engines, rolled up hoses, repairing or replacing broken ones. Wolfe turned to his brother and Billy. 'I think the bombing has just begun. With the Victoria close to the docks we need to discuss whether we should take a chance and keep it open, or close it.'

'I think we must close it,' said Asher, adding, 'We cannot put our workers, or gamblers in danger.'

'I'm sure that after tonight many of the men and some of the women would want to enlist,' Billy pointed out.

'We could transfer the Victoria croupiers over to the Hanover,' said Wolfe.

'I think we should leave it to Frank to organise the transfer of chips, and perhaps some of the tables over to the Hanover as spares,' Billy said.

'Good idea,' Wolfe pointed a finger at Billy. 'If you shoot over there now, Frank could get the ball rolling. I think we should offer those that are enlisting a week's pay.'

'I agree with that,' Asher said and Billy nodded in agreement.

*

In the sky above Dover, Isaac was sticking to Cole's tail as he turned to attack a Heinkel 111. Isaac wove to the left, glancing into his rear view mirror. His heart skipped a beat on seeing the black shape of a ME109 on his tail. There was nothing else to do but leave Cole and save himself. He pulled back on the stick, curving in behind the German, but before he could fire the ME went into a steep dive. Isaac followed it down and for a second he was in his sight; Isaac pressed the gun button on the stick, the fighter shuddered slightly, he let out yell on seeing bits drop off the opposing fighter, but his jubilation was short lived as he was attacked by another ME. He instantly hauled back on the stick and streaked upward. The German followed for a second and then broke off the attack. Isaac eyes followed the enemy plane as it flew towards the English Channel, and breathed a sigh of relief.

Low on fuel he headed back to Hornchurch. He hadn't shot anyone down, but then, he was still in one piece and his first combat mission was over. He landed to refuel, rearm, have a cup of tea, and then took off once again, weaving from side to side along the grass airstrip watching the speedometer as it quickly reached eighty miles an hour, pulling gently back on the stick and was airborne, the squadron of twelve Spitfires climbing steeply into a darkening sky and gaining height at two thousand feet a minute as Squadron Leader Spalding voice came over the radio.

'Top Hat control, Castle Leader here, squadron airborne.' A minute went by, and then the controller said over the radio telephone. 'Top Hat to Castle Leader, Vector 160 two hundred plus bandits, Angels one eight.'

'Roger control, your message received.' As one, the squadron headed towards the enemy.

The early warning radar chain was working well, and even though the Germans had knocked some out, mobile units quickly filled the gaps until they were back working once again.

Isaac scanned the sky and the distant horizon for German planes as the squadron climbed another thousand feet, when someone yelled, 'Tallyho, ten o'clock.' Isaac looked quickly in that direction and his heart beat faster. He gulped back the bile of fright; the sky was full of German aircraft, Dornier and Heinkel bombers with their fighter escort in tiers a thousand feet deep.

Isaac said, 'Fucking heck,' as he switched on his reflector sight, flicked the gun switch to fire and lowered his seat till the circle and dot on the reflector sight shone dark red. Spalding's voice was calm over the RT. 'Blue and Yellow sections take on the bombers, Red and Green the fighters.'

Isaac swallowed nervously as the squadron hurtled ever closer to the enemy bombers and their escorts. Sweeping round with the sun behind them and on Spalding's order dived down on the enemy.

Isaac was calm now that the butterflies had disappeared as he put the fighter into a steep banking dive, coming in behind a Dornier which now filled his sights. He fired a short burst and then he was past, turning to have another go, but before he could, bullets past over his canopy as an ME110 swung in behind.

He yelled angrily at himself, 'You fucking idiot, Brown,' knowing he hadn't been careful enough.

He turned his fighter onto its port wing, the enemy plane following, and then pulled back on the stick. The German suddenly broke off the attack. Breathing heavily, Isaac knew that it was the second time in one day he had gotten away with being an idiot and not careful enough, forgetting all he had learnt from Cole. He climbed to twenty thousand feet to see German fighters heading for home.

Today he had learnt a valuable lesson in survival. It did not worry him like it had some pilots that he hadn't shot down an enemy plane. He knew that would come one day, but he was gaining experience every time he took to the air. He wove left and right, looking around. The skies were empty; the German bombers on their way back to their bases. He could see London Docks, and his mouth formed a tight line; East London looked like Dante's Inferno. He hoped his family were safe in their shelters.

When he landed he would phone Ginger at Manston. Perhaps he had a kill.

*

Lily, carrying baby Daniel, emerged from the garden shelter, with Eva behind her. The air filled with the smell of smoke and other obnoxious aromas. Eva clapped her hands on seeing their house still standing and untouched, but her main thoughts were of her family scattered around London and the country.

Sally had stayed in the shop, even though they were closed, hiding under a table. She crawled out and smiled, shining the torch around the darkened shop thinking, *it's all here, a bit dusty, but there was no damage thank goodness.*

The following morning, April walked slowly down Burdett Road. Her step quickened on seeing the bombed-out shops and houses, but her salon and the two shops either side were still standing. There was a big smile on her face as she stepped through the door with the open sign to see her sister Dora washing Mrs Benning's hair. Abraham would be home tomorrow. She wondered how he would take the news. She gently rubbed her belly and then put on her working jacket, a dreamy smile on her face.

*

Abraham and Gus sat opposite each other, playing cards. They stopped playing as the train came to a halt and the lights went out. The conductor walked along the coaches saying, 'Ladies and gentlemen, sorry for the delay, but there's a raid on at the moment. As soon as it's clear we would continue our journey.'

He carried on to the next coach. Through the window they could see a red skyline, and searchlights moving across the sky like the spotlight on a theatre stage. Fifteen minutes later the carriage lights came on and they continued their journey towards Kings Cross and London.

Since Dunkirk there had been a bond between Abraham and Gus that surpassed their rank.

'What's the girl's name, and where did you meet her?' Abraham asked.

Gus looked up from the cards for a moment, a smile lighting up his face. 'Freda, I met her at Brady Street Jewish Club. My father told me there was a dance on that Sunday. My mother said I should get out of the house and enjoy myself. So out of boredom I went, and there she was. It's the first time I've been on leave since our training began. I've written and she had replied. I'm picking her up at her parent's house tomorrow.' He looked out of the window. 'We're here. That went quickly.'

The two men parted, Abraham headed towards the taxi rank eager to get home and make sure April was okay. The taxi wove its way through the streets, having to take a detour as the road was blocked by still smoking rubble. The devastation of the bombing shocked Abraham, not recognising some of the street they were passing through. A bus stood on end in a crater and people – many in army uniform, wardens, police and firemen – scrambled amongst the rubble looking for survivors. He paid off the driver and turned to be met by April, kissing his face and lips.

'People are watching – a man and lady – over the road stopped to have a look,' he said between her kisses.

'I don't care,' she took his hand and they moved towards the salon. 'I have some news for you.'

He stopped in mid-stride turning to face her. 'Good or—'

'I think it's good, I hope you do too. I'm pregnant.'

He looked amazed, then a big smile lit up his face. 'That's wonderful, when? Have you told our parents?'

'June, and no, I wanted you to know first.' He picked her up and kissed her. 'I can't believe it, me a dad.'

Just then the sirens pierced the air. Hand in hand they ran to the nearest shelter.

*

As usual, Isaac's heart beat faster and he breathed heavily into his oxygen mask at the sight of so many aeroplanes in one place at one time. The squadron climbed above the enemy bomber stream, the sun reflecting on the chrome parts and windshields of the enemy bombers as they flew steadily towards London.

Isaac lowered his seat and went into the usual drill and was now calm, for a second hoped that harmonising his guns from 500 yards to 250 on Cole's recommendation would give him better accuracy.

The order was given to attack. Isaac pushed the stick forward and the nose of the Spitfire dropped going onto a shallow dive gaining speed in a

full throttle attack. Isaac doesn't flinch as the bombers' gunner fired at
him, the tracer bullets racing over his canopy. He fired a short burst; the
recoil shook the Spitfire as he zoomed past the Junker 88, pulling back
the stick. Looping into a climbing right turn, coming up and below the
German bomber at 250 yards, he thumbed the trigger button and cordite
fumes blew back into the cockpit. He saw bullets strike the belly of the
aircraft, and was quickly past manoeuvring pedal and stick, glancing
over his left shoulder to turn the fighter around for another attack, but
there was no need. The port wing of the Junker fell slowly away from the
main body; its nose dropped and it began to spin, rotating slowly towards
the earth below.

Isaac pointed the Spitfire skyward to gain height, levelling out at
twenty thousand feet and immediately spotted another victim, a Heinkel.
He pushed the stick forward. The speed of the Spitfire reached 400 miles
per hour, and once again he was fired upon. He fired a short burst, but
the intensity of the enemy's firepower spoilt his aim, so he dived under
the belly of the bomber. His fighter buffeted by the draft of its propellers,
he dropped away into an inverted roll, pulled back the stick, looping the
fighter up and firing a two-second burst at the engine streaking quickly
past. He flipped the fighter over for another attack to see the enemy's
engine on fire and the bomber going into a shallow dive, the doomed
crew tumbling from the blazing aircraft as its downward path became
steeper and steeper, hurling like a fiery comet towards the ground.

He didn't follow it down, but glanced quickly into his rearview
mirror, and around the sky, jerking backward in his straps with shock on
seeing an ME 109 hurtling straight at him. Tracers flew above his
canopy. Gritting his teeth, Isaac kept the Spit level as he pressed the gun
button, yelling at the top of his voice, 'Fuck you, fuck you!'

For a second his heart jumped as he saw bits flying off the propeller
of the Messerschmitt. He pulled hard right on the stick and the German
flew past. Isaac came round looking for him, but the German was gone,
and suddenly as quickly as it had happened the sky was empty. He
glanced at his fuel gauge; he had enough to make it back. Smiling, and
patting himself on the back, he headed for Hornchurch. He had downed
two enemy bombers and damaged or maybe shot down a fighter. He
must phone Ginger.

Once he had been debriefed and had a shower, he phoned Manston,
asking to speak to Ginger. A couple of seconds went by when a strange
voice came on the line.

'This is Flying Officer Thompson, I'm sorry to tell you that Ginger
was shot down today and killed...' There was a slight pause. 'I saw it
happen and he didn't bale out, I'm so sorry.'

'Thank you for telling me. Good night.' Isaac walked slowly back to his room, head slightly bowed, Ginger had been in combat twenty-one days. Isaac realised how precarious his immortality was, and how aware he must be of all that was happening around him in the sky if he was to survive. He saw the telephone wasn't in use and decided to see if he could get through to Lily, and hopefully persuade her to evacuate to the country. He sighed. Why waste his breath? He knew the answer already.

*

After agreeing to close the Victoria, Wolfe, Asher and Billy hurried home to get changed. There had been no let up by the German bombing raids, day or night. Thirty minutes after arriving home they were on the way to the Victoria Casino to help load two lorries they had been able to hire to take roulette, card tables and other gaming equipment to the Hanover.

They had lost much of their workforce to conscription, and volunteers into the armed forces, but they still had enough people to keep the Hanover open.

When they arrived, the two vehicles were in the driveway, and loading had begun under the leadership of their capable manager Frank Mullin.

Billy could see by the dour expression on Frank's face that something was wrong, and pulled him to one side, 'What's the matter, what's happened?'

'A bomb landed on our house last night. Elizabeth is there seeing if anything can be salvaged.'

'Don't worry, we'll find you a place near the Hanover.'

'Go and help your wife,' Wolfe said.

Frank looked around. 'Are you sure, I've left Elizabeth to—'

Billy waved an arm. 'Go and help Elizabeth. We will be able to manage here,' Billy said.

Asher looked at his watch. 'If they run true to form, the Germans should be here in a couple of hours, so we'd better get a move on.'

The trio had been home a short while when the sirens began their piercing shrill.

Wolfe and Eva ran for their shelter in the garden just as they heard the familiar drone of approaching aircraft. Suddenly Wolfe turned and headed for the shelter door.

'Where are you going?' Eva screamed, in anguish as Wolfe left the safety of the shelter as bombs fell, yelling over his shoulder.

'Won't be a minute,' closing the door with Eva staring at it, yelling and swearing at him in Yiddish. The door suddenly opened, the sky behind Wolfe a flaming red, and the noise deafening in an everlasting sound of crashing bombs and buildings.

'I left the kettle on the gas.' He pointed at the kettle in his hand. She smacked him on the arms, wiping away the tears on her cheeks. 'You frightened me, you idiot, you could have been killed.'

He placed the kettle on the floor and wrapped his arms round her. 'I'm sorry, I didn't mean to frighten you like that.' He pulled slightly away. 'Tea?'

She smiled. 'Yes please.'

Eva was calm now that he was there as she cut a slice of cake, handing it to her husband, both ignoring what was happening outside. The all-clear sounded and hand in hand they emerged to see their house still standing.

Wolfe's first thoughts were to the family. He looked skyward hoping Isaac was safe.

Asher and Sarah looked over the fence. 'You okay?' they asked.

'Fine, except your *shmoe* of a brother ran over to the house when the bombs were falling to get the kettle.'

'I had left the gas on,' Wolfe said defensively.

That afternoon Wolfe was getting his fireman's gear together when there was a knock at the door. With a puzzled look on his face he opened it to see a rabbi standing there with another man. 'Yes, may I help you?'

'Is this the home of Eva Brown?'

Wolfe stared at the rabbi for a moment. 'Yes, what can I do—'

'I'm sorry to interrupt you, but could we—'

Wolfe's heart was in his throat, thinking it could be one of the children. He took a slight step forward, saying quietly. 'Has something happened to one of—'

'It's her sister, could we—'

'Eva,' he called loudly in Yiddish, 'there's someone here who would like to speak to you.'

Eva ran down the stairs. 'What's happened?' She came to a stop beside Wolfe.

'Mrs Brown, I'm Rabbi Shultz. This is the warden of our synagogue, Mr Davis. I'm sorry to tell you that your sister Rachael and her husband Amos were killed last night when a bomb struck their shop. Unfortunately they were in the cellar and the building collapsed on top of them, I'm sorry but we were unable to save them.'

Eva clung to Wolfe, tears streaming down her face, unable to speak.

'We understand they had two daughters and—'

'Naomi is in Palestine with her husband, and Ruth married a rabbi.

They live in New York,' Wolfe said softly, adding, 'I could write to my nieces and let them know of this tragedy.'

'We would be holding the funeral tomorrow,' Mr Davis said. 'Eleven thirty at Montague Road. We will supply a car if you need it.'

Eva looked at Wolfe. 'What should I do?'

'Don't you worry,' he said softly, arm around her shoulder. 'Leave it to me.' He turned to the rabbi. 'That would be fine, and the car would be gratefully accepted.'

The rabbi nodded. 'Sorry for your loss, the car would be here at eleven.' He turned to go; Wolfe held out his hand, the rabbi clasped it. 'I would like to reimburse you for the petrol, and I have coupons.'

'Thank you, Mr Brown, that's very generous of you.'

Family and friends gathered at Eva and Wolfe's house, where her daughters and daughter in-laws, including Hannah, had made a buffet for all those returning to the house after the funeral. The afternoon was interrupted by another raid, but no one left, just congregated in the cellar.

Although still devout, Eva felt she should not sit the full week of mourning, just the two days before the Sabbath. 'Are you sure this is what you want?' Wolfe asked.

'Yes, it's the safest thing to do.' She took his hand. 'I could always sit when the war is over,' she whispered. 'Please tell the Rabbi for me at evening prayers.'

*

The sirens began their nightly piercing song, which was the signal for the thieves of the Blitz to go into people's houses and steal whatever they could lay their hands on while the owners were in the shelters.

One of the most notorious of these unscrupulous people was Spider Munroe.

'The night shift's on time. Let's go,' he said to his three companions with a smile.

As one, they moved to a door leading to a garage where a black van was parked. A man in a fawn Crombie coat slid onto the driver's seat with Spider settling onto the passenger one. The other two men opened the garage doors, closing and locking them once the van was through, and then moved into the rear of the van. 'Take the usual route,' Spider ordered, 'and watch your speed.'

'I know,' the driver said belligerently.

A fire engine turned in front of them, its bell ringing a puff of the exhaust blowing back as it accelerated away.

'Turn left here,' Spider ordered, placing an ARP armband on his sleeve, and picking up an ARP helmet from the floor. He had bought it for fifty quid and to Spider and his cronies it was worth every penny.

The houses either side of the street were in darkness. The four men took no notice of the explosions or noise as a couple of miles away German bombers dropped their loads once more on London's docks.

Spider touched the driver's arm. 'Stop here, Bob.'

Bob Burns brought the van to a stop. Spider got out of the van donning the helmet and walked a few paces along the street, coming to a halt, his eyes moving from house to house, and then he turned slowly, surveying the rest of the street. He looked at the van, making a motion for Bob to switch off the engine, and walked across the road through an open gate along a path to the front door of a house, placing his hand on the door and pushed it.

Spider wasn't surprised as the door swung open and he stepped boldly into the house. Burns watched Spider disappear, and then checked the street for any movement. Spider emerged gesturing for Burns to come over.

'Come on, you two,' Burns said over his shoulder as he got out of the van. They left the rear of the van open and the three men holding bags quickly made their way across the road following Spider into the house.

'Johnnie you and Bob upstairs,' Spider ordered quietly.

The two men nodded and headed towards the stairs. 'George, you're with me.' As one they split into different rooms, opening draws taking anything sellable. Spider looked behind paintings on the wall in case there was a safe.

Upstairs Johnnie found a jewel box, emptying its contents into his bag. He lifted the mattress of the bed, nothing hidden there. In the next room Bob was doing the same, but he was more fortunate in finding a wallet with ten pounds inside it.

Suddenly there was an almighty bang outside; Bob moved to the front window: a bomb had landed at the end of the street a house was on fire. He ran down the stairs to find Spider. 'House on fire, won't be long before a fire engine gets here.'

'Okay, let's take the paintings, go get the others.' While Bob gathered the other two, Spider took down the paintings. The three men ran across the road to the van, while Spider placed the painting into the rear of the van, and then calmly walked across to the house on fire. Johnnie had just closed the rear door of the van when the fire engine arrived.

Wolfe and Asher leapt from the fire engine. While Wolfe attached the hose to the hydrant, crossing his finger it would work, Asher and the others pulled out the hoses from the fire engine.

'You call this in?' Wolfe asked Spider.

'Yes, I was about to see if anyone was in the—'

A scream of 'Help, help,' came from a second-floor broken window. Wolfe didn't hesitate but ran into the house ignoring the flames, with Asher close behind him, while Billy extended the ladder to just below the window where the scream had come from, and ran up it. The other firemen poured gallons of water onto the flames trying desperately to stop it spreading to nearby properties.

Wolfe and Asher raced up the stairs; the wallpaper curling from the heat, the flames moving down the wall. Wolfe opened the door to the bedroom. A woman and a man had their bodies wrapped around two children. Wolfe gathered the children into his arms, moving to the window. He handed a little boy to Billy who moved quickly down the ladder, handing the boy to McNamara and then climbed up again to take the other child.

Asher moved onto the ladder, helping the woman climb down, while Wolfe was about to climb through the window when the man collapsed. He did not hesitate, but lifted the father onto his shoulders, climbed through the window onto the ladder, and with Billy a few steps behind for safety, descended to the ground just as the roof caved in.

With the family safely on their way to hospital to be checked over, Wolfe looked for the ARP man, but he had disappeared.

The all-clear sounded. Bleary-eyed people emerged from their garden shelters or basements. Sleep had been virtually impossible with the continuous drone of aircraft, anti-aircraft fire, exploding bombs and bells. Some stood with disbelief on their faces to see their home a pile of smouldering rubble. Tears ran down their cheeks as they moved amongst the wreckage, seeking what memories they could salvage from their home. Rescue workers called out, hoping to find someone alive. Bomb disposal units began the dangerous task of making safe unexploded bombs. WVS vans appeared to supply homeless families with hot food and drink.

Despite the chaos and heartache, London still functioned as a commercial city. Buses picked their way around bomb craters, delivering passengers to work. Every shop window, some without glass, had a notice saying 'Business as Usual'. The sign outside a police station read 'Be Good We're Still Open'. That notice didn't worry Spider as he and his men upended their bags onto a long table.

'Not bad,' George Edwards said, picking up a diamond ring and looking at it through a jeweller's eye glass. 'We'll get fifty quid for this one.' He pointed to a necklace. 'Same for that.'

Bob picked up one of the paintings, looking intently at the signature.

'Nice painting – not a master, but I know someone who would have these.'

The twenty-one-year-old, Tom Spider Munroe, was a person without a conscience, who had been in trouble with the law since he was fourteen when he beat up his father, who, in a drunken rage, knocked out his mother's front teeth.

He was sent to Borstal, but instead of changing his character for the better it only made him worse. Within three months he was top dog. His coal-black eyes could stare into your soul, intimidating opponents before a blow was struck.

He loved his mother, money and women, in that order. He didn't care how he obtained the money, even murder. The nickname came with the tattooed spider that covered his right arm and the cobweb between thumb and forefinger.

Spider was called up, but after two weeks of being told what to do, he absconded becoming a deserter.

The bombing of London played into Spider's hands as he took advantage of the confusion the bombing did to people. His philosophy was, if I don't take it, someone else will. In some cases the public unwittingly helped him in his endeavours as he emptied a house of furniture.

'What going on here?' someone would ask Spider, his ARP helmet on his head.

'Unexploded bomb, I'm helping the owner get his belongings out.'

With that one of his cronies would appear. 'I'll give you a hand,' the passer-by would say, or would just quickly turn and walk away.

10

Wolfe, Asher and Billy had been away from home for a week. They, like many firefighters, had stayed at the fire station even though they were off duty. With the relentless day and night bombing, they had been needed. They were tired, having had very little sleep, but were still prepared to carry on, but their fire Chief McNamara had said, 'If you three don't go home for a rest, you'll be no use to me.'

'But we would be—'

'Have a look in the mirror,' McNamara interrupted Wolfe. 'You're about to drop, and slowing down. Go home, have a bath and a good meal.' He turned to go and looked back. 'What are you waiting for – a piggyback?'

'He's right,' Billy pointed out, lifting his arm and making a face at the smell, strolled over to a chair and picked up his uniform jacket. 'Coming.'

The three men walked out of the station. There were black rings under their eyes and they hadn't shaved for three days. Asher saw a cab and hailed it, giving him Billy's address first and then his and Wolfe's.

The house was empty when Wolfe entered. The first thing he did was have a shave and bath. He had just reached the bottom of the stairs when the door opened and Eva walked in. For a second he didn't say anything, an astonished look on his face on seeing her attired in a WVS uniform. She smiled and turned a full circle. 'You like it?'

'What the—' he pointed. 'Why the WVS, you know it's dangerous?'

'So big shot, it's okay for you,' she put her hands on her hips, 'but not for me.'

'You're a—'

'Woman,' she interrupted, adding, 'Sarah and Esther had also volunteered.'

He stepped forward, grabbing her around the waist, pulling her gently towards him, crushing his lips onto hers, and then picked her up onto his shoulders. 'Wolfe, what are you doing?'

'You need to take those clothes off and I'm going to help you, but I do like a woman in uniform – it's very sexy.'

'Wolfe Brown you are—' She burst into laughter.

On the landing he gently put her down. 'There's no children here are there?'

She touched his face. 'Not at this moment.' She wrapped her arms around his neck. 'What do you have in mind?'

The following morning the brothers and Billy were on their way to the synagogue when Frank suddenly emerged.

'I'm sorry to appear like this, but the Victoria was bombed last night. Incendiaries set it alight, I thought you should know.'

'Thanks, Frank,' Billy said. 'We'll have a look after the service.'

'Have you settled into the house?' Eva asked. The partners had bought a house in Blandford Street, within walking distance of the Hanover from their contingency funds after Frank's house had been destroyed.

He smiled. 'Yes, it's great thank you. You'll have to come and see what Elizabeth had done to the place.'

'That would be nice,' Eva said.

'That's if the bloody Germans would leave us alone for a while,' Billy said angrily.

'I'll be over tonight,' Wolfe said, 'to look over the books.'

'I'll have it ready for you. I'll see you all soon.'

Frank left and they carried onto the synagogue.

Once the service was over the three partners left their wives and walked to Queen Victoria Street. Asher let out a slow whistle on seeing the still-smouldering ruins of the casino. 'We would have to pull it down and build from scratch,' Asher said.

'We were lucky, it could have been worse,' Billy pointed out. 'We could have stayed open.'

'Well, there's nothing we would be able to do now,' Wolfe said. They began to walk away. 'We must put in a claim with the Government. I think the most they give on property is five hundred pounds. I'll get Frank to get the forms and we'll fill them in.'

Wolfe arrived at the Hanover just after nine o'clock in the evening. The casino was packed. He found Frank in the office. 'By the look of the crowd out there.' He gestured towards the casino. 'I'm pleased we put in the tables we brought from the Victoria.'

'If things carry on that way we might have to expand,' Frank said.

'I'll have a talk with the others, and see what we could come up with.'

For the next hour, Wolfe checked the books. 'Everything is in order, as usual,' he said to Frank. 'I'll have a stroll around the casino before I leave.'

'I'll come with you,' Frank said locking the office door.

There was a noisy crowd around one of the crap tables, Wolfe wandered over, curious to see what the fuss was about. He stood just behind Frank and one of the croupiers. His head jerked forward slightly, a frown creasing his forehead on seeing a well-dressed man at the end of the table, a stack of chips in front of him, shake the dice in his hand and showing his fist to the women by his side who blew on it.

Wolfe stared at the man as he threw the dice that landed on a three and four to the cheers of the people around the table. Wolfe was sure he was the ARP warden he saw the other night. Just then the man looked up, and for a second stared straight at Wolfe. If he had recognised him, the man didn't show it as he picked up the dice and threw again.

Wolfe whispered in Frank's ear, 'Had that man been here before?'

'He comes in at least once a week, sometimes more, big spender. He's winning at the moment, but most of the time he loses.' Frank frowned. 'It doesn't seem to bother him as it does other people.'

'I'm going, I'll be in touch, and you're doing a great job, regards to Elizabeth.'

Wolfe walked out of the casino taking the last underground train home, his thoughts on the ARP man. He had heard about thieves of the Blitz, not wanting to believe that someone would take advantage of people's fears by entering their homes and stealing while the owner was in a shelter.

He didn't say anything to the others. Maybe he was wrong and the man was genuine, but he would keep an eye out for him in the future.

Early Monday morning, refreshed, the three men reported to McNamara for duty.

Asher looked at his watch. 'Better get changed they'll be here in an hour.'

How right he was. Once again, Wolfe, Asher and Billy were rushing towards the River Thames. The fire engine came to a screeching halt by a group of warehouses and factories along Narrow Street in Limehouse. Two converted lorries stood close by in case they needed water. A fireman shouted that there were people on the roof of one of the factories. They quickly ran out the two-wheeled narrow ladders until they were a couple of inches short of the roof.

As soon as it was secure Wolfe ran up the ladder, carrying a hose over his shoulder, quickly followed by Asher. He reached the top, attaching the hose to the ladder, opening the nozzle and playing the jet of water onto the roof while yelling at the people to come to him. A very frightened young girl was the first. Holding the hose under his arm Wolfe stepped onto the roof to see flames creeping slowly towards them, and turned the jet of water onto the fire as one by one Asher helped the six people onto the ladder.

As the last one left the roof, the flame fanned by the slight breeze leapt towards Wolfe. Realising he was fighting a losing battle Wolfe climbed reluctantly down. Reaching the bottom of the ladder Wolfe looked towards the end of Narrow Street to see an ARP warden with another man pushing a cart with furniture on it. A man stopped, spoke to them and quickly continued on his way towards Wolfe, who pointed to the two men asking him, 'What's going on there?'

'ARP man said there's an unexploded bomb in the house and he was helping the owner move his furniture.' He left Wolfe looking intently back to the two men who were disappearing around a corner. He shrugged his shoulders, turning away to help fight another blaze.

More tenders arrived, adding their hoses to the others. The flames gradually disappeared, to be replaced by a spiral of smoke, but their respite was short lived as more bombers arrived and once again the firefighters like boxers in a ring knocked out the flames.

Thursday, 5 December 1940

Claire Wilson's brown eyes sparkled, a beaming smile on her face as she walked towards the entrance to the registry office. She held a posy of flowers in her hands and wore a white satin wedding dress with a taffeta petticoat. The skirt flared out from the waist with a grey waistband and white taffeta rose on the right hip. The bodice was sculpted at the neck with shoulder straps. Hannah, also smiling, walked beside her in a blue silk bridesmaid dress that hung to just above the ankle with a V-shaped neck. Behind them were the invited guests who were Claire's friends from Hannah's establishment.

Dr Stephen Franks stood by the doorway, looking dapper in his navy-blue suit, a white carnation in the buttonhole. Standing next to him, having obtained a week's leave, was Saul in RAF dress uniform with the Military Cross on his left breast, as best man.

'You are so beautiful,' the doctor said to his bride.

Saul disappeared for a second returning to say, 'It's time.'

Two hours later they arrived back at Compton Terrace, where Hannah had hired a caterer for the bridal dinner. Many of the guests were long-standing clients, not Claire's as she had for some time helped Hannah with front of house.

It was time for the couple to depart on a short honeymoon to Scotland. As they stood by the taxi that would take them to the station Claire hugged Hannah, 'Thank you for everything you had done for me. If it hadn't been for you I would never have been as happy as I am now.'

The two women hugged and kissed on each cheek before Claire climbed aboard the taxi. She threw the posy of flowers to the waiting crowd of women. The doctor had one foot in the cab then changed his mind, grabbed Hannah and kissed her on the cheek, saying, 'You were right, if you don't ask you don't know.'

He turned, entering the cab and closing the door. Claire hung from the window, waving goodbye. There were tears in Hannah's eyes as she entered the house to be met by Saul with a glass of champagne.

'It was a great party.'

She smiled, 'Yes it was,' she took his hand. 'And it's about to get better.'

He laughed, 'You or me?'

She punched him gently on the arm as they walked hand in hand up the stairs.

Saul hadn't told Hannah about applying for pilot training, firstly because he had not heard anything after his interview. He knew if he were accepted he wouldn't see Hannah as often as he did now. He loved her, and didn't care a damn about her past, but she was still a bit wary when they went out in case she saw one of Compton Terrace's clients.

He told her that the men frequenting her establishment would not want anyone else to know. If she did see someone she was to ignore them as they would do the same to her. Three times in the past they had seen someone, and as Saul had said, completely ignored them. He had thought of asking her to marry him, but with the war on and the uncertainty of everything, he decided not to broach the subject just yet. He knew that Isaac was coming home on a week's leave tomorrow. He would have a talk with him and see what he said about him being a pilot.

At that precise moment, Isaac with Cole were chasing a lone Dornier as it tried to escape at treetop level over the coast near St Margaret's Bay.

'He's a cheeky little blighter,' Cole said over the intercom. 'I'm in two minds whether to let him go.'

'I'm not so sentimental,' Isaac said as he pushed the throttle lever forward, the Dornier now in his sights, and let off a short burst. Bits flew of the rear port wing and dorsal. The German bomber seemed to slip sideways as Isaac let off another burst. Again bits flew off the bomber. His button clicked: he was out of ammo.

'Blue leader I'm out of ammo, he's all yours.'

He throttled back slightly as Cole flew in behind and slightly to one side of the Dornier. Isaac could see Blue leader's bullets hitting home. The bomber suddenly nose-dived into the sea. They flew twice over the wreckage site, but there were no survivors.

'Let's go home Blue Two,' Cole said.

The two spitfires in formation flew back to Hornchurch. Isaac smiled: a week's leave awaited him on landing after being debriefed.

Isaac took the underground to Liverpool Street Station, deciding to walk home. His face showed the shock of seeing so much devastation.

Smoke spiralled upward from dampened down fires. Rubble littered the pavements, entire streets were missing. He had to walk around a large crater in the road, stood there for a moment wondering if he should go and help the people looking for survivors.

Men and women passed him pushing prams or carts with what was left of their possessions. His face hardened on seeing two bodies being carried from a bombed house with just one side wall left standing. It was like looking at the side of an open dolls house with a staircase running through it. He decided to carry on home and was pleasantly surprised to see shops open, even though in some cases there were no windows left.

He smiled on seeing a placard in the window that was still intact, MISSED. Open As Usual. He stood for a moment looking at his home, the walls pockmarked from flying shrapnel, and was just about to place the key in the lock when the door flew open. He just had time to drop his case as Lily flung herself at him, landing her lips on his. He wrapped his arms around her, closing his eyes inhaling her perfume. He reluctantly took his lips from hers.

'I think we had better go inside before you—' she grabbed his hand, pulling him into the house. He just had time to pick up his suitcase with the other hand. She kicked the door closed with her foot, crushing her body close to him,

'Now where were we?' she whispered.

'What about—'

'Mama has taken Daniel to your sisters, so we—' He picked her up in his arms and headed for the stairs. 'I think I better walk from—' He let her legs go and as she stood, took her hand and ran up the stairs.

The Friday evening Sabbath service was over. Isaac looked up to the women's gallery and smiled at Lily, pointing towards the entrance. She nodded and disappeared from view. He was just about to move into the aisle when his father came along with another man.

'Isaac, this is Moshe Goldstein.'

'Good *Shabbat*,' Goldstein said.

Isaac smiled, automatically answering, '*Shabbat shalom*.'

'He's a new member – unfortunately he supports Tottenham Hotspurs.'

Still with a smile on his face, Isaac said, 'Papa, why are you talking to a man who knows nothing about football?' He moved out into the aisle.

Goldstein glanced at the pilot's wings and undid the top button of Isaac's tunic,

'Fighter pilot?' It was said as a question.

'Yes.'

They reached the hallway and Wolfe went in search of Eva. Lily saw Isaac and waved, moving towards him just as a woman said, 'There you are.'

Moshe smiled at her, turning to Isaac. 'Isaac, this is my wife, Golda.'

Lily moved beside Isaac, taking his hand. 'Lily, this is Moshe Goldstein and his wife Golda.'

'Very nice to meet you,' Lily smiled.

'You must be very proud of your husband,' Moshe said.

Lily's eyes shone as she looked at Isaac, 'Yes, I am.'

'Are you on leave?' Moshe asked.

Before Isaac could reply Golda said, 'Lily you are just the person I need. We have just moved into the area. Where are the best shops for kosher meat and poultry?' She smiled. 'That's if you are able to get it.'

'Meat was hard to get, but chickens not too bad, but it's still rationed, and you must get to the shop early, especially on Friday morning.'

'The German bombers must be keeping you busy?' Moshe asked, giving his wife a glaring look at being interrupted as they walked slowly towards the exit behind a crowd of other congregants.

Isaac didn't answer for a second. 'So, so,' he replied.

'You at Biggin, I hear it took a pounding.'

Isaac turned his head to look at Moshe Goldstein, his eyes quickly roaming the man's face thinking: probably about thirty-five, blue eyes. 'Yes it did.' He looked towards Lily who was talking to Golda.

'Your squadron on leave?'

'I'm sorry, Moshe, another time, we have to meet family.' He stepped quickly to Lily. 'I'm sorry to interrupt, you can talk to Golda another time. We are late already.' He took Lily's elbow, steering her away from the couple.

'What's going on?' she asked.

'Please don't say anything. Just come with me.' He had just moved out into the street when they were joined by Wolfe, Asher, Billy and their wives.

'Sorry we were late. Had to sit on the other side of the synagogue,' Asher said.

Isaac moved over to Billy, giving him a hug and whispering in his ear, 'Man and woman over on my right, grey suit brown hat, she's wearing a dark grey coat, feather in her hat, see them?'

'What about them?'

'Have you seen them here before, or around?'

'No, but we have been pretty busy at the fire station. Why?'

'He asked me some awkward questions about my squadron, and Biggin Hill, although he said it as Biggin.'

'You think he might be a spy, pretending to be one of us.'

Isaac pulled away. 'It has been known, and he has blue eyes.'

'If you're sure, go to the police.'

'What are you two hatching up?' Wolfe asked.

'Uncle Billy would tell you.'

Billy quickly told Wolfe about Isaac's suspicions. 'Go to the police.'

'I don't know where they live.'

'Follow them,' Asher suggested.

Isaac nodded and turned to Lily. 'Go with Mama and the others, I won't be long.'

As luck had it, the Goldsteins lived in a street opposite Sally's shop in Myrdle Street. They watched the pair enter a house, the four men pretended to be talking as they walked by in case the Goldsteins looked their way. Just then two couples came from the opposite direction and entered the house.

'I don't like it,' Billy said.

'It does look suspicious, 'Isaac implied.

'Could be a German spy ring pretending to be Jewish,' Asher pointed out.

'We thought of that already,' Billy said.

'I'm for us doing something about it,' Wolfe said.

'They could be guiding the bombers to strategic targets,' Isaac commented, 'and he did say Biggin, we would add Hill, and he has blue eyes. Papa, did he tell you where they're from?'

'He said Hamburg.'

'Anyone got any suggestions?' Billy asked.

'Let's go to my place and make a decision, do it ourselves, or go to the police,' Wolfe suggested.

The four men sat around the table throwing ideas at each other as to what they should do about the Goldsteins and their so-called accomplices. Asher looked at Billy. 'What about your policeman friend, O'Brian – is he still around?'

'Last I heard he was at Scotland Yard.'

'In the past we had always—' The door opened, interrupting Wolfe, and Saul walked in.

'Not interrupting something big, am I?'

'We think there are some people at the synagogue posing as Jews, and we were wondering what to do about it,' Isaac told his brother.

'Have you come up with any ideas yet?' Saul asked.

'The first idea was get in touch with our old friend, O'Brian,' Billy told him.

'We had always done better ourselves – you know, come up with a plan, and if need be tell O'Brian when we were ready,' Wolfe said.

Leaning forward in his seat, placing his elbows on the table, Saul looked at his brother. 'What made you think he wasn't who he was?'

'He started asking questions about my squadron and my leave, but he mentioned Biggin.' He pointed a finger at Saul. 'How would you say Biggin?'

'Biggin Hill.'

'See,' Isaac stood in agitation. 'Any English person would say Biggin Hill.' He looked at Wolfe. 'Papa had always told us go with your gut feeling, that's it, a gut feeling.'

'That's good enough for me,' Saul said, adding, 'Papa I think we should do something about it ourselves.' His face hardened. 'I'm at Biggin Hill, I know I shouldn't tell you that, but what those Germans did, not only bombing us, but low-level strafing attack, killing many of my friends.'

'Do we know anyone from Hamburg?' Isaac asked, adding, 'About the same age as the Goldsteins.'

'Myer, the croupier.' Wolfe frowned. 'Why?'

'They would be going to the synagogue for morning services. We would introduce them to Myer, who would talk to them about the people he knew in Hamburg. Let's see who they know?'

'If they are spies acting as Jews, wouldn't they have done their homework in case they were questioned?' Asher pointed out.

'I don't think so,' Wolfe said. 'The Germans believe we wouldn't think it could happen. Tomorrow morning we, Asher and I, will stand either side of Goldstein to see how much Hebrew he reads.'

'And before we go in, we'll introduce Myer to them,' Isaac said, adding, 'but he won't ask anything about who they know until the service was over.'

They all agreed on the plan. Wolfe and Billy would get in touch with O'Brian immediately.

As Wolfe and Asher left for Whitehall, Saul pulled Isaac to one side. 'I'd like to talk to you about something.'

'Okay, let's go into the kitchen and have a cuppa.'

The brothers sat opposite each other, mugs of tea between their hands. 'Okay, what's bothering you?'

'I'm a mechanic on Spits and Hurries at Biggin Hill.' He took a sip of tea, pulled out a pack of Players and offered a cigarette to Isaac, who took one, holding the lit match to his brother's cigarette and then his own. Letting the smoke trickle through his nostrils, Saul said, 'I was fed up with being shot at and not able to retaliate – you know me, that's not me. I put in a request for flying training school. Could you please advise me if it's the right thing to do?'

Isaac looked at his brother for a second then leaned forward in the chair. 'If that's what you want, go for it, but … do you want to be a fighter pilot, or just a pilot?'

'What do you mean, just a pilot?'

'Firstly, you may not make the grade as a fighter pilot. That means you would be transferred to bombers, or you may not make the grade as a pilot and your navigation is shit hot, that's where you'll go. You are a trained mechanic, you could be part of the crew as an engineer, or you might get washed up all together, that would piss you off, and knowing you, air gunner would be your last port of call.'

'Shit, I never thought of it like that.'

'Don't get me wrong, flying is fantastic, but I would be lying if I didn't say it's frightening.' He pointed a thumb at the ceiling. 'Up there people want to kill you as much as you want to do it to them, and to tell you the truth, as much as we need pilots, we need good mechanics too.' He pointed a finger at Saul. 'It's men like you that ensure we have the weapon to fight the Luftwaffe.'

Saul sat staring at his brother and sighed. 'Lots to think about, thanks.'

*

Billy and Wolfe entered Scotland Yard. Once their credentials were checked they were shown along a hallway to an office with a sign on the door, CHIEF INSPECTOR J. O'BRIAN.

Their guide knocked on the door, opening it on hearing 'Enter', standing to one side to allow Billy and Wolfe to move into the room, closing the door behind them.

O'Brian stood moving from behind a desk piled with papers, holding out his hand as he approached the two men, saying as they shook hands, 'What trouble you in now?' He gestured to two chairs. 'Please sit down.' He walked back to the chair behind the desk, dropping on to it and folding his arms.

'We're sorry to bother you this late, but we think there are a group of spies posing as Jews at our synagogue.'

'Think or know?' O'Brian said in his soft Irish brogue, looking from one to the other.

'Let's say ninety per cent sure,' Wolfe said, leaning slightly forward.

'And you want me to—'

'Nothing at the moment,' Billy interrupted, 'but we need to run our plan through you to—'

'Why not go to MI5?' O'Brian interrupted.

'We don't know anyone at MI5,' Billy pointed out.

O'Brian smiled. 'I do.' He stood. 'Drink?'

'Tea please,' they said in unison.

O'Brian picked up a phone. 'Three teas please and some biscuits.'

There was silence between them for a few minutes. There was a knock at the door. 'Come in,' O'Brian said.

The door opened and a young woman carrying a tray with three cups and a pot of tea, plus a plate of biscuits entered placing the tray on O'Brian's desk. They watched as she poured the tea handing each a sugar bowl to take the amount they wanted. When she had finished she left the room.

O'Brian dunked the biscuit in the tea. 'So what's the plan.'

*

They stood outside the synagogue talking amongst themselves waiting for the Goldsteins to arrive. Wolfe was speaking to Myer, and Eva stood on the other side of him talking to Lily and Myer's wife.

'You know what to do?' Wolfe said to Myer. 'Just ask innocent questions, truth with fiction. We would be by your side the entire time. If they are not who they say they are, you smile, and touch your right ear.'

Myer was about to say something, but Wolfe continued. 'I know it's stupid but,' he smiled, 'they are here.'

Wolfe moved forward. 'Good *Shabbat*,' he said to Moshe and Golda.

'*Shabbat shalom*,' the Goldsteins said in unison.

'May I introduce my wife, Eva. You know my daughter-in-law Lily, and this is an old friend of the family, Joshua Myer.'

They all greeted each other with 'good *Shabbat*' and together entered the synagogue. As arranged, Goldstein sat between Asher and Wolfe, who watched and listened to him throughout the service.

As they were walking down the aisle to leave, Wolfe said, 'By the way, Moshe, Myer comes from Hamburg.'

'Really,' Goldstein quickened his step. 'I have—'

'It's been a while since I had spoken to someone from home,' Myer said, moving in front of Goldstein. 'Have you ever been to the jeweller Guttmann? What a *gonif*,[9] the *chutzpah*[10] of the man. He's worse than Cazlebach.'

Moshe tried to move past Myer, but he touched his arm, stopping him

---

[9] thief.

[10] brazen cheek.

from going any further. 'I used to buy my bread at—'

'I'd love to reminisce, but—' he interrupted Myer, who clicked his fingers and touched his ear asking, 'Did you go to the Bachmann Talmud Torah?'

Goldstein turned to meet his wife. Wolfe and Billy stood either side of Moshe, placing a hand on his elbow.

'Please join us for lunch,' Wolfe said quietly as Eva, Sarah, Lily, Esther and Myer's wife moved close to Golda.

'Yes, please come to our house,' Eva joined in. 'It would be nice for Myer and his wife to talk to you, and for us to get to know you. There's enough food for everyone.'

'But we have…' stammered Moshe.

'We have friends coming,' Golda's voice quivered.

While the family guided the Goldsteins to their home, the police led by O'Brian and members of MI5 entered the Goldsteins' house.

Wolfe and Billy were deaf to the excuses and loud protest by Moshe Goldstein as they took him down to the cellar. He struggled to get free as they tied to him to a chair.

Upstairs the women surrounded Golda, tying her to a chair as well, protesting loudly at her treatment in broken Yiddish and accented English.

In the cellar, Myer faced Moshe. 'If you were any Jew from Hamburg you would know the name Cazlebach very well. He is a prominent rabbi.' He slapped Moshe very hard. 'There is no such place as Bachmann Talmud Torah. You should have protested immediately.' He slapped him again. 'And you should have agreed with me about the jeweller.'

Billy pushed Myer gently aside. 'So, who are you?'

The man on the chair stayed silent for a second. 'I told you, my name is Moshe Goldstein.'

Billy smiled. 'We know you are not a Jew.' He pointed at Goldstein's crutch. 'I wonder if that would tell us the truth.' He stepped back. 'Take his trousers down.'

Isaac and Saul moved quickly forward. The man in the chair held his knees tightly together, but a backhander from Isaac soon put a stop to that, and his trousers were pulled down to his ankles. His pants were next, revealing no circumcision.

'If you want to impersonate a Jew,' Wolfe touched the foreskin with a scissors, 'you must be one in every way.' The prisoner tried to move away, eyes wide, shaking with fear.

'Unfortunately for you,' Billy punched the man very hard, splitting his lip, 'you don't know us, but to—' he punched him again '—avoid any unnecessary pain, you should answer all our questions.'

The prisoner spat at Billy, '*Juden*, piece of shit, scum of—' he got no further as Billy punched him so hard the chair toppled sideways. Isaac and Saul kicked him a couple of times before picking him up.

'Apart from the woman upstairs and the four at your house, is there another group impersonating Jews in London?' Wolfe asked.

Mayer spoke to him in German. 'I think you had better answer as in a very short while you are going to be in a lot of pain.' He shrugged his shoulders. 'You could tell them what they want to know, and they would make sure you're handed over to the proper authorities.'

The man was silent, his eyes showing their hatred of them. As quick as a flash, Wolfe grabbed his penis and cut the foreskin.

Billy clamped his hand over the German's mouth, stifling the scream and whispering in his ear, 'Tell us what we want to know, now you've had your circumcision or—' He left the rest unsaid. They all knew that beating the man would not get the answers they needed, but there were other ways, which Billy had done many years ago.

He let go the German. 'Gag him,' he said, walking over to the corner of the cellar, picking up a toolbox, placing it on a bench and opening it. The prisoner turned his head, which was suddenly jerked backward as Asher placed a gag in his mouth. The German began to struggle, trying to topple the chair, making noises behind the gag as he saw Billy turn towards him with a hammer in one hand and some nails in the other.

Isaac and Saul held the chair as Billy stood in front of the prisoner, whose eyes showed his fear. 'Nod if you want to tell us something,' Billy said, smoothing out the right testicle sack against the chair, placing the point of the nail against it and brought the hammer down, moving quickly to one side as the man wet himself. He was breathing heavily through his nose and trying to scream through the gag.

'Did he nod?' Billy looked around at the shaking heads. He gave a grim smile as he smoothed out the other testicle. 'If you don't answer any questions after this it will be your dick, which may I say is in a bit of a state already. As we said, you don't really know us, but you can see we have done this before.'

The prisoner tried to pull his testicle away, but the other was nailed to the chair. Billy brought the hammer down. The prisoner's face went red, trying to open his mouth and yell; sweat poured from his forehead and mucus from his nose. The blue eyes that were defiant a few moments ago now had tears streaming from them.

'So what's it going to be?' Wolfe asked. 'Tell us what we want to know and the pain will stop.' He smiled, but not with the eyes, which were hard. 'The pain we are about to inflict on you will—' He turned to

Billy, holding out his hand. 'May I, as it's my hammer?'

Billy nodded, handing him the hammer and another nail. Wolfe turned back to the prisoner. 'We,' he gestured round the cellar, 'have heard what you Nazis had been doing to the Jews of Germany and other countries, so we are wanting—' he waved the hammer '—to in some way avenge our brethren, so to speak.' He bent forward. 'And here you are.'

He slammed the hammer down on the prisoner's hand, which was resting on the arm of the chair, and while he was making noises behind the gag Wolfe placed the point of the nail against his penis. The prisoner nodded vigorously. Wolfe moved away as the door opened to the cellar and O'Brian walked in with another man.

'You're just in time,' Billy said, taking the gag from the prisoner's mouth.

Wolfe gently placed a hand over the German's broken one. 'What were you about to tell us?'

For over an hour, as O'Brian and the other man took notes, the prisoner gave them the information they wanted. The man with O'Brian looked around the cellar. 'Thank you, you have saved a lot of lives.'

Within minutes soldiers came to take the German spies away.

'What will you do with them?' Wolfe asked as they climbed the stairs to the hall.

'Hang them,' was the terse reply.

Wolfe's eyes opened on seeing the woman known as Golda walking by with two policemen on either side of her. She was completely bald. Eva moved beside him, holding a pair of scissors.

He looked at her, 'Did she say anything?'

She smiled, nodding her head. 'Oh yes.'

The next day, Billy and the brothers were back at the fire station as if nothing had happened.

11

A haze drifted like cigarette smoke across the airfield, as fitters and riggers sat relaxed, waiting by their aircraft for the yell of 'Scramble.'

There was a faint sound of music coming from a dispersal hut some fifty yards away. Inside there was an air of tension as pilots waited to be called into action. Smoke spiralled lazily towards the ceiling from cigarettes held between fingers, or hung loosely from the corner of a pilot's mouth. Some played chess, draughts or cards, while others read well-worn magazines.

Isaac sat with the back of his chair tilted on its rear legs against the wall, eyes closed, thinking of Lily. He let the chair fall forward onto its front legs, taking a cigarette case from the top pocket of his uniform, extracting a cigarette and flamed it alight, exhaling smoke rings towards the ceiling. He glanced over to the table by the window where a corporal sat by a telephone, willing it to ring and unconsciously tapping his fingers on his knee to the rhythm of the music coming from the radio. He blew another smoke ring across the room and the telephone rang.

Like a game of statues, everyone stopped what they were doing, eyes on the corporal, who yelled, 'Scramble.'

Before he had replaced the receiver Isaac was on his feet and striding towards the door. Other pilots followed him; some in their eagerness and haste tried to get through the door at the same time. Isaac ran towards his Spitfire, putting on his Mae West. His fitter, Fred, pressed the starter button on the battery cart connected to the twelve-cylinder Rolls Royce Merlin engine.

Isaac grabbed his parachute from the wing, expertly put it on and climbed into the cockpit. Tom the rigger helped strap him in and then jumped down. Isaac checked the oxygen through his mask and pressed the start button. There was a slight whine, a yellow flame and a puff of white smoke from the exhausts. He pushed the throttle slightly forward foot on the brake. The three-bladed propeller began to turn, spinning faster and faster until it was a smooth blur.

He held up a thumb to the fitter, Fred pulled away the chocks and gave a mock salute. Isaac eased the throttle forward and the Spitfire emitted a roar of power. He returned the mock salute with a smile, taking his foot off the brake. The fighter leapt forward, rumbling faster and faster across the grass. He could see Cole and Jones slightly in front and to his right as he eased back on the stick, the fighter with its three foot roundel and XTG on the fuselage lifted off the ground. The Squadron moved into formation as Squadron Leader Spalding said over his radio, 'Hello Top Hat control, Castle leader here. Squadron airborne.'

'Top Hat control to Castle leader. I have trade at Vector 120, hundred plus Bandits Angels one nine.'

'Roger Top Hat, on our way.'

At twenty-two thousand feet the squadron reached the vector on the Kent coast and someone yelled, 'Tally-Ho at eleven o'clock.'

Isaac looked in that direction, at the same time lowering his seat, adjusting the reflector sights and taking a deep breath.

'Be alert for fighters,' Spalding said as he led the squadron in a diving attack on the German bombers.

Isaac had eyes on a Dornier. At three hundred yards it began to fill his sights. He pressed the gun button, seeing bits fly off the tail, which suddenly broke away from the main body, and the rest of the bomber went into an immediate dive.

He looked around: planes were going down in flames, black smoke pouring from damaged engines and parachutes were opening. The sky was full of planes and falling bodies. He pointed the nose of his Spitfire skyward levelling out at eighteen thousand feet and spotted a Heinkel, white smoke billowing out from its port engine.

Isaac's face behind the mask was contorted in rage as the bomber dropped its bombs, not caring where they landed as it turned back for home. Swearing, Isaac pushed the throttle forward, diving in a frontal attack and wanting to kill the pilot.

Even though he was angry, he waited until he was close enough to fire; pressing the button in a two-second burst and seeing with satisfaction the German's Perspex glass disintegrate, and then he was past, coming quickly around to see the Heinkel diving into the sea, but he didn't dwell on it. Instinct made him pull the stick to the right, the wing came up and tracer bullets passed by, as did the Messerschmitt 109.

He tried to calm his fast-beating heart as the German turned for another go at him. Quick as a flash, he dived down into an inverted outside half-loop, pulling out close to the ground, glancing quickly into the mirror and yelled, 'Thank you, Morgan, for teaching me that.' He pulled back the stick, pushing the throttle forward, gaining height and streaking towards the bombers, eyes roaming the skies for fighters.

He came up underneath a Dornier and pressed the trigger button but after a second the guns were silent. He dropped away and then felt the Spitfire shudder. His head span around to see the ME109 on his tail, with lights twinkling from its guns, and then it was past him. His fighter was badly hit, the fabric on the port wing full of holes, the controls sluggish. He dragged the damaged fighter around, the ME following.

This is it, he thought, when suddenly the ME pulled away as a Hurricane attacked it. 'Thank you, thank you!' he yelled to the Hurricane pilot. In one quick movement he undid his straps and the mike lead, sliding back the canopy. Cold air tugged at his clothes as he pulled back the stick. The nose pointing slowly upwards, he stood on the seat, dropping out of the stricken fighter as it stalled, diving sideways towards the ground.

He had heard of some German fighter pilots killing British pilots as they hung helpless in their parachutes. He was falling fast, waiting for the last possible moment before pulling the ripcord. He was suddenly jerked upward as the parachute opened and air filled the canopy. He dropped his head onto his chest, feigning dead, and smiled slightly, recognising that he was just beyond the sea at Portsmouth.

Luckily there was a slight breeze blowing him inland. He looked down, the ground coming towards him at what seemed an alarming rate, and pulled down on the straps, placing his feet together, and hit the ground, rolling over to his right. He banged the quick release with the palm of his hand and got to his feet, wrapping up the parachute in his arms as people ran across the park. He smiled as an elderly gentleman with a cricket bat in his hand yelling, 'Put your hands up.'

Isaac smiled. 'What do you think you would do with that—' he pointed a finger at the bat '—against an armed German pilot? Stick it up his bum?'

By now there was a crowd of people around Isaac. 'Oh, you're British,' a young woman said, moving close to Isaac and rubbing the parachute between thumb and forefinger. 'Nice piece of silk. Give you two bob for it.'

Isaac laughed. 'Sorry, no sale. This piece of silk just saved my life.' There was a beeping of a car horn as a camouflaged army car skidded to a standstill and a lieutenant got out of the car. For a second they just stared at each other, and then Isaac said with surprise, 'Abraham.'

Abraham smiled. 'Isaac.' The two men converged and hugged.

Abraham stepped back. 'You okay?'

'I'm fine, got caught napping by a 109, had to get out pretty quick otherwise I'd be … let's not talk about that. What are you doing in this neck of the woods?'

'My battalion was sent here as protection against any invasion by the Germans. Come on, I'll give you a lift back to my barracks.'

Once at the barracks, Abraham's commanding officer phoned Hornchurch.

Abraham was called to the CO's office. 'Your cousin's CO has asked if Brown was uninjured to bring him back to Hornchurch. Do you fancy the trip?'

Abraham smiled. 'Yes, sir.'

'Okay, drive him to Hornchurch, stay in London one night. I'm sure you would like to see your wife. Here's a chit for forty-eight hours' leave. Take Warrant Officer Newark with you.'

'Thank you, sir.'

'Don't lose my car.'

Isaac smiled. 'Thank you very much, sir.'

'By the way, your request and Newark's to transfer for a combat posting has been denied.' He held up a hand. 'Not from me. If you're both in a hurry to get killed, who am I to stand in your way? I'm sure they would need a replacement lieutenant and warrant officer with combat experience very soon. Okay, off you go.'

Abraham left the office at the run. He explained very quickly to Gus, who said, 'What are we waiting for?'

Isaac was a little peeved at Abraham and his staff sergeant spending the night in London, but by the time he arrived at Hornchurch he realised he could on his day off go home as he wasn't far from East London. Before the two cousins parted, Isaac said, 'Do not say anything to the family about me bailing out, just that you returned a pilot to say, Biggin Hill. Make up a name if you have to.'

'I promise I won't say a word,' Abraham said. Gus nodded his agreement.

Isaac watched them drive away. 'About bloody time you got back,' Cole said.

Isaac smiled. 'I knew you would miss me.'

'You are now a bona fide member of the Caterpillar Club. I've already sent your details through to the club secretary.'

Isaac smiled. 'Thanks.'

Monday, 23 December 1940

There was the usual smell of smoke and burning wood in the early morning air, but also an atmosphere of expectancy, as the population of London went about their business. Some looked skyward, hoping the weather would be too bad for flying and give them some respite from the constant bombing by the Luftwaffe. There was no thought of surrender, just a grim, spirited determination to outlast whatever the Nazis threw at them.

Wolfe and his fellow firefighters checked equipment and cleaned their engines. After so many days and weeks of continuous bombing, there were additions to the station's firefighting capacity. Fire pump escape engines were rigged with a two-wheeled portable ladder that enabled the firemen to fight fires in London's narrow streets. A nozzle of a hose could be attached to the top step to attack the fire from above. Hundreds of taxis had a hook-up device attached so they could tow a water tank, and carry five men and their equipment wherever they were needed in the city. Three were parked beside the fire engines. Every day the raids caused over seventy breaks in the six thousand miles of water pipes. It was imperative for vehicles to transport replacement water pipes to any part of London.

In the next street stood a flatbed truck carrying steel pipes; nine firemen could join a thousand foot of steel pipes in sixteen minutes. Next to it was a lorry carrying six thousand feet of rubberised canvas hosing, which could be laid as the truck moved slowly forward. Lorries equipped with a thousand gallon tanks of water were also available. Firefighters were learning to fight fires the hard way.

The Government and fire services knew the Germans would try and raid London when the River Thames was at low tide. The Government in their wisdom had forty pumps stationed along London's bridges, which could suck up three thousand tons of water a minute, even at low tide.

It was four o'clock in the afternoon when the shrill screech of the sirens echoed throughout the City. The first wave of bombers approached the British coast.

McNamara received the call to a fire in Valance Road, close to Bethnal Green Station and the viaduct across the road. Within seconds of the fire engines arriving, water was cascading into and on the buildings. A woman ran up to McNamara, tears streaming down her face. 'Three people are trapped on the third floor,' she told him.

McNamara sent Wolfe, Asher and Billy into the building which had twenty flats. He ordered two turntable ladders with hoses attached to attack the blaze from above, especially the roof of the properties adjacent to it.

As they climbed the stairs with their Proton breathing equipment, yelling through the mask, 'Anyone in there,' ever vigilant for the hidden dangers, Wolfe's eyes stared intently through the goggles at the corners and bottom of doors to see if there were puffs of smoke that changed colour from black to grey or yellow, like a breathing effect. This would tell him that behind the door the room was starved of oxygen, which, if ventilated in any way by opening a door or window, would form a chain reaction resulting in an ignition with the force of an exploding bomb, a firemen's nightmare.

They reached the third-floor hallway, the window at the end rattling from the force of the fires draft. 'We better get out of here pretty quickly!' Billy yelled above the crackling wood and roaring flames, pointing at the flame licking the ceiling.

Inside one of the flats they found two small boys and a woman.

'Is there anyone else in the building?' Asher asked the woman through his face mask, covering her with his jacket.

'No, just us.'

Wolfe picked up one young boy, covering him in his jacket; Billy picked up the other youngster, with Asher bringing up the rear with the woman. As they raced along the hallway and headed down the stairs, Wolfe wondered why the woman hadn't taken her children to the country, but then that thought left him as he heard an almighty crash: the hall window had caved in. Knowing what was happening behind them, the three firemen raced down the stairs as a wall of flame charged along the hallway following them. They exited the building, running towards the line of firemen, who were playing their hoses on the building as the second and third floors were engulfed in a fireball.

Wolfe was about to join the others in dousing down the adjoining flats and houses when something made him look to the right; a frown creased his forehead on seeing two men, one in an ARP helmet loading a cart outside a block of apartments. He squinted through the smoke and took a few steps towards them to check whether it was the same man from a few nights ago. The ARP man looked in his direction and said something to his companion, who glanced in Wolfe's direction, and quickly assisted the ARP man in pushing the cart. Wolfe turned back to help the others, making a mental note to speak to Asher and Billy about it, but in the future he would keep an eye out for the ARP man.

Spider was in no doubt that the fireman from a few nights ago had seen him and recognised him. Spider and Bob Burns cut through some back streets, ending up on the Hanbury Street corner of Brick Lane. Spider came to a halt on seeing the jewellers shop. He moved away from the cart, whispering, 'Follow me, Bob,' looking around as he crept slowly towards the front door.

The street was empty. Spider grasped the handle of the front door and turned it, finding no resistance, and opened the door a couple of inches, running his hand along the edge and top of it, his fingers coming into contact with a bell. Taking a handkerchief from Bob's top pocket, he placed it in the bowl of the bell and stopped the clacker from sounding. He and Bob quietly entered, moving behind the counter, opening cupboards and drawers. All they found were a couple of watches and half a dozen bracelets. Spider found the safe, but then the all-clear sounded and the pair quickly left the shop, making sure they closed the door. They had left the few bit and pieces they had found because Spider said, 'We'll come back another day, and try to open the safe.'

Gradually Wolfe and the other firefighters got on top of the fires, making a strong effort after each raid to ensure the fires were out so they couldn't be used to guide a new wave of bombers to their target. Other services cleaned up debris and restored normal services as best they could to help bolster the morale of the civilian population.

*

The air in the shelter was stale, mingling with the smell of unwashed bodies. Sally placed a scarf around her mouth and nose, breathing in the fragrance of her perfume as she moved slowly up the stairs as the throng of people in front and behind moved as quickly as they possibly could to leave the shelter.

She was angry with herself, having spent more time than she anticipated with Mr Bloomingfeldt, the draper. She hadn't been there for some time and was shocked at the small amount of stock he had.

'I'm so sorry, Mrs Hyams, but there is a war on; and the shipment I was expecting from America is now at the bottom of the ocean.' He spread his hands, looking around his store and tut-tutting. 'The mills here are busy turning out uniforms for the armed forces.' He touched her arm. 'Take your pick. It might be some time before we receive more stock, or get bombed.'

She left the drapery, having chosen some materials which the draper would deliver the following day.

On her way home the bus driver had stopped by a shelter as sirens screeched their warning. The bus was empty in seconds as the passengers joined the line of people waiting to enter the shelter. Sally was angry as she moved down the stairs. She should have been home and in her own shelter. Some babies cried, children played, running between the people, arms outstretched, pretending to be aeroplanes. Someone began to sing, trying to drown out the sounds above them.

Now she couldn't wait to get out of the shelter, at last reaching the exit and thankful to be out, but then different senses and smells engulfed her. She moved quickly in and out of the slowly moving crowd of people, some standing on the kerbside staring at piles of rubble where there once stood a row of houses. She eventually approached her shop. Taking the front-door key from her handbag, she was about to insert it into the lock when an army sergeant ran towards her shouting. She turned to look at him, and was about to take no notice when he breathlessly arrived by her side. 'I'm sorry, Miss, but you cannot go in there.'

'Why not, this is my shop.'

'We think there's an unexploded bomb in there.'

'What makes you think that?'

He took her arm. 'Please come with me.' He led her across the road and pointed to the roof where there was a gaping hole. 'That's why, there's no fire and—'

'I must get in there.' She stepped off the kerb to cross the road. 'All my designs are in there.'

Sally was suddenly thrown onto the ground, a wind passed over her, carrying bits of stone, glass, cloth and other debris that swirled dangerously through the air, and then came the deafening explosion, followed by an eerie silence. Sally heard muffled voices and tried to get to her feet, not yet realising what had happened. Someone was helping her to stand and speaking to her, but the voice seemed far away. She felt faint and dizzy; she shook her head and gradually opened her eyes to see an ARP man, concern on his face and voice far off, asking, 'Are you okay, Miss?'

Sally looked towards her shop. 'No, oh, no.' The front windows had completely disappeared, bits of dummy and ragged clothing littered the pavement and road as gradually her hearing returned. She shook herself from the ARP warden's hand and staggered across the road.

He ran beside her. 'Where are you going? The building could collapse any moment.'

'I have to see if there is anything I could salvage.'

'Please, miss, don't go in there.' He stood outside as Sally entered the shop. It was a mess. She couldn't go upstairs as half the stairs were missing. Her eyes moved across the room, coming to rest on a small chest of drawers that was originally upstairs in the workroom. She walked across the rubble-filled room to the chest of drawers and pulled open the middle drawer. Her dusty face smiled as she pulled out her notebook with her designs.

'Please, miss, come out now,' an army sergeant stood by the door. 'This building could collapse any moment.'

Sally nodded, stepping gingerly across the room till she stood beside the sergeant. 'It's a miracle,' she whispered, taking his hand and walked from the shop.

Suddenly there was a noise like someone groaning. 'Run,' said the sergeant.

Side by side, they ran across the road as the rest of the roof and top floor collapsed in a cloud of dust, leaving a gaping hole between the shops either side of hers untouched.

'Phew, that was lucky. Another minute...' The sergeant left the rest unsaid.

As she took a taxi home, Sally whispered, 'Just one foot either side my shop...' She shrugged her shoulders, and began to cry. If she had not been late she would have... She shook her head: it didn't bear thinking about.

After a bath and cup of tea she felt more like her old self. Sad but philosophical about the shop, she walked the short distance from her home in Buxton Street to the shop of her parents-in-law in Commercial Street. Her mother-in-law was in the shop when she arrived, but Phillip and his father were at the factory. Half the factory was on war work, making frames for aeroplanes; the other half making furniture from plywood as furniture timber was hard to come by.

'What are you going to do now?' Sally's mother-in-law asked.

'I could work from home, but it's not the same.'

'Is there anything left that you could rebuild?'

Sally gave a wry smile. 'The roof and first floor collapsed, it's just a pile of rubble.' She got to her feet. 'But, miracle of miracles, the book with my designs was untouched. I'm going to the factory; perhaps I could do something there.'

Shock showed on Phillip's face as Sally told him about the shop. 'What made you want to go in there, you could have been killed?'

'You know, when I think about it I didn't believe there could be an unexploded bomb in my shop.' She shrugged her shoulders. 'So I walked towards it, two minutes more and I would have been in there, or if I wouldn't have been late from the drapers, I might be dead.'

She dropped onto a chair, her face changing from surprise to wonder to disbelief, her hands went to her chest. 'Two...' She began to cry as the ordeal of the morning caught up with her. Phillip wrapped his arms around her, cuddling her to him, gradually lifting her to her feet. 'Come on, I'll take you home.'

*

Spider smiled, looking up at the searchlights moving across the night sky as they left the house. It was time to get down to business, and business was Kinsky, the jewellers on Brick Lane. He and the boys needed money to spend on Christmas and New Year, especially on Spider's mother.

They parked the van in Buxton Street; because the roads were blocked by fire engines, their hoses spreading from Commercial Street, Fournier Street into Brick Lane.

With his white warden hat and armband, Spider walked leisurely along streets he had known since childhood. Bob Burns walked beside him, George and John a few paces behind, their faces lit by the fires and ack-ack shells exploding above them. They arrived at the corner of Chicksand Street, George, John and Bob walked a few yards up Brick Lane, making sure there were no people around, and moved back to Spider, standing by the door to the jewellers.

'All clear,' they reported.

'There's a fire further along. The firemen are too busy to notice us,' Bob said.

Spider nodded and tried the door. It was locked. Spider took a jemmy from the inside pocket of his overcoat, placing it in the door jamb, waited a second until there was a loud bang of a bomb exploding, and prised open the door, at the same time reaching for the bell above the door, stopping it from ringing. He looked around before entering the jewellers, placing a piece of cloth over the bell's clacker.

'John – the safe,' Spider ordered in a whisper. 'Look around,' he added to Bob and George.

He knelt beside John, 'Do you need anything?'

'No, I'm fine, but this is going to be a bugger to open. It's American.'

Further along Brick Lane, at the corner of Fournier Street, standing on a turntable ladder, Wolfe was pouring gallons of water from his hose onto the raging inferno below him. From time to time the water dampened the roof of the Great Synagogue nearby and Wolfe hoped the fire would soon be under control as there were irreplaceable holy scrolls and relics within the building. He glanced to his left along Brick Lane to see four men by Kinsky's, the jewellers shop. He stared through the smoke, seeing one of them holding a white helmet, and knew immediately who it was, and what they were about to do.

He climbed quickly down the ladder, running over to McNamara. 'Chief, I need you to relieve Asher, Billy and myself.'

'Whatever—' he stopped in mid-sentence seeing Wolfe's face, knowing he wouldn't ask unless it was urgent. 'Okay,' he nodded, 'get back here as soon as you can.'

Wolfe ran up to Asher and Billy. 'Come on, those four are at it again.'

'Where are they?' Billy asked.

'Kinsky, the jewellers,' was the quick reply.

The three men ran up Brick Lane, slowing down by the jewellers. Wolfe peered through the window, seeing John kneeling by the safe with Spider behind him. Wolfe moved back to the other two. The guy with the white helmet was standing behind a man trying to open the safe. 'I'm assuming the other two are upstairs.'

'What do you want us to do?' Asher asked.

'They'll not be expecting us; as soon as we enter the shop you two run upstairs and grab the men up there.'

Wolfe moved to the front door which was ajar, pushed it open and walked into the shop. The two men by the safe hadn't heard him because of the noise outside. Asher and Billy ran up the stairs as Wolfe said, 'Good evening.'

Spider whipped round, a surprised look on his face. John tried to turn and overbalanced. 'You are one nosey fireman,' Spider said harshly.

'Need to recuperate your losses?' Wolfe asked.

'What do you know about my losses?' Spider looked quickly round as George and Bob, their hands tied behind their back, stumbled down the stairs with Asher and Billy holding onto their collars. They pushed the two men roughly against the wall.

'Sit,' said Billy, hooking his foot round the back of George's leg and sweeping him off his feet.

'You too,' Asher said, placing a hand on Bob's shoulder, pushing him down.

'I think we should take this lot to the police,' Asher said, taking a step forward and dropping the metal end of his axe onto John's wrist. John screamed dropping the pistol from his hand, his wrist broken. Asher scooped up the weapon. 'You're lucky I was going to chop your hand off, but I don't like the sight of blood.'

Spider suddenly leapt at Wolfe, a knife in his hand. Wolfe sidestepped to the left, knocking the arm away. Billy took a step forward. 'No Billy, he's mine.'

'I'm not that easy to beat, fireman,' sneered Spider.

Wolfe dodged and with another thrust grabbed the wrist, bending it backward and making Spider drop the knife. 'You were saying?'

Spider went into a boxer's crouch, the sneer still on his face as he moved in, his punch finding air. 'What I want to know, is—' Wolfe's right hand buried itself in Spider's solar plexus '—why do you steal from your fellow Londoner, especially—' he blocked a punch, landing one on the side of Spider's head that rocked him back onto his heels '—with all the heartache and death—' he stepped in, landing another punch to Spider's stomach '—you steal. To me, it's as low as a person could get.' Spider landed a punch to Wolfe's face, receiving two back in exchange, followed by a quick one-two to his right eye, which was beginning to swell.

'If I don't take it, someone else would,' Spider said, just before he was hit with a flurry of punches, lifting his hands to protect his face, but the punches still got through his guard.

'So, it must be you?' Wolfe said.

'Why not, haven't you—' Whatever he was going to say stopped as he received a left and right to the face. His right eye was puffed and he could hardly see out of it. He had already spat out two teeth. 'No I had never ever even thought about it.' With that, Wolfe stepped in, landing an uppercut to the jaw. For a second Spider stood there and then crumpled to the ground, out for the count.

Carrying the hapless Spider over his shoulder with the other three tied together, they moved back to fire tenders as the all-clear sounded. The fires along Brick Lane had now been extinguished. They handed Spider and his cronies over to the Leman Street police station.

12

Fire, Fire, London's Burning
Sunday, 29 December 1940

There was a lull in the bombing over Christmas, the sirens were silent, and the people of London breathed a sigh of relief, speculating on the resumption of hostilities. Some dared whisper that the Luftwaffe were on holiday until the New Year, but then at exactly six o'clock on the evening of Sunday, 29 December the sirens shattered the silence of the City of London as five hundred German bombers and their fighter escort covering some twenty miles of sky passed Margate, heading due west along the River Thames.

Once again Germany's war on London resumed, and London's civilian front line troops braced themselves for the night ahead.

Freda and Max had just arrived at Whitechapel Station when the sirens went off. They were about to leave the station but were pushed back by the amount of people descending the stairs. 'If I were you,' one old man said, 'I'd stay here till the all-clear. By the sound up there—' he pointed a thumb towards the ceiling '—there are hundreds of the buggers.'

'Let's stay here, it might not last long.' Freda took Max's left hand, the right holding their suitcase and they descended the stairs.

Abraham, April, Gus and his girlfriend Freda ran laughing across Leicester Square towards the underground station as the droning buzz of bombers came ever closer.

In the WVS centre, Eva, Sarah and Esther made sandwiches. 'I thought the Germans liked New Year,' Sarah said.

'They're making sure we don't,' Eva muttered.

'I hope Abraham and April are okay. They went to the cinema with his … oh, what's his name?' she snapped her fingers and smiled, 'Gus something or other and his girlfriend, Freda.'

Before the war the fire situation in London's Square Mile of the City was called The Danger Zone. Even in peacetime the narrow, congested, cobbled streets and alleys, filled with centuries-old houses and offices, livery halls, medieval buildings and churches, backed by warehouses filled with inflammable goods, made the possibility of a conflagration in this area an ever-present anxiety and fear for London's fire chiefs. Now their fears were a reality.

At Fire Services Headquarters reports were coming in of large amount of falling incendiaries, and it was soon apparent the Germans' intention was to set the City of London ablaze.

All local fire stations close to the City were soon empty of their first-line engines, but they weren't enough, and more fire tenders arrived, some as far away as Bristol.

Wolfe's face was a grim mask as he and his fellow firefighters fought the blaze, trying to stop it spreading, their ears filled with a stomach-churning cacophony of sounds, the hum of aircraft engines, whistling of the bombs as they fell towards the ground, ear-splitting detonations of high explosives that literally sucked the air from a person's body. The unmistakable plop of incendiaries that sizzled with a bluish white light that suddenly turned into flame. Finger beams of searchlights moved around the sky, searching for an enemy plane; pounding ack-ack, exploding glass and shrapnel flew through the air, compounding the dangers to the firemen, who ignored everything except for putting out the fires.

Sewers ruptured, adding to the smells. Water mains burst, cutting off water supplies, telephone poles on fire, their lines falling onto the pavement, buildings collapsing, entombing their occupants. The hospitals were stretched to the limit, tending the wounded who had been brought in by brave ambulance crews that heroically returned to the streets to pick up more wounded.

Wolfe looked to his left on hearing a groan, yelling a warning to two firemen, who were already running from the collapsing building. McNamara called for reinforcements as tens of thousands of incendiaries rained unrelentingly down onto the city.

It quickly dawned on the fire chiefs and firemen on the ground that this was the most determined and callous effort by the Germans to set London ablaze, with St Paul's Cathedral its main target. Luckily the City was empty of workers as banks, insurance companies, the Stock Exchange and law offices were closed.

In Whitechapel Underground Station a young girl began to cry. Her mother tried to placate her but to no avail. That started other children off as they looked up at the ceiling and heard the sounds above them, the fear showing on their young faces. Freda slid beside the young girl, saying quietly, 'What's your name?'

'Doris,' the young girl sniffed.

'How old are you, Doris?'

'Seven and a half.' She wiped the tears with the back of her hand. Her mother wiped her nose as Freda said, 'That's old enough to know lots of nursery rhymes.'

The little girl smiled, 'Do you know Bo Peep?'

Freda began the nursery rhyme, and a now-smiling Doris joined in. Gradually the other children moved towards Freda, making a semi-circle in front of her, singing the nursery rhymes at the top of their voices. Freda pointed to a young lad. 'You have a good voice,' she smiled at him. 'I bet you could sing.'

His face went white. 'I…' He stammered. Freda began to sing 'Roll Out the Barrel'. The boy began to sing with her and suddenly the station echoed to old familiar songs, drowning out the noises from above.

Leicester Square Underground was full of men and women in uniform. Some played cards, others chattered amongst themselves, until three girls from the Windmill Theatre decided to put on an impromptu show. Gus and Freda joined in the singing between kisses, and someone played the accordion. Some of the soldiers and their girls danced cheek to cheek. Abraham had his arms wrapped around April, who was leaning against him as they swayed to the music, oblivious to the sounds above them, as Wolfe, Asher, Billy and hundreds of firemen fought valiantly to douse the flames around them. Century-old wooden buildings in the narrow, cobbled streets went up like tinder boxes. Small fires joined up with others as the breeze fanned the flames, causing a firestorm from Islington to St Paul's. The city was now a sea of flames.

Paternoster Row, the centre of the publishing trade, was afire as irreplaceable old books and manuscripts added to the enormous bonfire.

Using a fire pump escape engine in the narrow street, Wolfe climbed the ladder with a hose attached to the top rung, playing water onto the roof of the next building, hoping to stop the fire spreading. His heart sank as the breeze grew stronger, carrying the dancing flames onto the next building. But there was no let up. The Germans had planned this raid to coincide with a low tide and it became increasingly difficult for the pumps to maintain pressure. And still the incendiaries fell.

The Prime Minister, Winston Churchill, came to the same conclusion as the fire chiefs and sent a message to Fire Service Headquarters to save St Paul's at all costs.

With the electric grid and telephone lines out, young men on motor and pedal bikes bravely ignored all that was happening around them, scrambling their bikes over the maze of snaking hoses that littered the streets, intent on delivering their messages.

The city was an inferno, from Aldgate to Cannon Street, Cheapside to Moorgate, including Pudding Lane where the Great Fire of London of 1666 had begun. London was surrounded by a ring of fire, the flames shooting hundreds of feet into the air, and in the midst of it stood the dome of St Paul's Cathedral.

One hundred thousand incendiaries had been dropped on London, the firefighters having to cope with temperatures in excess of 800 degrees centigrade.

Across the river, firemen worked feverishly to get emergency pumps into position on the Thames Canal. Lines of hoses were laid over mud flats to the fire area. Powerful hose laying lorries set out twin hoses towards the city and danger zone, while in the City fireman climbed on roofs and entered buildings to douse incendiaries before they burst into flame.

Asher's sweat-streaked blackened face showed despair as he turned to Wolfe and Billy. 'I feel that I am looking at the destruction of the City of London.'

'Come on, Asher, it's not like you to be like this. We won't let that fat, arrogant Goering defeat us.' Billy said.

Wolfe, Asher and Billy hugged each other as the pumps began to work, spewing out gallons of water. They moved through narrow passages and streets dousing out incendiaries while being showered with embers from burning rafters; flames rolled across streets, clouds of choking smoke filled the air, but the firemen fought on. Asher suddenly grabbed Wolfe, who was slightly ahead of him, as a wall swayed, making a cracking noise as the brickwork crumbled and tumbled to the ground, brick dust adding to the lung-searing heat. Wolfe looked at his brother and hugged him. 'Thanks.'

Gradually the firemen took back the buildings, stopping the fires short of St Paul's.

By nine o'clock the bombers had gone. Three hundred fire engines had been sent to the city. Gradually the firemen began to control the flames. Wolfe stopped for a moment to look towards St Paul's. 'Hey, you lot, have a look at that,' he yelled.

The firemen stopped for a minute to look in awe. The sky around St Paul's was a bright red and through it all could be seen the dome. Some incendiaries had landed inside St Paul's, but the firewatchers had doused all of them. One man had hung one-handed on a rafter while sweeping an incendiary into a bucket of sand. There were many heroic and some stupid moments. A rookie fireman put his helmet over an incendiary. It glowed red hot and then disintegrated the helmet.

As dawn streaked the sky, their seemed to be an air of change over London as people emerged from their shelters. No matter what their religion was, they looked towards the dome and smiled: Hitler had been defeated.

The raid had focused on the ancient city. The Germans had dropped over a hundred thousand incendiaries, and one thousand fires were started. Along with other firefighters, Wolfe, Asher and Billy, wet and soot-stained, faces black, had performed brave and daring feats; they had fought the fires and extinguished the flames.

The brothers and Billy stood in a line in Paternoster Row. 'My goodness,' Wolfe said, 'there are thousands of them.' He bent to pick up a sodden book.

The cost was high: sixteen firemen lost their lives, many more had been injured. Historical building and churches had disappeared, but the symbol of London and the country, St Paul's, stood tall amidst the second Great Fire of London.

Wolfe turned to Asher and Billy. 'This was the day that Germany lost the war.'

The all-clear sounded. Eva, Sarah and Esther helped homeless people with sandwiches and tea, giving them blankets to keep warm as most had lost their homes.

'We need to find these people some kind of shelter,' Sarah said.

'There's no—' Eva stopped in mid-sentence. 'Come on, and get into the van.'

'Where are we going?' Esther asked.

'The club.'

'What cl—' then a smile lit up Sarah's face. 'But is it still standing?' She clapped her hands on seeing the youth club they had helped run still standing. Eva took a key-ring from her pocket, placed a key in the lock and turned it. There was a slight click. Esther opened the door and walked in. 'Smells a bit musty but.... All we need is mattresses, pillows and blankets. We can get the kitchen started more or less right away.'

'We have to get the men involved; we can't do it on our own. If we could get hold of Hannah, she knows plenty of people.'

No sooner had Abraham and April arrived home than they were accosted by Sarah. Next door was the same story when Freda and Max surprised Eva. 'Oh I'm so glad to see you both, we need your help.'

Leaving their children to clean up the club, Sarah and Esther went to WVS HQ to obtain the food and as much bedding as they could.

Eva was on the way to Highbury to speak to Hannah, stopping at Sally's home. Leaving Sally to make her way to the club, Eva continued on to Highbury. Hannah was immediately businesslike as Eva explained what she wanted to do. With spare blankets and pillows, Hannah, two of the girls and Eva headed back to the club.

By late afternoon the club was ready. Rows of mattresses with pillows and blankets were lined along the top floor. Downstairs they had made a counter from doors and timbers rescued from the rubble. They were dog-tired, having had no sleep or respite for over twenty-four hours, but with the thought of helping people who had lost their homes and possessions, rest never entered their minds.

A few streets away, having helped all they could with the club, Wolfe and the other firefighters looked for survivors, moving piles of bricks and rubble.

'Quiet everyone,' Asher suddenly shouted, and there was instant silence. He knelt, placing his ear against the still-warm bricks, then raised an arm. 'Here, there's someone alive here.'

He began frantically throwing bricks back towards the road as the others ran over to help him. Thirty minutes later a smiling group of men pulled out a woman and two young boys, all unharmed. To Wolfe and the others it was a victory. Tired as they were, they continued with their unenviable task.

Hannah was helping Eva when she said, 'Why don't we decorate the place like Christmas? And for the Jewish children a menorah. New Year's Eve is only a day away – we could have a little party, perhaps get some toys for the children. What do you think?'

Eva smiled. 'It's a brilliant idea. I'll go to WVS Headquarters and see what they have.'

'I'll go back to the house with one of the girls and get some decorations.'

'How long are you staying for?' Eva asked her daughter Freda before heading for WVS HQ.

'We don't have to go back for a fortnight. Max and I asked for this break. It's been non-stop shows since Dunkirk.'

Eva smiled. 'I'm sorry, now I've roped you into this.'

'Mama, at the moment we are the lucky ones.' Just then the sirens went off, and everyone headed for the basement.

Hannah had been lucky she had just reached Ruby's when the sirens sounded. She rushed to the basement with some of girls who had stayed behind. While they were together she outlined the plan for the Christmas decorations for the club. The girls offered to help. The all-clear sounded. The girls packed away the decorations, at the same time looking for some suitable gifts for the children. They decided to ask the shopkeepers in Upper Street to help with donations for the children's Christmas and Chanukah party explaining about the club.

Hannah was overwhelmed by people's generosity to the extent that she had to hire two taxis to take her, the girls and presents back to Wapping.

*

'Top Hat, Castle Squadron airborne,' Squadron Leader Spalding spoke into his radio.

'Hello Castle leader Top Hat calling, Vector 19, Trade at Dover, 20 plus heading west Angels twenty.'

Isaac lowered his seat, realising for the first time there were no butterflies in his stomach. 'Tally-Ho ten o'clock,' Cole called out.

Isaac automatically looked in that direction for a second, and then his eyes slowly roamed the sky around them. There was a slight twinkle of light above them. He slit his eyes, and yelled, 'ME's coming down fast eleven o'clock.'

He pulled back the stick not wanting to be at too much of a disadvantage, as Spalding ordered, 'Blue and Red section take on the fighters. The rest go for the bombers.'

Isaac saw the ME hurtling down towards him. He had already decided not to dive away but kept heading upward towards the Messerschmitt, wondering who would crack first. There was a twinkle of light from the Germans guns, but he was too far away to hit Isaac, who smiled, not looking through his sights saying, 'Wait, wait, now...'

He fired a ten second burst and then pushed the stick forward, diving under the belly of the fighter. He came around into a screaming turn, hoping not to black out, and saw the fighter heading towards the ground. The canopy opened and the pilot bailed out.

Some miles ahead, the bombers that had got through were dropping their bombs. Isaac headed in that direction, gaining height. As he closed in on the bombers he could see their fighter escort heading back to the coast and across the Channel, the German fighter pilots watching their fuel gauges all the way back to their base. Spitfires and Hurricanes swept down on the unprotected bombers.

Isaac spotted his prey and dived in a beam attack, racking the Dornier from rear to front, and then he was past, turning quickly around. The German gunner fired at him as he attacked again; smoke appeared from the German's port engine and it began to lose height. Two forms left the aircraft as its downward journey became steeper.

Isaac decided as there were no fighters to worry about to follow it down. He could see two crew members at the corner of his eye floating safely to the ground below. The Dornier straightened out slightly. Isaac moved beside it. There was blood on the windscreen and he could see the pilot struggling with the controls glance in his direction and gave a slight smile and then turned away.

They were now about a hundred feet from the ground. Isaac pulled back on the stick, climbing above the stricken bomber. He could see the nose go up slightly, but not enough to stop it from crashing nose first into the ground. Isaac made a mental note of where they were, to see if the pilot survived the crash. He glanced at his fuel gauge: it was time to go home, refuel and rearm.

On landing he was told to report to the adjutant's office. After being debriefed he knocked on the adjutant's door.

'Come in.'

Isaac opened the door, walked into the office, closed it, turned and saluted. 'You wanted to see me, sir?'

Squadron Leader Phillips smiled. 'Yes. At ease.'

Isaac relaxed, but a perplexed look remained on his face.

'Right, good and bad news; as you know,' he reached for the pipe in front of him, 'we are going back to Scotland, but after a week there, you are being transferred back here to 54 Squadron.'

Isaac's looked surprised and shocked at the news. 'But I'm—'

Phillips held up a hand, stopping Isaac from saying anything more. 'You are as from today promoted to flying officer, and granted a DFC. I'm sorry, Isaac, we are sad you're going, but you have been requested. Is your wife joining you in Scotland?'

Isaac smiled. 'Yes sir, a week would be nice, we haven't had much time together.' He stood to attention and saluted.

Two hours later, Isaac and the rest of the squadron flew to Scotland. That night he joined Lily and baby Daniel at the hotel he had booked.

13

Spider stared at the cell wall, his face twisted in anger. He stood and hit the wall with the palm of his hand, the anger centred on the fireman that put him there; because of him he had missed Christmas and New Year with his mother. He had persuaded the police to notify her of his arrest, and that he wasn't allowed any visitors.

Spider had so far spent a month in Wandsworth Prison awaiting transfer to a military prison to stand trial for desertion. All he could think about was how to escape, and the pain he would inflict on the fireman and his friends when he got out. His thoughts were interrupted by the key in the lock and the cell door opened. He stood, thinking they had come to transfer him, but instead the warden said, 'Your new home, Bull – well, for a while anyway.'

Spider's eyes widened as the huge six foot four man entered the cell. He sat back onto his bed as the door clanged shut and the key turned in the lock. Spider was silent as the man called Bull threw his pillow and blanket onto the top bunk. The bunkbed tilted slightly as he climbed up and sat on the edge of the bed, but within seconds swore and dropped onto the floor, the pillow in his hand. He looked at Spider. 'Name's Bull Burgess.'

'Spider Munro.' Neither man held out his hand as Bull dropped the pillow onto the floor and sat on it, leaning his back against the cold wall.

Spider looked at him, the bald head sitting on broad shoulders. He looked strong enough to pull the bars from the window. He frowned, wondering how many policemen it had taken to overcome such a strong man. Curiosity took the better of him. 'How did they arrest you?' he asked, adding, 'Probably took an army, going by the size of you.'

Bull looked up, a slight smile on his face. 'Six of them, two others grabbed my legs and tripped me up and put chains around my legs. I'm being sent for trial as a deserter. What about you?'

'Some meddling firemen caught us robbing jewellers.' Spider pointed to his mouth. 'He could fight, knocked out two of my teeth. He had two other firemen with him; one of them broke my friend's arm. One was called Billy. I owe them for making me miss Christmas and New Year with my mother.' He got to his feet. 'My friends received bail. Like you, I'm destined for a military prison to stand—'

'Say that again,' Bull interrupted.

'I'm also going—'

'The one called Billy – did he have an Irish accent?'

'Yes ... why?'

'The other two are Jew brothers – Wolfe and Asher Brown. The three of them own the Victoria Casino.'

'It's a pile of rubble.'

'Oh, didn't know that, I'm from South London, but they own another, the Hanover Casino in the West End.'

'I go there, but I've never seen them there.' He frowned and squatted in front of Bull. 'How do you know the Irishman and the brothers?'

Bull ignored the question. 'How do you intend to get out of here? Have you got people that could help?'

'Not allowed visitors.' Spider got to his feet, taking his pillow and blanket from the bottom bunk. 'You can have the bottom bunk. It's easier for me to get up there.'

'Thanks, I was preparing to sleep on the floor.'

Spider hardly slept, trying to think of a way out of his predicament, the face of the fireman named Wolfe etched in his brain, his lips tight, the tongue flicking to the two empty sockets of his missing teeth.

It was late afternoon when Spider, his face intent in thought, got to his feet, the blanket wrapped around his shoulders, and began pacing up and down the cell like a caged animal, his breath like smoke from a cigarette in the cold damp air.

'Without help from the outside, all the pacing in the world wouldn't solve the question of escape,' Bull said quietly. He got to his feet. 'What we must do is wait, play it as it comes. I'm sure that at some point during our transfer there would come a chance to—' The key being placed in the lock interrupted what he was about to say. Both men faced the door as it opened and the Guvnor of the prison entered, followed by two soldiers, one carrying a clipboard, a third stood outside. 'You're being transferred to an army facility.'

Bull looked at the armed soldiers and held out his hands to be handcuffed, as did Spider.

'Not you Burgess, just Munroe.' One of the soldiers stepped forward with a pair of handcuffs. The Guvnor took the clipboard with the order for the transfer on it, and as he was handed the pen, dropped it.

'I'll get it,' he said, bending down to pick it up, glancing at the soldier's shoes, he frowned. They weren't army shoes. He picked up the pen and straightened up, 'Oh, ah, I'll be forgetting my head soon, I have Munroe's file in my office, I'll go—' A rifle butt crashed down onto his skull and he crumpled to the floor.

'I told you to put on the boots,' Bob hissed angrily at George.

'I'm sorry, but they hurt my flat feet.'

'Shut the fuck up,' Spider said. Just handcuff Bull and me, and let's get out of here, before they miss the Guvnor.'

Locking the Guvnor in the cell, the two prisoners and their soldier escort walked out of the prison. Bob Burns let down the tailgate of an army lorry, helping Spider and Bull into the vehicle John and George following them. Bob dropped the flap into place, hiding the four men from sight and hopped onto the driver's seat, started the engine and let out the clutch. He slowed down at the gate, hoping the Guvnor hadn't woken up yet, waiting for someone to shout and wanting desperately to put his foot down on the accelerator. The two guards opened the gate waving them through and drove out onto Trinity Road as the skies began to darken. He slid back a small communicating window. 'Where to, Spider?'

'I think it would be safer if you stayed south for a while,' Bull said to Spider, who stared silently at him. Bull knew that Spider was weighing up what best to do. 'They won't think of looking south for you.'

'You're right, but what about you, won't they be looking for you?'

'Yes, but not where I would take us.'

While they were talking, John and George changed into civilian clothes.

'Bob, how you going to dump this lorry without being seen?'

'Don't worry, it's all sorted. I figure we've got about thirty minutes before the shit hits the fan.'

They crossed Wandsworth Bridge.

'Do you know where you're going?' Bull asked.

Bob smiled, won't be a moment and we'll be there.' Three minutes went by and they came to a stop. 'We're here,' Bob said, sliding from the seat and moving to the rear of the vehicle. Letting down the tailgate he leapt up moving into the interior. 'Won't be a moment, have to change.'

He emerged from the lorry, smartly dressed as usual. The others got down, following him to where a black Humber was parked. He opened the door and slid behind the wheel, with Spider as usual on the front passenger seat. Bull, George and John slid onto the back seat.

'We had to leave the van back home,' Bob said, 'but I have someone bringing it to us when we have an address.' He looked round at Bull. 'Where to?'

It was just after five in the morning when the fire tenders returned to the fire station. Wolfe jumped down from the cab as a man moved out from the shadows. Wolfe looked at him and yelled, 'Hey, Billy, we have a visitor.'

Billy walked around from the other side of the fire engine. 'Who could be visiting us at this time?' He stopped in mid stride on seeing O'Brian.

Asher had joined Wolfe as O'Brian moved closer, saying quietly so only they could hear. 'Spider Munro escaped yesterday evening. I know you were the ones that caught him, so I thought you should know.'

'What, how did they—'

'Three men dressed as soldiers said they had come to take him to a military prison. The Guvnor didn't realise till too late that they weren't soldiers. They knocked him out and locked him in the cell. By the time he came to, they were gone. We searched the usual places in East London, but Spider had disappeared. He escaped with another prisoner named Burgess, who was also waiting to be transferred to a military prison.'

'Burgess – not Bull Burgess?'

'The very same, why do you—' He pointed a finger at Wolfe. 'Is that the man Saul fought?'

'The one and only,' was the reply.

'What about Munroe's three friends?' Asher asked.

'They were the soldiers, plus they did not appear in court, having been granted bail, so they are also on our wanted list. I suggest you three be very vigilant. I'm given to understand that Munro was pretty verbal on what he was going to do to you three.'

'And for good measure we have Burgess as well,' Billy said.

'He's from South London,' Wolfe said, adding, 'I bet that's where they are holed up, somewhere south.'

'Okay, I'll get some of my men checking Burgess's haunts, see if they come up with anything. In the meantime keep vigilant and if you need me, you know where I am.'

18 January 1941

The searchlights crisscrossed the sky as a dark-blue van crossed Battersea Bridge into Beaufort Street crossing Kings Road Chelsea and slowed down. The eyes of the driver, Bob Burns and Spider next to him moved slowly along the houses either side.

'Stop here,' Spider said, opening the door and donning a white ARP helmet and armband he had bought a few days ago. He stepped from the slowly moving vehicle just before it came to a stop and walked slowly along the street, pausing to face the houses opposite.

'What's he doing?' Bull was nervous as he asked George and John, who sat in the back with him, the German bombers dropping their usual high explosives.

'He's seeing which houses might be empty,' John told him.

'How does he know that?'

'Instinct,' John replied softly, eyes on Spider as the latter crossed the street, opened the gate of a house and walked boldly up the stairs to the front door. Spider stood still for a moment and then pushed the door. It was locked. He took something from his pocket, looking around to make sure he wasn't being observed, then placed the object into the lock. Opening the door, he went inside, emerging seconds later waving them forward.

'Okay, let's go,' Bob said, opening the driver's door. The three men emerged from the rear of the vehicle, leaving the door open and quickly ran across the road to join Spider.

'Each takes a room. You have ten minutes, and then we are out of here. If you're not by the van by then, we leave without you.'

Ten minutes later the five men ran towards the van and within seconds were driving away, crossing Albert Bridge and heading south as the all-clear sounded.

Bob turned the van into Cubitt Terrace near Stockwell where they had been staying for the last couple of weeks. Before that they went into hiding at a house in Bromley owned by an old friend of Bull's, who was doing six years in Brixton Prison.

The reason for the change of abode was, as Spider had put it, they were running short of cash and needed to get back to their own manor, plus he was getting itchy feet, wanting his revenge against the brothers and the Irishman.

Not wanting to go to prison, John, Bob and George had broken their bail agreement and missed their court hearing, so with Spider and Bull, they were now wanted by the police.

That night they had two visitors, friends of Spider's from East London, Fred and Brian Moss.

'We have done as you asked. The three firemen are at Commercial Road Fire Station, and own the Hanover Casino—'

'Fuck it, Fred, I know all that,' Spider yelled at him in frustration.

'Sorry, their wives are in the WVS and they house homeless at an old youth club the brothers and the Irishman set up. I tell you what, Spider, those—'

'Get on with it,' Burgess stood, leaning towards them.

Fred held up his arms, leaning back. 'There's nothing.'

'What about their children? Could we get at them through them?' Spider asked.

'Two sons in the RAF, one's a fighter pilot. The brother's son is a captain in the army. The fighter pilot has a wife and young baby son. The other son—' he looked at Bull. 'His girlfriend runs a brothel in

Highbury. The army man has a wife who owns a hairdressers in Burdett Road.'

Spider sat staring at Fred as if he wasn't there. 'I told you, the only way was to kill them,' Bull said.

'I want to hurt them where it hurts the most.'

'It's not in their pockets,' Bull moved towards Spider. 'They are very deep. Their children are grown men and women, so, like I said, you would have to kill them, because I'm telling you, if you do anything against them, they would come back at you two fold. I know that from experience.'

Spider was silent, his eyes on Bull for a moment and then he looked away, his thoughts interrupted by the man beside Fred. 'There was one other thing.'

He seemed to shrink in his seat as Spider turned his gaze on him. 'And that was?'

'Whenever they are off duty. They all meet on a Sunday.'

'All? Who would "all" be, Brian?'

Brian's voice quivered as he said quietly, 'The entire family, the brothers, Reid, their wives, and children.'

'There you go, kill the lot with one blow,' Bull said vehemently.

Spider stood looking up at Bull. 'What's all this about killing? It's easy to kill someone, but it's more satisfying if you can hurt them first, and hurt them badly so it stays with them for the rest of what's left of their lives, so stop for a moment with the fucking killing.'

Bull took a step forward. It wasn't very often someone spoke to him that way, but one look into Spider's eyes made him stop.

They stood like that for a couple of minutes, and then Spider said quietly, 'Fight fire with fire.'

'What's that mean?' Bull said belligerently.

'What do firemen fear most?' Before anyone could answer, he said, 'Not being able to save anyone trapped in a building.'

'So what's that got to do with you know who?' John asked.

'What if a building was on fire with their loved ones inside it – on separate floors, of course, and they were unable to escape?'

'You're not thinking of setting the club on fire?' Bob asked.

Spider stared at Bob, a slight smile on his face.

Bob leapt to his feet. 'You can't do that; there are innocent women and children in there – mothers, like yours – and the people running it are helping those that have nowhere to go, and have lost everything.'

'You don't mind robbing them so why be squeamish now?'

Bob took a step towards Spider. 'We have been together for some time, but I would not be a part of that.' He spread his arms. 'We may be many things to certain people, and yes we have done things I'm not proud of to survive, but this is murder. I'm out.' The others murmured their agreement, except for Bull.

Spider was silent as he lit a cigarette. There was a slight sneer of contempt on his face. 'Okay, we'll find a building, four stories high, placing one wife in a room on each floor.'

Bob looked around the room, his face impassive, shocked at what Spider was planning. He had known Spider for a few years, before they teamed up with the others.

Bob Burns used to be an art dealer with a business in Sloane Street, Chelsea, and was not averse to selling stolen masters for collectors who would pay a lot of money to obtain what they desired. Like Spider, he loved money and women, but had a passion for the card game chemin de fer, and suddenly he was down a lot of money.

He had never had such a run of bad luck. He borrowed on the business, but his luck did not change. Like many gamblers Bob was chasing good luck. If he won one day he lost the next three days. Suddenly the bank wanted its money, and they foreclosed on his business. He went to the recruiting office, hoping to get into the army and, with his educational background, to be an officer, but he failed the medical. He tried to get employment at an art gallery, but they knew about his gambling habit. He was making a cup of tea, wondering what to do next, when there was a knock at the door. He opened it to find Spider facing him. Without saying a word Spider walked past him and into the hallway.

Bob closed the door. 'What's going—'

'I have a painting here,' Spider interrupted.

'I no longer have a business.'

'I know, but you still know people.' He unwrapped the painting.

'Where did you get this, it's—'

'Can you sell it?'

Bob looked at Spider, 'I thought you were in the army.'

'Let's say it's not for me so I left.'

'You deserted?' There was shock in Bob's face and voice.

'Can you sell it?'

'Yes, but its twenty per cent for me.'

'That's a bit steep.'

'I need the money. I've the kettle on, would you like a cuppa?'

'Okay, but I can't stay long.'

They sat opposite each other drinking tea, when Spider said, 'Join me.'

'What does that mean?'

'In a little while the Germans are going to bomb London. Many people would leave their homes to go to shelters. We enter their homes and ... well, you get the picture. I thought you would be an officer by now.'

'I failed the medical.'

'So would you join me? I have two friends who are reliable.'

'I have nothing better to do.'

Bob had never killed anyone, although he had suspected Spider of doing that. There had been times when quarrelsome competitors had suddenly disappeared. He had been with Spider and the others for over a year.

Bob took a pack of cigarettes from his pocket, not offering them around as he pondered the problem in helping Spider have his revenge without involving the wives.

As far as Spider was concerned there was only one thought on his mind, revenge against the men who did the unspeakable: took away his Christmas and New Year with his mother. It didn't occur to him that it was his fault for being the criminal he was.

*

Across London the three men uppermost in Spider's mind were sitting around a table, discussing Spider's escape and his union with Bull.

'They are a dangerous duo,' Billy said.

'We have to try and be one step ahead of them,' Wolfe pointed out.

Asher looked down at the mug of tea in front of him. 'In the past we would have some idea what to do, or more to the point what the terrible duo would do next—' He took a sip of tea. 'There's a war on, and from what O'Brian had told us, Spider is not your usual psychopath.'

'There are five of them,' Billy said, 'and they want to kill us—' he pointed at Wolfe '—well, you.'

They were silent, for the first time in many years they were stumped on what they or Spider would do next.

The firebell rang and they ran to their tender, Spider disappearing from their thoughts for a while.

20 January 1941

Isaac arrived at Hornchurch to join 54 Squadron. He went immediately to the officers' quarters, dropped his case on the bed and walked across to report to the CO. He knocked on the door, opening it on hearing the order, 'Come in.'

On entering he stopped in mid-stride on seeing the man behind the desk. It was Martin Ainsworth, now a squadron leader, who smiled on seeing Isaac. 'Close the door.'

Isaac saluted, but Ainsworth didn't return the salute, instead picked up the phone and pressed a number. 'Could you pop over please.' He replaced the receiver. 'Stand at ease.'

There was a knock on the door. 'Come,' Ainsworth said.

The door opened and Isaac stepped back in amazement. It was Cole, now a flight lieutenant. 'You look surprised.'

'Excuse me, sir, flabbergasted would be more appropriate.'

'Sit down, Isaac,' Ainsworth said quietly, shocking Isaac by the use of his first name when he had always been so formal. 'You too, Ron.' Ainsworth waited for them to sit. 'Smoke if you want.'

Isaac took a cigarette case from his top pocket, a present from Lily, offering it around. Cole took one, while Ainsworth pointed to his pipe. Isaac flamed a match, lighting his and Cole's cigarettes.

Ainsworth waved the smoke away from his pipe saying, 'This squadron took a bit of a beating, and I had been given the task of making it operational ASAP.' He pointed the pipe at Isaac. 'I requested you and Cole to be here because I believe you two could help me do that. There are a few young, inexperienced pilots straight from flight training; I'm giving you both the job of getting them combat ready. Ron, you take over B flight as Squadron Flight Instructor. Isaac, you're his number two. Okay, off you go.'

Both men stood to attention and saluted, which Ainsworth returned, and they left the office.

'Have you unpacked yet?' Cole asked Isaac.

'No, not yet, I—'

Cole looked at his watch. 'Meet me in an hour, I have an office, if you could call it that,' he pointed, 'at the end of the hall.'

'Yes sir.' Isaac went to salute. 'No need for that. By the way, how's the baby...' he snapped his fingers '...Daniel?'

Isaac smiled. 'He's fine sir.'

'See you in an hour.'

On returning to his room Isaac checked the cupboards and drawers to make sure the gear he had left before leaving for Scotland, knowing he would be returning, was still there. All his shirts and clothes had been cleaned, his uniform pressed. He unpacked and changed into everyday uniform. He was about to leave and meet Cole when a pilot officer entered.

'Oh, I'm sorry sir,' he stammered. 'The billet sergeant said I could bunk in here until—'

'Name's Isaac Brown.' Isaac held out his hand.

The young officer wasn't sure if he should salute or take the hand. Instead he stood to attention and saluted. 'Pilot Officer Jack Jones, sir.'

Isaac burst into laughter. 'Okay Pilot Officer Jones, I must leave now, but I'll see you later.'

He walked from the room thinking, *My goodness he's only a child.* The door to Cole's office was open, he knocked and entered.

'Please close the door and take a seat.'

Isaac did as he was asked and sat facing Cole.

'Isaac, I want you to take over Blue and Red Sections, the—'

'Both? But they are—'

Cole held up a hand, stopping Isaac from saying anything else. 'I know we should have another flying officer to take one of the sections. They would be here in due course, but in the meantime Squadron Leader Ainsworth wants what pilots we have to be combat-ready by March. We are at the moment a stand-down squadron, but we are also in reserve if needed. I have put Pilot Officers Jones and Fielding in Blue Section, and there is another three in Red Section.' He searched the papers in front of him. 'Ah, here they are – Riley, Booth and Dunhill.' He handed Isaac a sheet of paper. 'Just in case you forget their names. I'm sorry to land this on you, but,' he smiled, 'you should know what it's like.'

Isaac smiled back, 'Yes, I do know, and I must admit, if it hadn't been for you and Jones, I … thanks.'

'I'm going to help you get them ready from being killed. Okay, I'll see you in the mess for a drink. Off you go.'

Isaac got to his feet, and saluted. Cole returned the salute and as Isaac opened the door Cole said, 'And by the way, Jones is the brother of our old Flight Instructor.'

'It would make no difference to the way you and I would teach him to stay alive. You and Jones taught me well. I hope to do the same with his brother.' He waved the piece of paper, 'and these others.' He turned and walked out of the office, closing the door behind him.

'Rattatat,' Isaac yelled over the radio. 'Come on, Jones, concentrate. Okay, let's return to the field.'

On landing, Isaac went in search of Cole, finding him in the officers' mess having a cup of tea. He plonked himself onto the seat facing Cole. 'Ron, I can't train them on my own.'

Cole didn't reply, but just took a sip of tea.

Isaac's lips tightened. 'You remember what Jones did with me; he made me follow you on all the manoeuvres on how to defend myself from an attack by another fighter.' He stabbed a finger onto the table. 'It was the best lesson I ever had, and we need to do the same with this bunch.'

Cole looked at Isaac, 'After lunch, we'll start with Jones.'

*

Eight days later, Squadron Leader Ainsworth, at Isaac and Cole's request, took B flight on a mock attack by German fighters. On landing he told the station commander that the squadron was combat ready.

Spider paced up and down like a caged animal. He had hardly slept, trying to think of ideas how to best hurt the three firemen and it was consuming him. He suddenly turned on Brian. 'You said they always meet on Sundays?'

'Only if the firemen are not on duty...' stammered Brian '...but if they are, the women would probably be at the club or handing out sandwiches and teas after and during a raid.'

'Fuck it,' yelled Spider. 'Can't you be sure about something?'

Brian cowered in his seat, expecting a backhander from the volatile Spider. 'No one could be absolutely sure where they would be during a raid.'

Spider stared at Brian and then turned away. Everyone could see that he was wound up like a clockwork toy and would explode at any moment. He turned back to face the men in the room, and said calmly, 'We'll grab the wives wherever they are.'

'So what you're saying,' Bull said, 'is that we choose a Sunday when Reid and the Jew boys would be called to any building we set alight.'

'Yes, that's correct,' Spider said softly, adding, 'We set the wives alight.'

Bull's face was like a horror mask at Halloween, imagining what he was going to do to the Irishman and his wife.

Bob was appalled by the callousness of setting someone alight. He moved beside Spider. 'It's a horrible death; no one deserves to die like that.'

Spider's face contorted with hatred. 'I owe them for the worst Christmas and New Year my mother and I ever had.' Spider's face was a mask of hatred at the mention of the firemen.

Bob moved away not wanting to antagonise Spider any more and leant against the wall, lighting a cigarette and letting the smoke trickle from the side of his mouth, knowing that Spider would not think twice in killing him if he betrayed him in any way. He hoped he could come up with a different plan in the next week or so. If he couldn't the consequences... He dropped the half-smoked cigarette on to the floor, stubbing it out with the toe of his shoe.

The weather forecast read early morning cloud, and any rain easing off in the morning with sunny periods in the afternoon.

Isaac smiled, sitting comfortably in his seat, legs stretched out, his cap over his eyes. With low cloud the Germans wouldn't risk sending bombers over.

There was a sudden yell, 'Scramble!' Isaac was out of his chair and running for his Spitfire. Within minutes he was in the cockpit and speeding along the grass. He pulled back the stick as he heard Squadron Leader Ainsworth reporting to control they were airborne.

'Vector Nineteen, Trade over Dover Forty plus bandits heading west along the Thames Angels Seventeen.'

'Roger Control, Bulldog Leader understood.' The squadron turned towards their targets climbing steadily to intercept.

'Tally Ho,' young Jones said excitedly. 'Seven o'clock.'

Isaac looked around at the formation of Spitfires, and gave a slight smile, thinking they were like knights of old, charging on their trusty steeds towards the enemy to defend their country, knowing death was real, but putting it to the back of their minds as they charged the enemy.

The bombers were below them just above the clouds. Ainsworth's voice came over the intercom. 'Blue and Red flights the fighters, Green and Yellow the bombers.'

The Messerschmitts peeled off, climbing to meet the threat to their bombers as the British fighters moved in to attack. Isaac pushed the stick to the left in a gliding dive, closing quickly on the enemy fighters. He straightened the Spitfire out, not flinching as the 109 streaked towards him, his mind yelling *Wait, wait!* as he saw the tinkle of light from the 109's guns, knowing he was too far away to hit him. His mind yelled, *Now!* and he let off a two-second burst, seeing bits flying off the enemy plane. He pulled back on the stick and looped round for another attack. The Messerschmitt was sliding downward in a gentle slope.

He moved behind it and was about to fire when it turned over spinning downward as it stalled. He must have hit the pilot. He felt the Spitfire shudder and knew he was hit kicking himself for not being more alert as the enemy fighter shot past him, he turned quickly away, but the 109 was quickly upon him. He dived and then pulled back the stick, looking in his mirror. The Spitfire stalled, and for a second his stomach churned with fright. Instinct made him flick the fighter onto its back out of the reverse, a trick he had learnt from Morgan. The engine started and he pulled out of the dive a thousand feet from the ground, yelling happily at the grim reaper, '*Fuck you! Fuck you!*' and sped for home.

He brought the Spitfire to a stop by the dispersal area. As he climbed from the cockpit, Cole, who had landed before him, stood with a look of amazement on his face. 'Termites are flying high these days.'

Isaac jumped down. 'What are you—' Isaac turned around on seeing Cole pointing at his aircraft. 'Oh my.' His face showed his shock on seeing a line of holes from the tail to just before his cockpit, the fabric of the tail rudder hanging like a curtain. He placed a hand on his forehead wondering how he made it back in one piece. He turned to his fitter, 'Sorry,' he said, slung the parachute over his shoulder and walked back with Cole to be debriefed.

That evening Isaac took a crate of beer over to the hangar where his Spitfire was being repaired. He handed the beers to Fred, his fitter. Tom the rigger was sitting in the cockpit.

'Will she be ready for tomorrow?' he asked Fred.

'Yes sir, we're going to work all night if need be.'

'Can I help with anything?'

'No sir,' Fred said, holding up a beer. 'This is what we need.'

'Just make sure the CO doesn't see them.'

'He won't be able to smell it on our breath.'

Isaac smiled. 'Thanks.' He turned and walked out of the hangar.

27 January 1941

Saul grit his teeth as he, Hannah, the girls and their patrons sat in the cellar. When there was a loud bang everyone looked up at the ceiling, hoping it wasn't the house. There had been some near misses in the last few weeks. The pub over the road had received a direct hit, incendiaries followed and the building caught fire, and then a second bomb landed on the pub. Firemen stood with an astonished look on their faces as the blast had put out the fire.

Saul got to his feet, looking down at the floor as he paced up and down a couple of times. Hannah also stood up, moving beside him. 'It will all be over soon.'

He smiled and gave her a peck on the cheek. 'I'm not worried, or scared about the bombing, just the fact that I am down here wanting to have a go at them and can't.'

She smiled. 'I have a whip upstairs.'

He stopped pacing, turning to face her. 'You never brought it with you. What if a German airman parachuted into the garden? What then?'

One of the girls lifted up her blouse. 'I'd show him my tits.'

'Mavis, that's not nice,' the woman sitting next to her said. 'You'd frighten the poor man to death.'

Everyone laughed, easing the tension around the cellar

At last the all-clear sounded. Hannah took the lead with Saul beside her as they emerged into the hallway. A deep sigh escaped her lips on seeing the house intact, followed by a chorus of similar sighs from the women behind her. Hannah walked from room to room, making sure the windows were still intact. She didn't have to say anything to anyone. The women knew what to do. The brooms and dusters came out and they began to sweep the dust of the floor, chairs and tables. An hour later everything was clean and ready for their clients.

*

Their bodies close together, the perspiration from their lovemaking was still on their bodies. 'I need to see someone in Brick Lane first thing in the morning,' Saul said. 'Would you come with me, it won't take long.'

'I haven't been down there for months, can we go to Blooms?' said Hannah. 'I love their Viennas.'

The following morning they walked hand in hand along Brick Lane. Twenty yards from Hanbury Street, Saul came to a stop, turning to stand for a second in front of Hannah. Taking her right hand, he dropped to one knee.

'Hannah Grozenski, I've been in love with you since the first time I saw you. Would you please do me the honour of marrying me?'

Hannah's left hand was at her cheek, a look of amazement in her eyes as she gazed down at Saul; then a smile lit up her face and she said, 'Yes, oh yes.' She bent down to kiss him.

Once their lips had parted, he said, 'Let's get a ring,' and took her hand, leading her along a few yards. 'Guess what, here's a jewellery shop.'

The bell above the door rang as they entered the shop to see a smiling Mr Kinsky and his wife behind the counter.

'Good morning Saul,' the jeweller said and Miss—'

The smile had not left Hannah's face as she said, 'Grozenski, Hannah.'

Mr Kinsky took a box from a drawer and handed it to Saul, at the same time saying to Hannah, 'Could I please see your left hand.' She held it out. Mr Kinsky's touch was soft; his head turned towards Saul who had opened the box, looked at the contents and then closed the box.

'Mr Kinsky you have excelled yourself.'

Kinsky smiled. 'It should fit perfectly.'

Saul opened the box, showing Hannah the ring. 'Oh dear me, it's so beautiful,' she whispered.

'Put it on,' Mrs Kinsky said.

Saul lifted from the box, taking hold of Hanna's left hand and sliding the diamond ring with baguettes on either side of the diamond onto her finger. She held out her hand to see, and then wrapped her arms around Saul and kissed him, as the Kinskys clapped.

Thirty minutes later they entered the house. They could hear Eva in the kitchen singing in Yiddish. Her face lit up when she saw them. Hannah placed her left hand onto her right breast, the ring prominent. It did not take Eva a second to see it. She let out a screech, hands full of flour towards Hannah.

'Mama, wash your hands.'

Eva stopped in mid stride, turning towards the sink to wash her hands, wiping them on her apron as she moved across the kitchen to take Hannah's hand, looking at the ring. 'Hannah, it's beautiful.' She then placed her arms around her, kissing both her cheeks. '*Mazeltov*, I'm very happy.'

She turned to Saul, giving him a hug and a kiss and then moved away saying, 'Sit, I'll make a cup of tea.'

That evening at the dinner table after a very exciting day Saul said, 'I'm being posted, I cannot tell you where, but I might not be able to see you for a while.'

'How long is a while?'

'Six to nine months, maybe more.'

She stared silently at him, her eyes sad, a tear moving slowly down her cheek.

'I'll send you the details of where to write as soon as I know where I am.'

'You're going out of the country?'

'I cannot tell you that but truthfully, no, I'm not.'

She wiped the tear from her cheek. 'That's okay then. When do you have to go?'

'I have one more day of my leave left.'

'Well then, what are we waiting for?'

Saul had not told her that he had been accepted for pilot training and was to report at Number 3 Training Squadron. He had spoken to his CO, who told him that it was to train bomber pilots. Saul had smiled when he was told that. Now he would show the Germans what he had been going through.

Night flight

Isaac could hear the controller in his ears, 'Blue One Bandit's vector one-two-zero, Angels 20.'

'Blue one, Roger Control,' he replied, levelling out at twenty thousand feet, saying, 'Top Hat control, Blue One, have reached twenty thousand feet.'

'Blue One Bandit's three miles ahead of you, closing to port.'

Isaac was hunched up and tense. This was his first night flight since training. He gave a wry smile, staring into the darkness. It was his idea for this night flight. He had persuaded Ainsworth to let him go.

'I'm fed up with just sitting around,' he had told the Squadron Leader. 'The Germans have all but given up on daylight bombing.' Ainsworth had laughed at first, but Isaac had been persistent, so here he was staring into nothing, gnawing his bottom lip under the oxygen mask.

The controller's calm voice broke into his thoughts as he directed Isaac towards the enemy bomber. 'Blue one, you should be making contact.'

Searchlights crisscrossed the sky, flack bursting like coloured fireworks.

Isaac stared ahead, eyes moving left and right like windscreen wipers, and spotted a slight glow in front of him, and suddenly the Heinkel was outlined by the bursting shells of ack-ack, one a little too close for comfort. For a second he hoped his IDF was working, he would look stupid if he were shot down by friendly fire. The bomber's gunners must have seen him as tracer whizzing past his cockpit, but ignored it as he closed in, and pressed the gun button in a two-second burst.

Nothing happened. He must have missed, and then suddenly there was a glow, which grew brighter, spreading along the bomber's fuselage; its port wing dipped and it slid downward as dark forms left the stricken bomber, which was now a flaming comet diving towards the ground. Isaac averted his eyes, looking at the instrument panel and pulling back the stick climbing back to twenty thousand feet, calling, 'Top Hat control, Blue One here, shot down enemy bomber.'

He looked down at the City which was aflame, when a voice said, 'Blue One bomber ahead of you.' He couldn't help but swear. 'Fucking Ada!' there it was – its bomb bay doors open. He moved in fast, giving it a two-second burst, and pulled the stick over when without warning the bomber blew up. Debris flew through the sky. He reacted quickly, pulling back on the stick and trying to avoid the debris, sucking in lungfuls of air through his oxygen mask, knowing he had been lucky not to have sustained damage. He was running short of fuel and was happy with his night's work, two kills. 'Top Hat control, Blue One, I'm heading home.'

'Roger Blue one, well done.'

As he neared Hornchurch he dropped to fifteen hundred feet; the Aldis lamp lit up, giving him the okay to land, and there it was: the Chance light to starboard. He turned towards it, unclipped his oxygen mask and slid open the hood, breathing in the cool night air. Lowering the wheels, he landed with a slight bump and taxied to the dispersal bay, turning off the engine and jumping down. He shouldered his parachute and frowned, noticing something protruding from under the wing. He moved towards it and then stepped back.

'Fucking hell.'

Just then his fitter and rigger moved either side of him. 'You were lucky, sir,' Tom whispered.

Isaac stared at the piece of metal. An inch to the left he would not have been able to lower the wheels. He looked up at the sky and gave a silent 'thank you'.

14

Bob wasn't happy. They had returned to East London, but Bull Burgess had come with them. They had exchanged their small van for a larger one to accommodate three in the back. Spider had found them a house in Finnis Street, Bethnal Green with a lock-up garage opposite in Three Colts Lane.

It wasn't so much that Bull was with them, but Spider's moods were a problem, pacing up and down like a caged tiger, muttering to himself, and then suddenly against advice from Bob and the others, go out during the day looking for a house to put his plan against the brothers and the Irishman in motion. Usually he would came back in a worse mood than when he went, but today his face was creased in the biggest smile they had seen for many months.

'What you smiling about?' Bob asked.

The black eyes shone. 'I've found it.'

'Found what?' Bull asked.

'The house, where—'

'You are still going ahead with that plan,' Bob interrupted, adding, 'Where's the house?'

Spider stared at Bob, not happy at being interrupted. 'Cephas Street.'

'That's not far from here,' George said.

'Off Cambridge Heath Road, and close enough to the bastards' fire station for them to get the call,' smiled Spider.

'So what's the plan?' John asked.

'There are three floors to the house, which still has some furniture and curtains. My plan was that on the top floor—' he looked at Bull '— what are the brothers' names?'

'Wolfe and Asher,' was the quick reply.

'Asher's wife will be on the top floor,' he pointed at John. 'I'm sure you want to avenge your broken wrist. When you've finished with them, you set fire to the curtains and leave.'

'Thanks,' John smiled.

Spider looked at Bull, a slight smile on his lips. 'I'm sure you would like to take care of the Irishman on the second floor.'

'I've been waiting a long time for that, but I want to watch them burn.'

Spider's face changed, the eyes hard. 'Wolfe's mine,' was all he said.

'What about George and me?' Bob asked.

'You will be in the van parked outside the house for our getaway.'

'And me?' George asked.

159

'We won't come back here. You get all our gear and take it to 33 Camden Street.' He handed George a key. 'Make sure the kettles on.'

'When?' asked Bob, holding the flame to his cigarette, trying to hide his feelings at the plan.

'Next Sunday.'

'Give us time to get some more cash,' John said.

*

That night Bob couldn't sleep, trying to think of a way that would not involve the firemen's wives. He had to get away from Spider for a couple of days and think. As soon as Spider was awake, Bob said, 'I spoke to my mother yesterday. She isn't too well so I'm going to stay with her for a couple of days.'

'When would you be back?'

'Saturday.' He picked up a small case and was about to leave when Spider said, 'Should I go over the plan with you again?'

'No I'm fine.'

'Okay, see you Saturday.' Bob was at the door when Spider added menacingly, 'Make sure you're here on Saturday.'

Bob nodded and left.

Bob took the underground to Shepherds Bush. Knowing Spider, he might have him followed. He left the station and walked along Goldhawk Road, stopping now and again to look in shop windows. He smiled, giving a sigh of relief: he was alone. He needed to get away from the intensity and insanity of the situation with Spider, and a bit of normality. Perhaps being at home with his mother for a few days, and away from the bombing, he might come up with a solution that would prevent anyone being killed. He turned into Ravenscourt Road, hesitated for a second before climbing the familiar five steps to the front door. He had a key, but knocked on the door, not wanting to frighten his mother as he hadn't told her he was coming.

The door opened and his mother stood there, smiling and opening her arms. He moved into them and she wrapped them around his neck. He kissed her cheek as she said warmly, 'It's lovely to see you, Robert.' She always called him by his full name and would be shocked to hear anyone calling him Bob.

'And you, Mother.' He moved slightly away. 'I hope you don't mind me suddenly appearing like this. Could I stay a couple of days?'

'You don't need to ask. This has always been your home.'

She stepped to one side. He entered the hallway and she closed the door behind him, moving in front and leading him into the kitchen.

'Tea?' she asked over her shoulder.

'Yes please.'

They sat opposite each other as she poured the tea from a pot into china cups. He didn't take any sugar, knowing how hard it was for her to obtain.

She took a sip of tea, looking at him over the rim of the cup, and frowned. 'There's something bothering you. You're not in any trouble?'

He didn't say anything for a minute. She could read him like a book. 'No, Mother, I'm not in any trouble.' He leaned forward. 'Could we please talk about it later, I'm still trying to analyse it, and yes, perhaps talking openly about it would give me the solution I need.' He finished his tea and said, 'I'm going to have a bath and change, I won't be long.'

He entered his bedroom; it was exactly as he had left it a year ago. Thirty minutes later, dressed in dark blue trousers and a light blue silk shirt open at the neck, he made his way downstairs, finding his mother in the dining room listening to the radio. He moved to sit in an armchair, taking a pack of cigarettes from his pocket. 'Do you mind if I smoke, Mother?'

She smiled. 'Of course not. There's an ashtray on the table.' He stood, reaching for the ashtray, turning back and lowering himself onto the armchair. She turned off the radio and he knew it was time. She had known about his indiscretions as she had put it in the past. He looked at the photos on the mantelpiece: his brother was a captain in the guards and his sister a nurse. 'Where's Helen now?' he asked, noticing the photo of him at the far end.

'She is a sister now at St Bartholomew's.'

Shock showed on his face. 'That area's taking a pounding from the Germans every day.'

She sighed. 'I know, she doesn't say much about it, but I can put two and two together from the news. James is in Africa.'

'I wish I was with him, flat feet.' He looked down at the ashtray on his lap, saying quietly, 'I never thought I had flat feet.' He wiped his eyes, trying not to cry.

She was quickly beside him, cuddling him to her, knowing how it hurt him not being able to be with his brother.

For a moment he felt like a little boy again when she would cuddle him if he cut his knee, taking away the pain.

She moved away, taking a few strides to a drinks cabinet, turning slightly, a smile on her lips. 'I think a nice glass of sherry is in order. Would you like a brandy, Robert?'

'Yes please, Mother.'

She poured the drinks, and with a glass in each hand walked back, handing him the brandy. They touched glasses. 'Cheers,' she said, taking the few steps to the armchair and lowering herself on to it. 'So what is the problem?'

He took a sip of brandy, holding the glass between his hands, and began telling her about Spider. He lit a cigarette before telling her about Bull.

'Mother, they're so twisted and bitter with hatred, it's all they can think about. Bull keeps whispering in Spider's ear to kill them, but Spider wants to do more, set the firemen's wives alight.'

His mother's face registered shock. 'They are heartless.' She shook her head. 'No one should ever—'

'Even think of something like that,' he agreed. 'Spider had.' He leaned forward. 'The trouble is, they do not realise it's their own fault.'

She took a sip of sherry, eyes on her son, knowing that he was here for some sort of guidance. He had always been like that, knowing that talking about it might give him the answer. In this case should he help his so-called criminal friends or tell the firemen and put his life in danger, knowing that Spider would kill him if he found out? She knew the answer, but it needed someone else's help.

She frowned. Her ex-husband might refuse. She had never asked him for anything since he had left her and their three children for his secretary. Robert was his son too; he had not seen Robert since he was seven, which had been Robert's choice. She nodded to herself, finishing the rest of her sherry, placing the glass on the table beside her and got to her feet.

'Be a dear, could you – go to the grocer and see if they have any potatoes, perhaps some peas, I don't have enough for dinner.'

He knew it was a ploy; she needed time to think over his predicament.

He smiled. 'Of course, Mother, is there anything else? I have some coupons.'

'That's all dear.'

As soon as her son had left, Mrs Burns moved across to the mantelpiece, taking down Robert's photo, undoing the back and extracting a folded piece of paper. Opening it, she moved across the room to the telephone, picked up the receiver and dialled the number written on the piece of paper. It rang a couple of times before being picked up. 'Mayfair 326.'

'Could I please speak to Brigadier Burns?'

'Who's calling?'

'Mrs Cathleen Burns.'

'I'm sorry but the Brigadier isn't here at the moment.' She knew that voice, and her face hardened, but her voice was calm. 'I'm sorry to bother you, but I need to speak to the Brigadier. It's urgent, I'm sorry but it cannot wait.'

'Oh, I see, phone Whitehall 263. They would put you through.' The line went dead.

She immediately dialled the number which was answered immediately, 'Whitehall 263.'

'Good afternoon, could I please speak to Brigadier Burns?'

'Who should I say is calling?'

'Cathleen Burns.'

'One moment please.' There was a slight click. 'This is a surprise,' came a deep bass voice.

She ignored the pleasantries. 'Edward, I need your help, more to the point Robert does.'

'Go on.'

'He wanted desperately to enlist and become an officer, but was turned down because of flat feet. He's always been sporty and it had never shown up before. Not being able to get into the army and join his brother has taken away his self-esteem. Now there is a problem he must solve, but it means him disappearing into the army. Can you please help?'

'Firstly, how are you,' he said softly. 'It's been—'

'Many years,' she interrupted. 'I wouldn't ask you unless it was important.'

'He could get killed, there's a war on.'

'I know, but he could be killed if he does the right thing here.'

'Could you give me more details, perhaps there's another way.'

'I'm afraid there is no other way. If he does the right thing, which he wants to do, they would kill him, and these are bad people.'

There was a slight pause, and then the Brigadier said, 'Tell him to report to Mons Barrack Aldershot 8am on Monday morning, I'll have everything ready at that end. Tell him not to worry everything will be okay. It's the least I can do for him, and for what it's worth, I'm sorry I hurt you.'

'All I want you to do is look after our boys. Helen's at Bart's.'

'I know. I wish she worked somewhere else. The bombings pretty bad. I'm going to send all the documentation Robert needs to your home tonight. If you ever need me again don't hesitate to call.'

'Thank you, I will, goodbye.' She replaced the receiver staring at the phone, his face etched in her mind, knowing she still loved him, but at the same time hating him for what he had done. She heard the front door open.

'I'm back,' Robert called out.

She quickly hid the piece of paper in a drawer and strode into the hall, a smile on her face. 'Help me make supper.'

Mrs Burns waited until they were having their meal before telling her son what she had done. Robert placed his knife and fork on the side of his plate, stood and in two strides was beside his mother, cuddling her.

'Thank you, Mother, thank you.' There were tears in his eyes as he let go and returned to his seat, but before he could sit down, there was a knock at the door.

'I'll go,' he said. Opening the door he was surprised to see a second lieutenant standing there.

'Mr Robert Burns?'

'Yes.'

The second lieutenant handed him a large brown envelope. 'From Brigadier Burns.'

Robert took the envelope. 'Thank you very much.'

Without another word the officer turned and running down the stairs to a waiting car, he slid into the driver's seat. A face appeared at the side window as the car moved away from the kerbside. He watched it disappear around the corner before closing the door and returning to the dining room.

'It's from father.' He sat down, no longer hungry. Opening the envelope, he extracted two papers from it. He read the first and then the second, and looked across the table at his mother. 'The first one is from the court; all charges had been dropped against me. The other was orders to report at Mons Barracks on Monday morning.' There was a big smile on his face, as he whispered, 'Thank you, Mother, I knew you would know what to do.'

'No, Robert, we did it together, and a decision had been made.' He picked up his plate. 'I'll help you wash up.'

He couldn't stop smiling: he was happy for his father's help. Today was the first time he had seen him since he was seven. He made a mental note that once he had passed out from Mons he would meet his father, but most important of all he now knew what he had to do in regards to Spider and Bull; the problem was how to do it before Sunday.

*

At the Hanover Casino Billy had thought long and hard about their predicament with Spider and Bull, not knowing where, how or when – he stood and walked across to the drinks cabinet, pressing a button on the side, the cabinet slid to one side revealing pistols, rifles and shotguns. He picked out three pistols, Colt M1911 with a seven-round magazine and ammunition, pressed the button and the drinks cabinet slid into place. He spent the rest of the evening cleaning the guns.

Later Wolfe and Asher met him at the casino to discuss the Spider and Bull situation. As the three men sat around the desk Billy handed them the pistols, saying, 'From now on we go armed. It's a certainty that Spider and Bull will be too.'

1 March 1941

No sooner had Bob closed the door than Spider was on him. 'Where the fuck have you been?'

'I told you my mother wasn't well and I went to see her.'

'Oh, I forgot.'

Bob could see a difference in Spider since he left; he was jumpy, excited, eyes wide as though he was on drugs. He shouted, 'Everyone in the kitchen now.'

Spider leant against the sink while the others sat around the table. 'I want to go over the plan for today and Sunday.'

'We know what...' Bull's voice trailed off on seeing Spider's face.

'Sunday night the firemen are on duty and we—'

'Are you sure about that,' George asked.

'Brian has given me a copy of their roster. Any more interruptions before I carry on,' Spider looked around the room; everyone averted their eyes accept Bob who took a packet of cigarettes from his pocket, lighting one and leant against the wall.

'Tonight we capture the firemen's wives and hold them overnight.'

'Wouldn't it be easier to capture them tomorrow morning or afternoon?' Bob said quietly, moving away from the wall. 'That way we don't have the worry if someone's missing them. We know the daughter-in-law lives with Wolfe and his wife. We could prepare the house at Cephas Road tonight so all we have to do is take the wives there and sound the fire alarm.'

Bob expected a tirade from Spider, but for a second there was only silence everyone waiting for Spider to erupt, but he didn't. He moved from the sink to stand in front of Bob. 'That was fucking brilliant.' He slapped Bob on the shoulder. 'It's great to have someone with brains in the group.' He moved away, saying, 'We are going with Bob's plan. Tonight we prepare the house for our guests.'

Bob felt as though Spider was rubbing his hands together with glee. He stubbed the cigarette in the full ashtray. He needed to get away for a couple of hours. 'I'm going to Fred's and fill up the van,' he told Spider.

An hour later he was at the side of the fire station. He looked at his watch; he had thirty minutes before the German bombers arrived. He moved out of the shadows and as luck had it the fireman called Wolfe was standing just in the doorway and noticed him. Wolfe put a hand inside his jacket pocket to grip the handle of the pistol. 'What are you doing here?'

'I need to speak to you, and the others, it's very important.'

Wolfe called the others, who were standing on the other side of the fire engine. 'What the fuck are you—'

'Spider has a plan to kill your wives.' It came out in a rush of air.

'What did you say?' Asher said, stepping in front of Bob.

'Could we please go into the shadows. If someone sees me speaking to you...' Bob looked around, but there was just the usual traffic and pedestrians.

They moved to the side of the fire station and for the next twenty minutes Bob outlined Spider and Bull's revenge. He gave them the address of the house in Cephus Street.

'Why are you telling us this?' Billy asked.

'I am nothing like Spider or Bull; I just got caught up in the stupidity of it all.'

'If Spider finds out he will kill you,' Wolfe said.

'Hopefully by Monday morning he would not be able to find me.'

'What's your name?' Asher asked.

'Robert Burns.'

'Well, Robert Burns, let me shake you by the hand and thank you for saving our wives' lives.'

'Yes, Thank you,' Wolfe and Billy said in unison, both shaking Bob's hand.

Spider and co. set up the house with buckets of petrol behind each chair to douse the wives.

The next morning, having left Bull and John at Cephus Street, Bob, Spider and George were parked fifty yards from Wolfe's house, making sure his wife was home alone. To Spider's surprise and glee, just after midday the wives of the other two firemen arrived at the house.

'Well, fuck me,' Spider smiled. 'It couldn't be better if I had planned it, all the eggs in one basket.' He turned to Bob and George. 'We'll wait a little longer to make sure there aren't any other visitors.' They nodded silently.

Bob was surprised he thought the firemen would have taken their wives somewhere safe.

Spider looked at his watch; it was just after two o'clock. 'Okay, let's go,' he said.

Bob drove the few yards to park outside the house. The three men walked quickly up the path to the front door. In seconds Spider had it open and entered the house, followed by the other two. Halfway along the hallway he came to a stop on hearing voices coming from behind a door in front of him. With a silly grin on his face he pushed it open saying, 'Good afternoon ladies.' Three heads turned in his direction as Spider, George and Bob moved into the kitchen.

'What do you want?' Eva said belligerently.

Spider ignored the question. 'Tie them up,' he ordered. 'If any of you scream—' he took a pistol from his belt '—I will kill you.' Bob and George tied the women's hands behind them.

'Our husbands will be back soon,' Sarah said, showing no fear.

'No they won't – they are on duty till Tuesday,' Spider sneered, adding, 'Get up.'

Esther, like Eva and Sara, stared defiantly at him. He grabbed Esther, lifting her roughly onto her feet and leaning forward, his face close to hers. 'Don't fuck with me,' he said loudly, the spittle from his mouth falling onto her face. 'Let's get them into the van.' He pushed Eva roughly forward and smiled. 'Perhaps I'll return later, you have some nice pieces of furniture.'

She turned and spat in his face. 'You don't scare us,' she said. 'We've survived worse men than you.'

'You won't think like that when I've finished with you.'

Without warning they gagged the three women. Before leaving the house they made sure that no one was around to see them, and then quickly moved the women to the rear of the van. George followed them into the back.

As he slid onto the driver seat, Bob wondered what the brothers were thinking of, especially their wives being in the same house.

'That was a piece of luck,' Spider said as he moved in beside Bob.

'They are family,' Bob replied as they moved away from the kerbside.

Five minutes later they pulled up outside Cephus Street, dragging the women roughly from the back of the van and into the house. No sooner had they entered than Bull was in front of them.

'Which one's the Irishman's wife?'

'Why?' Bob asked.

Bull stood in front of him, leaning close. 'I have my reasons.'

Spider stepped between them, facing Bull. 'I'll tell you which one when the time is right.' He wagged a finger in front of Bull's face. 'You are not going to start something now,' his eyes were wild, the lips tight, 'or spoil my plan, otherwise.' He left the rest to Bull's imagination.

Bull moved back, lips curled pointing a finger at Spider. 'I want my bit of vengeance too, and you would be wise not to stop me.'

Bob could see things were getting out of hand, and someone – perhaps one of the women – could get seriously injured, and he did not want that to happen. 'We're getting a little heated here for no reason,' he said, stepping between them. 'Spider's plan was working, so let's not let a little pettiness get in the way. You will very soon have what you want—' he looked at his watch '—in two hours.'

'Bob's right,' said John.

Spider and Bull seemed to relax, both lighting cigarettes and moving to opposite sides of the room. Bob moved across to the women, placing a chair behind them to sit on. The eyes of all three were wide with fright, looking at Bull.

*

At the fire station the brothers and Billy stood in front of Chief McNamara, who leapt to his feet, his face showing the shock of what he had just heard. 'So this whatshisname—'

'Spider,' said Wolfe.

'—and this Bull would set your wives on fire because this Spider missed Christmas and New Year with his mother.'

'That's it,' said Billy.

McNamara rubbed his brow. 'And you want us to respond to a fire call at Cephus Street, but you three want to be there before the alarm.'

'That's it, Chief.' Wolfe nodded.

'What happens if it all goes wrong?'

'We have to make sure it doesn't,' said Asher.

'They want to set the house alight. I'm assuming they would use some form of an accelerant—'

'Petrol,' Wolfe interrupted.

'In that case the place would go up like a tinder box.' He looked from one to the other. 'What if we don't get there in time?'

Billy stepped forward, placing a hand on the chief's shoulder. 'We know you will.'

'What's going to happen to these criminals once you save your wives?'

'We have told a policeman friend of ours the situation,' said Wolfe. 'He will be there to arrest them.'

'Okay, off you go, and be careful.'

Leaving their uniforms at the fire station, carrying a long ladder between them, they headed for Cephus Street.

'What if they're armed?' Billy asked.

The three of them had talked about the possibility that they might have to kill Spider, Bull and John, who had done the unthinkable in involving their family in their anger to get at them, and from what O'Brian had told them about Spider, it could well be a fight to the death.

'Make sure we fire first, although I hope we don't have to use our weapons,' said Billy, adding as he looked at Wolfe. 'Did you tell O'Brian we were armed?'

'Yes,' he said. 'We have to do whatever it takes to save our wives. He knows us, Billy.'

They reached the top of Cephus Street and cautiously looked around the corner, seeing the van parked outside the house, but otherwise the street was empty of vehicles and people. They moved quickly along the street, moving to the side of the house where the windows on each floor were broken, just as Bob had told them. They placed the ladder against the wall close to the windows. Asher was the first to climb the ladder to the top floor. He looked quickly through the broken window and then down at the others, giving a thumbs up sign, and climbed through the window. Billy was next, climbing through the second-floor window, its glass missing. Wolfe followed, glancing through the first-floor window, making sure the room was empty before climbing through. The three of them, using rubber gloves, pulled the curtains away from the window to ensure an easy escape route.

On the ground floor Spider cocked an ear to listen, hearing the faint drone of aircraft in the distance. He stood, saying, 'It's showtime.'

John moved towards Sarah, carrying a long piece of rope and tying it around her waist. 'Stand up,' he ordered.

She got to her feet and he pulled on the rope. 'Come with me.' She stood her ground. John gave a sharp tug. Sarah had to move, otherwise she would have fallen to the floor. At the stairs she tried to stop him from pulling her up, but he was too strong for her and she had to follow him. On reaching the top floor he tied her to a chair. 'It won't be long before your husband should be here to save you, but I can assure you he won't.' Spider stood in front of Esther. 'Hey, Bull,' he said loudly. 'This is the Irishman's wife.'

In two strides Bull was in front of Esther, a ghoulish grin on his face, and without a word picked her up, hoisting her onto his broad shoulders and carrying her to the second floor where he dumped her unceremoniously onto a chair, tying her to it. 'I've waited a long time for this,' he said. She cringed back as he touched her breasts. 'Mmm, once I've dealt with your husband, you and I.' He moved across the room to stand by one of the windows.

The drone from the skies above was become louder. Spider turned to Bob and George, 'You two know what to do.' They both nodded and went to leave. 'Bob,' he called as he pulled Eva to her feet, 'I'm relying on you, to be there, see you later.'

Bob waved an arm and moved into the hallway to the front door, making sure George had left. He could see him halfway along Cephus Street, going into the phonebox. He hoped it worked. He turned, walking back into the hallway, moving a piece of sacking aside to reveal a suitcase. He picked it up, walking very quickly to the van and within minutes was driving away, a smile on his face, ignoring everything around him.

Spider tied a rope around Eva's waist, and as he went to pull her up she lifted her feet off the ground and for a second took him by surprise, nearly pulling him to the ground. He moved close, looking into her eyes, a slight smile on his face.

'You won't win,' he said, then turned, placing the rope across his shoulder.

Eva couldn't help but stand, otherwise she would have fallen onto the floor, but she was determined to make it as hard as she could for him. He dragged her into the hallway, moving up the stairs. She tried to resist, pulling backwards, when he suddenly let go the rope and she tumbled down the three stairs. He quickly followed her, picking up the rope and hauling her to her feet.

'Two can play at that game,' he hissed close to Eva's ear and licked it. He then shortened the rope, pulling her quickly up the stairs, her shins scraping on the edge of the steps as she tried to keep up. When they reached the first floor, he turned angrily, swiping her across the face with the back of his right hand and pulling a knife from a sheath tied to his leg with his left hand.

'If you persist in this resistance, I'll cut your face.' She stared defiantly into his coal-black eyes, realising he would do as he had said. He moved across the room, dumping her onto the chair and tying her to it, a red welt appearing on her cheek where he had struck her.

On the top floor John smiled on hearing the fire engines approaching, moved across to a curtain and lit a match, placing it against the bottom of the petrol-soaked curtain, which caught fire immediately. Asher moved from behind the door where he had been hiding. John turned, taking the few steps towards Sarah, but stopped on seeing Asher, surprise showing on his face.

'Where the fuck did you come from?' He waved an arm. 'Never mind.' He took another few steps towards Sarah, but Asher stepped in front of him. The room was bright from the burning curtains, a slight breeze from the broken windows fanning the flames.

John smiled. 'No one to help you now, and no axe.' He pulled a stiletto knife from a sheath inside the sleeve of his jacket attached to his wrist. Bending slightly at the waist and holding the knife in front of him, he moved his right arm left and right

Asher smiled. 'It seems your wrist's okay now.' He could have pulled out his gun and shot John, but that would be too easy. As quick as a flash, he moved forward, his left forearm pushing the knife hand away, landing two quick punches to the stomach. 'Bit flabby there,' taunted Asher. He blocked the knife thrust but was unable to stop the punch with the left, realising that his opponent was no pushover.

'Did you like that?' John sneered, moving quickly in, but his knife met air, receiving a punch to the mouth for his trouble.

'That might keep you quiet.' Asher glanced around the room. He had to end this fight pretty quickly. The curtains were now a roaring inferno, but in that second of taking his eyes from John, he was unable to block the knife entering his left side. He grabbed John's hand with his left as he withdrew the knife, chopping down hard with the edge of his right hand, making John drop the knife.

Asher moved forward, throwing punches at John's head and ignoring the pain and blood coming from the knife wound. At first John was able to block the punches, but the ferocity of Asher's attack had him back-peddling across the room. Asher suddenly realised that John was too close to the curtains but before he could warn him, John tripped over the curtain, landing against it. The fire caught his clothes, which had dabs of petrol on them. He attempted to douse the flames with his hands, at the same time trying to get away from the curtain, and in so doing became entangled in them. He screamed in agony, his hands aflame from the petrol-soaked curtains.

Knowing he could do nothing to save John, Asher was quickly beside Sarah, untying her from the chair and carrying her to the window, quickly realising they needed something for Sarah to stand on to reach the windowsill. He placed her on the floor.

'You're bleeding,' she yelled against the noise from outside and in the room.

He smiled. 'I'm okay, stay here.' He ran across the room, picking up the chair and in a second was beside her. 'There's a ladder against the wall for you to climb down.' He could see the fear in her eyes, and grinned, adding assuringly, 'I've done this hundreds of times.'

He climbed from the chair onto the windowsill, stepping onto the top rung of the ladder and turned to Sarah. 'I'm going to put you over my shoulder.' She shook her head violently. 'It's the only way unless you are able to get onto the ladder yourself.' He could see she was frightened. 'There's nothing to be frightened of, I'm here, it's your choice, but we cannot stay here much longer.'

Just then they were doused with water as firemen below played their hoses onto the building. 'I'll climb down myself,' she said.

'Okay, I'll help if you need me too.'

Sarah climbed onto the chair and windowsill, seeing a river of flame moving quickly down the walls. She turned, lowering her left leg and reaching for the first rung of the ladder. Asher helped place her foot there and gradually they moved down the ladder to where McNamara was waiting.

'What about the others?' he asked.

'I don't know, Billy and Wolfe ordered me not to interfere. Hey, you're bleeding.'

'Knife wound, not sure how deep it is.'

'Stretcher bearer,' McNamara yelled.

Two men ran over, taking Asher's hand away from the wound. 'It's not very deep, but you'll need stitches and it has to be cleaned. We'll take you to the hospital.'

'Sort me out here – I'm not leaving until the others are safe.'

'We'll take your ladder down and put our own against the second-floor window,' said McNamara. He ran over to some firemen, directing them to put their turntable ladder against the second-floor window below the one Asher and Sarah had just escaped from.

On hearing the screams coming from the room above, Bull roared with a loud, shrill laugh. He walked across the room setting the curtain's alight, turning towards Esther that ghoulish smile on his face as he moved towards her.

Esther wanted to scream but knew that's what Bull wanted. She cringed back into her seat as he leant across her, picking up the bucket behind the chair and threw the contents over her head. She gasped from the coldness of the fluid. Placing the bucket on the floor, he went to touch her breasts. 'It won't be long now.'

Suddenly his arm was pulled away and bent backward up his back. 'I'll chop that hand off if you touch my wife again,' a voice he recognised said into his ear.

Bull elbowed Billy in the face with his free arm. Billy let go the arm, reeling back from the blow as Bull turned quickly to face him, going into a boxer's stance.

'I've been waiting a long time for this.' Bull threw a punch, which only found air, receiving two to the face for his trouble.

He shook his head. 'Is that all you've got.' He lumbered forward.

Billy knew he must do something very quickly, knowing that as the fight went on Bull would be able at some point to grab him. He could shoot Bull, but that was not his way. Billy stepped backward, his heel caught on something and he began to fall. As quick as a flash, Bull was on him, wrapping his arms around Billy, entwining his hands in a bear hug. Billy could feel the pressure on his ribs. He kicked Bull in the shins but he ignored it.

In the meantime the flames were catching hold, the walls were now alight. Billy could feel his bones being crushed. He looked around for some way of escaping Bull's hold. The curtains and wall were a flaming mass and if he didn't do something soon he and Esther would be trapped by the fire. He took Bull by surprise by back-pedalling across the room but before Bull could react, Billy's back slammed into the flaming wall. Bull let out a bloodcurdling scream as his hands caught fire. He let go of Billy, stepping back slightly and looking at his hands, trying to out the flames by slapping them against his sides as he hopped around the room, screaming in agony.

Ignoring the pain of his smouldering clothes, Billy stepped in front of Bull, landing a flurry of punches on his face as he had taught Saul. The big man tried to avoid the punches, back-peddling as quickly as he could. Billy saw a window behind Bull. He ducked his head and with a yell ran at Bull, catching him in a rugby tackle, using all his strength to lift the big man off his feet. The momentum took them to the glassless window, and in one movement heaved Bull through it.

As Bull disappeared Billy his one thought was Esther. He staggered over to the chair and untied her. 'We have to get out of here.'

He took her hand, leading her to the window, the room now ablaze. He let go her hand to climb onto the windowsill, glancing behind to make sure the ladder was there. Stepping on to the top rung, he leant over the windowsill, grabbed Esther under the armpits and ignoring the pain in his back, he lifted her onto the windowsill.

Below, McNamara could see Billy was hurt. He grabbed a fireman. 'Steve, run up there and help Billy.' It took a minute for Steve to reach Billy. 'I'm here if you need me, Billy.'

Billy looked round. 'Thanks, Steve.' He turned back to Esther. 'Let me help you down.'

'I can do this,' she said, lowering her foot onto the rung of the ladder.

Billy smiled. 'Of course you can, my angel.' Billy was feeling faint from the pain and his foot slipped, but Steve grabbed him. Billy let out a cry of pain. 'I'm sorry,' said Steve.

'I'm okay.' As they descended, Billy could see Bull lying on the ground. 'How is he?'

'He's dead, broken neck,' Steve said.

On reaching the bottom, Billy collapsed. Two ambulance men were waiting for him. They cut away his clothes covering his burns with a special dressing. Esther was immediately by his side, stroking his face. 'I love you,' he smiled and stroked her face. 'You were so brave.'

'Where's Asher?' he asked the Chief.

McNamara stood by the ambulance as they lifted the stretcher. 'He was stabbed, but he's okay, he won't go to hospital until Wolfe comes out.'

Billy gave a wry smile. 'Brotherly Love, I'd like to stay as well, but,' Esther was holding his hand, 'I have to go.' The two ambulancemen lifted the stretcher into the ambulance.

McNamara took the other hand and shook it. 'See you soon.' He watched the ambulance drive away before turning to the men. 'Get that ladder up against that first-floor window. Let's try and control this fire.'

Spider was leaping around the room, a big smile on his face on hearing the screams from the floors above. He picked up the bucket behind Eva, pouring the contents over her. A high-pitched sound like a demented laugh escaped from his mouth as he ran to the windows and lit a match. Placing the flame to the petrol-soaked curtain, he jumped up and down as each one caught fire. He came to a halt by a window without curtains; a frown creased his forehead and his eyes narrowed. He turned to look in Eva's direction, lips drawn tightly together and took a couple of long strides towards her, pulling the pistol from his waist band.

'I know you're here,' he yelled, lighting a match, stopping a few feet in front of her. 'You'll never be able to save her in time.' He threw the match onto the damp floor in front of Eva. It just fizzled out. He stamped his feet in anger, turning a circle, the pistol held out in front of him. 'Where the fuck are you, firemen?'

Wolfe, who like the others had hidden behind the door, now moved out into the room as water cascaded in, but it wasn't enough to put out the flaming curtains.

'I'm here,' Wolfe said, his voice just audible against the sounds outside and the raging fire inside the house.

Spider turned to face him. 'Do you know what you did to me and my mum?' he screamed, taking a couple of steps towards Wolfe and waving the pistol. Wolfe ignored him as he ran across the room to Eva and began untying her.

Spider's eyes were wide and wild. 'No!' he screamed. 'She was supposed to burn like the others!'

'Are you sure it was they who burnt?' said Wolfe, trying to undo

Eva's bonds and hoping Spider wouldn't suddenly rush him. But Spider just stood there, a perplexed look on his face. 'What do you mean?'

Eva was free. 'Have Bull or your mate John come down the stairs. Look up, the place is an inferno.' He lifted Eva to her feet, whispering, 'Stay behind me. When we reach the stairs run as quickly as you can, McNamara and O'Brian should be waiting outside.' He sidled towards the door with Eva behind him his hands behind his back holding her close as they slid step for step sideways. They had nearly reached the door when Spider yelled, 'No you don't.' He moved quickly across the room to stop them.

Wolfe turned his head. 'Eva, run now,' he ordered. He felt her turn and run towards the door. Spider went to intercept her, but Wolfe stepped in front of him saying, 'I don't think so.'

Spider virtually skidded to a halt, a slight smile on his lips, as he sneered, 'I'll still have her once I've dealt with you.'

'Brave words for someone who let his mother down over Christmas,' goaded Wolfe.

'It wasn't me.' Spider pointed a finger at Wolfe, but before he could say anything else Wolfe said in a calm voice, 'Who stole from innocent people, and got caught trying to rob a jewellers? You, you demented idiot.'

Spider fired, Wolfe dropped to the ground, blood seeping from under him. Spider stood over Wolfe. 'You bastard, you can't die yet, I need vengeance, I need to watch you—'

Eva, on hearing the shot, turned back and saw Spider standing over Wolfe, who was trying to get to his feet. She ran and leapt onto Spider's back. The pistol fell from his grasp, sliding across the floor as she clamped her legs around his thin waist, the forefinger of her left hand digging into his eye, the other scratching his face, tearing off skin as she yelled obscenities at him in Yiddish.

He tried to unseat her like a bucking bronco at a rodeo, but she stuck to his back as he raved and ranted every swear word he knew in anger and pain, stomping unseeing around the burning room. She saw the pistol and leapt from him, at the same time pushing him in the back. He staggered blindly across the room, holding his hands in front of him as a blind man does, but couldn't keep his balance. Spider's hands entered the flames as he tried to cushion the fall. Screaming in agony he got to his feet, shaking his head and trying to open his eyes. His right eye opened to see Eva pick up the pistol. As he lumbered towards her she pointed the pistol at him and pulled the trigger as fast as she could until the hammer clicked. Spider moved slowly towards her, his flaming arms held out, blood pouring from chest wounds.

Hearing gunshots, O'Brian and McNamara with two firemen ran into the building.

Eva stared at Spider as he staggered closer, unable to move. Suddenly someone grabbed her.

'Come on Eva,' O'Brian said, lifting her off her feet.

'Wolfe, what about Wolfe?'

'McNamara has him, we must hurry. This building is about to collapse.'

Behind them Spider fell face down onto the floor. He was dead as the flames moved over his body.

Asher looked anxiously towards the door of the house, ignoring the medics' pleas for them to take him to hospital. He smiled on seeing Eva and Wolfe, but showed concern on seeing the blood gushing from Wolfe's wound. 'Go and see to my brother,' he yelled at the medics.

They moved quickly to Wolfe's side, tearing away his clothes to look at the wound.

'You were lucky,' one of the medics said. 'It hasn't hit any vital organs.' He turned to Asher. 'Could we take you to the hospital now, as I'm sure there will be a lot of other wounded people there after the raid, and you've lost a lot of blood.'

Asher with Sarah's help got to his feet and walked over to his brother, giving him a hug, both not saying anything as they let the ambulancemen put them on stretchers and into the ambulances. McNamara patted Wolfe on the shoulder.

Wolfe said, 'He was so angry, but what got me was, he couldn't see it was his own fault. Where's Billy?'

'Hospital burnt his back, we don't know how badly.'

'Anyone know which hospital?'

'The London,' McNamara said. He suddenly moving towards his men, waving his arms and yelling, 'Get back.'

There was a groan from the house bricks and other debris cascaded down as it collapsed into a pile of rubble dust rose in the air covering those close to it.

'Are we going to the London?' Wolfe asked the medic.

'Yes and your brother.'

The all-clear sounded as Wolfe and Billy were brought into the hospital. The first thing that struck Wolfe was the low moan of wounded patient's, and the swish of the nurses' uniforms as they passed by stretchers or makeshift beds, and their quiet efficiency which seemed to calm the patients. Nurses checked the wounded as they came in to make sure the worst cases were seen first, while other helpers took patients' names, making a copy and pinning it to a board so that any relatives looking for them would know they were in the hospital.

While Sarah stayed with Asher and Wolfe, Eva went in search of Billy and Esther. She looked on the lists on the wall, finding Billy's name: Ward Five. She hurried up the busy stairs to the ward and found the pair.

Billy was asleep. 'How is he?' Eva whispered, not wanting to wake Billy.

'His back is not as badly burnt as we thought; Bull's big hands stopped it from catching fire, but there's an outline of Bull's hands burnt into his back and superficial burns to the skin. The doctor said that they would keep him in for a while to make sure the burns don't become infected, and thankfully he won't need a skin graft. What about Asher and Wolfe, where are they?'

'Asher was stabbed and Wolfe shot.' Eva touched Esther's arm. 'They're okay.'

'What about Spider and Bull?'

'Both dead, as is John. Look I must go and see how the others are. I'm sure we'll catch up later. As soon as I know something I'll come back.' The two friends hugged. 'It could have been worse,' Eva said as they parted.

While the brothers waited to see a doctor, Bob parked the van in Burrell Street, just off the Blackfriars Road. He looked around; the street was empty as people were still in their shelters. Placing a suitcase on the pavement, he opened the rear of the van and took a small bottle wrapped in a rag, nearly jumping out of his skin as the all-clear sounded. Bob undid the cap, spilling the fluid into the van and then, taking a box of matches from his pocket, lit a match and tossed it into the rear of the van. He closed the doors and picked up the suitcase, heading for Waterloo Station whistling 'It's a Long Way to Tipperary'. He didn't look back as the van erupted in flames.

George put on the kettle and lined the cups ready for Spider and the others to return. He didn't hear the bomb that exploded on the house or feel the splinter of glass that cut like a knife into his heart.

12 March 1941

Wolfe, Asher and Billy were playing cards at the Hanover. 'If Sarah doesn't stop fussing over me I'm going to shoot myself,' Asher said.

'We know what you mean,' Billy dealt the cards. 'If that doctor doesn't give me the all clear soon I think I'll shoot him.'

'It's okay for you two, but my wound takes at least seven weeks to heal. I let them keep the bullet.'

'Why didn't you shoot him?' Asher asked.

Wolfe pointed a finger at his brother. 'Okay, I'll ask you the same question, why didn't you shoot John?'

Asher smiled, 'I asked you first.'

'I thought about it when I was trying to get up and he was ranting, but I also thought that would be an easy way out for Spider, and I wanted him to suffer in prison for the rest of his life.'

'Eva stopped that from happening,' Billy laughed. 'I had always said if we want to win the war, send our three wives to Germany.' Wolfe and Asher laughed, nodding their heads.

'Now you know why I always say yes to her.' Wolfe lay down his cards. 'Gin.' He turned to his brother. 'And?'

'I know he wanted to kill me, I could see it in his eyes, but truthfully for what he had done, and was going to do too Sarah, I wanted to punish him.' Asher's face was hard-lips tight. 'I wanted to look in his eyes as I beat him to a pulp, but it was a fitting end, fire with fire.'

For a minute there was silence between them. Wolfe broke the silence, picked up the newspaper. 'That President Roosevelt is a *hamesha mench.*[11] He signed a Lend Lease Pact with the Britain to supply military equipment without payment until after the war.' He pointed a finger at Asher. 'You know what he said?' Asher shook his head. 'He said it's like lending a neighbour a hosepipe to put out a fire. I like him, Roosevelt, must be Jewish.'

'Talking about America, have you heard from Adam?'

'Yes, had a long letter from him yesterday; he said the mood there is they would soon be at war with Japan very soon.' Asher lit a cigarette. 'Sarah was happy that he was there and an American citizen and not in the army here, but if what he said was true, then he would be called up into the American army, but he seemed happy.'

Asher took a wallet from his jacket pocket, sliding some photos from it and showing them to Billy and Wolfe. 'These are my grandchildren: Joseph, he is three and Judy, who is eighteen months.'

'They are gorgeous,' Wolfe said.

'It would be nice if you could visit them,' Billy said, handing back the photos.

'It would have to wait till the end of the war,' Asher said philosophically.

Despite the increasing raids on London docks, with the help of the fire service it continued to function, coping with the flood of imports that kept London's economy flowing. The yards and factories along the river

---

[11] a good person.

still manufactured products vital to the war effort, but for one Government official it wasn't enough.

With the shop gone, and unable to have the heart at the moment to start up again, Sally went to the club in Wapping to help her mother and aunts with the homeless people staying there.

Children ran about the place playing tag; outside they had chalked out hopscotch on the pavement, some of the girls skipped between long ropes, while the boys played war games or football on the flat roof.

As she helped Lily dish out food, Sally said, 'Did you hear about Bevin's idea to recruit women to work in industry?'

'Yes, I saw the poster by the shelter wall. Women of Britain come into the factories,' she said in a deep voice.

Sally smiled at Lily's joke. 'He makes sense, and it would release men for the armed forces. We, the women, could make a difference. I'm tempted to work in a war factory.'

'Why would you want to do that?' Lily asked.

'If I were a man, I would have joined up, but working in a factory producing something that could defeat the Nazis would give me immense satisfaction. Would you want to work in a factory?'

Lily looked at the pram beside her with baby Daniel asleep. 'I would. It beats washing nappies, cleaning the house and all the other things of motherhood, and if I didn't have your mum to help – well, I don't know what I would do.'

'You could join Sophie, her son Samuel and parents in Wales.'

'I asked Jack if he would be joining them. He said no, the Bakery must keep going. Although he's missing them he knows they're safe.'

There was silence between them for a second as they dished out food, smiling at the person holding the plate. 'You know,' Lily looked at Sally, 'I would join Sophie if Isaac was stationed there, but even then I couldn't leave Mama or Papa. Are you really serious about the war factory? You could join the forces.'

'Mmm, very tempting, but like you I couldn't leave Mama or Papa or for that matter Phillip. By staying in London I could still help the war effort, and before you say it, I couldn't work with Phillip as much as I love him.'

'Bevin also said that he would arrange day and night nurseries for young mothers wanting to work, and like you I'm tempted, but I would have to run it past Isaac, Mama and Papa first.'

Just then the siren's sounded, Eva ran out to the street, gathering up the children as they all moved down to the basement.

On 17 April, Wolfe, Asher and Billy were given the all-clear to return to the fire station and the gym. As they left the outpatients department they were like little kids let loose in a playground.

15

The moon shone round and bright in the starlit skies above London. It was a night made more for romance than for war. Some Londoners wondered what the German had in store for them after a few days and nights of relative quiet. Others just wanted to live for the day and enjoy themselves, dance, sing, go to the cinema and the theatre, so that for a moment in time they could forget about the horrors of the Blitz and war.

It was just before eleven o'clock in the evening when the sirens had people throughout the capital running for their shelters.

There seemed to be an angry buzz from the engines of the five hundred and fifty German bombers, which covered some thirty square miles of sky in tiers of a hundred, the Heinkels and Dorniers outlined in the bright moonlight flying over the Kent coast.

At Fighter Command control room they scrambled the night fighters. Isaac waved to his ground crew to take away the chocks. As usual they gave a mock salute, which he returned with a smile, pushed the throttle lever forward and the Spitfire sped across the grass. He pulled back the stick, following Cole's Spitfire as it lifted off the ground.

Just before Tilbury the bombers changed formation as if closing ranks. Flak burst lit up the sky like fireworks, the bomber seeming to lead a charmed life.

Suddenly the moon was hidden by a carpet of bombers that seemed to hover over London and as one they dropped their loads, which literary rained high explosives and incendiaries. The combustion blasts pushed and pulled the the bodies of the firemen, who were trying to contain the flames. Wolfe, Isaac and Billy held the bucketing hose as it poured water onto the houses. The firefighters ignored everything around them as they battled to put out the fires, and keep them from spreading onto other buildings. Luckily the bombs missed the bridges across the Thames whose pumps were helping to pump gallons of water onto hundreds of fires.

'I don't think the Germans like us,' Ashley yelled.

'The feelings mutual,' Wolfe yelled back.

Bombs and incendiaries were still falling, but the firefighters fought on. Asher let out a yell, 'Oh my God,' his face showing disbelief pointing to the street next to them. Wolfe and Billy just had time to see an entire terrace of houses disappear before their eyes, leaving just a pile of bricks and a cloud of dust.

'I hope everyone from that terrace were in their shelters,' Billy yelled, the heat from the fires and wet uniform making his back itch.

Wolfe glanced up, seeing bomber after bomber dropping their bombs. He gave a loud whoop. 'Got you, you Nazi bastard.' The others followed his gaze to see a bomber on fire, diving towards the ground, followed by two parachutes. The airmen struggled as the wind from the flames buffeted them around the sky, trying to control their chutes as they dropped into the flames they had created.

'Whatever happens next,' Billy said, 'that has made my day.' The others nodded in agreement.

*

Isaac looked down; London was a mass of flames. In the bright moonlight he could clearly see the German armada ahead of him, and went through the familiar drill, reflector light on, lowering the seat, gun button to fire, press the emergency boost override. He pushed the throttle lever forward and the Spitfire sped towards the enemy.

The feeling of apprehension he used to have had now disappeared to be replaced by the excitement of combat – some would call it an adrenalin rush. Isaac saw a Dornier ahead of him and manoeuvred for a beam attack. Automatically glancing into the rearview mirror, closing fast on his prey, he judged the distance and pressed the gun button, racking the bomber from tail to front, seeing his tracers hit home.

The Dornier began to lose height its nose dipped, he must have hit the pilot. Tracers come towards him; the gunner of the stricken bomber returning fire, but thankfully missed. His eyes followed the Dornier and as its dive became steeper, black forms left the stricken bomber. He turned away, heading towards the bomber stream slipping behind a tail end Charlie Heinkel. Again he received fire from the alert gunners; he was hit, but not badly.

The intensity of the fire made him break off the attack, diving under the Heinkel. Moving stick and rudder, he came around and up, giving him a two-second burst, and then he was past, dropping, then port wing, coming around for another attack. But there was no need, it was on fire. Isaac wasted no time in moving quickly away, having had one scare of being in close proximity of a bomber blowing up, but not this time.

For a second it seemed to hover and suddenly its port wing dropped and it turned over, going into a slow spin towards the inferno below. Low on fuel, Isaac turned for home and looked down, the shock showing on his face. London was now a conflagration from the east as far as Wanstead to Chiswick in the west, Islington in the north and Elephant and Castle in the south. He hoped Lily, baby Daniel and the rest of the family were safe.

*

Eva, Lily and baby Daniel were in the shelter, the baby fast asleep seemingly oblivious to the sounds outside. 'I wonder how the chickens are,' Eva said.

Lily looked at her mother-in-law, surprise on her face and voice. 'With all that's going on outside, you're thinking of chickens?'

Eva smiled. 'I know it sounds silly, and I should be thinking of the family, hoping they were safe, but it just popped into my head. I mean, what would happen if an incendiary fell near one?'

Lily laughed. 'We wouldn't have to cook it.'

'Do you think it would be kosher? ' Eva laughed.

'Mama, you are silly at times, but that was funny.'

It didn't take long for the Prime Minister down to the firemen to realise the Germans' intentions of setting London aflame. Fire tenders arrived from outlying areas and the various airfields surrounded London.

Some firemen like McNamara's men were inside the fire zone, forming an inner ring. The buzzing sound of engines faded as the Germans made their way back to their bases in Europe, leaving the familiar crackle of flames and crash of falling masonry. Repair crews were quick to mend water mains, but it was a back-breaking job. Gradually the firefighters had begun to win the battle.

As Wolfe, face black, a white film of dust on his wet uniform, walked towards the WVS van, he turned to McNamara. 'This was worse than the night of December 29th. It was as though those—' he pointed skyward '—*mamzers*[12] wanted to set London on fire.'

McNamara gave a wry smile. 'I'm sure that was their intention.'

The all-clear sounded, and with a feeling of apprehension Eva emerged from the shelter; Lily followed with Daniel in her arms. Both looked towards the chicken coop and then at each other and laughed, turning towards the house. Eva said a prayer of thanks to God that it was still standing, and then looked over to see that Sarah and Asher's home was safe and walked towards the fence calling, 'Sarah, Sarah.'

A head popped over the fence. 'I'm here.'

'How are your chickens?'

'What, no I heard that, some people were now homeless,' she shook her fists at the sky, 'because of those *chozzers*[13] and you think of chickens.

'It just popped into her head,' Lily smiled.

---

[12] bastards.

[13] pigs.

Sarah looked across at her coop. 'Mine seem okay; Eva, what's with the chickens?'

'I know it sounds *meshuggah*.'[14] She shrugged her shoulders and turned towards the house.

As the sound of the all-clear died away, people emerged from their shelters; nearly all turning a circle, horror showing on their faces at the devastation they were seeing, which for a minute shook them to the bottom of their boots as they wondered how much more London could take. The raid had lasted six hours and fifty minutes – the longest and most destructive of the war so far.

Many historical buildings were destroyed. The Chamber of the House of Commons with its Gothic variations was just a pile of rubble. The roof of the twelfth-century Westminster Hall was set alight, but most of it had been saved by firefighters. The square tower of Westminster Abbey had fallen, and Big Ben was scarred, but the clock still kept perfect time. The British Museum and St Paul's were damaged, as were all mainline stations. Firemen and rescue workers began the unenviable task of searching for survivors.

Throughout the day the army of rescuers found people alive, or injured, but then there was the sadness of finding those that did not survive.

There were stories of miracles. A couple had their bath land upside down on top of them, protecting them from falling masonry. A baby was born in a cellar as the house above caved in. Day turned into night and still the search went on, many glancing skyward, but the sirens stayed silent.

Wolfe, Asher and Billy and the rest of their fire station moved amongst the rubble calling softly, ears cocked to one side, listening for the slightest sound.

Thousands of Londoners' homes had been destroyed, their possessions – many irreplaceable – lost for ever. The City of London had in the past faced two Great Fires, but this time the Germans had tried to put the entire capital ablaze.

Centres for the homeless were erected in schools and church halls that were still standing. Neighbours offered neighbours a room or two, and the great Blitz spirit that the world had witnessed over the last six months continued. Firefighters were being called 'Heroes with Grimy Faces'.

Wolfe, Asher and Billy stood by the WVS van, enjoying a mug of tea and a cheese sandwich. They had been on the go for thirty-six hours, but

---

[14] mad.

the thought of going back to the station, or home never entered their heads. There had been highs and lows throughout the day, and as night came, once again they left the van to join their team that still searched through the rubble. Volunteers made walls from the bricks as they gradually cleared a street. No one wanted to leave, hoping on hope to find people alive.

Wolfe heard a sound just in front of him and yelled, 'Quiet everyone.' The people stopped what they were doing. Wolfe lay on the ground, ear to the rubble and then, 'We'll get you out,' waving people forward to clear away the bricks and other bits of rubble until they made room to bring a mother and child who were still alive to safety. There were smiles on the dirty faces of the rescue workers as they returned to their arduous task.

It was two o'clock in the morning when McNamara walked slowly among his men who were taking a break. 'When you've had your tea we'll return to the station.'

'We want to carry on searching,' some, like Wolfe, had protested.

'I'm sorry lads, but look at yourselves. You all need a shower and some sleep, so if there's a raid tomorrow we would be prepared.'

Wolfe looked at Asher and Billy, and smiled. 'Why are you smiling?'

'I never noticed before, but you two look like you've been dragged along by a bus.'

The men slowly got to their feet and climbed aboard their fire tenders. Once back at the station, they gave all their attention and last bit of energy to cleaning the tenders and replacing broken equipment.

16

Wolfe was reading the paper when Asher walked into the fire station. 'Have you looked into the Saltzman Brothers' window?'

Wolfe lowered his newspaper looking over the top of the page. 'No, why?'

They don't only have the price of a suit or coat, but also how many coupons you need to buy them.'

'What – we have to give coupons for clothes?' Billy interjected.

'Sixteen for an overcoat, two for—'

'In Petticoat Lane you could buy clothes without coupons, and do you realise there haven't been many raids lately?' Billy interrupted.

'That's because Germany invaded Russia,' Wolfe said, turning the page of the newspaper. 'And if you remember, I told you they would.'

Chief McNamara walked into the room. 'I need you three to help clear some rubble.' They didn't grumble, just put on their jackets and followed the Chief.

At the club, Eva, Sarah and Esther were looking for volunteers to help when there was a bombing raid and they were not around. Freda and Max had returned to ENSA; Sally – who said she never would – and Lily were working in Phillip's factory, producing wings for the new aircraft made from wood. Phillip had a Government contract to produce as many as he could, which meant employing women under the new directive, releasing his men who were eager to join the armed forces. There was a children's nursery where mothers could leave their children while they worked. For Sally and Lily it was an ideal situation, although Eva wasn't too happy about leaving Daniel with a stranger, but Sally won her round by telling her how wonderful the nursery was.

'Does that mean that you might—'

'Not at the moment, Mama,' Sally interrupted with a smile.

Eva found two women she could trust to look after the people at the club and also found two teachers setting up a school in a room upstairs, obtaining help from some of the men to partition the room for younger and older children. The bombing raids were now spasmodic, giving Londoners time to return to their bombed houses, and help clear the rubble.

On 29 June, April gave birth to a little girl whom she called Miriam. On 20 July, at midnight, zero hour in Britain, the BBC began every broadcast to Europe with the opening notes of Beethoven's Fifth Symphony, which was the same in Morse code as V for Victory. Throughout France Belgium and other countries, the V sign suddenly appeared on walls, doors and German vehicles.

The year passed quickly. In October Sally fell pregnant, to her mother's delight. There were raids on London and other cities by the Luftwaffe, but nothing like the scale earlier in the year. The people of East London had prevailed, their fortitude and never-say-die attitude had won the hearts of the people of America and Europe.

'Hey, did you read this?' Asher asked no-one in particular.

'Read what?' Billy asked.

Churchill had pledged to join America within the hour if they went to war with Japan.

'Do we need that kind of *tsoris*?[15] We have enough of our own,' Wolfe said, and held up his hands, stopping someone from saying anything as he hadn't finished. 'Yes, I know about the Lend Lease Agreement, but I didn't know we had a problem with Japan.'

'Even without that declaration,' Billy interjected, 'we might not have a choice if the Japanese attacked Singapore, as that belongs to us.'

'Everything's doom and gloom,' Asher said.

8 December 1941

The music from the radio was suddenly interrupted by the announcer.

'This is an important bulletin from the United Press. On December 7th 1941 there was a surprise attack by three hundred and sixty Japanese war planes on the American Fleet at its home base of Pearl Harbor, in Hawaii. There were over two thousand people killed, five battleships and other smaller craft were destroyed, including two hundred aircraft. A state of war had been declared by America and Britain on Japan.'

Within hours Germany and Italy declared war on America.

'The world's truly at war,' Billy said, looking towards the radio, and then at the brothers as they sat around the table playing cards.

Wolfe fanned the cards in his hand. 'And the war to end all wars twenty-three years ago forgotten.'

'From what I've been reading in the newspapers it was inevitable,' Asher joined in, laying his cards on the table. 'Gin.' The others threw their cards on the table in disgust.

'How come you always win?' Wolfe asked.

'He cheats,' said Billy, glaring at Asher.

'You two are bad losers; anyway I'm a better player.' He picked up the cards to shuffle them when the fire bell went.

---

[15] misery.

*

Lily watched her niece Barbara getting ready for a night out to the West End; she turned to Sarah, a shocked look on her face. 'What's she using for lipstick?'

'Boiled beetroot juice. You can't buy lipstick, or any other sort of make-up unless you know a spiv.' Lily watched her niece go to the fireplace to place some soot on her finger using it as eye make-up. Lily shook her head as Barbara took a pot from the cooker, smearing the contents onto her legs to make them brown. Lily was appalled at what she was witnessing and leapt to her feet walked over to her niece, holding out her hand. 'Barbara Brown, you come with me,' she ordered, turning to Sarah. 'Look after Daniel for a while.'

Barbara looked at her auntie, taking her hand, wondering where she was going to do. Lily led her to her home next door and up the stairs into her bedroom. 'Firstly go to the bathroom—' She waved her, shooing her, 'and take off that stuff on your face and legs.'

Barbara did as she was told and walked back to her auntie's bedroom, wondering what was going to happen next. Her eyes opened wide on seeing the abundance of make-up in a box. 'Pick your colour lipstick; take whatever you need for your eyes, and these.' Lily held out a pair of nylons.

'Are they real?'

Lily laughed at seeing the joy on her niece's face. 'Just try not to ladder them.'

Barbara threw herself at Lily, tears in her eyes, wrapping her arms around her. 'Oh thank you, thank you, I'll be careful.'

Lily held her at arm's length. 'You enjoy yourself, but don't tell anyone where you got them.' Barbara made a zip motion on her lips. 'Go on, get dressed.' Lily returned with her niece to Sarah who asked, 'What have you two been up to?'

'Put the kettle on. I need a cuppa tea, and then you'll see.'

They were sipping tea in the kitchen when Barbara walked in. Sarah's hands went to her face whispering, 'You're so beautiful.'

'Thank you, Mama.'

Sarah looked at Lily, 'Thank you.' Just then Daniel woke up. Lily picked him up, making a face. 'If I smelt like that I'd cry too.'

*

Isaac touched his lips with his forefinger and then the photo of Lily and Daniel that was taped to the dashboard of his Spitfire. The sun shone on the Perspex of the twelve fighters as they slid easily into formation. 'Top Hat control Bulldog squadron airborne,' Squadron Leader Ainsworth said.

'Bulldog leader, Top Hat control, Vector nine zero, thirty plus, Angels twenty.'

'Roger Top Hat control, we are on our way.' As one, the squadron turned towards Dover. They had just reached the coast when someone yelled, 'Tally-Ho, eleven o'clock.'

'Watch out for fighters,' Ainsworth warned.

'Fighters coming down fast,' Cole's voice was calm in Isaac's ears. Ainsworth cut in, 'Blue and Red flights the fighters, Yellow and Green the bombers.'

Isaac had already set his sights and lowered his seat as he pulled back the stick, a smile on his lips, heading towards the diving fighters. He liked this tactic as it was like a game of dare: which one would pull away first? He knew it wouldn't be him. The Messerschmitt and Spitfire closed in at over 300 miles an hour. The German dipped his wing, pulling away slightly and exposing the belly. Isaac gave it a two-second burst and yelled on seeing his bullets strike home following the German round, giving it another short burst.

Fire suddenly appeared along the fuselage. The nose of the stricken fighter came up, the canopy opened and the pilot dropped away, followed by the stalling Messerschmitt. Isaac felt his fighter shudder, he glanced in the mirror: no one there and then to port as a ME turned to come at him beam on. For a second time stood still; he rolled and dived quickly away, the bullets flying past. The ME followed him down he felt the bullets strike home, thinking *this was it.*

Smoke blew backward from his stricken engine. The ME suddenly broke away as a Spitfire attacked it, Isaac yelled, 'Thank you,' and then looked down through the smoke thinking of baling out, but he was too low. He dipped the wing slightly to see if he could recognise where he was and smiled as flames began to lick the canopy. He dipped the wing ever so slightly so he could adjust his descent and straightened out, took his hands off the controls and quickly slid back the canopy, grabbing the controls again. He could see Gorleston beach through the flames. Lifting his arm to keep them away from his face, he glided down, pulled back the stick and the nose came up. There was a slight bump and the fighter slid along the water line; seawater cascaded into the cockpit, dousing the flames and soaking Isaac. The fighter came to a sudden stop, the straps preventing him from moving forward.

He unclipped his mike, took the wet photo from the dashboard and undid the straps, hauling himself out of the cockpit and onto the wing. He could hear the hot engine hissing like a boiling kettle. His left arm was painful. He looked to see his jacket smouldering and knew he had had a lucky escape thanks to the Spitfire pilot. He walked along the wing, carrying his parachute wading through the water and onto the beach to see soldiers running towards him. He walked a couple of steps and collapsed. They lay him on the stretcher and carried him to a waiting ambulance.

Isaac opened his eyes to see a white ceiling; there was a slight smell of disinfectant and another he didn't know. He turned his head to the left to see a line of beds; some of their occupants had their faces and hands bandaged. He went to turn his head the other way when a woman in a nurse's uniform appeared with a smile on her face.

'That's good, you're awake.'

He went to say something but it came out as a croak.

'Have a sip of water,' she said, placing a hand under his head, which she lifted slightly so he could drink from a miniature teapot. She placed the snout in his mouth, tipping it up slightly so he could drink, then took the teapot from his mouth.

'Where am I?'

'You're at the Burns Unit at Queen Victoria Hospital RAF in East Grinstead. You have burns to your right arm and thigh.'

He tried to lift his arm, uncontrollably crying out in pain. 'How bad?' he asked, looking down at the bandaged arm and flexing his fingers. The skin felt tight. *They're okay*, he thought.

'The doctor would give you a better idea than me. Now you're awake, I'll get him.'

She moved away, returning a few minutes later with a white-coated, bald-headed man. He took hold of Isaac's right hand, but did not shake it as he bent slightly forward, a slight smile on his lips.

'I'm Dr Brayden, I operated on you yesterday.' He held up his left hand, seeing that Isaac was about to say something. 'Let me explain your injuries and what we have done so far. We have cleaned the wounds; although I must say you were very clever landing on the edge of the ocean. The salt water stopped you from having some nasty burns and infections to your hands and face. There's a tightness of the skin on your hands and your face, but they are the sort of burns you would get from lying in the sun for too long. But your arm and thigh are a different matter: you have second degree burns. We have bound your wounds with a tulle gras adhesive bandage. Tomorrow we will start you bathing in a saline solution to keep your wounds clean.'

'When can I return to my squadron?'

The doctor sighed and patted his arm. 'I'm afraid I cannot tell you at the moment how long it takes you to heal. You will need a skin graft to your thigh, and I'm not sure about the arm yet.' He stepped back. 'You were lucky, look around you, some of these airmen weren't.'

'What about going home?'

Brayden smiled. 'That's different.' He patted Isaac on the shoulder. 'If you are free of infection, then we'll see.' He turned to the nurse. 'More cream on his hands and face.' He turned back to Isaac. 'The nurse will show you how to apply the cream. I'll see you tomorrow.'

Isaac tried to telephone Lily, but the lines were down. He sent a telegram telling her he had been injured, but was okay.

Two days later Squadron Leader Ainsworth and Cole came to see him. They brought Lily with them. His mother was looking after Daniel.

Lily was crying when she saw him, but they were tears of relief that he wasn't as badly injured as some of the men in the ward.

Isaac quickly realised that he had saved himself from horrific burns by landing on the edge of the sea. He felt guilty at being there as his wounds were nothing compared to most of the men's wounds. They told him they had put themselves in the capable hands of Dr McIndoe, a New Zealander known as The Boss, who gave them hope for a normal life with his ground-breaking plastic surgery and skin grafts. They jokingly called themselves Guinea Pigs and formed a club to that effect.

In the evening, in the nation's hospitals, homes, factories, airfields and army camps, people were glued to the radio listening to the comedy show with Tommy Handley called *ITMA* (*It's That Man Again*) famous for its catchphrases. One favourite was Mrs Mopp, who would say, 'Can I do yer now sir?' Or Colonel Chinstrap saying, 'I don't mind if I do.' Which referred to anything that could be taken home or drunk. Laughter resonated throughout the country.

Four weeks after being shot down, having had a skin graft to his thigh, and with the wounds to his arm healing well, and armed with medication, Isaac went home with strict instructions to keep the wound clean and to return if he was worried in any way, but all he was worried about was how soon he could return to flying.

17

The beginning of 1942 had been comparatively quiet in London as far as bombing raids were concerned. The country settled down to war work with women taking over from the men, releasing them for active service.

It gave Londoners who had lost their homes a chance to find accommodation and for auxiliary services to replenish and renew stocks. In the evenings the cinemas were full, as were the dance halls. The Hanover was booming.

'Did you read about this?' Wolfe looked over the top of the newspaper.

'Read what?' Billy asked as he poured the tea.

'On 16th April the King awarded the George Cross to the Island of Malta.' He dropped the newspaper onto his lap. 'What about the East End – haven't we suffered from the Germans bombing?'

'Malta's a small island, and in a very strategic position to stop the Germans from receiving vital supplies.' Asher nodded his thanks to Billy as he handed him a cup of tea.

'Thanks,' Wolfe said to Billy, shook the newspaper open, shrugged his shoulders and carried on reading. 'Well, blow me down with a feather.' He leant forward. 'Princess Elizabeth has turned sixteen and registered for war service. Now that's one plucky royal.'

Suddenly on 29 April the Germans seemed to remember London, and once again the sirens wailed around the capital, and once again the Germans tried to bomb St Paul's and Westminster Abbey, and at the same time bombed the cities of Exeter, Norwich, York and Bath, trying to destroy Britain's historic buildings and churches. They missed their targets.

Most if not all war information came from the BBC News broadcasts, newsreels, and newspaper reports, but the Government knew how important it was to keep up people's moral by giving them positive war information. The newscaster said, 'Last night one thousand of our bombers raided Cologne dropping two thousand tons of bombs and incendiaries. Our bombers destroyed two hundred factories. This is the end of the bulletin.'

'At last the Germans are getting a taste of their—' the sirens interrupted Asher as they ran towards their fire engine '—own medicine,' he yelled as the bell of their fire engine peeled to ring.

*

It had been six months since Isaac was shot down. He sat impatiently in the waiting room for another check-up of his graft by Dr Brayden, hoping that this time he would give him the all-clear to fly again. He knew he wouldn't be returning to 54 Squadron. Ainsworth told him the squadron had been posted to Australia. Isaac was to stay put for the time being.

The door in front of him opened and a nurse called, 'Flying Officer Brown.' Isaac stood and entered the room.

Dr Brayden walked from behind his desk to greet him asking, 'How are you?' holding out his hand.

Isaac took the offered hand. 'I'm fine, bored out of my mind sitting at a desk while I hear aeroplanes taking off and landing, and fed up with running to shelters every now and again.'

'Okay, let's have a look at the graft.' Isaac stripped down to his pants. 'Lift your arm,' Brayden ordered, bending to touch the graft and skin around it.

'When can I start exercising?'

'Mmm, yes you can start now.' He moved to stand in front of Isaac. 'Light workout at first.'

'What about flying?'

Brayden didn't reply as he took hold of Isaac's right hand. 'Flex your fingers.'

Isaac did as he had been ordered.

'Clench your fist.'

Isaac obeyed again.

'I think you should be ready for flying duties by about September, but I'll need to see you before then, let's say...' Brayden moved back to his chair behind the desk to look at his diary, '3rd September. Get dressed.'

Isaac smiled. 'Thank you sir.'

The Prime Minister announced to Parliament on 20 April that as there was no longer a threat from invasion, church bells could ring once more on Sundays.

'This is the BBC News on June 20th 1942. We have received a report from Czechoslovakia that the Germans have slaughtered all the men and boys from the village of Lidice to avenge the killing of Reinhardt Heydrich, who was the brains behind the Final Solution. All the women and children were taken to a concentration camp.'

'That *mamzer* got what he deserved,' Asher said as he dealt the cards.

'Look at the cost, all the men and boys in one village murdered,' Billy said quietly.

'The Cossacks were just as bad as the Nazis,' Wolfe said.

'Did you read the report in the *Jewish Chronicle* from the Polish underground?' Billy asked the brothers.

'The one about the murder of seven hundred thousand Jews? Yes,' said Wolfe.

'The Nazis won't get away with that,' Asher said.

That evening the family went to the cinema. Newsreels showed Winston Churchill meeting President Roosevelt in Washington. The reporter said, 'The British Prime Minister Winston Churchill's hazardous journey was shrouded in secrecy as he met President Roosevelt in Washington to discuss maximum allied war power on the enemy.'

As they left the cinema Wolfe said, 'Churchill's a brave man flying to America for a meeting with the President.'

'If it were me I'd think twice before doing that,' Asher said.

'I'm sure the entire cabinet were loud in their protests,' Billy said.

Later at the fire station Wolfe was twiddling with the radios knobs. 'Hey, you must listen to this.'

'What's he saying?' McNamara asked. 'And who is it?'

'It's Air Marshal Harris, Head of Bomber Command,' Wolfe said. 'He's speaking in German to the German people saying they should expect devastation by day and night, no matter whether by the RAF and USAF, and he's promised to scourge the Third Reich from end to end.'

'Now that's fighting talk,' McNamara said.

On 11 August as the new Waterloo Bridge was opened, Abraham with the rest of the battalion was notified that they would be leaving for North Africa in November.

In homes, factories, airfields and army camps, the music was interrupted by the newsreader. 'This is a special announcement from Buckingham Palace,' the voice was quiet and solemn. 'The Duke of Kent, the King's younger brother, was killed while on a visit to Iceland when his Sutherland Flying Boat crashed. This was not due to enemy action.'

On the first Sunday in September Sally and Phillip announced they were expecting a baby, in late May or early June. There was a big smile on Eva's face as she cuddled her daughter. Two days later Freda and Max paid them a surprise visit to tell them that Freda was pregnant. It looked like May or June 1943 would be a busy month, but Eva didn't care. Her daughters were at last pregnant.

18

The flight sergeant stripes were still comparatively new as were the pilot wings on Saul's left breast as he entered the hangar to be greeted by the hundreds of loud voices. He was here to find six men to make up a bomber crew. He had made up his mind before entering the hangar the sort of men he wanted. He wandered around, shouldering his way through the crowded hangar, and then he saw him, a slightly built sandy-haired man with navigator wing, a red and white scarf around his neck. Saul approached him, 'Arsenal fan?'

The navigator smiled. 'Red and white through my veins,' he said with a slight cockney accent.

'Care to join my crew, Sergeant?'

The navigator smiled and held out his hand. 'Harry Silver.'

Saul took the outstretched hand. 'Saul Brown.' He let go the slim-fingered hand, 'Two down, five to go.'

'What sort of person you looking for?' Harry asked.

'No officers, but I'm sure I'll know them when I see them. What sort of crewman do you want in your aircraft?'

'People with a good sense of humour, who don't gripe, and are good at their job.'

'How do you know I'm a good pilot?'

Harry smiled. 'You support Arsenal.'

They walked slowly around the hangar. 'Over there,' Saul said, gesturing to a flight sergeant reading a Polish to English dictionary. Above the sergeant stripes on his sleeve was the word 'Polish', the half wing on his left breast showing he was a bomber aimer and front gunner. 'Would you care to join my crew?' Saul asked.

'Are you sure?' the Pole said, his accent pronounced. 'I must tell you that I'm Jewish, and if—'

'That isn't a problem,' Saul interrupted in Yiddish. 'My name is Saul Brown.'

The man smiled holding out his hand, 'David Cheskowski.'

Saul gestured to the navigator. 'Harry Silver.'

Cheskowski took Harry's hand who said in Yiddish. 'Where in Poland you from?'

'Warsaw,' was the surprised reply.

'Oh my,' Saul said, 'what are the chances of this happening?'

'Thousand to one, probably more for three of us to meet,' Harry said.

'David, have you met anyone you think could join our crew?'

A big smile lit up the Pole's face. 'Radio operator, he was the only one apart from you that spoke to me.' He pointed. 'He's just there.' Cheskowski led the way, his broad shoulders shrugging other airmen aside until they were in front of the radio operator.

Saul leant forward to be heard amongst the sound of hundreds of voices. 'Have you found a crew yet?'

'No, not yet,' was the yelled reply.

'Would you like to join my crew?' Saul gestured towards the other two.

Brown eyes stared at Saul for a second as though summing him up, and then at the other two. He smiled and held out his hand. 'Flight Sergeant Andy Anderson at your service.'

Saul took the outstretched hand. 'Saul Brown, Harry Silver and David Cheskowski.'

'Now we are four, three to go,' Saul said.

'Who do we need?' Andy asked, adding. 'I know a great engineer.'

There was a big smile on Saul's face, which changed as he asked. 'Is he an officer?'

'No, Flight Sergeant Names, Oliver Moore met him on the train coming here. Stay here I'll go get him.' Five minutes later Andy returned with a slightly built young man with slicked-back brown hair; the hazel eyes smiled on being introduced to the others.

'Would you like to join the crew,' Saul asked, somehow knowing the answer before he asked it, but he had to ask.

'Love to,' was the reply.

'All we need is a couple of gunners and we are complete, just then a ginger-haired man, who looked about fourteen with a big smile on his face moved in front of him, the half-wing on his tunic having the G on it.

'Would you like to join our crew?' He swept an arm around the other four.

He nodded. 'Yes, Guv,' he said in a broad cockney accent grabbing Saul's hand to shake it as he said, 'Paul James, everyone calls me Ginger.' The others introduced themselves.

Taking a chance that Ginger might know someone from gunnery school he asked, 'Ginger, we need a tail gunner. Do you know anyone?'

Ginger gave a nod. 'Won't be a mo.' Within minutes he arrived back with a sergeant. 'Here's your tail gunner, Guv. Name's Derek Dickenson.'

'Hey you're the jockey that won the third race on the last day of Ascot,' Andy said. 'I won a few bob on you that day.'

Dickenson smiled. 'You owe me five per cent.'

The crew laughed at the joke.

'Okay lads, let's go over to the NAAFI and get to know each other,' Saul said.

The following day they were given travel documents to RAF Station Wigsley, Lincolnshire, part of Five Group, for conversion to heavy bombers. Saul was excited that at last he would be able to fly the Lancaster, but before the crew could do that the gunners were sent to Fulbeck a specialist gunnery school, where they were taught deflection shooting, which was essential because of the movement of the attacking aircraft and that of their own. The gunners used camera guns so at the end of their session they could see how well they had done. Ginger was a natural and cottoned on right away, he had an 80 per cent kill, but it took Dickenson a little while to adjust; the surprise was Cheskowski with 95 per cent.

Saul with an instructor and the crew took to the air in a Wellington Bomber. The instructor showed Saul an evasive action called the corkscrew by doing a steep dive and a climbing turn in alternate directions. It was thought that this made it difficult for a fighter pilot with fixed-wing guns harder to aim.

Against the size of the Wellington the Lancaster mark 111 was huge, nearly twice the size, being sixty-eight feet in length, a wing span of a hundred and two feet. The armament consisted of four Browning .303 machine guns in the rear turret, two in the mid-upper turret, and two in the nose turret.

There were day and night flights, which simulated operational conditions as much as possible; bombing runs with a variety of fighter aircraft pretending to be Germans attacking them. The crew were given a pass by the instructor; they were ready – well, as ready as they would ever be – for operations.

The crew were excited as they entered RAF Station Elsham Wold in Lincolnshire to join 103 Squadron whose emblem was a swan, its wings elevated and addorsed. The squadron's Latin motto was *Noli me tangere* ('Touch me not').

The crew were given a new mark 111 Lancaster and with the Squadrons Flight Instructor, Flying Officer Martins took to the air. After their second flight Saul spoke to the flying instructor. 'Excuse me, sir, but would it be possible for me to swap my crew around? For example, if my radio operator was killed or badly wounded I would have someone else in my crew that could take over the job.'

'It's a good idea, and I see no reason why you couldn't as long as it doesn't jeopardise the aircraft.'

'Thank you, sir.'

Saul gathered the crew in a circle around the table. 'I would like to run through my idea with you.' He took a pack of cigarettes from his pocket, handing it around as they lit up he said, 'I want you to change positions with various members of the crew, so if anything happened to one of us, another crew member could take his place. Everyone must learn to handle the machine guns. I have engineering experience, so I'll be Oliver's second. Anyone have flying experience?'

Harry raised a finger. 'Failed on landing, although I thought it was okay.'

'Harry is the second pilot.'

'I know a bit about radios,' said Cheskowski.

'Right you'll be Andy's second.'

'I'll second Harry as navigator,' said Andy.

'Ginger, you're the medic with Derek.' Saul pointed to them.

'Okay, Guv,' they said in unison.

'Anyone want to add anything else?' There was silence. 'Okay, starting tomorrow you will learn your second jobs.'

On the last tutored flight, Saul had the crew changed over to their allocated second jobs. At the end of the exercise Flying Officer Martins shook each crew member by the hand. 'Very impressive,' was all he said.

The next day they reported with the rest of the squadron to the ops room.

*

For Isaac the months since his crash landing had gone slowly. He was itching to get back into the cockpit of his fighter. The only good thing was spending more time with Lily and Daniel. He waited with baited breath for Dr Brayden to stop writing his notes. He blotted the page and looked up with a smile on his face. 'You have healed very well and you are fit to fly combat missions.' Brayden stood holding out his hand. Isaac took it. 'Thank you very much for all you have done for me.'

'All in a day's work, but it was your quick thinking that saved you from some nasty injuries.' Isaac left the office with a spring in his step, virtually running to the station, knowing that the squadron based at Hornchurch flew Spitfires.

On reaching Hornchurch Isaac went straight to the Commanding Officer's office, and knocked on the door, entering on hearing, 'Come in.'

Squadron Leader Baxter smiled on seeing Isaac who stood to attention and saluted, 'Flying Officer Brown reporting for duty, sir.' Isaac smiled as he handed Baxter a brown buff envelope.

Baxter took the envelope slitting it open with an ivory handled stiletto knife, saying as he extracted the papers from it, 'Dr Brayden warned me to expect you, and that you would want to go on ops immediately.'

'Yes, sir, that's the general idea.'

'Sorry, Brown, but I have orders to send you to number three advanced training school.'

'That's for twin aircraft training. I'm a fighter pilot.'

I know you're a very good fighter pilot, but they need you for something else, and I'm sure in a couple of months you'll change your mind.'

Isaac stared silently at Baxter waiting for him to add to the statement, but he just picked up a folder, giving it to Isaac. 'Hand this in to the orderly room when you get to South Cercey and here are your travel documents.'

For a second Isaac couldn't believe that after all the months of waiting to fly a Spitfire again, he was being sent to a training squadron. Then it hit him: advanced training, now he was intrigued; advanced training for what? He took the documents and saluted.

Baxter returned the salute with, 'Good luck.'

Isaac managed to send a message to Lily, telling her he had been posted, and would get in touch as soon as he could.

*

The propellers gradually slowed to a stop, and there was silence, except for hissing sound of the hot engines cooling down. Saul sighed and wearily lifted himself from the seat, walking slowly and carefully amongst the spent shell casing towards the open doorway following the others as they stepped from the aircraft. Saul hoisted his parachute onto his broad shoulders.

'Well done, lads,' he said. 'Let's get debriefed and have some breakfast.'

Later, after a shower he decided to try and get through to Hannah, who had been in his thoughts constantly, wondering what she would say when she saw him with his pilot wings. On his last leave, before the end of training he went home in civilian clothes. He dialled the number which was answered immediately. 'Ruby's.'

He smiled. 'Hello my angel, how are you?'

'I'm fine, and you?'

'I'm okay; look I've been thinking, when I get there, please make sure the whip is nowhere at hand.'

'Why, you done something wrong?'

'I'm not saying anything that might incriminate me. I'll see you soon.'

11 November 1942

As Abraham and Gus sailed for North Africa, Isaac took to the skies in a twin-engine Oxford. He did not hear church bells ringing throughout the country in a peel of jubilation in recognition of the British victory against Rommel's Africa Corps at El Alamein. Over the sound of the bells was the radio announcer's excited voice. 'Could you hear that in Occupied Europe? Do you hear that in Germany.'

People watched in awe as newsreels showed the British advance, and the capture of thousands of German prisoners. Captured German film showed Rommel Africa Corps retreating.

Wolfe looked over Billy's shoulder at the newspaper laid out on the table, pointing to the article about Sir William Beverage's plans for a postwar welfare state where the entire population would pay into a compulsory insurance scheme giving protection against sickness, unemployment and old age, with free medical and hospital treatment to everyone. He recommended that the Government establish a Ministry of Social Security to handle it.

Billy turned his head to look at Wolfe. 'Firstly, get your own paper, and secondly, yes I agree, it's a great idea, but as sure as eggs are eggs, people would find a way to abuse it.'

It was the first time in many weeks that on the last Sunday in November Wolfe, Asher and Billy had been able to have a weekend get together.

Although Isaac, Abraham and Saul were not there, Lily and April were there with the children, Daniel and Miriam. There was a lot of banter amongst the men as usual, but the talk amongst the women was the pregnancies of Sally and Freda. It was then that Lily said quietly, 'I'm pregnant again.'

Eva a big smile on her face asked, 'When?'

'July, I haven't told Isaac yet.' She gave a wry smile. 'I don't know exactly where his is.'

Isn't that typical, Hannah thought. *I don't know where Saul is either, just that he is on a special course and would be home soon.* In reality she was slightly jealous that her future sisters-in-law were pregnant. She had been toying with the idea for some time, but hadn't had a chance to talk to Saul. She wanted to get married as soon as possible, but where was the potential groom?

Her thoughts were interrupted by a knock at the door. Wolfe went to answer. A young boy handed him a telegram. 'Thank you,' he said in a surprised voice, thinking the worst. He walked slowly back to the dining room opening the envelope. He took out the message, looked at it for a second and then up at Eva, who placed her hands on her chest, whispering. 'Who?'

'It's Jack.'

'How, it's supposed to be safe in Wales,' Sally said, looking shocked.

'There's a phone number here. I'll call; perhaps the line will have been repaired by now.' He moved across the room to the phone, picked up the receiver to hear the dialling tone and dialled the number on the telegram, which was answered immediately.

'Hello Sophie,' he said softly. 'I have just received the telegram that Jack was killed – how?'

Wolfe listened intently to the voice at the other end, now and again saying, 'Yes,' until the voice had finished speaking. 'What do you want us—' Wolfe nodded silently as the voice interrupted him. 'Okay, we would meet you at the station. I'll make the burial arrangements this end and they would meet the train. Okay, thank you.'

He replaced the receiver looking down at it for a second then up at the people in front of him and said solemnly, 'Jack was on his way to be with Sophie and the baby for the weekend, he had just left the station when a low-flying German bomber trailing smoke from one of its engines dropped its bombs, which fell onto the houses Jack was passing. He was caught in the blast; a piece of shrapnel pierced his heart. Sophie wants me to make the funeral arrangements; they will arrive tomorrow with Jack.'

Hannah just caught Eva as she began to fall and helped her onto the chair, tears streaming down her face as she repeated over again, 'Poor Jack,' rocking backward and forward as Wolfe cuddled her. Gradually she stopped, looked at Wolfe, but not really seeing him. 'Eva, I'm going to make the funeral arrangements, we must let everyone know.

Wolfe went to see the rabbi with Asher, explaining that his son's body would be arriving on ten past two train to Euston.

'Don't worry, Mr Brown, we will be there and do all that would be necessary for the funeral on Tuesday,' he looked at the book in front of him, would 12.30 be convenient?'

'Yes, thank you, Rabbi, for your help.'

'That's what I'm here for.'

Whilst Wolfe and Asher were making funeral arrangements Billy sent telegrams to the addresses the women had for Isaac and Saul.

On receiving the telegram Saul went to his CO. 'Flight Sergeant, you and your crew are due a week's leave. You can start tomorrow. I'll have the orderly room set it up.' He stood holding out his hand. Saul took it, 'I'm sorry to hear about your brother.'

'Thank you, sir.' Saul stood to attention, saluted and left the office to tell the crew. Cheskowski had nowhere to go, so Harry invited him to spend his leave with him, his wife and children.

As luck had it, Isaac was not too far away, having arrived two days earlier at RAF Horsham St Faith near Norwich to join his new Squadron flying Mosquito 1Vs.

On receiving the telegram he went immediately to his CO, who showed compassion to his new Flying Officer with the DFC on his chest. 'I am only able to give you a seventy-two-hour pass, I need all the pilots I could get.'

'I understand, sir, thank you. What about my navigator?'

'I'll make sure he isn't too lonely without you,' the CO smiled.

Isaac saluted and left the office to pack a few things explaining to his navigator what was happening. 'I'm sorry Fred to leave you like this. The CO did say you wouldn't be too lonely without me.'

'Sorry to hear about your brother.' Fred Summerton gave a wry smile. 'I could imagine what the CO has in store for me; you better hope it's nothing nasty.'

Isaac picked up his gas mask. 'See you in a couple of days.'

Outside the base he took the bus to Norwich Station to get the train to Liverpool Street.

Saul took the underground to Aldgate, wondering what Hannah would say on seeing the pilot's wing on his left breast. He had promised her and his mother not to put himself in danger, if they only knew what it was like dropping bombs on Essen with the flak and night fighters trying to shoot him down, she would kill him herself. He walked slowly towards the house, remembering how his brother Jack loved to bake; Sundays were a feast of his skills. He wondered what would happen to the bakery now.

He decided to knock on the front door. Within seconds it was opened by Wolfe, who stood for a second staring at Saul, noticing the pilot's wings. He stepped forward and hugged his son, kissing him on both cheeks.

'I'm happy you were able to come.' He let go of Saul and took a step sideways. 'Hannah is here.'

Saul nodded and stepped into the house, saying, 'Where is she?'

'She's in the kitchen with your sisters.'

Saul strode towards the kitchen and entered. Hannah had her back to him, pouring water into a teapot. Eva was the first to see him.

'Saul.' There was sadness in the way she said his name, which made him move towards her, kneeling to cuddle her. He kissed the tears from her cheeks not saying anything. Hannah turned from what she had been doing and stepped towards him, coming to a full stop on noticing the pilot's wings. He moved away from his mother and got to his feet to face Hannah. 'I was going—'

'When?' she asked quietly. 'When we get a telegram that you had been killed?' He moved towards her. 'How long have you?' She pointed to the wings.

'A few months, I'm—' He was at a loss what to say, knowing full well he should have told her sooner.

Hannah stayed silent, not wanting to cause a scene; there was enough sadness in the house. 'When do you have to go back?'

'I have a week's leave.'

Isaac arrived just as Wolfe was about to leave for Euston. Isaac and Saul decided to go with their father to make sure he would be okay.

Everything went as the rabbi had promised. They all hugged Sophie as she got off the train with her parents and young Samuel.

*

The ceremony at the burial ground was over, the mourners and the families went back to Eva and Wolfe's house where the Shaffers had insisted on catering the table for those coming back to the house.

'Are you going to stay in London now?' Eva asked Sophie.

Sophie looked down at her hands around the cup, which was now empty, and then looked up at her mother-in-law. 'We would be returning to Wales at the end of the week of mourning.'

'But Sophie, we are here. It's best you be amongst family.'

'What happened to Jack was a freak accident...' tears streamed down her face '... and it's my fault.'

Eva took the cup from her hand. 'How is it your fault? You never dropped the bomb.'

'I asked Jack to come as I was missing him. He was due to come next week. If I hadn't pleaded with him to come, he would still be alive today.'

'It's not your fault, please don't blame yourself. As you say, it was a freak accident, but I wish you would reconsider staying in London. This is your home.'

Sophie stayed silent, knowing that whatever she said wouldn't be appropriate at that time.

'You've been pretty quiet,' Isaac said to Lily. 'Is anything the matter?'

'I'm pregnant.'

A smile lit up his face. 'That's fantastic.' He moved towards her, but she stepped back.

'That's fantastic,' she mimicked. 'It's fantastic for whom? You? It's okay for you traipsing around the sky, but how many times have you been in London during the Blitz? Two, three times? Why would I want to bring a child into a world war?'

He was silent for a moment, and then said, 'Would you like to go with Sophie to Wales?'

'No, not really, it's just—'

He smiled. 'Would you like to go to Paris?'

Lily burst into laughter and stepped closer to him. 'I suppose I am happy about the pregnancy, and your mother is over the moon, two daughters and a daughter-in-law pregnant. When do you have to go back?'

'Thursday night.'

People arrived to pay their respects and for evening prayers. Saul was pleasantly surprised when Harry and Cheskowski arrived. He introduced them to his family and Hannah who smiled at them. 'Thank you for coming.'

At the end of the week of mourning, against Eva's pleas, Sophie, her son Samuel, and her parents returned to Wales.

Hannah had waited till everyone had left and the house had returned to normal before confronting Saul. She cornered him in the kitchen. 'I want to talk to you.' He stood still as she moved in front of him. 'Of all the scheming conniving things you could have done was not telling me you were training to be a pilot.'

He looked at her hands, making sure she wasn't holding the whip. 'I knew you wouldn't approve, and I didn't want to worry you.'

'I'm worried already, but before you think you've got away with it, you owe me.'

Inwardly he breathed a sigh of relief, expecting a tirade of abuse. 'What is my debt?' He tried to keep a straight face, but couldn't help a little smile. 'No whip, that's a relief.'

'Yes, you're lucky I'm not at home. I want to get married as soon as possible and have a baby.' She smiled. 'Otherwise the whip would see daylight.'

'I only have two days of my leave left; I don't think I could arrange a wedding and baby in two days.'

She smiled. 'I can.'

'We need the rabbi's permission, and I think I need to get permission from my CO—'

'So, what are you waiting for?'

'We have to speak to Mama and Papa first, don't we?'

'Yes, you're right.' She grabbed his hand. 'Don't just stand there.'

By the time Saul returned to Elsham Wold, everything but the date of the wedding had been arranged. All he had to do now would be to get permission from his CO and find out when he could have leave to marry.

As the year came to an end, cinemas were showing war films, the most popular being *In Which We Serve*, written by Noël Coward. Audiences cheered at the end of the film. Bogart and Bergman steal the screen in *The Maltese Falcon*.

19

The synagogue was packed with family and friends. Wolfe was amazed that everyone they had invited was able to attend. Saul with Isaac in their best blues the pilots wings proudly on their left breast looked back waiting for Hannah to appear. Harry Silver winked at Saul, who sat in a line with the rest of his crew and Isaac's navigator Fred Summerton. Freda sat next to her sisters Sally and Lily, their bulge of pregnancy showing on them. The girls from Ruby's sat behind them.

Across the other side Phillip and Max were deep in conversation when suddenly the synagogue went quiet as Hannah stood framed in the doorway on the arm of Asher. She had asked Asher and Sarah to give her away in place of her parents. There were gasps from the women at her beautiful wedding dress. The V-neck of the empire line showed just enough cleavage to be tasty with folds that flowed down to the ground with a small train. She carried a bouquet of long-stemmed lilies. The veil could not hide her smile with just enough make-up to show off her beauty. At last she stood beside Saul, who grasped her hand, whispering, 'You're beautiful.'

The ceremony over, the smiling couple walked hand in hand from the synagogue to make their way to the Shaffer's restaurant for the reception.

Isaac was pleasantly surprised when speaking to his brother-in-law Phillip that his furniture making factory was turning out parts for the Mosquito. He didn't tell him that he was flying one. Saul introduced his crew to Hannah, each giving her a peck on the cheek.

Only too soon the party was over and people parted, not knowing when or if they would see each other again. Hannah and Saul took a taxi to the Dorchester hotel for a honeymoon weekend as he and the crew had to report back for duty on Monday. Isaac and Fred had not been so lucky: they only had a twenty-four-hour pass.

On 3 March tragedy struck the East End. It was a very orderly crowd of people that made their way to Bethnal Green underground station shelter, when a woman carrying a baby tripped and fell, as she did so she knocked over an elderly gentleman, and they blocked the way down the steps. Within seconds a hundred and seventy-eight people were crushed to death as those outside, unaware of what was happening in front of them, pushed forward. It was the worst civilian disaster of the war so far.

On the same day, Wolfe, Asher and Billy played their hose as usual onto a raging fire. Large splinters of glass from exploding windows flew through the air like arrows. Suddenly Billy fell to the floor, his face a grimace of pain. Yelling as loudly as he could, Wolfe called Chief McNamara, who seeing Billy on the ground called other firemen to take over the hose.

'What's the matter?' Wolfe asked as Billy clutched his thigh, blood seeping through his gloved fingers.

Wolfe and Asher knelt beside him, concern on their faces as Wolfe gently pulled Billy's hand away for them to see a long piece of glass protruding from his jacket. 'Fucking Ada,' said Asher.

'I second those sentiments,' Billy said between tight lips, his face showing the pain he was in.

McNamara took one look at Billy. 'Asher go get the ambulance crew,' he ordered.

'It must have been travelling at some speed to penetrate his jacket,' Wolfe said, looking up as the ambulance crew arrived. Within minutes Billy was on a stretcher and being carried into the ambulance. Wolfe turned to McNamara with a questioning look. 'You and Asher go with him; we can manage here.'

The brothers leapt into the rear of the ambulance, which with bells ringing sped off as the medic tended to Billy the brothers looking on with worried faces.

'Is he going to be okay?' Asher asked the medic as he listened to Billy's chest and gave him a painkiller injection. They pulled into St Bartholomew's Hospital. Billy was quickly wheeled into the accident centre. Wolfe and Asher were made to wait in the waiting area as wounded from the bombing began to arrive.

'Should one of us go and tell Esther?' Wolfe asked, knowing already what they must do. Wolfe spotted a messenger boy and ran across to him. 'Are you doing anything important right now?'

'No sir.'

'Could you run a message for me?'

'Yes sir.'

Wolfe quickly wrote a message on a piece of paper. 'Do you know the old youth club in Wapping?'

The boy smiled. 'I know you, mister; you taught us boys how to box. I'll go as quickly as I can.' He took the paper and was off as quick as a flash.

The doctor came from behind the curtain and the brothers converged on him. 'How is he, doctor?'

'He's been lucky, it missed any vital organs, but we'll have to take him to the operating theatre to get the glass out, making sure there are no other fragments there. Sorry we had to cut his clothes away to get a good look at the wound.'

Just then Esther arrived with Eva and Sarah in tow. 'How is he? What happened? Did he fall off a—'

'Slither of glass in his thigh,' Wolfe interrupted her.

'Is it—' Esther couldn't get the rest of the question out as she began to cry.

'The doctor said it missed any vital organs,' Asher said.

'They have to take him to theatre to get the glass out.'

They sat in the waiting room while they operated on Billy. An hour and half later a nurse came in. 'Mr Reid is back from surgery. Just two of you. At a time he's still a bit groggy.'

Esther sighed and for the first time since arriving at the hospital smiled. 'Thank you nurse.'

She took Eva and Sarah's hand. 'Come with me?'

'But the nurse said—'

'I'm sure they won't mind,' Esther interrupted Sarah.

The three women left the waiting room, moving into the ward. Billy saw them, and smiled. Esther grabbed his hand, bent and kissed him. 'I'm okay, and they got all the glass out, I'd show you, but I'm naked and I don't want to make Eva and Sarah jealous.'

Esther slapped him gently on the shoulder.

Eva could see he was groggy from the anaesthetic. 'You look tired, she said, the boys want to see you, and then we'll go, we'll return tonight.'

Esther could see her friend was right. 'You rest my darling; I'll be back at visiting time.'

No sooner had they left than Wolfe and Asher entered the ward. 'How are you feeling?' Asher asked.

'A little tired, and sore.'

'At least you're okay,' Wolfe said.

'That piece of glass could have gone anywhere. The doctor told me it was twelve inches long, and just over two inches thick. The end that penetrated my thigh was pointed like a spear.'

'You were lucky,' Asher pointed out.

'Anyway, you're okay.' Wolfe patted his friend's shoulder. 'We'll let you sleep.'

Three days later the doctor told Esther, 'Mr Reid could go home tomorrow. Make sure he doesn't do anything for two weeks.' He gave a wry smile. 'No running up ladders or weights in the gym. I'll make an appointment for three weeks to take out the stitches. He's driving me mad to let him go back to work. Here are some tablets if he is in any pain.'

'We'll put him in chains if we have to.' Asher smiled.

Esther took the tablets and prescription. 'Thank you doctor.'

He patted her arm. 'He will be okay with a few weeks' rest. Sorry but I must go. You can take him home in the morning.'

Billy had only been home a couple of days when they received a telegram that their youngest child, Ariel, was dead, and who to get in touch with for any funeral arrangements.

The following day they went to the morgue to identify their son, who had just received his call-up papers. They had already spoken to the rabbi and the funeral was to be the following day.

'How did he die?' Billy asked, stroking his son's red hair.

'He was on a bus when the air raid went off. The driver tried to get them to a shelter, but he wasn't fast enough. The concussion of the blasts sucked the air from his body. There were ten other people on the bus.'

'Thank you,' Esther said, the tears streaming down her face.

20

While Billy sat at home healing, Wolfe and Asher were heading once more towards the docks. The heavy drone and beat of bombers' engines drowning out the wail of the sirens.

'It's strange not having Billy here,' Wolfe yelled to Asher.

'I saw him last night. You could see the frustration, and if he does something he shouldn't, Esther is there in a second.'

'Esther's having a hard time. It's like trying to tame a lion, but it's a good thing after Ariel's death.'

Wolfe's face was grim. 'That's a tragedy.'

The fires were contained. Soaked and soot-faced as usual, Wolfe and Asher with the rest of the crew headed back to the fire station, knowing that apart from a nuisance raid by one or two German fighters, the Germans would not return tonight. Maybe tomorrow. The big armada of bombers were now a thing of the past as Germany's Luftwaffe was needed in other theatres of the war.

As they cleaned the fire tender Wolfe said to Asher, 'What Billy needs is a hobby.'

'What do you have in mind?'

'We could take him some knitting needles and wool.'

Asher burst into laughter. 'If you did that, he'd probably stick the needles up your bum.'

'I know that sounds silly, but we need to find something to keep him busy, but what?'

'In Billy's case, that's a dilemma.'

Not far away, Billy took his coat from the hanger in the hall, but before he had even done the buttons up Esther was beside him. 'And where do you think you're going?'

'It's a pretty nice day, I thought I'd—'

'Go to the gym, the fire station.'

He sighed: she could read him like a book. She stood in front of him and stroked his cheek. 'I know it's hard for you this sitting around, but you were lucky. You have to let the wound heal, and then you would be able to exercise, within reason, and be at the fire station.' He went to protest, but she held up a hand. 'Why don't you take a cab to the Hanover, have a look at the books, stroll around and make sure everything's okay. I'm sure Frank could do with a break.'

He smiled, taking her hand and kissing it. 'You're right as usual, and that's a good idea, but I'll take the underground. The walking would be better than sitting here.' He kissed her. 'See you later.' He put on his fedora hat, taking gloves from his pocket as he strolled up the street, a slight smile on his face.

*

At the fire station the men were as usual listening to the war news. 'We have reports from Warsaw that Hitler has given orders for General Stroop to clear out the Jews from the Warsaw Ghetto. The Jews are fighting back against troops armed with machine guns and rockets.

'Saul's bomb aimers from Warsaw,' Wolfe butted in on the announcer's last bit of news.

'On the home news, the Prime Minister has said that as there is no threat of invasion church bells can ring once more throughout the country. This is the end of the news.'

Just then Billy walked into the station holding his uniform, Wolfe and Asher leapt from their cheers with a whoop of delight, Wolfe and Asher giving him a hug. 'Welcome back.'

Chief McNamara, a big smile on his face, walked over to Billy. 'I received a report from the doctor that you would be returning to duty; it's nice to have you back.'

'Chief, it means I'm fit for work, no mollycoddling.'

'You won't get any from me.'

Tunisia, April 1943

Abraham and Gus were tired; sweat ran down their dust-streaked faces. They and the rest of the 1/16th East Surreys had been in the thick of the fighting since landing in North Africa in November. They had just retaken Djebel Djaffa after a hard-fought battle, as it overlooked the road through the Djaffa Pass. All they wanted to do at that moment was have a shower and sleep, but now they had been ordered, with the rest of the battalions making up the 78th Division, to attack, and take Longstop Hill, known locally as Djebel el Ahamera. It was two miles long and eight hundred feet high and overlooked the entire Medjerda Valley. Until Longstop Hill was taken the Allies' left flank was insecure, and the Division could not begin their main attack on Tunis.

From the original compliment of eight hundred officers and men the Surreys were down to a meagre two hundred.

At 11.30 on the morning of 23April with the rest of the Division, Abraham and Gus began the slow climb. Abraham ran his hand over the spring corn and flowers that grew on the hillside, body bent slightly, nerves jangling as they advanced.

Abraham licked his lips and for a fleeting moment wondered how April and Miriam were, and then he dived for the hard rocky ground as German machine guns opened up, followed by artillery. Abraham tried to burrow into a dip in the rock, and looked to his right to make sure Gus was okay. He had his head down, left hand holding onto his steel helmet. Abraham looked at his men; what were left of them were easy targets lying there; he took a whistle that Isaac had given him, saying to him, 'It's better than shouting.' He smiled, placing it to his lips and blew. As one, the men looked in his direction and he pointed forward. They all nodded, even though they were scared, and crawled slowly upward, stopping now and again to fire at the enemy.

After a five-hour battle some forty officers and men reached the summit of Longstop hill.

A hundred yards from the summit, Abraham and Gus were having their wounds attended to by a medic who was tying a tourniquet around Gus's left arm; his shirt open revealing a blood-soaked dressing. Next to him was Abraham, his leg broken, the medic busy trying to stem the blood from a nasty shoulder wound.

'Don't move your leg sir,' said the medic, giving him a painkilling injection. 'I'll get to your leg in a second.'

Abraham reached for his blood-soaked tunic next to him, taking a pack of cigarettes from the right-hand pocket. 'That's lucky, no blood. Would you like one corporal?' he asked the medic.

'Sorry sir, blood on my hands, could you stick it behind my ear, I'll have it later.' He bent slightly and Abraham placed the cigarette behind his ear. Abraham stretched his hand across to Gus lying next to him, lighting the cigarette and handing it to him. 'You saved my life Gus, I never saw the grenade.'

'This isn't the cinema. You're being melodramatic.' Gus smiled.

Abraham wasn't going to argue now. He could see that like him Gus was in a lot of pain. Suddenly Gus was being lifted off the ground; the stretcher-bearers came to take him to the medical tent.

'Hey, wait for me,' Isaac called out.

'You're next,' the medic said, pinning a tag onto his trousers.

'What's that for?'

'Tells them the wounds you have and the painkiller I've given you,' the corporal said, wiping his hands, and taking the cigarette from his ear. 'Thanks for the fag, sir.'

On 7 May Allied armour rolled into Tunis, by then Abraham and Gus were on their way back to England to recuperate from their wounds.

Four days earlier, on 3 May, as Sally had gone into labour, Bevin the Labour minister announced that women between the ages of 18 and 45 would be called up to do part-time war work of up to thirty hours a week so as to release more men needed for the armed forces.

Eva sat by her daughter's side holding her hand, giving her words of encouragement. They had called the midwife, who didn't seem too worried about the length of time Sally had been in labour. Phillip had stayed most of the night, but had to return to the factory at six in the morning.

'Is she okay? Is the baby okay?' Eva asked the midwife, who smiled as she looked up from looking at the cervix.

'Everything's okay, I could see the head and it won't be long now.' She looked at Sally. 'Mrs Hyams, when I say push, push.' She disappeared for a moment and then said, 'Please push now.'

Sally let out a yell, her face red as she pushed, gripping her mother's hand so tightly that Eva thought she would break it.

Suddenly the midwife popped her head up, holding a baby. 'You have a very healthy, handsome son.' With expertise she cleaned the baby, saying to Eva. 'Would you like to cut the cord?'

'Oh, yes please.' Eva smiled at her grandson as she cut the cord. The midwife wrapped the baby up and then handed him to Sally, who couldn't stop smiling at the little bundle in her arms. Eva cuddled her daughter, saying, 'Thank you. Have you decided on a name?'

'Solomon, after *Zaida*[16] – and his English name would be the same – Solomon, it's a strong name,' Sally said.

Eva nodded, tears in her eyes that they had thought of continuing her father's name. 'Thank you, he would have been proud of you.'

Four day later on 8 May, Freda went into labour. It was so quick that the midwife arrived just as the baby was born, another boy. Max arrived late in the afternoon and knelt by the bed. 'He's so good looking, he has your colouring.'

'Don't be silly. You can't tell yet.'

'Do you have a name?' Eva asked.

'Max and I decided Yaakov for the Jewish name, after Max's father, and Jeffrey as the English name.'

A week later both boys were circumcised, to the joy of their parents, grandparents and those of their family that could be there.

It was later that day, when everyone had left, that Hannah took her mother-in-law's arm. 'By February there would hopefully be another addition to the family.'

---

[16] grandfather.

Eva couldn't contain herself, wrapping her arms around Hannah's neck and kissing her. 'My goodness, I've waited a long time for my grandchildren, and now there would be an abundance of them.' She hugged Hannah. 'If that Hitler comes anywhere near you, I would kill him with my bare hands.'

Hannah had no doubt that she would.

*

The dawn found the brothers, Billy and the other firefighters cleaning their fire engines and replacing broken equipment after another night of bombing when the newsreader's voice broke into the music being played: 'This is the morning news on May 18th, read by Alvar Liddell. This morning the Air Ministry announced that walls of water swept through the Ruhr and Eder valleys, destroying everything before it, after British bombers successfully breached the Mohne and Eder dams, swamping coal mines and iron works, causing immense damage to the German war machine. This is the end of the special bulletin.'

Wolfe stared at the radio, hoping that Saul was safe and not on that raid, as successful as it was.

The, two days later: 'Good morning, this is Stuart Hibbard with the latest news on May 20th. The Prime Minister Winston Churchill addressed the United States Congress yesterday, pledging to keep up the fight against Japan. He had been staying with President Roosevelt at the White House. Further news, the first wartime race meeting at Ascot on Saturday was a great success. This is the end of the morning's news.'

The three men sat around the dining room. Wolfe was playing a game of patience while Asher and Billy read the latest news.

'Did you know the King went to visit the troops in North Africa?' Asher asked Wolfe.

'No, I must have missed that.'

'What, you read the paper from end to end. How come you missed that?' Asher said sarcastically.

'Is he still there?'

'Don't be silly. They wouldn't write that in the paper unless he had returned.'

Eva burst into the room. 'Wolfe, get the midwife. Lily's started labour.'

On 27 July, as her husband took off for a raid on Hamburg, Lily gave birth to a baby girl, naming her Rosalind in memory of her mother, Rose.

Unaware that his wife was giving birth, Isaac dropped the markers on target for the following bomber stream; neither was he aware that his brother Saul was part of the attacking force as he turned for home.

As the bomber stream approached Hamburg it encountered a huge storm that caused the phenomena of St Elmo's Fire. Blue flames flickered around the gun muzzles, propellers and wing tips, and any pointed objects like antennas. Andy's radio equipment seemed alive, and there was no way the crew could communicate. Saul lost no time in losing height, trying to get below the storm clouds, keeping an eye out for other aircraft. As they cleared the cloud, Saul regained communication with the rest of the crew. Without hesitation, even though his instruments had gone haywire, Prof said over the intercom, 'Eight minutes to target, Guv. Stay on this heading.'

'Roger, Prof. Andy, let go window,' Saul ordered.

'Roger, Guv.'

This was the first time 'window' was being used. These were small strips of shredded tinfoil that the pathfinders and following bombers dropped to confuse German radar that guided their night fighters to attacking bomber streams.

Saul and his crew successfully dropped their bombs and headed for home.

*

Abraham picked up his Sten gun, hoisted the backpack from his bed to his back in one movement and walked out of his barrack and across to billet B, where his troop were lining up under the watchful gaze of Gus, who on seeing Abraham approaching, yelled, 'Troop Attention.' There was a crash of boots on the concrete as Gus turned and saluted, 'Troop ready for inspection, sir.'

Abraham saluted back. 'Thank you Sergeant-Major, stand them at ease.'

Abraham and Gus were now fully recovered from their injuries, having had operations aboard the ship bringing them back to England. Their wounds healed pretty quickly after they had convalesced in an army hospital, following this with two weeks' leave, in which Gus got married before returning to barracks. They were then put through, with others recovering from their wounds, a four-week fitness course by a physical training instructor.

They didn't return to the East Surreys, but at the end of September were posted to the 1st Suffolk Regiment training in Scotland. Abraham vaguely remembered them from Dunkirk, but instead of having hardened battle troops under him, he was given B troop raw recruits straight from training.

That first night he talked it over with Gus. 'I'm assuming we're going to be part of the invasion force.'

Gus nodded, handing him a cigarette, which Abraham took with a smile, lighting them both up from a box of Swan Vestas. 'We took a hammering up that mountain in Tunis. Could you imagine what it's going to be like charging through sand with backpack and rifle?'

'Very difficult, and those Nazis have been waiting for us for four years.'

'My uncle, who was in the army many years ago, gave me a bit of advice. Train them hard, but make sure I do what they do.'

'He's right, we did that last time, and it paid off.'

'Okay, first thing in the morning after inspection, rifles only.'

While Abraham trained his men, there was loud protest when the very ill fascist Mosley was released from prison.

As the country moved into the last months of the year, young men enlisting in the armed forces were shocked to find that one in every ten must work in the coal mines. This was introduced by the Labour Minister Ernest Bevin because of the loss in manpower as many miners had enlisted in the armed forces to get away from the pits. These men became known as the Bevin Boys.

While new troops trained in boot camps throughout the country, the Supreme Commander of Allied Forces, General Dwight D. Eisenhower, returned to Britain with General Montgomery to plan the invasion of Europe.

21

Eva, a big smile on her face, looked around the extended table to accommodate her grandchildren's highchairs. She didn't care about the chickens they had used, or the amount of vegetables from the allotment at the back of the garden. It had been a long time in coming, but at last her entire family and friends were celebrating the New Year, be it a day late as yesterday was the Sabbath. No one was in uniform, and as usual the banter was just fun. She looked at Hannah, who was showing her pregnancy, and winked.

All too soon, their leaves over, Isaac, Saul and Abraham returned to their units.

Britain was crammed with men and equipment as day by day American, Canadian and other Allied Troops arrived, and the country became a huge army camp, with armour and supplies from eggs to motor oil. Troops were forbidden any contact with the world outside their camps. The south was covered with row upon row of armoured cars, tanks and aircraft. In Kent steel containers with ammunition lined the grassy verges of country roads. Depots were piled high with every imaginable item for an invading army. A joke went around that the thousands of barrage balloons in the skies stopped Britain from sinking beneath the waves.

In the meantime General Eisenhower and his advisors completed their plans to invade Hitler's Europe.

The Americans brought a new type of music and dance to Britain called, Swing. Glen Miller's Air Force Band wowed youngsters and the troops across the country.

Troops trained with mock-ups of the places they would be attacking. Abraham had his men run along the beach in zigzag patterns. 'Shaw,' he yelled, running alongside the soldier. 'Not in a straight line. You'd be dead by now.'

'Yes sir,' the soldier moved to the side, ran a few steps forward and ran the other way.

20 January 1944

The sun finally disappeared over the western horizon as the Lancaster V for Victor with the rest of the Squadron climbed steadily towards their rendezvous over the North Sea.

The twenty-nine painted bombs under the pilot's window indicated the amount of missions she'd flown. Newly painted sections on the fuselage and wings showed she hadn't always come through them unscathed.

The dark hazel eyes of Oliver Moore, the twenty-one-year-old flight engineer, moved slowly across the gauges in front of him, head tilted to one side, listening to the four Rolls Royce Merlin engines. A smile creased his face; everything looked and sounded okay as he took off his right-hand glove, sliding his hand inside his flight-jacket pocket to stroke the head of his lucky teddy bear. He looked across at Saul, whose mascot, a laughing elf, hung from his parachute harness.

Saul looked outwardly calm, hands steady on the control column, but inwardly he was very nervous, with butterflies in the pit of his stomach, and he felt sick. Saul knew that it would soon pass as he felt like this at the start of every mission. He swallowed nervously, licked his lips and took a deep breath, exhaling slowly and the nerves disappeared. This was a trick Billy had taught him. He smiled inwardly at how the big Irishman had pestered the doctors to let him go back to work and training until they caved in.

He clipped on his oxygen mask, turning to look out of the window at the dim silhouette of the Lancaster on his port wing and raised a hand to the pilot of F for Freddie, who waved back.

Once again their target was Berlin, Germany's capital city, which covered an area of eight hundred and eighty-three square miles. With a population of four and a quarter million people, and was the most heavily defended city in the Reich.

Apart from being the political capital, it was also an industrial city, with factories consisting of textile, iron and steel works situated along its railway routes and waterways of the rivers Spree, Haver and Lake Wanasee. Its factories produced fifteen per cent of the Luftwaffe's aero engines, plus Dornier, Heinkel and Folk-Wolf aircraft. A quarter of the army's tanks, half its field artillery, submarine motors, precision instruments, and a third of Germany's electrical output were produced in Berlin. No wonder it was so heavily defended.

Enormous cones of searchlights and flak towers surrounded the city in groups of eight that fired salvos every ninety seconds to a height of forty-five thousand feet. Apart from that there were night fighters, ME

109s and 110s, a daunting task for allied bomber crews.

Saul touched the laughing elf, as a picture of Hannah came to mind, the bump of pregnancy prominent. She hadn't moaned about her swollen ankles or morning sickness, just about how grotesque her dress was. He smiled under the oxygen mask.

Reaching their rendezvous point, Prof broke into his thoughts. 'Two minutes to turning point, Guv. One hundred and twenty degrees magnetic, and climb to nineteen thousand feet.'

'Roger, Prof, thanks.'

The navigator, Flight Sergeant Harry Prof Silver, the only other married man in the crew, was busy with his calculations, having to know the aircraft's position at all times, regardless of their conditions, be it weather or enemy action. Prof, the practical joker of the crew, was very superstitious and a fanatical supporter of Arsenal football club. He placed his fingers to his lips, touching the photo taped to the bulkhead in front of him, his wife Sandra and their three children.

In the observation dome, the brown eyes of Sergeant Andy Anderson, the radio operator and fire-controller, slowly roamed the sky. It was his job to direct the pilot and gunners in the event of visual combat with enemy fighters. He automatically rubbed the lucky rabbit's foot inside his flying jacket.

V for Victor joined the main bomber stream of seven hundred bombers, each crew member of every aircraft with their own thoughts and dreams.

In the nose turret, the front gunner and bomb aimer Flight Sergeant David Cheskowski, a Polish Jew, stroked the cold metal of his Browning machine guns. This being Mission 29 made no difference to him. He smiled under his oxygen mask, remembering a passage from the Bible: *Saul could kill his thousands, David his tens of thousands.* He hummed to himself a tune thousands of years old as they flew through the darkness towards a hostile coast, dark brown eyes roaming the sky ahead.

Prof clicked on his microphone. 'Guv, climb to twenty thousand feet, five minutes to the Dutch coast.'

'Roger Prof,' Saul acknowledged. 'Gunners, test your guns, and please don't shoot down the Lancaster next to you; stay alert for fighters.'

The guns in the mid-upper turret shudder in the hands of the youngest crew member, Sergeant Paul Ginger James. His freckled face set in its usual grin. Ginger like many cockneys was always talking, his light blue eyes twinkling with good humour at Cheskowski's unsuccessful imitations of Ginger's *Apples and pears and plates of meat.*

Two days ago Ginger's parents, brother and sister were killed when a bomb hit their house. He was told to go on leave, but declined, saying he was better off with his mates.

Ginger touched the St Christopher medallion his mother had given him on his last leave, bringing it to his lips, a picture of the four of them waving goodbye, and his brother shouting, 'See you next week.'

Ginger looked through the gun sights of his Browning, hoping a German fighter would attack them so he could shoot it down and in some way avenge his loss.

In the distance searchlights pierced the darkness, their beams crisscrossing the sky, searching for enemy aircraft as the squadron flew ever nearer to their target, with the moon playing hide and seek behind broken puffs of cloud.

In the rear turret, ex-jockey Derek Dickenson had a sense of detachment from the rest of the crew as he looked back at the formation of six hundred bombers stretching out behind them.

Like Prof, Derek was very superstitious. On each mission he wore the same pants and socks, washed of course, and not RAF issue. Inside his flying jacket was his lucky riding cap, which he wore when they drove out to the dispersal area.

Derek's eyes, like the other gunners in the formation, searched the darkness as tension mounted and the distant searchlight beams over Berlin speared upward.

Since leaving the coast of Holland the bomber stream had been under constant attack by night fighters and ack-ack. Some bomber had been shot down; parachutes blossoming out as crews abandoned their doomed aircraft, while others had not been so lucky. Saul and Ginger watched F for Freddie going down in flames, as a voice inside Saul yelled, '*Jump, jump,*' but no one did.

'Break left, break left,' Andy yelled in Saul's ear as a Messerschmitt attacked them. Mac and Ginger fired together and the ME flew straight into the stream of bullets, flipped over onto its back, streaming black smoke as it nose-dived towards the earth below. Saul pulled back on the column, returning the Lancaster to its original height.

The night sky was alight with searchlights and exploding ack-ack shells. The River Spree lay ahead as the crew of V for Victor prepared for their bombing run. Cheskowski left his guns for the bomb aimer's position just as an ME109 attacked them. Ginger yelled that he had been injured – it was a shoulder wound. He still had that silly smile on his face as Andy helped him from his turret to dress the wound.

'I'll get a gong for this, won't I, Andy?'

'There's no doubt about it, Ginger.' Andy smiled at the young gunner beneath his oxygen mask as he administered a painkilling injection, wondering if the grin was a grimace of pain.

'Look 'ere, Andy, I'm as good as ninepence, and I'll take your position in the dome. I'll spot the buggers fur yah.'

'Are you sure you're up to it?'

Ginger winked. 'Piece of cake. Come on, there's MEs to be shot down.'

Andy helped Ginger strap himself into position in the dome. 'Guv, I'm swapping over with Ginger. He has a shoulder wound, not too serious,' Andy said over the intercom.

'Roger, Andy, thanks.' Saul was relieved that the young cockney's wound wasn't too serious. There was the familiar clump-clump of exploding flak shells outside the Lancaster and a sound like hailstones on the roof. The bomber shuddered.

'Bloody heck, the inner port engine's on fire,' Ollie yelled.

Saul glanced over to his left to see tongues of flame straddling the wing, knowing that the high octane fuel could explode at any moment. 'Kill it,' he said quietly.

Ollie was already throttling back the engine, feathering the prop and pressing the fire extinguisher button, while at the same time cutting off the fuel and transferring it to another tank. Ollie breathed a sigh of relief as the flames were extinguished.

'Fire out, Guv,' he said, looking across at Saul, who was about to say something when Ginger yelled, 'Fighter coming in fast two o'clock.' Derek and Andy returned fire. Holes appeared in the fuselage and Prof was hit in the leg.

'My turret's jammed,' Derek yelled over the intercom.

Saul turned to Ollie. 'Go and help Derek and assess our damage back there.'

Ollie found the Prof tying a tourniquet around his leg. He knelt to have a look. 'It's a flesh wound. The bullet went straight through.' Harry gave the thumbs-up sign and turned back to his charts.

Ollie moved along the fuselage towards the rear, coming across Ginger hanging from his straps in the dome. He was dead. He gently undid the straps, lowering the little gunner onto the floor and covering him up. He moved to the tail section and plugged into the intercom. 'Ginger's dead, Guv. I'll check Derek.'

Andy felt guilty; it should have been him in the dome instead of Ginger. He gripped the handles of the machine guns, his eyes moving steadily across the sky, the wind whistling through the bullet holes in the fuselage.

'Ollie, you able to release the turret from your end?' Dickenson asked.

Ollie tried to move the turret manually. 'I can't budge it; do you want to come out of there?'

'No, not for the moment. I can still fire the guns, but not rotate the turret.'

'Okay, give me a shout if you need me.' Ollie returned to the cockpit, plonked onto his seat, strapped himself in and switched on the microphone, looking at Saul. 'Ginger's dead, Prof's injured but he's okay for the moment. The rear turrets jammed, but if need be Derek can get out. Andy's manning the upper turret.'

Saul looked out to the inner port engine, the propeller turning lazily, caught in the current. *Fuck it,* he said to himself, mulling over their predicament, *one dead, one wounded, rear turret jammed and flying on three engines.* He could see the target a few miles ahead lit up by green and red markers. Should they go on or turn back? Saul gnawed his top lip under the oxygen mask. They were still flyable. He decided to go on, but it was going to be a long trip home.

Lying flat on his stomach, Cheskowski didn't flinch at the brightness of exploding shells around them. This was, for Saul, the hardest part of the mission, the run in to the target. There was no jinking right or left now as their target crept slowly towards the cross-hairs of the bomb sights.

'Bomb doors open,' Cheskowski said softly, concentrating on the ground below. The night sky was alight with searchlights, exploding flares and anti-aircraft shells, as hundreds of bombers prepared to drop their bombs.

A Lancaster to their right was caught in a cone of light, which was quickly joined by others. The pilot tried to escape the glare, moving left and right, but the cone of searchlights stayed steadily on him. The Lancaster suddenly dived away but couldn't escape, caught like a moth in the light as shells exploded all around it, until at last it was hit, falling in flames towards the ground. Two shapes left the stricken bomber, their parachutes open and drifted slowly towards the cauldron below.

Saul fought the drag from the open bomb bay doors and the loss of one engine as David's calm, accented voice said, 'Left a little, a little more, hold it, *hooollled* it.' The intensity of the flak shells seemed to have increased, shooting hot pieces of metal around the sky. David pressed the bomb release, said something in Polish and then, 'Bomb's gone,' his eyes following the four thousand pound bombs and incendiaries plummeting towards their target, a smile on his face.

The Lancaster leapt forward, free of its load, and Saul pushed the throttles of the three remaining engines forward, trying to gain more speed and leave the target area as quickly as possible.

David was still looking down as they turned away, a big grin on his face, yelling in triumph, seeing the bombs hit their target.

Halfway into their turn a fighter braving its own ack-ack flashed across the front of them firing. A blast of cold air gushed into the cockpit; the big bomber shuddered as if coming to a full stop and then dived towards the ground. Saul fought to control the shuddering aircraft as it plunged downward, the wind howling like a banshee into the cockpit as their downward airspeed increased. Hooking his right arm around the control column, Saul pulled back with all his strength. Slowly, ever so slowly, the nose came up and they levelled out at three thousand feet.

Breathing heavily from his exertions, Saul looked across at Ollie, yelling over the wind, 'Have a look at David,' and then called the crew over the intercom, 'Anyone hurt, Prof, you okay?'

'I'm okay, Guv, but there's a few more holes back here.'

'Andy?'

'I'm okay, Guv, and as Prof said, there are a few more holes here.'

'Derek, you okay?'

'Yes, Guv, fine.'

Saul could see a few holes in the wings. Thankfully the fuel tanks hadn't been hit.

The wind buffeted the jagged edges of the shattered nose cone as Ollie checked on the bomb aimer. David was dead, his safety harness stopping him from falling into the dark void below. Ollie wondered how he and Guv had escaped injury. He returned to the cockpit and told Saul, 'David's dead, it's a mess; his straps are stopping him from falling through the shattered nose cone.'

Saul let out a stream of swear words, and then calmed down. They were flyable and... 'Break left, break left!' Andy yelled.

Saul tried to turn the damaged bomber, but she was slow to respond. Holes appeared in the roof, the bullets narrowly missing Andy as the Messerschmitt came around for another attack and in the instant that it showed its underside Andy fired, yelling in jubilation on seeing the bullets strike home, mentally thanking the German pilot for being such an idiot.

Flames appeared from behind the wounded ME's cockpit, the nose pointed skyward, the canopy opened and the pilot dropped out of the stricken fighter that stalled turned over and nosedived towards the ground.

Derek yelled, 'Fighter one o'clock,' and then gasped in pain as he was hit, blood quickly soaking his flying jacket. He fired his Browning at the same time, yelling at the German pilot, 'Bastard, fucking bastard, I'm hit.'

'How bad?' asked Saul, struggling to control the shuddering bomber.

'Pretty bad, Guv. Could someone get back her and help me out?'

'Okay, Derek, I'll send Ollie.'

Ollie freed the badly wounded jockey, helping him onto a bunk, unzipped his blood-soaked flying jacket and shirt, pressing a field dressing firmly against the gunner's stomach and trying to stem the flow of blood, while at the same time injecting a heavy dose of morphine. There was nothing more he could do for the ex-jockey so he returned to the cockpit as once again they were attacked. Saul pushed the control column forward, trying to escape the fighter levelling out at two thousand feet, hoping the darkness would hide them. 'Andy, do you see him?' he asked.

'Yes, Guv, but it seems he can't see us?'

Saul breathed a sigh of relief, and pulled back the column. The bomber shuddered as its nose pointed upward. Saul's mind raced. He clicked on the microphone. 'Prof, the shortest way home please, try and avoid any ack-ack.'

'Roger, Guv.'

Saul looked across at Ollie to see a blood stain on the shoulder of his flying jacket. 'Why didn't you tell me?'

'You had other things to worry about, and—' He was cut short as the outer starboard engine coughed and cut out. Ignoring the pain, Ollie checked the instruments and tried to restart the engine, but it wouldn't fire up. He looked over at it, the propeller like the inner port engine turning lazily in the slipstream.

Saul gave up trying to gain height, the damaged nose making it very difficult to keep the big bomber stable, but at four thousand feet the aircraft stopped shuddering.

'How's the fuel?' He looked at Ollie. 'We could have sustained damage and lost some fuel – no, forget that, we would have caught fire if we had.' Like Ollie he knew the engine very well.

'We seem to be okay. The gauge tells me there's still petrol in the tank.'

'If it's leaking, trying to start the engine would not be the best thing to do.'

'Mmm, you're right, but we only have two engines.'

'The manual said we could fly on two, and we had tried it in training, so we are capable of doing that, but—'

'Do we have enough fuel?' Ollie interrupted.

'Guv, Braunschweig is to our right,' Prof said over the intercom. 'Keep on this heading.'

'How many miles to home?' asked Saul.

'We are lucky, we have a tailwind; I reckon about two hundred.'

'Thanks Prof. Andy could you come into the cockpit? Ollie's hurt.'

'What about the guns?'

'We'll have to take a chance.'

Suddenly searchlights pierced the darkness. 'They can hear us, but hopefully they won't realise how low we're flying.'

Andy entered the cockpit area. Ollie turned in his seat to face him and pointed. 'Shoulder and it hurts like bugger.'

Andy smiled. 'Let's have a look.' He unzipped Ollie's flying jacket. 'Made a mess of your shirt, better save it for—'

'You're trying to kill me by worrying about my shirt,' Ollie laughed. 'If I weren't in pain I'd kick your arse.'

'Here am I trying to help you with the pain and you... This is going to hurt.'

'Fucking shit, what are you doing?' Ollie gritted his teeth, trying not to yell.

'I'm trying to see the bullet, and if possible get it out. This may hurt.' Andy couldn't see or feel the bullet. 'Sorry, Ollie, I couldn't see it. We'll have to wait till we get home.' He poured some disinfectant powder into the wound and bound it up, giving Ollie a painkilling injection. 'I'll help you on with your jacket. You okay to carry on?'

'Thanks, Andy, that's much better. If I need you I'll call.'

Andy looked out at the two dead engines. 'We okay, Guv?'

Saul gave a wry smile. 'At the moment yes, Andy.' Hunched in his seat, his mind went over the variables in his mind. *Two hundred odd miles back to England, two engines fuel consumption...* the maths rolled together. He sat up straight on the uncomfortable parachute. *As fuel consumption plus minutes, well, hours really at lowest speed before stalling is around ninety-five mph, we are above that. If we transfer fuel to the two engines, keep them at a steady rev so as not to overheat them at 190 mph, we can make it.* He glanced at the altimeter, three hundred and fifty, *not bad.* He looked across at Ollie. 'Engineer, could you please transfer all fuel to our two remaining engines.'

'Roger, Guv.' Ollie's lips were stretched in a straight line against the pain as he obeyed the order.

'Transfer completed, Guv.'

'Thanks, Ollie. Look everyone, we're flying on two engines. With the transfer of fuel, I estimate we should just reach home a little later than we would have liked. Andy, you keep a lookout for fighters, but in the darkness and at this altitude we should be okay. As soon as we reach the North Sea, send a radio message home.'

'Roger, Guv.'

There was silence between them except for the steady beat of the two Merlin engines.

Saul was cold, the collar of his fur-lined flying jacket was up, but he was also thankful for it. The cold was keeping him awake and alert. He knew that just one moment of lack of concentration could see them diving into the ground.

There was the familiar click of a microphone being switched on. 'Guv, how's Ollie?' Andy asked.

Saul looked across at the engineer; his face was white against the darkness and the bloodstain on his flying jacket seemed to have grown larger. 'He doesn't look too good. Leave the turret and come here. I don't think we'll be bothered by fighters now.'

As Andy made his way forward, Prof's voice was in his ears. 'Five minutes to the coast.'

Saul breathed a silent sigh of relief. 'Thanks, Prof. How are you?'

'I'm okay, Guv, legs a bit stiff, but I'll live. Stay on this heading; we have a tailwind, so all is well.'

They crossed the coast of Holland as Andy checked Ollie's wound. 'Won't be long, Ollie, and we'll be home. Once they get the bullet out, you'll be okay. I'm going to give you another shot of painkiller.'

'Thanks, Andy,' Ollie whispered.

'Once you've done that, Ollie, get on the radio. We don't want to be shot down by our own people.'

They crossed the North Sea, and Saul slowly turned the crippled bomber so as not to make it shudder towards their base.

'Beacon light would be flashing for you, Guv,' Andy said quietly.

'Thanks, Andy.' He was wondering how he would drop the wheels, one-handed, and how the Lancaster would handle when they dropped, but to his surprise Ollie pushed the lever forwards. The aircraft's nose began to drop and the shuddering began. Ollie settled the pitch of the engines to compensate, and the shuddering stopped.

'Thanks, Ollie.' He could see the flashing beacon welcoming them home, and there was the runway. He decided to go into a gentle glide. 'Ollie, would you be able to count me down?'

'Yes Guv.' Now they were virtually home his voice seemed stronger.

Saul could hear the engineer's voice in his ears as he concentrated on landing the crippled bomber. It began to shudder, but he held her in an iron grip as they dropped lower. They brushed the perimeter fence, then there was a slight bump as the wheels touched down. He gently applied the brakes and pulled back the throttle. Out of the corner of his eyes Saul could see ambulances and fire engines speeding beside them. Saul turned into their dispersal area, and switched off the engines as an ambulance and fire engine pulled up beside them.

Ollie and the badly wounded rear gunner were stretchered from the aircraft, while Harry climbed gingerly down, helped into a waiting ambulance by one of the ground crew, while others gently lowered Cheskowski onto a stretcher.

'Hey, George, look at him,' one of the stretcher bearers said.

'What about him?'

'He's smiling – must have seen his bombs drop onto the target before he bought it.'

A very tired Saul and Andy walked into the Nissan hut for a cup of hot tea and biscuits before being debriefed by the adjutant.

The following afternoon, Saul and Ollie made their way to the hospital to see how their fellow crew members were doing. Ollie, his shoulder heavily bandaged, was sitting up talking to Harry, who was sitting on the edge of the bed, holding a couple of crutches.

'How are you both?' Saul asked.

'They took the bullet out of my shoulder,' Ollie said. 'I was lucky it didn't hit any bone, or vital tendons. Doc said I should be okay within a couple of months.'

Saul looked at Harry who smiled. 'I could play for Arsenal in two months if there was no infection.'

'Where's Derek?' Andy asked.

'Next ward, he isn't that good,' Ollie said.

'You'll have to ask a nurse or doctor before you could see him,' Harry said.

Saul nodded. 'Okay, I'll speak to someone first.' He moved towards the ward, meeting a nurse leaving it. 'Excuse me, nurse, would it be possible to see Sergeant Dickenson?'

'And you are?'

'I'm the pilot of his Lancaster, Flight Sergeant Brown.'

'One moment, I'll ask the doctor.'

Two minutes later the nurse returned with a doctor. 'I'm sorry, Flight Sergeant, but he's pretty poorly, and he's heavily sedated. His parents are on their way to see him. Perhaps you could come back later.'

'Excuse me, sir, but does this mean he might not make it?'

'All I could say at this moment is the next forty-eight hours – well, we'll see. Pop back later, I'm sure his parents would like to talk to you.'

'Thank you, sir, I'll do that.' Saul returned to the others to tell them the news.

Saul and Andy left the hospital to report to their CO as ordered when they were debriefed. They knocked on his door, entering on hearing. 'Enter.'

They entered, stood to attention and saluted. The CO smiled. 'Stand at ease, smoke if you want.' They both declined smoking, wondering what he wanted with them.

'You have exceeded the odds and finished thirty missions. I'm sorry about Ginger and Cheskowski. It will be some time before the rest of your crew will be ready for combat flying.' He held up a hand, seeing Saul was about to say something. 'We have new crews arriving every day; they need someone with your experience to show them anything they need to know that would help them survive. There are three new crews that arrived yesterday, all in B flight.' He picked up a folder. 'Here are the names of the crew, and their grades.'

Saul took the folder from the outstretched hand. 'You have a week to get them ready, I'll need a report from you then.'

Saul looked at Andy, shrugged his shoulders and said, 'We'll do our best, sir.'

'This is the news on January 23rd Yesterday Allied troops landed on Anzio thirty miles from Rome the Italian capital.'

Wolfe slammed his hand on the table, making the other firemen look in his direction. 'This is it.'

'Is what?' Billy asked.

'It's the beginning of our offensive against Hitler. Haven't you realised that the victory at El Alamein was the Nazis death knell. We are taking the offensive.'

Asher was silent, wondering what Abraham was doing. At that moment Abraham was snaking through a barbed-wire complex with shells and hand grenades exploding around, and bullets flying overhead as he led his men through the assault cause. At last he was free of the wire, running to and leaping over a wall, landing on his feet on the other side with Gus on his right shoulder, the rest of the men following. Their faces black and sweat-streaked, uniforms mud-splattered, they quick-marched back to camp, entering a large building with a mock-up of their objective, when they got the green light that the invasion of Europe was on.

In a map room deep under Horse Guards Parade, Generals Ike and Monty, with their advisors, reached a verdict of when the invasion would begin. To fool the Germans, tanks and heavy armaments were concealed under yards of camouflaged netting as Allied soldiers awaited the order that the invasion was on.

On 12 February Hannah went into labour. She had one of the girls telephone Eva and Saul's air base. That evening with her mother-in-law beside her, Hannah had a little girl, naming her Ruby.

The following afternoon with just a twenty-four-hour pass, Saul arrived to see his wife and baby daughter.

22

March 1944

While the war in Africa moved forward with German troops on the retreat, much of Europe was still occupied by Germany and her allies. Plans to invade Britain were now a thing of the past.

Since January the amount of night bombers the Germans sent were significantly lower than three years previously.

As they sped towards Upper Thames Street, Wolfe yelled above the sound of the bell, 'Where do you think all the rubble caused by the bombing goes?' he asked Asher sitting next to him.

'No idea.'

'They use it to build runways for the heavy bombers. Clever, don't you think?'

Asher looked at him in surprise. 'I thought they dumped it out in the Channel.' He turned to Billy. 'Did you hear that?'

'Yes, and like you I never knew that.' He pointed at Wolfe. 'I'm sure he reads every article in all the newspapers we get at the fire station.'

'You're probably right.'

'What'd he say?' Wolfe asked.

Asher smiled. 'I'll tell you later.' The engine came to a screeching stop and within seconds they had a hose out and pouring water onto a blazing warehouse. Suddenly the firemen let out a cheer as they watched a German bomber plummeting downwards.

Eva shook her fists at the departing German bombers as she, Sarah and Esther drove their van to Shoreditch, where most of the bombs had fallen. Within minutes they were dishing out tea and sandwiches to people emerging from shelters.

Saul knocked on his CO door, entering when he heard, 'Come.' He stood to attention and saluted. The CO looked up from the papers in front of him and smiled. 'What can I do for you, Brown?'

'My crew, except for the bomb aimer and gunners, have recovered from their injuries. We are bored out of our minds and to put it bluntly, sir, I'm fed up with training crews that fly off leaving me on the ground. We would like to go on ops again, sir.'

'What about making up the rest of your crew?'

'Well, sir, I have approached some men, who are also missing members of their crew who are available.'

'What are their names?'

'Mid-upper gunner was Sergeant Roy Burnett; the bomb aimer, Flight Sergeant Tom Wilson; and tail gunner Sergeant Rob McGregor.'

The CO thumbed through a book he had in front of him, made a few notes and looked up at Saul. 'Okay, Brown, you have your crew, are you sure about this? As you've already done one tour, that's—'

'Yes, sir, I know,' Saul interrupted, 'but I need to be doing something more than write report, and test crews.'

'Okay, get your men together, there's a new Lancaster that's just arrived. See the ops officer to put your names down for it.'

For the next three days Saul took their new Lancaster S for Sugar on trial runs, and to get the crew used to each other and once again give them other jobs than their own.

On the ground, Abraham took his men to the beach with just their rifles. He and his men ran up and down the beach for an hour, with Gus in the rear egging on the stragglers. As they rested he had them in a circle around him.

'Sip your water,' he ordered. 'Don't guzzle it down, otherwise you might be sick and feel dizzy.' He paced up and down in front of them. 'You're wondering why I'm running you up and down the beach.' He took a pack of cigarettes from his pocket. 'Smoke if you want to.' He lit his cigarette and blew out the smoke. 'It's so you get used to running on the sand.' He took a puff of the cigarette, letting the smoke trickle through his nostrils.

'When you've finished your cigarettes, we are going into the sea. Hopefully when the time comes we won't have to wade through too deep a sea. From the sea we are going to run up the beach and down to the water's edge and halt. The last two men will give me twenty push-ups.' He finished his cigarette. 'Okay, on your feet and follow me,' he ordered.

They followed him into the water until they were just below knee high. 'Okay, on my whistle, run as fast as you can,' he yelled to make himself heard. Taking the whistle from his top pocket attached to lanyard, he placed it in his mouth and blew. The men ran up the beach with Abraham and Gus in the lead. Abraham turned, running backward and throwing an arm forward. 'Come on!' he yelled, turning to face the front and catching up with Gus. 'They're doing well,' he panted.

At the end of the beach they turned around and ran back to the sea's edge, many being sick, others bent over, gasping in lungfuls of air. Abraham took the last two a little way up the beach. 'I want twenty push-ups.' Without a word they dropped to the sand. He turned to face the men. 'In a real attack,' he pointed at the two men, 'they'd be dead.'

When they had finished, he said softly, 'Join the others.' He followed them, patting them on the back, giving them encouragement. 'Okay, we'll march back to barracks; clean your gear and uniforms, and check your weapons, all of them.'

The following day he had them dressed in fatigues with full gear and back to the beach they went. This time he had them running up the beach and dropping to the ground on his command, and then up again, running up the beach, and on the way down they did the same thing.

He had them rest for twenty minutes, standing in front of them saying, 'This time when you run up the beach I want you to zigzag, no running in a straight line. The sergeants are going to stand along the beach and at the end of the exercise tell me who didn't zigzag. Do you understand?'

They mumbled something back.

'Do you understand,' he yelled, and they yelled back, 'Yes sir.'

He smiled. 'That's better. Okay on your feet. Sergeants, take up your positions.'

On the sound of his whistle, they ran moving left and right up the beach, once again following Abraham.

Over the next four days he had them running everywhere and did a mock entry onto the beach as though they were in a landing craft. He then gave the men two days' complete rest, except for talks given by the CO on their objective called Sword Beach, which was split into four sections. Abraham's was Queen Beach.

*

'Good evening, it is 29th May, and this is Alvar Liddell. It has been reported that forty-seven British servicemen were shot by the Gestapo yesterday after escaping from the escape proof Stalag Three in Silesia. Ninety-six allied airmen tunnelled their way out of the camp. The Germans said the forty-seven were shot while trying to resist arrest. Fourteen are still at large. That was the latest news.'

'Bastards,' Billy said vehemently. 'I bet you a pound to a penny they caught them and shot them in cold blood.'

'I'm inclined to believe you.' Wolfe shuffled the cards and began to deal. 'That's all those Nazi scum are good for, killing unarmed people.'

Asher took the cards, holding them for a moment, a thoughtful look on his face. Then he sat bolt upright and said, 'Have you noticed there hasn't been a raid for some weeks now? Something's going on.'

Holding his closed cards in his right hand, Billy pointed a finger at Asher. 'I noticed that the raids we've had since January have not been as intense as the last couple of years.'

'The Germans are now fighting on many fronts and if the news reports are anything to go on, the Germans seem to have their backs to the wall.' Asher leaned forward. 'I told you when we won El Alamein it was the beginning of the end for the Germans.'

'Yes, you did say that,' Billy said, adding, 'Russia big mistake—' He gestured towards Wolfe. 'You said it at the beginning, and I bow to your paper-worm—'

'Paper-worm, what does that mean?' Wolfe interrupted indignantly.

Billy and Asher laughed. 'What it means,' said Asher, still smiling, 'is that instead of being a bookworm, where you read lots of books, you're a paper-worm because you read most of the papers from cover to cover.'

'It has always helped me with my English.'

'But you read the Jewish papers as well. Let's play,' Asher placed a bet.

'Have you heard from Adam?' Billy asked Asher.

'We had a letter last week. He's been called up into the Marines.'

On 4 June Rome fell to the Allies. German generals had ignored Hitler's order to blow up the Tiber Bridge and burn the city to the ground. The city's beauty was still intact, as was the Eternal City.

23

The wind blew across the Solent, flapping flags and ensigns on the ships moving with the swell against their moorings. On deck and inside the ships, sailors and soldiers waited. They had been waiting since 1 June when the Invasion of Europe, codenamed Overlord, was supposed to have begun, but sudden bad weather, rain and high winds made it impossible for General Eisenhower at his HQ in Southwick House, Portsmouth, to give the order to go.

He was well aware of the conditions his troops had had to withstand. The weather was just as bad on the other side of the Channel, grounding Allied and German planes. For the last four days he had fumed at the weather, but today the reports from weather ships had been favourable.

Eisenhower woke at four in the morning of 5 June and was told the rain would stop and winds abate by midday with visibility good. After some discussions with his team he stood silent, head bowed, pondering should we wait or should we go. After what seemed hours, he looked up. 'Let's go ahead.'

Throughout Britain, airfields received the word, paratroopers and glider troops checked their equipment, and had a last run through, by their officers to their objectives.

Ships' decks vibrated as engines burst into life, and the clank of raised anchor chains echoed around the Solent.

Abraham smiled at Gus. 'This is it, we're on the move.'

'I thought we'd be stuck on this ship for the duration of the war,' Gus snorted.

Just then a corporal approached Abraham and saluted. 'Sir, the CO would like to see all officers in the wardroom immediately.'

Abraham returned the salute. 'Thank you, Corporal.' Abraham picked up his helmet. 'I'll see you soon.' He smiled as Gus gave him a rude salute. 'I could put you on a charge for that.' Abraham entered the ward room to find it full of the Regiment's officers. He saluted, but it wasn't returned by the CO, who was standing in front of a map showing sixty miles of Normandy beaches set out in sections which were marked in large capital letters, SWORD, JUNO, GOLD, OMAHA and UTAH.

Sword was the beach where the Third Infantry Division was assigned to land, and was the most easterly part of the landings, and fifteen miles from their main objective, the city of Caen. For the next twenty minutes the CO ran through their plan to advance along the beach and the road to Caen. He looked around the men facing him. 'Good luck to you all.'

He donned his cap and a lieutenant said loudly, 'Attention,' and saluted the officer as he walked purposefully from the wardroom. In ones and twos the officers left to get their men ready.

Abraham found Gus arranging his knapsack. 'Just a reminder to where we're supposed to be at any given time.'

'Doesn't always work like that, and we could prove that.'

'I'm going to walk amongst the men. Care to join me?'

'Yes, must make sure their weapons are clean, and—'

'Casually, Gus,' Abraham interrupted. 'They're frightened enough.'

The two friends walked among the men who were getting their gear together, making sure their weapons were clean and muzzles covered, most with a condom, so the salt water couldn't go down the barrel as they waded onto the beach.

After speaking quietly to the men, Abraham cleaned his Sten gun and revolver. When he had finished he looked at Gus. 'Let's go on deck.'

Gus nodded. The cool, fresh, salty air hit them as they reached the deck. Gus pointed downward, 'That's no milk pond.'

Abraham turned a circle, saying quietly, 'My goodness me, there are thousands of ships. I tell you, Gus, we would never ever again see anything like this; it's amazing.' He looked up to see hundreds of bombers and fighters heading towards France.

Above the fleet Isaac couldn't believe his eyes as he looked down at the Armada of ships below him. 'Isn't that a fantastic sight.'

'Five thousand ships,' Fred muttered in awe, his head against the windscreen. 'Battleships, gunboats, troopships and tank landing craft. Hitler's in for a big shock.'

Saul's squadron rendezvoused with others over the Channel. Like his brother a few miles ahead of him, he looked down, his body tingling with excitement on seeing the attacking force of ships. 'Prof, Andy, come up here, you must see this, and anyone else that cannot see below.'

Prof and Andy squeezed into the cockpit. 'Isn't that a wonderful sight,' Prof said. 'We'll soon have those Nazis on the run.' A thousand feet above them was an umbrella of fighters.

Saul said, 'As the old saying goes, this is something to tell your grandchildren, and remember for the rest of your lives.' He waited a few minutes and then ordered, 'Everyone back to your stations.'

*

It was dull and overcast with a heavy swell as in a line the ships anchored a few miles from the Normandy coast, when suddenly there was an almighty roar as the battleships and other craft opened up a bombardment on the German positions. Throughout the fleet, British, American and Canadian troops lined the rails of the troopships to climb down nettings hanging over the side of the transport onto waiting landing craft.

The noise was deafening as salvo after salvo of shells and rockets flew across the sea onto and around the beaches, the flashes from the muzzles lighting up the faces of the troops.

Abraham stood by the rail, making sure his men climbed down safely onto the landing craft bobbing up and down with the swell against the troopship's hull. No one refused to go, their faces serious, lips drawn in straight, determined lines. Abraham and Gus followed them down. As soon as it was loaded, their landing craft pulled away from the troopship, circling until others joined them with the rest of the company.

At 0640 the circling landing craft moved into a flank position and headed towards Sword Beach west of Ouistrehem.

The company were packed together, faces white, eyes staring straight ahead, the sea erupting beside them, soaking the soldiers as the enemy's artillery opened up on the small landing craft speeding in line abreast towards the beaches, a white wake snaking behind them.

Many of the men were sick, no one spoke, but their lips moved in silent prayer, minds numb. As quickly as it started, the roar of the battleship's guns and rockets were silent, and in their place was the rattle of machine gun fire bullets pinging off the armoured landing craft. One blew up from a direct hit. Abraham swallowed back the bile of fright, peeking over the side to see they were almost at the beach.

He yelled above the exploding shells, 'Don't pack together. Remember what we've practised. Good luck, I'll see you soon.' Just then they reached the beach. The ramp came down and the men ran from it.

Bent at the waist, Abraham ran as fast as he could, zigzagging across the beach towards the dunes. Out of the corner of his eyes he saw some of the men fall onto the sand and yelled above the noise, 'Burgess.' The soldier looked in his direction. Abraham made a motion with his left hand. Burgess's white face nodded, and he raced Abraham to the dunes. Gus was already there with most of their men. Gus's sweat-streaked face smiled at his friend. 'That's the first time I've ever beaten you. Where've you been?'

Abraham grinned back. 'Had to take a leak. Nearly pissed myself.' The men closest to them erupted in laughter.

Gradually the battalion moved forward, capturing Ouistrehem harbour and its loch, but were unable to reach their main objective, Caen. It was the same with the Canadians who were supposed to capture the airfield at Carpiquet. By midnight the 1st Suffolks were dug in.

Tuesday, 13 June 1944

There was a new sound in the skies over Britain. It was like a motor bike without a silencer. Wolfe, like many others, watched the cigar-shaped object as it flew over London, a flame streaming out behind it. Suddenly the flame cut out. There was an eerie silence as the object suddenly dived towards the ground. For a second there was a bewildered look on Wolfe's face as he wondered what had happened. Then there was an almighty explosion.

Over the next week Londoners were overcome with hundreds of what they called doodlebugs or buzz-bombs that peppered London, capable of killing large numbers of people and leaving others with terrible injuries. The blast was a hundred times greater than the high explosives of the Blitz. On impact, buildings were totally demolished, with up to twenty terraced houses destroyed in one blast.

Fire crews, hospitals and ambulance services were at full stretch, rescuing people and dousing gas fires.

Wolfe, Asher and Billy worked tirelessly, their faces drawn, eyes red and tired. The air was filled with smoke that blew across the derelict street. To Wolfe it seemed an impossible task. 'I wonder how many more buzz-bombs Hitler has,' he said to no one in particular.

'From the news,' said Billy, 'we're bombing the rocket sights, plus our boys are making headway since their D-day landing.'

'I'm sure that High Command, or whoever, had them down as a top priority,' Asher chipped in.

'Well, I hope they hurry up—' He pointed to people looking through the rubble for some of their belongings. 'They won't be able to take much more of this.'

'Some of the children have been evacuated again,' Billy said.

'Best thing,' said Asher. 'You never know where that bloody doodlebug will land.'

'The thing is,' Wolfe stood, picking up the kettle, 'how to bring it down.'

The newsreel in the cinema showed King George VI visiting troops twelve days after the invasion, just a few miles from the front line; the excitement of the newscaster's voice enthralling the cinemagoers.

'I was just reading about that,' Asher said.

'That was a brave thing to do.' Billy looked over Asher's shoulder at the pictures of the King with the troops.

'Thank God that *mumzer* Edward wasn't king,' Wolfe said. 'The Nazis would already be in Whitehall and we would be in a concentration camp.' There was bitterness in his voice as he, like many, had thought

Edward would be a good king, but his liaison with and subsequent marriage to Mrs Simpson seemed to have changed people's opinion of him.

The radio as usual was loud in the firehouse as tired firemen cleaned their equipment, and no one seemed to be listening until the newscaster said, 'Today the allies have seized two V1 launch sites on the Cherbourg Peninsular.'

There was a cheer from the men. 'That should stop the buggers,' Billy said.

But it didn't, as the rockets kept coming, day and night.

*

Saul couldn't help thinking about the French civilians below him as they turned back for home after dropping their bombs, but very happy with the Allied air superiority not having to worry about German fighters. He looked down. Abraham had landed on Normandy; he hoped he was okay.

Fifty miles away, Isaac was strafing an armoured convoy, who didn't take kindly to him as mobile anti-aircraft guns fired back. 'We're hit,' Fred said in a quiet voice.

'Where? I can't see anything.' Isaac said, looking over what he could see of the Mosquito, opening the throttle and climbing away from the danger tracer bullets following them. There was a ping sound and the port engine began to smoke. Fred quickly pushed the fire extinguisher button, the aircraft seemingly coming to a halt. Their speed decreased by half with the loss of one engine. There was a banging noise from the rear. 'We took a hit just behind the cockpit,' Fred said. 'I cannot see what damage we may have.'

'Give me a heading for home,' Isaac asked, looking at the fuel gauge and calculating in his mind if they had enough fuel, quietly muttering the figures, when Fred said, 'We have just enough to get to the coast, maybe a little more.'

Isaac turned to look at Fred unclipping his oxygen mask as they were low enough not to need it, a big smile on his face. 'I knew you were a man of many talents; I did not know that you could read minds as well.'

Fred smiled back. 'Just keep your mind on flying this thing straight. You're beginning to drift slightly.'

'Okay, boss.'

They just about made the coast and were directed to the nearest airfield, landing safely with a thimbleful of petrol left, and a jagged hole just behind the cockpit.

*

In Normandy Abraham and his men's advance was slow as they struggled through a treacherous network of narrow lanes and high, tangled hedgerows called bocage, which to their cost hid the Germans who had lived there for four years and knew the area, having mapped out and camouflaged lanes of fire for snipers, tanks, machine guns and mortars.

Abraham was frustrated; if he could, he would have burnt the hedges to the ground. The buildings in the surrounding areas were mostly stone farmhouses and cottages, which were well constructed: a natural fortress for the defending Germans, who booby-trapped most things they left behind – bayonets, cigarettes, a bottle of wine, entrances and windows to buildings. Abraham had lost ten men, four to booby traps. If he was asked to describe the fighting, he would say bloody.

It wasn't long before someone came up with the idea of mounting rotating blades on a tank, which sliced through the bocage.

For three weeks since landing, Abraham and his men had fought continuously as the Germans slowly retreated, but the British troops were still miles away from their objective, Caen, with its hub of roads leading out towards Paris and Europe.

Abraham had just come away from a briefing with the CO. The Suffolks with the South Lancashires in support were ordered to take Epron and the Château de la Londe.

Abraham's company came under very heavy machine gun and mortar fire.

'Fuck it,' Abraham said angrily.

'What's the matter,' Gus asked as he moved cautiously through the cornfield.

'The South Lancashires have sustained very heavy casualties and had to withdraw, leaving us to stay the night here in the cornfield.'

'Well, that's not a bad idea,' Gus pointed out as they moved amongst the men. 'They can't see us and we can't see them.'

'No smoking, and be as quiet as you can,' Abraham ordered.

The following morning, with crocodile tanks in support, Abraham and the Suffolks attacked the château once again. The British tanks took heavy casualties from German Tigers that were dug in, but Abraham's men fixed bayonets and emerged from the cornfields to attack the château. The defenders stood their ground, but the Suffolks' momentum and determination carried them forward, and it became hand-to-hand fighting.

A corporal came at Abraham, who sidestepped the bayonet thrust, ramming the butt of his Sten into the side of the German's face. The corporal yelled angrily, turning quickly, eyes filled with hatred, his hand going to his blooded face, swearing at his opponent. Abraham drew a knife from a sheath attached to his leg and swore back at him, and for a moment the soldier stopped, surprise on his face. Abraham smiled, beckoning him on with his fingers, saying, 'You're so ugly, how could you look at yourself in the mirror?'

The German let out an angry yell and lunged at Abraham, who swayed away from the bayonet, thrusting his knife into the German's side, whose momentum wrenched the knife from his hand. The corporal carried forward a few steps before turning to face Abraham, blood pumping from the wound as he pulled the knife from his side. His knees buckled and he fell to the ground, trying to get to his feet, swearing at Abraham as he went to throw the knife, but fell flat on his face. Abraham retrieved the knife, wiping the blade on the dead German's jacket, and looked around, suddenly hearing the yells and shouts of obscenities from both sides. His men were getting the upper hand, moving slowly from house to house, clearing the way.

Abraham walked slowly up the stairs on hearing the crack of a rifle, quickly realising it was a sniper. He reached the landing, the Sten-gun in his hands, when there was another shot from a room to his right. He stepped slowly towards it, trying to be as quiet as he could, and pushed open the door to see a German soldier, a rifle with a telescopic sight at his shoulder. Abraham stood there for a second, deciding whether to shoot the man or ask him to surrender. While he hesitated, the German must have sensed his presence and slowly turned around to face Abraham and in a split-second raised the rifle to hip level, but Abraham was faster and a stream of bullets from his Sten gun knocked the German backward.

By nightfall the Suffolks had taken possession of the château at the cost of a hundred and sixty-one men killed, injured or missing. Wearily they dug in, expecting a counter-attack, but instead they came under heavy bombardment. Abraham covered his head with his arms, involuntary jerking with every bang. He looked quickly over the lip of his foxhole, hearing the cries of the wounded and a feeling of helplessness overwhelmed him, knowing how vulnerable he was. He wanted to get up and charge, and then as suddenly as it had started, the shelling stopped.

This gave the Suffolks a respite to write home and for the battalion to hold a service for fallen comrades.

The respite was short lived as they received orders to move to Beauville and attack Sannerville as part of a major Allied operation, codenamed Goodwood.

Abraham sat with his back to a tree, Gus lying on the ground next to him, smoking, head resting on his backpack. 'Do you notice the continuous noise? I mean there doesn't seem to be silence at any time.'

Gus moved onto his side to look at his friend. 'To be honest, I've been so intent on what we are doing through those bloody hedges, blocked road and lanes while the Nazis take potshots at me. So no, I haven't taken any notice of it, but—' he took a drag of his cigarette '—now that you mention it, those bloody Germans are a noisy lot. By the time we get to Caen there would be nothing left of the place, look,' Gus pointed. Abraham looked in the direction of Caen; all he could see was a wall of flame and smoke.

'I wouldn't like to be there right now. Our bombers are pounding the place, and I feel for the French families.' He got to his feet. 'Let's get the men together.'

The Germans fought ferociously for Caen and the surrounding areas with the knowledge that if Caen, the hub of twelve major roads, was captured, the road to Paris and Europe would be open.

Abraham felt the enemy's desperation as they fought in the narrow lanes, but the British and the Allies were also desperate to advance, which was slower than High Command had predicted or wanted. The fighting was so fierce that it often became fist fights.

Although they were supported by armour, it was nigh impossible for the armour to get through the lanes which were often blocked by broken-down vehicles.

After another bout of very heavy fighting, and losses, Abraham and his men entered the streets of Sannerville, on the outskirts of Caen. He was shocked by what he saw, which reminded him of Dunkirk. Black smoke drifted across the streets from smouldering tyres, and wood mixed with the stench of dead bodies, animals and machines of war that littered the streets, adding to the sombre scene he was witnessing.

He automatically dived for cover on hearing the crack of a rifle to see one of his men fall to the ground. He ran out, grabbed him by his webbing, dragging him to the safety of the house, while his men fired at the window where they thought the sniper was. Abraham called the medic to attend the injured man, who was whimpering, 'I'm going to die.'

'Jackson, you're not going to die, you were lucky. Now let the medic tend to you.'

'Yes sir, thank you sir.' Just then Abraham saw a slight movement on the third floor of a building. He whistled and the men looked in his direction. He pointed at the window and two men, who nodded. He then crawled to a window, placing the barrel of the Sten on the sill, gave a slight nod, and he and the others began firing at the windows of the houses opposite, hoping to keep the German occupied as the two men ran across the road.

Abraham crawled to the door, placing his helmet on the end of his Sten gun and moved it slightly out of the door. There was a crack and the helmet dropped to the ground. He didn't retrieve it right away until hearing a couple of shots and saw his two men wave through the window. He picked up the helmet with a hole in it, placing it on his head and the company moved forward.

He turned a corner, moving back very quickly, stopping Gus and the four men with them from going any further.

'There's a gun emplacement just around the corner, let's move carefully through the houses till we are level with them and attack.'

He looked at each of them, and then said, 'Let's go.'

Bent slightly at the waist, they moved slowly through the houses until they were level with the German emplacement and in a line walked slowly along the alley between two houses. The Germans were so intent on looking ahead that they didn't see Abraham and his men. He showed them three fingers and they all nodded. He held out his hand, showed one, two and then three fingers. Abraham ran at the Germans with Gus at his side, firing his Sten, and for some unknown reason found himself yelling, 'Fucking Nazis, bastards.'

Within minutes they had killed most of the Germans, and captured two, one to Abraham's pleasure an SS officer. He said to him in Yiddish, 'How does it feel to be captured by a lowly Jew?'

The officer spat in his direction. 'Bastard Jew, you're no lower than a worm on the ground. How did your mother get that nose through her infested—'

Gus wasn't having any of it. He smashed the German in the mouth with the butt of his weapon. The officer dropped to his knees, spitting out broken teeth, and then Gus kicked him in the groin, saying in German, 'That would stop you producing the Aryan race for a while, and if you say another word I'll kill you, but it won't be quick.'

The German officer suddenly showed fear and got slowly to his feet.

'What was that all about, sir?' a corporal named Sykes asked.

'He was just having a rant about my ancestry.'

The sergeant looked at Abraham and then Gus. 'Could you please translate what they say in the future, sir?' He turned and punched the officer in the face, and without looking at Abraham said, 'I'd always wanted to punch an officer.'

Capturing Sannerville, the battalion dug as it began to rain, and once again they came under heavy shelling.

Abraham was ordered to report to the CO. He entered the command house, stood to attention and saluted. 'You wanted to see me, sir?'

'Yes, Brown, I need you to take over Baker Company as well as your own. I'm short of officers, I'm bumping you up to temporary captain and you can tell Newark he's now a second lieutenant. It's just till we get some reinforcements.' The CO sat back in his chair and picked up his pipe. 'Thank you, Captain.'

'Abraham stood to attention and saluted.'

Returning to his men, he explained that what was left of Baker Company would be joining them for the time being, and that he had been promoted to captain and Gus to second lieutenant. Just then, led by a sergeant, Baker Company walked into their bivouac, and were greeted warmly by Abraham and his men, and in a short while, like fighting men throughout history, were soon horse playing.

With the fall of Caen and leaving the bocage behind, the Suffolks moved to a position overlooking Vire in preparation for an attack on the Falaise Gap.

Abraham listened to the brigade commander who explained that they would attack Tinchebray with the East Yorkshires and support from Churchill tanks.

Abraham returned to his men, and as he had always done, put them in the picture. 'Okay, get some sleep as I don't think we will have much of that in the next few days.'

Abraham was right, as they once again fought a determined but retreating army. The road and fields to Falaise were clogged with German dead, wounded, cattle and abandoned vehicles, making progress slow. Abraham and his men come to the edge of a corpse of trees.

'Okay, spread out, but quietly,' he said, gesturing with hand signals what he wanted.

He lay prone, resting on his elbows as he and Gus looked through binoculars at the surrounding area. Gus's lips were pursed as he looked intently at something slightly to their right, looked away and then back again.

'Tiger at three o'clock.'

Abraham gave a slight nod. 'Machine gun emplacement dead ahead. Just see the top of their helmets.'

'What do you suggest?'

'Take some of the men and try and circle around them.'

'You could get a Sherman tank up here.'

'The tiger would take it out before they even got a bead on it. No, it's up to us. I think before we do anything else I'll get Morgan up a tree back there a bit where he can't be seen and see if he spots anything else.'

'Fuck this,' Gus swore. 'It's so frustrating.'

'I know, but we're out of that damn bocage.' He placed the binoculars to his eyes, saying quietly, 'Let's kill them before they kill us.' He turned to the man nearest to him. 'Can you get Morgan for me, and keep low.'

'Yes, sir.'

A minute later Morgan was beside him. 'Can you go back a little way and climb a tree. Make sure you're not seen. There's a Tiger tank at three o'clock, and a machine gun team in front of us. See if you can spot anything else. We don't want to run into anything unexpected.'

'Yes sir.'

'Quick as you can, the Lieutenant's getting itchy feet.'

Morgan smiled and disappeared into the foliage. Ten minutes later he returned, crawling beside Abraham. He made a drawing in the ground. To the left of us is a howitzer and further back some soldiers. There's a cluster of houses. Looks like some of them may hide a sniper, but to tell you the truth, sir, I couldn't see any.'

'Okay, thanks.'

'We need the Churchills,' he said, turning to Gus.

'I told you that.'

Abraham punched him lightly on the shoulder, turning to the radio man and picked up the mike.

It didn't take long once the Shermans, and tank-busting Typhoons took care of the Germans.

For two days without any sleep, Abraham and his men advanced. He and Gus stood by what was left of a wall.

'He's in the third house on the opposite side,' Abraham said, turning to Gus. 'You and Johnson give me covering fire, on three. One-two-three.'

As Gus and Johnson fired the weapons in the direction of the enemy sniper, Abraham sprinted across the street, bullets kicking up the ground around him. He dived through a doorless opening of a house opposite, rolling onto his side and in an instant was on his feet. He gave a thumbs up to Gus and moved cautiously through the house, looking for a wire across the door, or something on the floor like a loose board that would release a pin and a grenade would explode.

He entered the next house from the garden, hearing the crack of the rifle and carefully checked the room before walking slowly across it and into the hallway. Again he hunched down, looking at every piece of floor and step. Satisfied, he moved slowly forward, trying not to make a sound, reaching the first-floor landing and hearing the sound of a rifle bolt sliding into place from a room further along the hallway.

He arrived at the room, checking for any trip wires or a floorboard that was not right, and pushed open the door to see a German sitting on a low stool by the window. Something – a feeling or whatever it was – made him turn his head and for a second he stared at Abraham. Like a slow-motion film, Abraham watched him leap from the stool and charge at him, not giving him a chance to aim the Sten gun at him, but Abraham fired anyway, the bullets hitting the German in the legs, but then he was on Abraham, hands wrapped around his throat, dragging him to the floor.

The German landed on top of him, letting go the throat hold with his right hand, leaning his weight onto the left arm and reaching down to his blood-soaked boot. Abraham knew it was time to do something so he grabbed the German's hand around his throat and twisted it away. It was then the Nazi grabbed the hilt of the knife handle protruding from the top of his boot. Abraham stuck his fingers in his opponent's eyes. The German screamed but grabbed the knife from his boot. Abraham held his arm away, but the Nazi was strong and was gradually getting the better of him when suddenly there was the sound of a shot and the German gave a sigh and slumped onto his side.

Abraham gave a sigh of relief as he looked up at Gus. 'Thanks.'

'Don't mention it.'

Abraham slowly got to his feet. 'He was fucking strong.'

Burning houses and flaming vehicle turned day into night. The streets and roads littered with engines of war, it was like seeing into Hell as the Falaise gap closed on the retreating German army. The Normandy battle was over at last, and the road to Paris was open. The fighting seemed to slow down as the Germans surrendered, but still Abraham was cautious.

It was their third morning in Tinchebray. Churchill tanks moved through the streets, picking up pockets of resistance. It was impossible to walk a few yards without encountering a dead body, army or civilian; it was like a horror movie. Suddenly Abraham found himself on the ground. He tried to get up, but couldn't. There was a lot of noise around him. He turned his head to see Gus lying a few feet away. He tried to crawl to his friend but blacked out.

24

Lily, with Rosalind and Daniel in her arms, danced around the kitchen as the commentator on the radio said loudly and excitedly, 'Paris was liberated today, and once again the Tricolour flies over the Eiffel Tower. People lined the streets, crying with happiness, shouting and singing La Marseillaise as Free French troops led the Allies into Paris.'

She stopped dancing on hearing the grating sound of the doodlebug. Her head turned upward, and the sound stopped. The smile left her face as she lay the children carefully down, following them under the table, then there was an almighty bang. The crockery shook on the shelf, the windows rattled, and then silence, except for the sound of bells. Lily crawled from under the table; the children had fallen asleep. Lily smiled at them and kissed their foreheads, turning towards the radio, the announcer still excitedly explaining the scenes of jubilation before him.

Wolfe watched the doodlebug as it flew over London with another following. A sudden feeling of fear came over him, not able to move, eyes transfixed on the two rockets with their fiery tails. His right hand went to his chest, trying to stop his pounding heart, thinking they were heading straight for him. Both engines stopped and the two doodlebugs plunged to the ground. There was an almighty explosion, dust and bricks flying into the air.

He ran towards the tower of dust, his brain yelling *Eva, Eva*; he turned the corner, suddenly coming to a halt. The entire left side of the street had been reduced to a pile of smoking rubble, and on the other side not a house had been touched except for broken doors and window panes. He joined the crowd of people rushing towards what was once a row of terraced houses to see if anyone had survived, but they already knew it was hopeless.

Two hours later a dishevelled Wolfe walked thankfully through his front door to be greeted by Eva.

'What have you—'

He pointed backwards. 'An entire row of houses demolished,' he interrupted. 'I thought like others that someone would have survived, but it was futile. I thought—' He stepped over to her, cuddling her to him, and then moved slightly back to look into her eyes. 'I thought the doodlebug was going to land here.'

She didn't say anything, just moved forward and kissed him. It was a long, lingering kiss, both thankful to still be alive.

'Would you like a cuppa?' Eva asked.

Wolfe smiled and nodded. A cup of tea cured all. They moved into the kitchen and he realised for the first time since the war began that he had been scared, and it made him angry, that the doodlebug was a threat that he, the other firefighters and the population of London had no control over; there was no hiding place from the bomb once it plunged towards the ground. He hoped the army would quickly come across the launch sites and destroy the V1 before it destroyed London.

The following day he sat in the synagogue, the feeling of dread still with him. He looked up at the women's gallery, seeing Eva looking down at him. A frown creased her forehead; she knew something was troubling her husband. She would speak to him when they got home.

Wolfe's eyes turned to the open ark, looking intently at the holy scrolls. He hadn't slept last night, as a feeling that something bad was about to happen would not leave him. He thought that if he stayed awake it would go away, but it hadn't.

He hadn't heard from Isaac and Saul for a couple of months. Asher, Sarah and April hadn't heard from Abraham since a week after the D-day landings, assuming he was still in Normandy. They were also worried about Adam, who had many years ago moved to America with his firm, met an American woman and married her, becoming an American citizen, and now he was also caught up in the war against Japan as a marine. The last letter Asher and Sarah had was a month old.

The service was over and he walked slowly behind Asher and Billy into the lobby where they met their wives and made their way out into the street. As usual the three men walked together with the women ahead.

'What's bothering you?' Asher asked.

'What do you mean?'

'You've hardly said a word to us all morning, and I know you. Something's bothering you. What is it?'

Wolfe came to a halt, turning to look at his brother, and then Billy. 'I don't know why—' he spread his hands '—but I've had a feeling of dread since watching two buzz-bombs crash not far from our houses yesterday—' His face showed his anguish.

'I suddenly realised how vulnerable we were, there's no defence against them, they destroy everything. I saw an entire terrace of houses destroyed in one blow, and look what it did to the guard's chapel, 120 soldiers and their wives killed. Some were on leave from fighting abroad. I know we've seen many terrible things throughout the Blitz, but nothing as devastating as this.'

For a moment Asher and Billy were silent, and then there was a shout. 'Come on you three,' Esther said loudly.

'Better do as she says, otherwise...' Billy left the rest unsaid.

Asher took his brother's arm. 'This conversation is not over yet, I'm—' he pointed at Billy '—we are pleased you confided in us about your feelings.'

'I can assure you, my friend, you are not the only one with those feelings.' Billy patted Wolfe on the back and the three men continued their walk home, with the loud off-beat engine of buzz-bombs overhead.

'Hitler has no consideration for our Sabbath day,' Wolfe said.

The three men didn't discuss Wolfe's fears until they were at the fire station on the Monday.

With his hands wrapped around a mug of tea, Wolfe said, 'I have never felt fear, against anyone or anything we three have been through in all our years together, but this doodlebug puts the fear of God into me. It's like someone rolling the dice at the crap table – will it or won't it it?'

'I know what you're saying,' Billy said quietly, 'but we are in God's hands.'

'This war is nearly over,' Asher said. 'The Germans are on the run on all fronts. We are giving them a taste of their own medicine by bombing their cities day and night. We just have to think positive a little longer.'

'I read that the buzz-bomb travels at four hundred miles an hour and has a ton of explosives in the nose cone. You cannot—'

'London isn't the only city being hit. Southampton, Norwich, Ipswich, Kingston, look—' Bill pointed at the newspaper in his hands '—even the Japanese are losing ground.'

Wolfe held up a hand. 'Okay, okay, you've made your point, let's play cards.'

*

With orders to destroy any German transport, trains or convoys, Isaac and Fred flew low over the German countryside. Fred kept a lookout for enemy fighters while Isaac concentrated on the ground before them.

'Tallyho,' Isaac said loudly.

'Where and what have we?' Fred asked.

'Convoy trucks and tanks at eleven o'clock,' Isaac spoke quietly, concentrating on his target as they sped towards it, trucks, tanks, armoured cars and men having scattered, though some not quick enough. A tank blew up, taking a couple of hits from the cannon. They flew along the road, firing at anything in front of them, and then they were past. Isaac brought them around for another go, but this time tracers headed their way from a Bofors gun mounted on the back of a lorry.

He turned the mosquito on his port wing, the tracer bullets flying harmlessly by. He quickly spotted the Bofors, and at over three hundred miles an hour brought the aircraft in a wide arc, coming in behind the Bofors and pressed the gun button. The mosquito shook as it spat out bullets that engulfed the Bofors and lorry.

Isaac stopped firing looking down at the destroyed Bofors. 'Let's go home,' he said.

'Roger that,' Fred replied, and gave Isaac the heading.

*

Abraham slowly opened his eyes, and then the sounds came: cries for help and low moans. He tried to sit up, but fell back onto the pillows as pain shot through his head. A male voice with a slight Irish lilt said, 'Great, you're awake,' and the face of a young man came into view.

'Where am I?'

'You are in an army hospital near the airfield of Carpiquet, awaiting transfer to England.'

'Is there a Gus Newark here? My left leg hurts like fuck.' He touched his forehead. 'And I have the mother of a headache.'

'Lieutenant Newark is in the next ward. Your headache will hopefully go once you've taken a couple of aspirin. You've had a slight concussion, and I'm sorry to tell you that we had to amputate your left leg below the knee. The pains you're getting are phantom pains.'

Abraham pulled away the cover, and stared at the bandage covering what was left of his leg. 'How's Gus?' he whispered.

'He lost his left arm below the elbow.'

'How long have I been here?'

'Mmm, just three days. As I said, you've had concussion.'

'Could I see Gus?'

'I'll have to ask the doctor. We might be able to move yours or his bed so you can be together.'

Abraham smiled. 'Thanks, is there anything to eat? I'm starving.'

'I'm Corporal Willis, your nurse. I'll find you something to eat, and see if I can get the doctor to talk to you. Are you still in a lot of pain?'

'No, since talking to you it's gone.'

The corporal smiled. 'I'll be back as soon as I can.'

It seemed like ages before the corporal returned, but it was only twenty minutes, carrying a tray with a cheese sandwich and cup of tea.

'You're a life saver.' He went to sit up.

'Let me help you.' Willis placed an arm under Abraham's. 'Push with the heel of your right leg,' he said, and Abraham sat up. The corporal adjusted the pillows behind his back. 'The doctor is coming.'

A captain arrived beside the bed. 'I'm Captain Gold, and I'm happy that you're awake, you had me worried for a while.' He pulled back the bed cover. 'I'm sorry about your leg. Your foot was a bit mashed up, but I've managed to save your knee, and we pulled out a bit of shrapnel from your right leg.' He carefully peeled back the plaster dressing, and turned to the corporal. 'Please clean it and redress it. Let's have a look at the other one. Corporal, could you please take off the dressing.'

Being as careful as he could, Willis peeled off the bandages. Abraham seemed to hold his breath, wondering what he would see. The blood had dried around the neat stitching and it was swollen. The captain put on a pair of rubber gloves as he touched the area. 'Mmm, that's good, redress this one as well. Any problems, call me immediately.'

He patted Abraham on the shoulder. 'The swelling will go down. We'll get you back home in a couple of days.' He turned to go, but quickly spun back. 'Oh! I've arranged for Second Lieutenant Newark to be transferred to this ward.' He turned and quickly left.

Minutes later, Gus was wheeled into the ward, his bed being placed next to Abraham's by Corporal Willis and another orderly. 'I have news,' he said, adjusting Abraham's pillows. 'You're leaving for Britain tomorrow afternoon. I'll have new uniforms for you in the morning.'

'Do you know where we'll be going?' Abraham asked.

'Not sure, it could be Queen Mary's at Roehampton as your wounds are healing and it's one of the best rehabilitation centres for artificial limbs. It's not far from Putney,' Willis said.

Both Abraham and Gus smiled. 'Couldn't be a better place for us,' Abraham said.

8 September 1944

As Abraham and Gus settled in at Queen Mary's Hospital, they were at last, after many months, able to tell their wives where they were. Hitler had sent another reprisal weapon onto the population of Britain, called the V2. This was a long-range rocket, carrying a one-ton warhead, diving vertically from fifty miles high at the speed of sound. There was no warning, just a tearing sound like an express train. The blast wave could be felt many miles away.

At first people thought it was a bomb that hadn't been discovered after the Blitz. Others said it was a delayed fuse on a buzz-bomb, but then a foreign correspondent released details to the papers, and once again Britain was in the firing line.

British and American bombers had bombed the launching sites, but the rocket could be launched from any concrete base.

Once again Churchill announced a relaxation on the blackout. Lights could be lit once more on trains and buses. Children were taken to town squares to see lights they had never seen before.

The papers and newsreel were full of the British and American Parachute Regiments defeat at Arnhem. The idea behind the attack was to open the Bridges across the Rhine for the Allies which would have shortened the war by several months.

At the beginning of November, President Roosevelt was voted in for a fourth term in office, which had never been done before. News reports told of the Allies' advances throughout Europe. In the East MacArthur landed in the Philippines and Britain send troops to help fight the Japanese. Wolfe was as usual reading a newspaper when he said loudly, 'No, it's not right.'

'What's not right,' Billy asked.

'Lord Moyne, British Minister to the Middle East, was murdered by two members of the Stern gang, a Zionist terrorist group. Two men gave themselves up.'

'What paper you reading?' Asher walked over to face Wolfe.

'The JC.[17] It also states here that after Churchill received the Freedom of Paris, he said that Zionist terrorist groups should be eradicated, and compared them to gangsters worthy of Nazi Germany.' Wolfe looked up from reading the article. 'That's terrible, and I'm ashamed. Knowing what the Nazis are doing to Jews in concentration camps, these idiots kill a British ambassador. It doesn't make sense.'

Asher picked up the paper and read the article. 'It says that if they don't stop, Churchill promised government action.' He looked up at Wolfe and Billy. 'You know what that means.'

Asher turned a couple of pages and slapped the page. 'The Jewish Agency had asked for an immediate cessation of any more terrorist attacks.'

'That's a relief,' Billy said.

*

'This is the BBC Home Service on 12th November 1944. Yesterday after four and half years of service, the Home Guard was disbanded. Every member will receive a certificate of service, and officers will retain their ranks.'

'That means we would soon be leaving too, isn't that right, Chief?'

---

[17] *Jewish Chronicle.*

Asher looked at Chief McNamara.

'I haven't received any such orders yet.'

Wolfe, Asher, Billy and their wives watched the lights go on at Piccadilly Circus after five years of darkness. They wandered arm in arm down to the Strand and along Fleet Street with its newspaper offices, and lingered at St Paul's Cathedral, and told their wives about the night the Germans tried to destroy the cathedral and set the city aflame, 'This is where we were,' Billy pointed out.

'By the way,' Eva said, 'we have been chosen, with other women throughout the country, to be at Westminster County Hall on the 6th. The Queen will be there with Princess Elizabeth.'

*

At Westminster County Hall there was a gathering of women from many parts of the country. The Queen, with Princess Elizabeth beside her, said, 'I praise you, the women, who have worked in civil defence, police, fire brigade, ambulance services, and the wonderful work of the WVS, who through your efforts have saved our children and grandchildren from another war.'

'What was it like,' Asher asked, 'when their wives returned home?'

'Wonderful,' Sarah replied. 'The Queen shook our hands.'

'Did she say anything to you?'

'She looked at the three of us and said, "Well done, ladies, I've heard what you had done at the club." It caught us by surprise. How did she know?'

'The head of the WVS probably told her,' Wolfe said.

Apart from the war news, there was concern about Glenn Miller: the bandleader's plane was missing on a trip to France, where his band was due to play. No distress call was made.

Throughout Christmas and New Year, Wolfe and the others read with trepidation the war news from the Ardennes, which had been covered in fog and four-foot snowdrifts, grounding Allied planes. German troops and tanks broke through, driving a sixty-mile wedge into Allied lines. At the end of the month the weather cleared, allowing Allied planes to take to the air, pulverising the German troops and supply lines, and causing them to be low on fuel and ammunition.

By 9 January it was over. 'Am I happy I didn't know about the Ardennes until now?' Billy said.

Lily clapped her hands happily as she watched the newsreel showing the first boat train in five years leaving for the Continent. The following day she received a letter from her Aunt Sarah, saying they were all safe and returning to Paris.

At last after months of rehab, Abraham and Gus were allowed home on a week's leave. Both were waiting for their prostheses to be made.

Abraham was surprised when Miriam walked towards him, still thinking of her as the baby he last saw, but quickly realised she was nearly three.

The *Jewish Chronicle* was full of the story and a photo of the railway line of death from the liberated Auschwitz concentration camp. Jews throughout the free world were appalled by what they read in the newspapers and what they saw in newsreels. And still the buzz-bombs and rockets rained down on London and other cities.

14 February 1945

Saul looked through the window of the Lancaster, his thoughts on Hannah and their daughter Ruby. 'Approaching the coast, Guv.' The navigator interrupting his thought. 'Stay on this heading.'

'Roger, Prof. Gunners, test your guns.'

Tonight their target was Dresden. Apart from the high explosives, they were also carrying incendiaries.

Time seemed to pass pretty quickly. Saul could see the marker flares ahead and the usual searchlights. They were forty miles from Dresden and getting ready for their run in, when the tail gunner yelled, 'Break left, break left.'

Saul yanked the column over, eyes on the bomber ahead and to his side. There was a pinging sound as bullets struck the bomber. He saw the Messerschmitt 109 pass over them and loop upward, coming around for another go.

'Roy, Bob, get ready. Andy, let me know when he's about to attack. Roy, Bob, as he does I'm going to dip the right wing so you can both have a go at him at the same time. Roger that?'

'Yes, Guv,' they both said.

'Steady, Guv,' Andy said quietly. 'On the count of three. Steady, one, two, three.'

Saul pulled up the wing. They were now flying vertical. Oliver, the engineer gave the engines a boost. Saul could hear their guns chattering away and then, 'Got the bastard,' Andy said excitedly.

Saul brought the bomber straight and level, climbing to their original height. 'Thanks, Ollie, I was a little scared we might stall.'

Ollie looked at Saul. 'You took a chance. Only you could have thought of something like that.'

The voice of the bomb aimer filled their ears. 'Bomb aimer in position.'

'Roger, bombardier,' Saul said, as flak came up fast and furious, the searchlights dancing around the sky. They were nearly there and Saul squared his shoulders. He, like many pilots, hated this part as they had to fly straight and level to drop their loads.

'Steady, Guv, steady—' Tom's voice was calm and calculated and then '—bomb's gone.'

Saul pushed the throttle levers forward, turning away from the bomb area. They had just levelled out when Andy yelled, 'Break right.' Saul turned as ordered, his reflexes a fraction of a second after the yell, but still they were hit. 'He's coming around again, Guv, your side on.'

Saul took a quick glance in that direction, just seeing the outline of the German fighter. Realising he was aiming for him, judging when he was about to fire, Saul pushed the column forward and they went into a dive, but he was too late – the fighter's tracer bullets hit the cockpit. Saul gasped as he was hit.

'He's following us down,' Andy yelled, panic in his voice.

'Where's he now?'

'Behind and closing fast.' Saul could hear the chatter from his gunners firing at the diving Messerschmitt. He pulled back on the column, giving the mid-upper gunner a chance to shoot at the fighter. His mind was working overtime: he was trying to avoid being hit again, but they had taken some heavy damage.

'I'm hit!' yelled Bob McGregor, the tail gunner.

'Me too!' yelled Andy as his observation dome shattered.

His face a grimace of pain, Saul twisted and turned the aircraft, trying to shake the aim of the enemy fighter, knowing his tail section was exposed, and then he saw it, a cloud just ahead of them as once again they were hit, and the outer port engine caught fire but Ollie was on it right away with the fire extinguisher button, closing down the engine.

Saul could sense rather than see the fighter, knowing that he was coming for him again. He glanced at the cloud. It didn't seem to be getting any closer, but knew from experience it was an optical illusion. Bullets pinged off the bomber just behind the cockpit. The fighter crossed in front of them and Tom the bomb aimer fired a long burst at it as they entered the cloud.

Saul hadn't heard from the mid-upper gunner. He called over the intercom, 'Report any damage, and if you're hit.'

'Tail gunner here, Guv. I'm hit, bleeding pretty badly, gun's jammed.'

'Mid-upper here, Guv. I'm okay and can fire the guns, but Andy looks pretty bad, the turret's shattered.'

'Prof here, Guv. I've been hit, but am able to carry on.'

Saul looked across at Ollie. Blood covered his jacket; he looked at Saul and winked. 'Tom, leave the guns and come up here,' he ordered.

As soon as Tom appeared he said, 'Could you go back and see what help you are able to give the wounded.'

'Roger.' The gunner disappeared aft.

They were still in the cloud. 'Guv, I've taken Bob from the rear turret. He's bleeding pretty badly. I've managed to stem the flow, and strapped him on the bed, but we need to get a move on. Andy's hit. Lucky he was wearing his goggles when the dome shattered. Prof's okay.'

'Roger, Tom. Can you man your guns.'

He quickly came to a solution – well, he hoped it was. The fighter might be waiting for them to clear the cloud. He looked at the horizon meter in front of him. The fighter would expect him to come out on a homeward-bound direction.

'Prof, I'm going to turn to port and come out hopefully behind the fighter – that's if he's waiting for us. Tom, you and Roy must spot the bugger quickly before he knows we're there.'

He turned to port, watching the horizon meter holding the aircraft dead centre, which was hard going on three engines, trying to ignore the pain from his wound. He could see the cloud thinning out and they burst into a starlit sky, but the fighter was nowhere to be seen.

Saul breathed a sigh of relief. 'Course for home, Prof.'

'Roger, Guv.'

They approached the white cliffs of Dover with Tom and Roy tending to the wounded. Ollie wouldn't leave his seat, but allowed Tom to bandage him. His face was as white as a sheet. Saul hadn't said a word about his wound as he said over the radio, 'S for Sugar to control. Permission for emergency landing. Badly damaged aircraft and wounded on board.'

'Control here, Roger, S for Sugar, understood.' There was a moment's silence and then, 'Control to S for Sugar, you're clear to land.'

A white-faced Ollie lowered the wheels and they began their run in. Suddenly a voice in Saul's ears said, 'S for Sugar, abort, abort, only one wheel down.'

Saul revved the three engines, climbing away, and made a circuit of the airfield as they tried to bring the wheels down, but still only one dropped down. He made another circuit of the field, looking at his petrol gauges. They were nearly empty. 'S for Sugar to control,' Saul called quietly.

'Control here, over.'

'I'm coming in on a belly landing. Two of my men are bailing out, but the others are unable to, plus we are low on fuel.'

'Understand, S for Sugar.'

'Roy, Tom, put your parachutes on. I'm going to gain height when we're over the airfield. You two bail out.'

'Roger, Guv,' they said in unison.

A minute later Tom came up to the cockpit. 'We've placed the others in as good a position as we could. We're bailing out now, Guv. Good luck.'

Saul nodded, holding the aircraft as steady as he could, nearly passing out with the pain from his wounds. Having judged they had both bailed out, he brought the aircraft lower, lining up the aircraft level with the grass verge of the runway lights. He shut off the engines a few feet from the ground and lifted the nose a fraction.

For a second there was silence, a heavy bump and a loud grating noise as the big bomber slid uncontrollably along the grass, the propellers bent. Fire tenders and ambulances raced alongside. At last they came to a stop, the firemen immediately dousing the engines in case of fire. The side door flew open and medics swarmed inside the aircraft with stretches, carefully carrying the wounded from the aircraft.

Saul was the last to leave and was met by Tom and Roy. Tom leaned over him, taking his hand. 'Bloody good job, Guv, you saved our lives.'

Saul tried to smile and could only whisper, 'A bit melodramatic,' and passed out.

Saul heard a sound and opened his eyes, and for a moment wondered where he was. He tried to sit up. Pain racked his body and he let out a yell.

A smiling face appeared. 'Try not to move too much, otherwise you'll break the stitches.'

'Where am I?'

'You're in a ward at the base hospital at Elsham Wolde.'

'How long have I been out, and how are my crew?'

'You've been here two days; we have notified your wife that you are safe.' She seemed to want to say something, but patted his bed clothes. 'I'll get the doctor. He would know more about your crew than me. Would you like a drink?'

'Please.'

She lifted his head slightly, giving him a sip of water. 'I'll fetch the doctor.' Saul closed his eyes and in an instant was asleep.

Someone was touching his hand. He opened his eyes to see a man in a white coat looking down at him. The man had brown eyes and the bushiest eyebrows Saul had ever seen.

'I'm Squadron Leader Ornstein. Before I say anything else, you're one hell of a pilot bringing in that damaged Lancaster; you saved most of the crew's lives.'

'What do you mean most of my crew?'

'Unfortunately Sergeant McGregor died. We tried to save him, but he had lost a lot of blood and was shot up pretty badly. The rest of your crew are in this ward. Anderson has a few cuts on his face, a broken collar bone, and we took out a couple of bullets, which miraculously missed his heart, as we did with you.'

Ornstein pulled back the bedclothes, placing two fingers on the left side of Saul's chest, which was bandaged. 'Two bullets somehow came through the side of your chest and went downward, missing your heart by fractions of an inch and broke two ribs. I'd call that a miracle.'

'What about my navigator and engineer?'

'Silver had a shattered left elbow. We couldn't save the arm, and a bullet went through the fleshy part of his thigh.' He picked up Saul's arm by the wrist, feeling the pulse as he said, 'Oliver has a collapsed lung, which will in time inflate itself and we had to repair his bowel. He's pretty weak as it was a big operation.' He let go the arm and patted it. 'You'll be as good as new pretty soon, and I'll get the nurse to sit you up so you can see your crew, who are in the next beds to you.'

'Thank you sir.'

Ornstein gave a grim smile. 'Sorry I couldn't save McGregor.' He turned and left.

Seconds later, the nurse appeared. 'Right, Flight Sergeant, I'm Nurse Susan Tendler and with Nurse Stephens's help I'll sit you up. Please ask us to stop if the pain gets to unbearable.' He gritted his teeth against the pain as they propped up the pillows and sat him up. 'Well done,' Nurse Tendler said, tucking in his bedcovers.

He looked to his right to see Prof smiling at him in the next bed, the sleeve of his pyjama jacket empty.

'Nice to see you, Guv, thanks.'

Saul frowned. 'For what?'

'Saving our lives, that was a nifty bit of flying.'

'I'm sorry about the arm.'

'I'm still here, and I'm sure Sandra would be pleased that I'm grounded.'

Saul looked to his left to see Andy, his arm in a sling, chatting up Nurse Stephens. 'Andy, leave the poor girl alone. She has patients to attend to.'

Andy smiled at Saul, the cuts on his face red. 'I'm glad to see you're okay, Guv, and well done.'

He looked around the ward. 'Where's Ollie?'

'In the bed next to mine,' Andy said.

'He's in an oxygen tent at the moment to help with the breathing, but he's awake and will be out of the tent in an hour.'

'I'm starving,' Saul said.

'I'm told a meal will be up soon,' Prof said.

*

Today there was much to rejoice about in Asher and Sarah's house as they and those of the rest of the family that could be there sat down to a family dinner, Sarah not caring that she had killed three of her chickens. Abraham was home for a few days before returning to Richmond for his last bout of rehabilitation. He wore his false leg and although confident with it, had a walking stick to keep him steady. April never left his side.

Naturally the talk among the men was the war, and as usual with the women with so many babies around, it was baby talk.

Wolfe sat, one hand playing with his knife, as he look around the table and for some unknown reason remembered the flu epidemic after the First World War, and how the family had escaped unscathed when many had been decimated. If the newspapers and newsreels were anything to go by, the war was nearly over, and it seemed God had spared most of his family and friends once again. His thoughts were interrupted by the grating sound of a buzz-bomb. Everyone looked up at the ceiling and the room went silent until it had passed by. There were tight smiles of relief and the conversations continued.

Two days later, as they raced towards another buzz-bomb attack, the news was all about the Germans' surrender in Italy.

'I'm telling you,' Billy yelled above the bell, 'the war will be over by June.'

'I hope you're right – not knowing when those bloody buzz-bombs are going to fall gives me the jitters,' yelled back Wolfe.

They arrived at Smithfield market to a place of devastation. People wandered dazed and aimlessly around as ambulance crews and army personnel tended the wounded and guided others to a WVS van where they were given hot tea, sandwiches and cigarettes.

Once again it was the heartbreaking task of crawling amongst the rubble, hoping against hope to find someone alive. Asher was slightly ahead and to the right of Wolfe when suddenly there was a sound like a moan and Asher disappeared as the rubble collapsed. Within seconds both Wolfe and Billy moved quickly and carefully towards the gaping hole, both yelling, 'Asher, Asher.'

Chief McNamara arrived with two other firemen. 'Get the longest rope you can find on the trucks,' he ordered them.

The dust had settled but it was still dark inside the hole. Wolfe shone a torch down into it, but still they couldn't see, and suddenly there was a yell. 'Anyone up there?'

'Asher, Asher you hurt?' Wolfe shouted down.

'I think I've broken my left leg, and my back hurts.'

'Don't move, we'll get to you as quickly as we can,' McNamara called down.

'We're going to need a stretcher and a medic with us,' Wolfe said to the Chief.

'Okay, you and Billy go down and let us know the situation so we know what we need.'

'Okay Chief.' Wolfe and Billy got themselves ready to be lowered into the hole. With helmet torches and ropes attached to the fire tenders they were slowly lowered down into the hole. There was a look of surprise on Wolfe's and Billy's faces, both believing that Asher would be badly injured from the fall, but there he was, lying on a bed.

Wolfe turned to Billy. 'I've seen many strange things in the last few years, but this beats everything: of all the luck, to fall onto a bed.'

'It must have been a thin layer of bricks covering the hole.'

Asher's left leg was broken. Wolfe looked up and yelled, 'We need a stretcher and two medics.' He stared at his brother and knew more than ever that God was looking out for his family.

Five minutes later, two medics with a stretcher were lowered down. They asked about his back, but until they got him to the hospital they wouldn't know more.

One of them placed a hand on Asher's shoulder. 'We'll put your leg in a splint and give you a painkiller before we hoist you up. It's going to hurt, but that won't matter after the luck you've had.'

Asher nodded. 'I hate to think what would have happened if the bed hadn't been there.'

Just then the stretcher began to rise, and whatever he was saying was lost against the side wall.

Once Wolfe and Billy arrived at the top, they with the Chief drove back to the station to clean their fire tender and change, knowing there was nothing they could do at that time for Asher. They picked up Sarah on the way to the hospital.

At the hospital Asher was just waking from his operation, left leg in plaster in a low hoist. The doctor was there when they arrived so they were able to speak to him, but before the doctor could say a word, Wolfe asked earnestly, 'How's his back?'

'Just a bit sore, no bones broken, but his left leg was pretty bad. He must keep that still so the bones can knit, otherwise it could mean an amputation.'

'Thanks, Doc,' Billy said, shaking his hand.

'Can I see him?' Sarah asked.

'For a little while he's still groggy from the Atheistic.'

While Asher was in hospital, the casualties from the V1 and V2 rockets grew, but the war news from Europe and the East was of advances made by the Allies as the Germans and Japanese retreated.

In February the American Marines captured Iwa Jima, a strategic island, but for Asher and Sarah there was sad news: their son Adam had been killed on Iwa Jima.

*

Saul was getting ready to leave hospital: his ribs had knitted well and he was raring to go. Harry Silver was leaving for rehab to obtain a prosthesis for his arm. Andy Anderson's collar bone had knitted well. Ollie Oliver's lung had reflated and he was as good as new.

They were packed and saying goodbye to the nurses and Dr Ornstein when the CO walked in with other high-ranking Air Force officers.

'Attention,' Saul said.

The men stood to attention as the CO approached. 'At ease,' he said, walking straight up to Saul. 'Flight Sergeant Saul Brown, I have been given the honour to tell you that the King would like to award you the George Cross at Buckingham Palace in two days' time. Apart from that you and your crew have been awarded the DFM.'[18]

'Thank you very much sir,' Saul said in embarrassment as the CO shook his hand.

Two days later, with Hannah by his side, the King awarded Saul the George Cross, saying, 'Flight Sergeant Brown, I have read the report of your bravery. It is well deserved.'

The Queen spoke to Hannah, 'I understand you have a daughter.'

Hannah smiled. 'Yes, Your Majesty, her name's Ruby.'

'A nice name. It is very nice to have met you.'

Hannah curtsied and as the Queen moved off to talk to another wife she wondered what the Queen might have said if she had known Hannah had been a madam in a brothel.

The following day a photograph of Saul and Hannah – with Saul's

---

[18] Distinguished Flying Medal.

George Cross prominently displayed – appeared in the *Jewish Chronicle*. He had a week's leave before reporting back to Elsham Wolde.

Asher was now back at the fire station and as usual the trio were listening to music as they played cards, when a voice said, 'This is the BBC Home Service on April 12th 1945. It is a sad day in the United States of America as President Roosevelt passed away today on the eve of victory. He will be sadly missed throughout the free world.'

Asher, Wolfe and Billy had the afternoon off and decided to go to the cinema, mostly to see the war newsreels. There was a sharp intake of breath from the three of them when pictures showing the liberation of Bergen Belsen appeared on the screen. Winston Churchill said, 'Words cannot express our horror.'

The latest news was of the Allies entering Berlin. Wolfe and Billy were cleaning the fire tender when Asher came in. 'Have you seen the newspapers today?'

'Have you got nothing better to do? And you're late,' Billy said.

'He's only joking with you.' Wolfe turned to look at his brother. 'You okay without the crutches?'

'Since they took off the plaster I'm fine. I'm late because they wanted to do another X-ray. Everything has knitted together.' He kicked up his leg. 'Everything's great.'

'What's the news?' Billy asked.

Asher took a folded newspaper from his pocket. 'They captured Mussolini and his mistress, shot them and then hung them upside down in a garage forecourt in Milan.' He held out the paper. 'Look.'

Wolfe took the newspaper from his brother, spreading it out on the table to look at the picture, with Billy looking over his shoulder. 'Couldn't have happened to a nicer pair,' he commented.

'Have you noticed that there have been no buzz-bombs or rockets for a couple of weeks?' Wolfe said.

'The Allies have crossed the Rhine, and entered Berlin, capturing the launch sites,' Asher replied.

'Stupid me, I should have known that.'

Billy turned back to the fire tender. 'No matter what, we still have to finish this.'

The newsreels and newspaper articles were all about the atrocities of the concentration camps. At Buchenwald, US troops fought to save those inmates still alive, many just walking skeletons. They were given milk until their stomachs were able to digest food. The Americans used ex guards and people from nearby towns and villages to bury the dead in mass graves, the protest at their treatment falling on deaf ears.

The music stopped and the excited voice of the newscaster said,

'Today, 8th May 1945, Germany has surrendered to the Allies. The war in Europe is over. Long live the King.'

In the fire station, Wolfe, Asher and Billy were dancing a circle, holding onto each other's shoulders. Within minutes the rest of the station including Chief McNamara had joined them.

A week later Londoners took to the streets. Whitehall and the Mall were packed with people. At Queen Victoria's Memorial, people formed lines doing the conga, but the three partners and their families went to the Hanover to join in the festivities with their patrons.

Through loud speakers placed at strategic points around Whitehall, everyone heard the Prime Minister say, 'Although Japan is yet to be subdued, the war in Europe is over. Advance Britain, long live freedom, long live the King.'

The place echoed with a crescendo of noise as the crowd moved slowly along Horse Guards Parade and along the Mall, people waving flags and dancing as they made their way to Buckingham Palace, and then the chanting began: 'We want the King,' over and over again until the King and Queen with Princesses Elizabeth and Margaret stepped onto a balcony to be greeted by a crescendo of cheers and singing. 'They are jolly good fellows' echoed for miles around. Those who could not get to the Palace watched it in cinemas throughout the country.

On 23 May the Coalition Government that had seen Britain through the worst of the war resigned. There would be a General Election in two months. On 26 July the General Election was over, and the three friends sat glumly around the radio, listening to the unexpected Labour majority.

'Well, that's a shock,' Billy said. 'I thought the country would vote for a Conservative government, seeing Churchill led us to victory.'

'We thought that, but it seems the majority want change,' Wolfe said. 'I voted Conservative.'

'Me too,' Asher and Billy said together.

On 7 August, the pages of newspapers, radio broadcast and newsreels told the world that America had dropped an atomic bomb on the Japanese city of Hiroshima. Two days later they dropped a second atomic bomb on the city of Nagasaki. Newsreels showed the utter devastation of both cities. At midnight on 13 August Britain learnt of the unconditional surrender of Japan.

The Prime Minister Clement Attlee said in his broadcast to the nation, 'The lot of our enemies is laid low.'

On high ground from Orpington to Ramsgate, bonfires were lit in celebration. People began to gather in London and by two in the morning Piccadilly was in full party mood. American servicemen wearing party hats, holding American flags, led a procession with beating drums, whistles and handheld fireworks. Two days later, street parties were held in London and other cities throughout the country.

In East London trestle tables, bearing an abundance of sandwiches and home-baked cakes, stretched along Wapping High Street from Thomas Moore Street to Wapping Lane.

In the club, Eva, Sarah, Esther, their daughters and daughters-in-law made sandwiches as fast as they could, taking them to the cheering, happy, hungry children. Gradually, as day turned to evening, all was quiet as the tired, happy children made their way or were carried home with smiles on their dirty faces.

On 22 September Hannah had a little boy, whom she named Jack after Saul's brother.

*

In October Wolfe, Asher and Billy said goodbye to their fellow firemen and McNamara, while in Nuremberg high-ranking Germans were sentenced to death for their part in the murder of millions of Jews.

Gradually life without war was getting back to some form of normality, and the rebuilding of a city began.

'I can't believe it.' Wolfe leapt from his seat. 'Of all the imbecilic things to do.'

Eva ran into the dining room. 'What you on about now?'

'They bombed the King David Hotel.'

'Who did?'

'The Stern Gang. There's going to be all hell to pay for that. If you ever wanted to turn people against Jews,' he slapped the paper with the back of his hand, 'this was it.'

Eva stayed silent, knowing how he hated what the Stern gang and Irgun had done in the name of freedom.

Wolfe sat down as he realised there was nothing he could do about it. Tonight he Asher and Billy would sit down to discuss their families' and their own future.

Epilogue

Wolfe watched as the Shaffers began to organise the New Year's Eve ball at the new extension of the Hanover Casino. The trio had bought the building next door six months ago, renovating the downstairs spacious rooms into a dining area for the casino's patrons.

He gave a slight smile as he leant against the door jamb and lit a cigarette. The last two years had been, to say the least, interesting and non-stop. The three partners had agreed to move homes and get away from the devastation of East London, and move to Clapton or Stamford Hill, but their wives would only move if their homes were next to each other. After three months of hard searching they had been fortunate enough to find three houses in leafy Cazenove Road in Upper Clapton. Naturally the wives wanted to redecorate their new homes before moving in.

'After what they have been through these last few years,' Wolfe said to Asher and Billy, 'if it makes them happy, I'm happy.' The other two agreed with him.

By August 1946 three contented wives moved into their new properties and the following weekend was the first family gathering in Wolfe and Eva's new home.

Wolfe moved away from the door, stubbing his cigarette out in an ashtray and taking a seat at a corner table as men manoeuvred tables to form a square space for the dance floor. Placing his right elbow on the table, his chin resting between his thumb and forefinger, Wolfe's brow creased in thought. As a family they had been lucky: many had lost their homes but miraculously there's and the club were still standing, and they were still okay financially, thanks to the Hanover.

The Government had compensated them for the bombed Victoria Casino and four of the brothers' houses that had been destroyed, including three of Billy's. All three agreed that their future finances were in property, and they had pooled their compensation money to buy properties to let, including their old homes. They decided not to rebuild the Victoria, but if they could buy the property next to the Hanover they could extend and make it into a restaurant, inviting clients to enjoy an evening meal and gamble. From the onset it had been a great success.

Isaac had bought a house in Filey Avenue, the next street to his parents. He was still the casino's accountant, but had also advertised for other clients while working from home. Lily was expecting their third child. Wolfe hadn't thought her maternal in the beginning, which just showed how wrong one could be. Isaac had won the DFC[19] and a bunch of other medals.

Saul had been awarded the George Cross, the DCM[20] and bar. Wolfe learnt from Harry Silver, the navigator, how Saul had saved the crew. Saul wanted to carry on flying so he applied to be a pilot with British European Airways but with the abundance of pilots it was a long process. Hannah had sold the brothel as soon as she became pregnant again. They bought a house in Warwick Grove, Clapton.

Abraham had opened a law firm in Lincoln's Inn, ending the war with the Military Medal and four campaign medals. He and April had moved with the family to Filey Avenue, next door to Isaac, not long after April had sold her hairdressing business and had a second daughter, naming her Nancy after her mother.

Abraham and Gus were still firm friends. Gus returned to the Prudential. He and Freda had their first child, a girl named Anne.

Sally opened another dress shop after having her second child, naming her Adrienne. Max had decided that he needed a regular job with two children to look after. Being good with figures he joined Isaac in his accountancy firm, while studying in the evening with the occasional gig with a band, doing what he loved the most – playing drums – with Freda singing.

Wolfe looked up to the ceiling and whispered, 'Thank you.' He stood up and walked over to Mr Shaffer. 'Everything looks great. Anything I can help you with?'

'No, Mr Brown, all is nearly ready.'

'Has the champagne arrived?'

'Yes, chilling as we speak.'

'This time, Mr and Mrs Shaffer, you are our guests. No cooking, leave it to the children – well, Mark, he's the chef here.'

Mr Shaffer smiled. 'Thank you.'

That evening Wolfe, Asher and Billy stood on the stage. The band had stopped playing as Big Ben rang the last chimes for 1946. All three had big smiles on their faces. Their first party since before the war had been a great success; the women in their magnificent ball gowns, and the men in dinner jacket and bow ties. The last chime of 1946 rang out and the three friends, with arms around each other, called out, 'Happy New Year.'

---

[19] Distinguished Flying Cross.
[20] Distinguished Conduct Medal.

CAST of EAST END BOYS AT WAR

Wolfe Brown married **Eva Goldberg**
Children:
Jack Brown married **Sophia Ginsberg**
Sally Brown married **Phillip Hyams**
Freda Brown married **Max Roth**
Isaac Brown married **Lily Gilbert**
Saul Brown married **Hannah Grozenski**

Asher Brown (Wolfe's brother) married **Sarah Rosenfeldt**
Children:
Abraham Brown married **April Reid**
Adam Brown
Barbara (Baruch) Brown

Billy Reid married **Esther Poznanski**
Children:
April Reid (child from Billy's first wife who died in childbirth)
Dora (Davora) Reid
Ariel Reid

Staff Sergeant Gus Newark
Ruby Newman
Nathaniel James
Derek Henshaw
Claire Wilson
Dr Aeron Franks
Squadron Leader Martin Ainsworth
Liam Ginger Robinson
Fred the Bull Burgess
Spider Munro
Bob Burns
George Edwards
Johnnie Jackson
Flying Officer Ron Cole

Saul's Lancaster crew
Flight Sergeant Harry (Prof) Silver
Sergeant Andy Anderson
Flight Sergeant Oliver Moore
Sergeant David Cheskowski
Sergeant Derek Dickenson

Sergeant Paul Ginger James

Saul's replacement crew members
Flight Sergeant Tom Wilson
Sergeant Roy Burnett
Sergeant Bob McGregor
Pilot Officer Fred Summerton (Isaac's navigator)

Fire Chief McNamara
Frank Mullen
Hymie Shaffer (Restaurant)
Kinsky (Jeweller)
Chief Inspector Jimmy O'Brian
Flight Lieutenant John Morgan